Asa Bird Gardiner, Fitz-John Porter

Argument of Asa Bird Gardner

counsel for government, after conclusion of the evidence in the case of Fitz-John

Porter before the Board of Army officers at West Point, January, 1879

Asa Bird Gardiner, Fitz-John Porter

Argument of Asa Bird Gardner
counsel for government, after conclusion of the evidence in the case of Fitz-John Porter
before the Board of Army officers at West Point, January, 1879

ISBN/EAN: 9783337402273

Printed in Europe, USA, Canada, Australia, Japan

Cover: Foto ©Andreas Hilbeck / pixelio.de

More available books at **www.hansebooks.com**

ARGUMENT

OF

ASA BIRD GARDNER,

Counsel for Government,

AFTER CONCLUSION OF THE EVIDENCE IN THE CASE OF

FITZ-JOHN PORTER,

BEFORE THE

BOARD OF ARMY OFFICERS AT WEST POINT,

JANUARY, 1879.

WASHINGTON:
GOVERNMENT PRINTING OFFICE.
1879.

ARGUMENT OF ASA BIRD GARDNER,

COUNSEL FOR THE UNITED STATES.

Mr. PRESIDENT AND GENTLEMEN OF THE BOARD: After a series of meetings, not equaling, however, the number held by the high military court which tried this petitioner sixteen years ago, the Board will soon exhibit to the reviewing authority, to the future historian, and to the judgment of the country a mass of statements respecting the campaign in Virginia in August, 1862, such as no other campaign, not even that terminating in Waterloo, has ever presented.

ERRATA.

On page 12, in the fortieth line should read "*Board*" instead of "Court."
On page 39, in the twenty-fifth line, the words "*desist from*" should be "*persist in.*"
On page 57, in the fifteenth line, the words "[the] road to Groveton" should read, "*right toward* Groveton."
On page 88, in the forty-fifth line, the word "battalions" should be "*batteries.*"
On page 122, in the forty-first line, the words "about 4 p. m." should be "about 2 p. m."
On page 129, in the eighteenth line, the word "forced" should be "*fired.*"
On page 129, in the twenty-fourth line, the words "Hampton's brigade" should read: "*Hunton's* brigade."
On page 135 the answer to question in thirtieth line is: "Yes; we were on his right."
On page 143 the answer to question in fifty-fifth line is: "I am certain it was at Hampton Cole's."

deprived of, as he terms it—

The inestimable advantage of having his case advocated by those who are practiced in the science and skill of advocacy, and who know how to bring out everything that can possibly make for the benefit of the client, whereby, in the end, truth, is elicited by all that can be said on either side, being heard, and the tribunal which has to judge is placed in the most advantageous position for deciding according to right.

In the American Army, the accused is, under the Constitution, always entitled to counsel as of right. This is exemplified in the case of this petitioner, who, on his trial, was defended by able counsel in the persons of the late Hon. Reverdy Johnson and Charles Eames, esq.

The history of the Army shows no instance of a body of commissioned officers assembled by executive order for the purposes which brought this Board together.

Necessarily the Board had to hear counsel for petitioner before determining its method of procedure. That statement, instead of formulating points as to what he desired to do, took the character of an elabo-

ARGUMENT OF ASA BIRD GARDNER,

COUNSEL FOR THE UNITED STATES.

Mr. President and Gentlemen of the Board: After a series of meetings, not equaling, however, the number held by the high military court which tried this petitioner sixteen years ago, the Board will soon exhibit to the reviewing authority, to the future historian, and to the judgment of the country a mass of statements respecting the campaign in Virginia in August, 1862, such as no other campaign, not even that terminating in Waterloo, has ever presented.

While the Revised Statutes of the United States provide for the institution of courts-martial or courts of inquiry to administer justice to those who are in the military service of the nation, and minutely provide for the oaths which have to be taken by the members and judge-advocate or recorder preliminary to any investigation or inquiry, Congress has never provided for any appeal or writ of error from the judgment of a court-martial after it has been finally acted upon by the convening authority. His decision is final and conclusive when the court which tries the case has jurisdiction over the offense and individual.

In the criminal practice of the circuit and district courts of the United States we find that, in many instances, judgment is final.

The present Lord Chief Justice Cockburne of England, in 1867, in the case of Colonel Nelson and Lieutenant Brand, said, when referring to general courts-martial:

No one, I think, can deny that the substance of justice is carefully attended to. There is nothing arbitrary, nothing capricious, nothing unsettled. * * * Perhaps there are no tribunals in the world in which justice is administered with a higher sense of the obligation which the exercise of judicial functions imposes, with a higher sense of honor, or a greater desire to do justice.

These, I think, so far as experience has shown, are, generally speaking, the characteristics of the *military* tribunals which exercise their functions under the name of courts-martial.

The eminent jurist who used this language did it after allusion to the fact that the accused, in general courts-martial in the British army, is deprived of, as he terms it—

The inestimable advantage of having his case advocated by those who are practiced in the science and skill of advocacy, and who know how to bring out everything that can possibly make for the benefit of the client, whereby, in the end, truth, is elicited by all that can be said on either side, being heard, and the tribunal which has to judge is placed in the most advantageous position for deciding according to right.

In the American Army, the accused is, under the Constitution, always entitled to counsel as of right. This is exemplified in the case of this petitioner, who, on his trial, was defended by able counsel in the persons of the late Hon. Reverdy Johnson and Charles Eames, esq.

The history of the Army shows no instance of a body of commissioned officers assembled by executive order for the purposes which brought this Board together.

Necessarily the Board had to hear counsel for petitioner before determining its method of procedure. That statement, instead of formulating points as to what he desired to do, took the character of an elaborate argument in detail, with presentation at the same time to each of us of the argument in printed form. From this it appeared that he proposed to introduce:

1st. So called newly discovered evidence;

2d. Cumulative evidence; and

3d. Evidence as to his conduct on the 30th of August, 1862, in order to show *animus*, which had been ruled out after argument on the original trial. In other words, he substantially proposed a new trial.

He also asked "justice"; alleged he had been wronged, and by another of his counsel declared that he desired the very fullest and most searching examination to be made of the facts of the case, so that the actual truth should be known, and would certainly expect that if it came to the knowledge of the Board in any way that witnesses can be had who are known to have knowledge upon the subject, even if it is inconsistent with the claims that he puts forth, they shall have opportunity to appear, and that all the knowledge that they should have on the subject should be drawn from them, and that the petitioner did not desire his witnesses to give any more *ex parte* statements, but that they should be subjected to the test of cross-examination so that the actual truth should be developed. (Board's Record, pp. 3 and 4.)

The petitioner's counsel also proposed to present the record of the court-martial and read evidence there taken to the Board preliminarily to introduction of what we may term, colloquially, oral evidence.

It also appeared that the names of a number of supposed witnesses, who had written letters, had been sent by the War Department and Army Headquarters either to the President of the Board or myself, who at that time in this case was merely the Recorder of the Board, with such duties as usually pertain to such office and mere regulation boards, where no law prescribes duties such as are prescribed for him on a court of inquiry. These names of witnesses I communicated to counsel.

With this state of facts the Board was called upon to decide what position it should occupy in the proposed action of counsel for petitioner.

Had this Board confined the petitioner's counsel to the presentation of affidavits in the nature of newly discovered evidence, so as to determine:

1st. Whether it was in fact *newly discovered* evidence, and,

2d. Whether, if it had been placed before the general court-martial which tried petitioner, it would have afforded ground for an acquittal, this was all he could, *under the circumstances*, have reasonably expected.

This Board, however, saw very plainly, that if evidence, so called, was to be presented and received by it as to the *merits*, and petitioner's counsel did not desire their witnesses to give any mere *ex parte* statements, some one must cross-examine and present rebutting evidence, if any there was.

This obligation, therefore, having been specifically devolved upon me by this Board on the 26th day of June, 1878, under the designation of "counsel for the government," with the full responsibility thus directly placed on me to cross-examine and to produce rebutting evidence, I have, with no knowledge of the case before that time, endeavored to elicit the truth, and the whole truth, irrespective of persons, so far as want of any judicial authority has permitted.

The representative of the government should never forget that justice is all that his government desires, but this does not demand of him a tacit or expressed acquiescence in whatever may be proposed by an accused.

The petitioner has come here with the assistance of three skilful, able, and learned counsel, after sixteen years' careful preparation, admitting also the legal assistance heretofore (by name) of some of the ablest counsel in the land, and that one of his present advisers here had been, when this Board first met, already a year engaged in his cause.

While, therefore, as representative of the government, I have never intentionally kept from petitioner's knowledge any properly admissible evidence which I deemed material to him (an obligation, by the way, which his counsel would not necessarily be under to the government), and while the record shows that I have even called new witnesses for government at his instance without knowing what they could testify to, thus giving him the privilege of cross-examination (Board's Record, p. 328), nevertheless, I have considered and do consider, despite some unthinking criticism, that the government has *some* rights, and that it is my duty to look out for them by the fullest endeavor to ascertain the truth, the Board itself being responsible for its method of procedure.

That obligation which, as I have said, this Board placed upon me I have not sought to avoid, for the reputation of the Army as well as the reputations of this Board as individual officers are concerned, that there shall be no one-sided, partial investigation of this case, if investigation like a retrial is admissible, and that the solemn record of a statutory court of nine duly sworn general officers shall not be reviewed without a previous exhibition of the most complete and conclusive evidence, so convincing that all may understand and acquiesce.

All examinations of a judicial or quasi-judicial nature have to take, for the ascertainment of truth, a well-defined course.

In all courts of criminal jurisdiction of the United States and in all its military tribunals, which are criminal courts of special and limited jurisdiction, the rules of common law in criminal cases, which are the result of matured experience of generations, prevail under the express ruling of the Supreme Court of the United States, except where such rules have been specifically modified by statute.

The proceeding before this Board is in the nature of a criminal case where these rules ought to apply; because, if we take the original record of evidence of petitioner's court-martial, with intent to compare it with other so-called evidence here introduced, certainly that which it is to be compared with must be such only as would be legally admissible on a court-martial in case it had been offered on the trial; for anything presented and received of a different character would have a tendency to impair the conclusion arrived at:

1st. Because it would be impossible to determine what weight had been given to it as against *legal* evidence in the original record; and,

2d. Because it would violate the only legal mode for the ascertainment of truth and satisfaction of public justice in military procedure.

These remarks I make preliminarily to future discussion of some portions of petitioner's evidence, so called.

When I heard and read the elaborate opening statement of petitioner's counsel, I was glad to perceive that it coincided with the opinions and sympathies I had hitherto entertained. With no knowledge of the facts, it seemed to me that the petitioner's case was strong—that injustice had possibly been done him, and I did not hesitate, in a private way, to express my sentiments, sentiments entertained by many others, on precisely the same grounds.

2 G

PETITIONER'S UNRELIABLE STATEMENTS:

After I began to study the case under the responsibility put upon me by the Board, several things in that argument or statement attracted my attention, and led me, on further search for the truth, to the reluctant conclusion I felt constrained to express in my opening argument. Those were—

FIRST. A suppression or avoidance of the fact (petitioner's opening statement, pp. 6 and 7) that the extraordinary exertions the petitioner made to embark at Newport News for Aquia Creek by midnight of the 20th of August, 1862, did not arise, as he would have had us believe, from eagerness to join General Pope and come under his command, but were because he had an express order to that effect *direct* from Major-General Halleck, the general-in-chief at Washington, and also a pressing telegram from Major-General McClellan, his then immediate commander, to push off, as it was a matter of life or death (G. C. M. Record, p. 233).

SECOND. An allegation in his argument that the regiments forming Piatt's brigade of Sturgis' division never reported to petitioner on the 29th of August, 1862, an allegation which the evidence of General Griffin (pp. 164 and 165) and also the testimony of General Sturgis or General Piatt show to have been directly contrary to the fact. This is also apparent from the opening statement (p. 89), in which he shows that this brigade was with him at Warrenton Junction.

THIRD. Another allegation in that deliberate and well-considered argument or statement (page 29), viz, that the petitioner knew Longstreet's separate force was strongly posted in his front and that it did not amount to less than 25,000 men, when in his equally well considered defense before the general court-martial which convicted him (G. C. M. Record, p. 266), he deliberately averred that this separate force, which he then also insisted was in front of him, amounted as he then (January 10, 1863) calculated it, at "from ten to fifteen thousand strong." Thus on his trial he advanced precisely the same line of defense as now, and in order then to make a reasonable excuse, alleged that the enemy before him on the 29th of August, 1862, was, according to his then assumed belief, "from ten to fifteen thousand strong"; but subsequently, in order to get a rehearing or review of his case, and to lead to the conclusion that he was the victim of circumstances, the presence of even 15,000 men before him would not have been sufficient to excuse his conduct, and he adds, for convenience, at least 10,000 more to the enemy, and presents to us the possibility generally offered by the Confederates (as see Longstreet's letter in petitioner's opening argument, p. 51, and his evidence, Board's Record, p. 64, also Beverly Robertson's testimony, Board's Record, p. 178), that if the Union forces had attacked, annihilation or destruction would have been the inevitable result. We know from our own military experience what forces three years later were placed in that category.

FOURTH. The fourth allegation which attracted my notice was one deliberately made by counsel for petitioner after concluding petitioner's opening statement (Board's Record, p. 9), to the effect that during the battle of the 29th of August, 1862, the petitioner did not have any belief whatever that the troops of General Pope were sustaining defeat and retiring from the field, and further that there was no ground for such a belief on petitioner's part or on the part of anybody else. This, it will be perceived, is directly contrary to a different part of the opening statement of petitioner, where, for another purpose, he introduced a dispatch he sent that very day to Generals McDowell and King, in which he said that—

• • • As they [the enemy] appear to have driven our forces back, the fire of the enemy having advanced and ours retired, I have determined to withdraw to Manassas. (Petitioner's statement, p. 35, dispatch No. 29.)

If the petitioner never had any belief whatever that General Pope's forces on his right were being driven back and retiring from the field, and if there was no ground for such belief, on his part or on the part of anybody else, or that they were even engaged, why did he actually send such a dispatch, a dispatch, it may be added, which he was proven on the original trial to have sent, and which he was willing to acknowledge for another line of defense before this Board?

If he sent that dispatch knowing it was false, but as an excuse for what he proposed in it to do, he intentionally sent thereby a notice the effect of which would have been to absolutely paralyze any offensive movement which the commanding general might have proposed to make at an auspicious moment, and thus ruin any plan of battle about to be executed, and possibly compel the commanding general, in the midst of success, to stop and order a retrograde movement to prevent being outflanked on his left by the advance of the forces from whose flank petitioner withdrew. If the petitioner did not believe what he said in that dispatch, he committed a great, a stupendous crime, for on those and previous exertions of General Pope depended the safety of the national capital.

The petitioner has stated in the part of his argument where he quotes this dispatch, that, "on going to the head of his column," he found he was misinformed, but he does not anywhere show (nor has he shown at any time in this case) that he notified either Generals Pope, McDowell, or King that he did not intend to carry out the determination expressed in that message.

We now know, and will see in the course of this argument, how he issued other orders and sent other messages of the same tenor, which, if they had come to the notice of the general court which tried him, would possibly have saved us all the trouble of reviewing this case.

FIFTH. The fifth point in petitioner's maturely considered opening statement which attracted my attention was in language as follows (page 57):

And I now repeat (and it is shown in the record) that at no time before dark had I or my officers knowledge of any other than an artillery contest going on, or of any *battle* pending, or that General Pope needed any aid.

On his trial he had called Col. E. G. Marshall, Thirteenth New York Volunteers (now colonel United States Army, retired, then a captain in the Regular Army), who commanded his advance skirmishers, and who said:

I could see General Pope's left and the enemy's right during the greater part of the day, about two miles off, perhaps more, diagonally to our front and to the right. The enemy set up their cheering and appeared to be charging and driving us, *so that not a man of my command but was certain that General Pope's army was being driven from the field.* In the different battles I have been, I have learned that there is no mistaking the enemy's yell when they are successful. It is different from that of our own men. Our men give three successive cheers, and in concert, but theirs is a cheering without any reference to regularity of form, a continual yelling.

Which evidence he also quoted in his defense. (G. C. M. Record, pp. 190, 269.)

The petitioner has since, as we have seen, recalled Colonel Marshall before this Board for additional evidence on other points.

That original evidence of this witness, just quoted, itself absolutely contradicts the petitioner's declaration in his opening statement or argument here. The Board will perceive that this is a little different from the state of affairs as described by the counsel who has last preceded me. The petitioner's troops at the head of his column saw and heard this firing and fighting on the left of General Pope's army, but he, away back to the rear, at junction of the Sudley Springs and Manassas and Gainesville roads, was in a position to hear Kearney's firing upon the right, near Sudley church. Additional thereto, in the opening statement itself, we find some of petitioner's own orders or dispatches, which he sent on the 29th of August, from which I quote, viz (dispatch No. 27, p. 94):

To Gen'l MORELL:

Push over to the aid of Sigel and strike in his rear. * * * See if you cannot give help to Sigel. If you find him retiring, move back toward Manassas.

If Major-General Sigel's corps of General Pope's army had not then been in action, and the petitioner did not know that it was, or that it needed help, why did he issue this order?

Again (dispatch No. 37, p. 96):

General MORELL:

" * * The *battle* works well on our right, and the enemy are said to be retiring up the pike.

Again (dispatch No. 31, p. 95):

General MORELL:

* * * All goes well with the other troops.

Again (dispatch No. 38, p. 96):

General MORELL:

* * * McDowell says all goes well and we are getting the best of the fight.

From these (from page 94 to 96 of his statement), over his own signature, despite his deliberate statement to the contrary, on page 57, it is apparent that both he and his officers knew there was a battle pending, and that he himself knew, by his order to his senior division commander to push over and help Sigel, that aid *was* needed.

He also knew a battle was impending, from a dispatch General Pope had sent to him that very morning, which was received by petitioner at Bristoe, at 5.30 a. m., August 29, in which General Pope ordered him up and said (see dispatch in petitioner's opening statement, p. 93, and G. C. M. Record, p. 235):

It is very important that you should be here at a very early hour in the morning. A severe engagement is likely to take place, and your presence is necessary.

It is apparent, therefore, from the admitted, heretofore proven facts set forth for other purposes by the petitioner in his own opening statement, that during all of that same 29th of August, 1862, both he and others of his command had knowledge of a pending battle, and that General Pope needed aid, despite the emphatic statement the petitioner has made to the contrary.

SIXTH. My attention was further drawn to still another paragraph in petitioner's opening statement (page 38), in which, referring to Friday, 29th August, 1862, he said as follows:

My troops were without food at this time, and so continued throughout the next day, except a small supply of hard-tack which they received that night.

On page 91, however, of that statement he printed a dispatch he sent to Maj. Gen. A. E. Burnside, at Aquia Creek, dated Bristoe, 28th August, 1862, 9.30 a. m., in which he said:

> I feel as if on my way now, and thus far have kept my command and trains well up More supplies than I supposed on hand have been brought, but none to spare. * * *

And on page 92, in another dispatch to Major-General Burnside, dated Bristoe, 6 a. m., 29th August (the very day of the battle), he said:

> I shall be out of provisions to-morrow night. Your train of forty wagons [provisions] cannot be found.

Thus, according to his own official reports, made at the time, he had—even without Burnside's forty wagons—enough subsistence for his command, not only for the 29th, but for the 30th, and yet he has stated here, apparently forgetful of these dispatches, that he had no provisions for his command that very 29th of August, when he reported he had.

SEVENTH. Another point in his deliberate opening argument which impressed me was the statement (on page 17) that he—

> Became informed (27th August) that the general policy of the campaign was to avoid a general action with the main forces of the enemy till large re-enforcements from the Army of the Potomac should join us.

Nevertheless, he knew that Major-General Banks' corps of General Pope's Army had attacked the enemy at Cedar Mountain on the 9th of August; and in his (petitioner's) opening statement (page 82), in a dispatch he sent on the 24th of August, 2 p. m., to Generals Morell and Sykes, he himself said:

> Pope attacked the enemy yesterday near Sulphur Springs, and the latter retreated. He was to renew the attack to-day, and it is probable Pope was pushing after him, knowing the river at Rappahannock was not fordable. General Halleck's orders are for us to hold the Rappahannock.

Again, in another dispatch of petitioner—this time to Major-General Burnside (petitioner's opening statement p. 84)—dated "Advance, 25th August, 1862," petitioner said: "Banks and Sigel are at Sulphur Springs fighting to-day."

Again, in another dispatch, which petitioner has printed (opening statement, p. 87), from General Pope to himself, dated "Headquarters Army of Virginia, Warrenton Junction, 26th August, 1862, 7 a. m.," the latter, after ordering him to move forward as speedily as possible * * * so as to "easily move to the front," said:

> I do not see how a general engagement can be postponed more than a day or two.

Again, in another dispatch to petitioner from General Pope, printed in the former's same statement (page 88), dated Headquarters Army of Virginia, Warrenton Junction, 27th of August, 1862, 4 a. m., General Pope said he wanted petitioner to march direct to that place as rapidly as possible, and, referring to the enemy, said:

> We will probably move to attack him to-morrow in the neighborhood of Gainesville which may bring our line farther back towards Washington: of this I will endeavor to notify you in time. You should get here as early in the day as possible, in order to render assistance should it be needed.

Again, in another dispatch of petitioner to General Burnside, which he prints in his opening statement (page 17), just after saying that the general policy of the campaign was to avoid a general action with the main forces of the enemy, he said: "I send you the last order from General Pope, which indicates the *future* as well as the present;" and in that order (page 18) movements of troops were ordered for "operation against the enemy," and for petitioner's corps to push forward to "assist the operations on the right wing."

Again, in another dispatch of General Pope to petitioner, which the latter also printed (page 91 of his opening statement), dated Headquarters Army of Virginia, Bristoe Station, 27th of August, 1862, 6.30 p. m., referring to General Hooker's fight at Bristoe, he said:

The enemy has been driven back, but is retiring along the railroad. We must drive him from Manassas and clear the country between that place and Gainesville, where McDowell is.

Again, at 9.30 a. m., petitioner sent a dispatch to General Burnside, dated Bristoe, 28th August, in which he said:

My command will soon be up and will at once go into position. Hooker drove Ewell some three miles, and Pope says * * * He hopes to get Ewell and push to Manassas to-day.

The statement, deliberately made by petitioner, that he became informed from General Pope at Warrenton Junction, on the 27th of August, that the general policy of the campaign was to avoid a general action with the main force of the enemy till large re-enforcements should join from the Army of the Potomac, is a statement made by way of preliminary justification or excuse for petitioner's subsequent conduct in not taking part in the battle of the 29th and his other offense of which he was convicted; but in the light shed by the dispatches and orders he himself has presented for other purposes, it is plain that General Pope was constantly on the offensive instead of the defensive, attacking the enemy on every possible occasion; that the petitioner knew it, and that his (petitioner's) deliberate opening statement as to the general policy being to avoid a general action is contradicted too pointedly in the dispatches just cited to require further illustration.

If, however, General Pope had been attempting to avoid any engagement until the Sixth and Second Corps of the Army of the Potomac joined him, then a treble, an awful responsibility, rests on whoever kept the gallant fighting Sixth Corps from joining General Pope at Centreville, which it did not do until late in the afternoon of the 30th of August, after our forces had been compelled to retire there after two days' battles (whose cannonade could be heard even in Washington), although the road by which it came from Alexandria was good and unobstructed—an easy day's march—and orders for its advance went to the commanding general of the Army of the Potomac on the 26th of August, and one brigade, Taylor's, of the Sixth Corps (Franklin's) was shoved up unsupported to Manassas Junction to meet the Confederate Major-General Jackson as he came in there. Brigadier-General Taylor himself lost his life while gallantly attacking, despite the enemy's superiority of force.

That the petitioner has no grounds whatever for the statement in his opening argument, that the general policy of the campaign was to avoid an action, is further evidenced by still later dispatches of General Pope, cited by him, as, for example, one of General Pope to petitioner, dated near Bull Run, August 29, 1862, 3 a. m. (petitioner's opening statement, p. 93), in which he was told that—

Kearney and Hooker march to attack the enemy's rear at early dawn * * * . A severe engagement is likely to take place and your presence is necessary.

We know from the charges of which petitioner was convicted that General Pope attacked the enemy at daylight of Friday, the 29th of August, 1862; and petitioner's own opening statement (on pages 26 *et sequitur*) shows that the *offensive* on that day was taken by the national Army.

Even on the 30th of August our forces again resumed the offensive, and petitioner himself says (opening statement, p. 65) that: "Early in the day [30th August] General Pope suggested plans of attack," thus showing all through General Pope's career with the Army of Virginia that that gallant officer was ever seeking to carry out the general policy of the campaign, " to fight like the devil," as previously ordered by Major-General Halleck, which was in strong and marked contrast to the conduct of the petitioner, who kept his command from becoming engaged until the *immediate* presence of that very commander, on the 30th, compelled him to make an attack. All this is in striking contrast to petitioner's unjustifiable remark that the general policy of General Pope's campaign was not to fight.

As we proceed in the consideration of this case, I shall be under the disagreeable necessity of presenting other instances which may compel the application of the maxim *falsus in uno, falsus in omnibus.*

STATUS OF PETITIONER AND METHOD OF PROCEDURE ADOPTED.

The petitioner in this case asked for "justice," not mercy. The pardoning power is an act of grace, clemency, or amnesty, and may be granted from the mere volition of the Executive, with or without cause; but whether or not it comes from compassion, from a settled policy, or as a mode of celebrating some joyful event, the petitioner, when he says he was unjustly convicted and wronged and wants to be " vindicated," does not appeal to that attribute of the Executive. As to a "review" which he asks for, we have seen Congress recently by law give the President power, specially and solely, to revise Ex-Surgeon-General Wm. A. Hammond's case (which this Board also had in charge), from which flows the necessary legal implication that without such legislative sanction such action would be *coram non judice.*

To take the original record of the court-martial as offered by the petitioner and compare it with other evidence and to report, is to review. Precisely, therefore, what the petitioner may lawfully demand and receive it is apparent he does not ask for.

It is to be regretted that this Board has no judicial or quasi judicial power; that is, power to compel attendance of witnesses, administe ran oath, or make any affidavit which may be presented "legal evidence," so that malicious false swearing to a material fact shall be perjury.

It is a great homage paid to justice and law that very few who are ever convicted of criminal offenses will admit guilt, but will declare to the last their innocence and the injustice of their punishment, even when about to suffer the extreme penalty of the law.

That this petitioner has on several occasions, as he asserts, sought by appeals to the Executive to obtain some sort of review or revision, I attach no importance to. It was not granted in the case of Brig. Gen. William Hull, U. S. A., but it has in this case permitted the fabrication of specious, and, in the case of his counsel (the late Reverdy Johnson), libelous pamphlets, which have gone to the files of the War Department, the public libraries and press of the country, and thereby manufactured unsubstantial sentiment.

My appearance in this case, under the ruling of this Board, was the first instance where any duly authorized representative of the government could publicly, and I believe honestly, say, during all these sixteen years of specious pleas, that the court of general officers which tried this petitioner, and convicted him of one of the gravest crimes, was composed of his personal friends, six of the nine being graduates of the United States Military Academy, and all men who he said on his trial knew him well, and as to each of whom he twice said, of record, he had no objection.

I have no desire to enter on an extended view of this case, nor have my current official duties and some considerable governmental counsel business in the civil courts during the recess afforded me that complete leisure to prepare such an elaborate argument as the three counsel on the other side present.

Furthermore, I do not deem it necessary. I have sought in this investigation to confine it to exactly what the petitioner did or failed to do under the orders he had.

The specifications and charges of which he was convicted are definite and precise, and the whole matter is really in a small compass, despite the collateral issues which counsel have skillfully presented, as to what this or the other did, or failed to do, so as to withdraw attention from their client and fix it upon somebody else, in order that the petitioner's disobedience, or criminal negligence, or positive willful offense, shall be lost sight of in the vague possibilities surrounding acts or omissions of others.

He comes before this Board, not with the presumption of innocence which attaches to those who plead "not guilty," but under a valid, subsisting, and executed sentence. Such fact, however, should not, and I believe has not, impaired the slightest of his rights, and I believe he has been treated, certainly by me, with courtesy and consideration. He has, however, everything to gain by this or any other rehearing, and nothing to lose.

When his counsel sought here (Board's Record, pp. 22, 23) to introduce:

1st. The very evidence as to his conduct on the 30th of August, in order to show *animus*, which had been, after careful argument by Reverdy Johnson, his counsel, ruled out on the original trial (G. C. M. Record, pp. 118, 133, 252, 280), it being the conduct of a day subsequent to petitioner's alleged offense;

2d. When he undertook to introduce cumulative evidence (p. 259);

3d. When he presented such evidence as General Pope's historical order to the Army of Virginia before petitioner joined him—an order known to petitioner on his trial—not produced there, but introduced here by way of justification or excuse as to *animus* (Board's Record, p. 278);

4th. When he undertook to recall some of his own witnesses who were witnesses on his trial in December, 1862, in order to *add* to and explain portions of their direct examination (Board's Record, pp. 282, 307, 440, 444, 461, 1127); and,

5th. When counsel declared, after referring to the "former trial," that the proceedings before this Board are a "full trial" (p. 293), and cross-examined government witnesses here on evidence given on the trial sixteen years ago (Board's Record, pp. 348, 801, 820), the effect was to make this Board an "appellate" tribunal to pass in judgment on the original court and to give weight to such evidence in its findings, and to make recommendations looking toward the revocation of this sentence on the ground, partially if not wholly, that in the judgment of this Board this special evidence, had it not been ruled out by the general court-martial, would have brought that tribunal to a different verdict.

In my opening argument of October 2 I went quite fully into certain branches of this case, both as to law and fact, stating, of course, as to the latter, only what I believed to be the real condition of affairs. The representative of the government, in a case like this, stands in a position that he need only pursue that line of reasoning which he believes to be just, with no obligation to a personal client to do the best that he can for him.

Thus have I approached this case.

Maj. Gen. Fitz-John Porter, of the United States Volunteers, and colonel of the Fifteenth United States Infantry, and brevet brigadier-general of the United States Army, was tried and convicted on two charges:

CHARGES AND SPECIFICATIONS OF WHICH PETITIONER WAS DULY CONVICTED.

FIRST.

Disobedience of orders, in violation of the [old] 9th Article of War, an offense punishable with death or such other punishment, according to the nature of the offense, as a court-martial might inflict.

SECOND.

Violation of the [old] 52d Article of War, in misbehaving himself before the enemy; also an offense punishable with death or such other punishment as shall be ordered by the sentence of a general court-martial.

These Articles of War are now known in the Revised Statutes of the United States respectively as articles 21 and 42.

The specifications of which he was convicted were briefly and substantially as follows, namely:

CHARGE 1ST.—VIOLATION OF THE 9TH ARTICLE OF WAR.

First specification.

That he received, at Warrenton Junction, Va., in the evening of 27th August, 1862, an order from General Pope, dated at 6.30 p. m., from Bristoe Station, announcing a severe fight there between Hooker's division (of Heintzelman's corps) and the enemy (Jackson's forces, Ewell's division), and directing him to *start at one o'clock at night, and come forward with his whole corps, or such part of it as was with him, so as to be at Bristoe Station at daylight the next morning, as it was necessary on all accounts that he should be there by daylight.* That if Morell's division (of accused's own corps) had not joined him (accused) yet at Warrenton, to send word to him to push forward immediately, and to send word to General Banks to hurry forward with his (Banks' corps) at all speed to take accused's place at Warrenton Junction. Further, that he, General Pope, sent an officer with this dispatch to conduct him to the place (Bristoe).

Second specification.

That the accused, being in front of the enemy at Manassas, Va., on the morning of the 29th August, 1862, received from General Pope a joint order, addressed to Generals McDowell and Porter, to move forward with their joint commands toward Gainesville, the accused having received written orders to the same effect an hour and a half before (see both orders hereafter set forth), and communication to be established between the two wings of the army; which order he did then and there disobey.

Third specification.

That the accused, being in front of the enemy during the battle of Manassas, on Friday, the 29th of August, 1862, did receive the following lawful order:

"HEADQUARTERS IN THE FIELD,
"*August 29th*—4.30 p. m.

"Major-General PORTER: Your line of march brings you in on the enemy's right flank. I desire you to push forward into action at once on the enemy's flank, and if possible on his rear, keeping your right in communication with General Reynolds.

12

The enemy is masked in the woods in front of us, but can be shelled out as soon as you engage their flank. Keep heavy reserves and use your batteries, keeping well closed to your right all the time. In case you are obliged to fall back, do so to your right and rear, so as to keep you in close communication with the right wing.

"JOHN POPE,
"*Major-General Commanding.*"

Which he did disobey, and fail to push forward his forces into action either on the enemy's flank or rear, and did in all other respects fail to obey said order.

CHARGE 2ND.—VIOLATION OF THE 52D ARTICLE OF WAR.

First specification.

That during the battle of Manassas, on Friday, 29th August, 1862, *while within sight of the field and in full hearing of its artillery,* accused received from Major-General Pope the 4.30 order (see above, Spec. No. 3), which he did then and there shamefully disobey, without any attempt to engage the enemy or aid the troops who were already fighting greatly superior numbers and were relying on the flank attack to secure a decisive victory and to capture the enemy's army; a result which must have followed from said flank attack had it been made in compliance with the order which accused so shamefully disobeyed.

Second specification.

That the accused, being with his army corps, on Friday, 29th August, 1862, between Manassas Station and the field of battle then pending between the forces of the United States and those of the rebels, and within sound of its guns and in the presence of the enemy, and knowing that a severe action of great consequence was being fought and that the aid of his corps was greatly needed, did fail all day to bring it on the field, and did shamefully fall back and retreat from the advance of the enemy without any attempt to give them battle and without knowing the forces from which he shamefully retreated.

Third specification.

That the accused, being with his army corps near the field of battle of Manassas, on the 29th August, 1862, while a severe action was being fought by the troops of Major-General Pope's command, and being in the belief that the troops of the said General Pope were sustaining defeat and retiring from the field, did shamefully fail to go to the aid of the said troops and general, and did shamefully retreat away and fall back with his army and leave to the disasters of a presumed defeat the said army, and did fail, by any attempt to attack the enemy, to aid in averting the misfortunes of a disaster that would have endangered the safety of the capital of the country.

In my opening argument in rebuttal, on the 2d of October, I discussed quite fully the composition of the court, the legal character of the court, and its jurisdiction over this case. As, however, the petitioner has, on various occasions, and even before this court, stated that he had been "improperly convicted and removed from the United States Army," and as the expression "improperly convicted" may be deemed to apply equally to the composition of the court as to the character of the evidence on which he was convicted, the exact condition of affairs, so far as the court is concerned, cannot be too prominently noticed.

JURISDICTION OF THE GENERAL COURT-MARTIAL.

The court consisted of nine general officers of the Army, appointed by Maj. Gen. Henry W. Halleck, then the General in Chief. On his trial, the then accused, before pleading to the merits, raised the question whether the court should not have been appointed by the President of the United States, under the act of May 29, 1830, for the reason that the officer who preferred the charges on which he was tried was inspector-general of the late Army of Virginia. That officer was Brig. Gen. B. S. Roberts, United States Volunteers, and at the time in the Regular Army. The implication in the point thus raised was, that as General Roberts had held this position by detail on the staff of the army commanded by Maj.

Gen. John Pope, therefore the latter must be assumed to have preferred the charges, or, that they were preferred " by his order." It further appeared on the record that there had been a previous military commission ordered to try the accused, but which was dissolved without action, and relative to which the then accused alleged (G. C. M. Record, p. 9) that " the subject-matter of its investigation was charges preferred against" him " by Maj. Gen. John Pope." In reply the judge-advocate of the court, the Hon. Joseph Holt, said (G. C. M. Record, p. 10), referring to the previous military commission, that " in point of fact no charges were ever preferred " by Major-General Pope; that the commission was dissolved and the general court-martial appointed, as first stated; that there was no reference in the order appointing the court-martial to General Pope at all; and further, that he wished to state distinctly that General Pope was not the prosecutor in the case, nor had he preferred the charges, nor did he, the judge-advocate, present them as being preferred by him. As the then accused did not pursue the matter further, the court was cleared for deliberation and very properly overruled the objection.

The general court-martial was appointed upon the 25th of November, 1862. Major-General Pope's connection with the Army of Virginia had terminated on or about the 7th of September. His army had been dissolved and incorporated with other forces, and he himself had, on the 16th of September, assumed command of the geographical Military Department of the Northwest, with his headquarters at Saint Paul, Minn.

The act of 1830, to which I have alluded, had been, it is pertinent to remark, made for a very different purpose than the one to which it was sought to be applied on the trial of this petitioner. It had been enacted for the purpose of preventing a commanding general from preferring charges against a commissioned officer and sending them before a court of his own appointment and then acting upon the proceedings in the case, as had been done but a short time before by a major-general commanding, who had preferred charges against the then Adjutant-General of the Army, had himself appointed the court and acted upon the proceedings, instead of forwarding the charges to the next higher authority, in order that a court might be appointed from that quarter, and the proceedings acted upon by the superior authority.

It will be perceived that in the case of this petitioner, Major-General Pope was not his commanding general at the time his court was ordered. He had not the slightest military power or authority in any particular over him; he was in a different sphere of duty; he could neither appoint the court for his trial, nor act upon its proceedings, nor carry the proceedings into execution. As to Brigadier-General Roberts, he was a general officer, detailed by the War Department for duty as inspector-general to that Army of Virginia, irrespective of who might be commanding general for the time being of that army. He belonged to the staff of that army, and not to the personal staff, like an aide-de-camp, of the commanding general. He had as much right to prefer charges against any officer in that army, or out of it, as anybody else. Therefore, as the petitioner was not under the command of Major-General Pope when the charges were submitted to trial or when the court was appointed, Major-General Pope was not his commanding officer, within the purview or intent of the act of 1830.

If anything further were needed in this case to show General Pope's connection with the charges, it is to be found in his evidence on the court-martial, where he testified, December 5, 1862 (G. C. M. Record, p. 23), that he did not of his own knowledge know who preferred the charges; that he had not preferred the charges against the accused.

He had, however, set forth in his official reports the latter's operations, as he did those of everybody else concerned in the campaign of August, 1862. It is quite needless to say that the making of his official report was but his duty, in order that justice might be done to all concerned. It possibly brought the accused to justice, because General Pope, as a sworn public officer of the government holding a high official position wherein the lives of thousands were within his control, was bound to state everything that he knew or believed bearing upon the events of the campaign which he had conducted, either in praise or censure of whoever might have been connected with that campaign. His reports were one source of information to the government and the public as to the transactions and the acts of commission and omission of the accused. The record shows that there were other sources of such information also.

General Pope's power or ability to bring the accused to justice after he became firmly convinced of his guilt was a power limited solely to the preparation and presentation of official reports; because, as we know from the Court-Martial Record, it was not until he arrived in Washington after the close of the campaign that he became firmly convinced of the criminal conduct of the accused, made evident to him beyond peradventure by the exhibition to him by President Lincoln of the dispatches and communications which the accused had sent to Major-General Burnside, and which that faithful officer had sent to the President (G. C. M. Record, p. 23). His, Pope's, power to act or command had then ceased, as Major-General Porter had resumed his connection with the Army of the Potomac, under a different commander. General Pope could not even order charges to be preferred by any of his staff except his personal staff, because he had no longer a military staff to the Army of Virginia, which was now dissolved. In military practice we know that when a staff officer prefers charges by direction of his commander he does so with the explicit statement, "By order."

I am constrained to enter into this collateral issue somewhat from the manner in which the petitioner has for a series of years, without the slightest warrant, held up Major-General Pope as his "prosecutor," because of General Pope's remarks in his report to the Committee on the Conduct of the War, made January 27, 1863, that he considered it a duty he owed to the country to bring Fitz-John Porter to justice, lest at another time, and with greater opportunities, he might do that which would be still more disastrous; and that with his conviction and punishment ended all official connection that General Pope had since had with anything that related to the operations he conducted in Virginia.

The petitioner knew as well as we know that it was a moral obligation and a duty on the part of the commanding general, as far as was in his power, to bring to the notice of the government anything that he believed would tend to bring a delinquent officer to justice. The verdict of the general court-martial which tried and convicted this petitioner of these grave crimes shows that General Pope had sufficient probable cause to induce a belief that the petitioner was guilty when he made his reports. This obvious official duty of General Pope should relieve him from any imputation of being animated by personal hostility to the petitioner, for whatever his personal feelings might have been towards the accused, friendly or otherwise, his duty would remain the same. If the accused, or his counsel, on the original trial had desired to know how or why or when Brigadier-General Roberts had come to prefer the charges against him, he could undoubtedly have ascertained when General Roberts was called and sworn as a witness, by asking him the question.

COMPOSITION OF THE GENERAL COURT-MARTIAL.

Having thus shown the legality of the general court-martial as a court properly appointed, merely for the purpose of again refuting the many insinuations and implications on behalf of the petitioner which have gone forth for so many years, next to be considered is the composition of the general court-martial.

The petitioner has deliberately asserted here, when referring to the court of nine general officers which tried him, that they "could not sit with that calm necessary for a judicial deliberation"; that his sentence was "undeserved," and that he was "improperly convicted."

In my opening argument I mentioned who those nine general officers were who, with the Hon. Joseph Holt as Judge-Advocate, formed the judicial tribunal under the military laws to administer justice. There had not been a court in the Army of the United States composed of officers of such rank since the close of the Revolutionary war. They sat, not as we are sitting, under the mere oath which we took when we accepted our commissions as officers in the Army years ago, but under the oath which the statute has wisely provided in cases of trials, "to well and truly try and determine, according to the evidence, and to duly administer justice without partiality, favor, or affection." When a court sits thus, it is only the most overwhelming and convincing proof which would justify in the slightest degree any one in saying that the sentence awarded by it was undeserved, or that the court "could not sit with that calm necessary for a judicial deliberation." The officers who tried the accused were, many of them, his intimates, and all his friends. • Even when he raised the point as to jurisdiction, he said it was "not with the slightest purpose of taking any exception to any member of the court" (G. C. M. Record, p. 10); and yet two of the members of that court had been active participants with him in the August campaign. Even before he raised the jurisdictional question he declared formally of record that he had no objection to any member of the court (G. C. M. Record, p. 5), thus, on two different occasions, deliberately placing himself on record in this matter. Of the nine general officers, six were graduates of the United States Military Academy, and the President of the Court was an intimate personal friend of the accused. The latter, in his defense on his trial, said, in addressing the court (G. C. M. Record, p. 256):

Yourselves most, if not all of you, have known me well. Your eminent official law adviser [meaning Judge-Advocate-General Holt], who has conducted this prosecution calmly and fairly, so far as on him depended, but with a vigilance which his duty demanded, himself, in the recent past, when numerous events hinged on the great sway which in his high post he bore, has trusted me, and has felt that his trust was in nowise betrayed.

It is plain from this that the court were his friends, and that the Judge-Advocate-General had respected him and esteemed him, or he would not have trusted him, or would have been prejudiced against him.

To the petitioner's carefully prepared written defense on the merits the Judge-Advocate made no reply whatever, but in alluding to the length of the investigation said (G. C. M. Record, p. 227):

I will simply remark that this case has been thoroughly and most patiently investigated. A continuous session of forty-five days sufficiently attests this.

I know of no instance in the history of the American Army where a general court-martial in the trial of a cause has devoted as many days to it as were given to the case of the petitioner. This fact of itself is sufficient answer to the remark he has made that they "could not sit with that calm necessary for a judicial deliberation." In his address here he has asserted that many of his witnesses were actively engaged in the Army and were unattainable. The record, however, of his trial does not show it. On the contrary, he specifically stated that he was ready to go on with his case (G. C. M. Record, p. 118). From then until its close there is nothing whatever to show that he did not have summoned and in attendance every witness he asked for. When all his evidence was in, the court gave him all the time he desired to prepare his written address (G. C. M. Record, p. 225).

Soon after his court had adjourned *sine die*, President Lincoln, over his own hand, by an order dated January 12, 1863, directed Judge-Advocate-General Holt, in his quality as head of the Bureau of Military Justice, and in the usual course in such cases under the law—

To revise the proceedings of the court-martial in the case of Maj. Gen. Fitz-John Porter, and to report fully any legal questions that may have arisen in them, and upon the bearing of the testimony in reference to the charges and specifications against the accused, and upon which he was tried.

We have seen this review which the Judge-Advocate-General made under the law the subject of severe animadversion on the part of the petitioner. In other words, as I have said in my opening argument, the reviewer has been reviewed, and no longer is "the eminent official law adviser" who, through forty-five days of trial, had "conducted the prosecution so calmly and so fairly."

It is a curious fact, among the many unusual defenses which the petitioner has set up here, that he has attempted to show that President Lincoln, who acted upon the proceedings and the findings and sentence of the court, which was that he should be cashiered and forever disqualified from holding any office of profit or trust under the Government of the United States, never read the proceedings at all, but came to his determination of approval from the review made by the Judge-Advocate-General under his order. If this even was true, it is none the less a fact that the sentence is a valid and subsisting and a final and completed act. But it must be borne in mind that while the case was still progressing the record was being printed and published in the newspapers of the day (pp. 653, 655, and 659 Board's Record), and that portion of it which composed merely the record of the prosecution was printed as soon as the prosecution was completed (p. 346, Board's Record). So that when the case finally came into the hands of Mr. Lincoln he was quite thoroughly conversant with all its principal points; and all that he practically would have had to do would have been to examine the questions raised by the accused in his defense, and consider them in connection with the review. I believe that the court which tried this convicted officer was a court of as honorable and just men as ever have been assembled on any court-martial in the Army of the United States.

I am constrained as the representative of the government to say this on behalf of the members of that court, many of whom I knew personally, because bound by their oaths not to disclose or discover the vote or opinion of any particular member, those who still survive have for sixteen years suffered with dignity and patience language of aspersion and reproach from this petitioner, and in his behalf. Had it been confined simply to a portion of the secular press of the day I should hardly in an argument like this have considered it my duty to notice it. But the petitioner has made himself a party to the slanders and libels by indorsing and making use of the pamphlet published by his senior counsel, the late Reverdy Johnson, shortly after his trial, in July, 1863. The language of that pamphlet (p. 994, Board's Record) in reference to the members of the court-martial was indefensible and unwarranted. To charge that the general officers who sat upon that court were promoted in rank by President Lincoln, with the consent of the Senate of the United States, on account of and because they had voted for conviction, was a reflection not only on the court, or the members who were referred to, but upon the President and the Senate. It contained an implication that certain members had been false to their oaths and had disclosed or discovered the votes and opinions of the members of the court. It was an implication that President Lincoln himself was corrupt, that he wanted the conviction of the petitioner, and sought it by corrupting the very fountain of justice.

This pamphlet to which I have referred (page 11) was, on the 10th day of June, 1869, forwarded by the petitioner to President Grant, in an appeal which he then made over his own signature, in which he spoke of the "unparalleled injustice" with which he had been treated. The fact that so bold and malicious an attack on respectable and honorable men who deserved well of their country should thus be made is but one of the indications of a systematic and sustained plan, since the time the court rendered its judgment, to abuse and hold up to contempt all who have been unfortunately, directly or indirectly, concerned in the prosecution and conviction of the petitioner, either as judges, as judge-advocate, as witnesses, or as executive reviewing authority.

We have seen here that instead of confining the evidence to what the petitioner did or did not do on the 27th and 29th of August, under the specific limited charges on which he was tried, it has been sought, directly and indirectly, at one time for one purpose, at another time for another purpose, either to test the recollection of the witnesses by cross-examination, or in order to have a connected narrative, or presumably to discover bias or prejudice or contradiction, to bring in detached portions of the campaign for the purpose of showing inconsistencies or seeming confusion or errors in the campaign as conducted by those who had been witnesses against the accused in his trial or concerned therein, without opportunity for them to defend themselves, or judicial sanction to such proceeding.

CONDITION OF AFFAIRS JUST PRIOR TO THE FIRST CHARGE.

In taking up the charges seriatim of which the petitioner was convicted, a preliminary sketch of military affairs as they then stood in Virginia will be desirable for a correct understanding of the merits.

In the report or rather statement made by General Pope, by request, to the committee of Congress on the "Conduct of the War" (subsequent to petitioner's conviction, and introduced by the latter before this Board against my objection, and for purposes quite apparent), occur some remarks which will illustrate the subject. Said he (Pope):

When I first assumed command of these forces the troops under Jackson had retired from the Valley of the Shenandoah and were in rapid march toward Richmond, so that at that time there was no force of the enemy of any consequence within a day's march of any of the troops assigned to my command.

It was the wish of the government that I should cover the city of Washington from any attacks from the city of Richmond, make such dispositions as were necessary to assure the safety of the Valley of the Shenandoah, and at the same time so to operate upon the enemy's lines of communication in the direction of Gordonsville and Charlottesville as to draw off, if possible, a considerable force of the enemy from Richmond, and thus relieve the operations against that city of the Army of the Potomac. The first object I had in view was to concentrate as far as possible all the movable forces under my command.

He then refers to the disposition of the troops :

King's division of the same corps it was thought best to leave at Fredericksburg to cover the crossing of the Rappahannock at that point, and to protect the railroad thence to Aquia Creek, and the public buildings which had been erected at the latter place. While I yielded to this wish of the War Department, the wide separation of this division from the main body of the Army, and the ease with which the enemy would be able to interpose between them, engaged my earnest attention, and gave me very serious uneasiness.

While these movements were in progress commenced the series of battles which preceded and attended the retreat of General McClellan from the Chickahominy towards Harrison's Landing. When first General McClellan began to intimate by his dispatches that he designed making this move towards James River, I suggested to the President of the United States the impolicy of such a movement, and the serious consequences which would be likely to result from it, and urged upon him that he should send orders to General McClellan that if he were unable to maintain his position upon the Chickahominy, and were pressed by superior forces of the enemy, to mass his whole force on the north side of that stream, even at the risk of losing much material of war, and endeavor to make his way in the direction of Hanover Court-House; but in no event to retreat with his army farther to the south than the White House on York River. I stated to the President that the retreat to James River was carrying General McClellan away from any re-enforcements that could possibly be sent him within a reasonable time, and was absolutely depriving him of any substantial aid from the forces under my command; that by this movement the whole army of the enemy would be interposed between his army and mine, and that they would then be at liberty to strike in either direction, as they might consider it most advantageous; that this move to James River would leave entirely unprotected, except in so far as the small force under my command was able to protect it, the whole region in front of Washington, and that it would then therefore be impossible to send any of the forces under my command to re-enforce General McClellan without rendering it certain that the enemy, even in the worst case for themselves, would have the privilege and power of exchanging Richmond for Washington City; that to them the loss of Richmond would be trifling, while the loss of Washington to us would be conclusive, or nearly so, in its results upon this war.

I was so deeply impressed with these views that I repeatedly and earnestly urged them upon the President and the Secretary of War.

After General McClellan had taken up his position at Harrison's Landing I addressed to him a letter stating my position and the distribution of the troops under my command, and requesting in all earnestness and good faith to write me fully and freely his views, and to suggest to me any measures which he thought desirable to enable me to co-operate with him or to render any assistance in my power in the operations of the army under his command. I stated to him that I had no object except to assist his operations, and that I would undertake any labor and run any risk for that purpose. I, therefore, desired him to feel no hesitation in communicating freely with me, as he might rest assured that every suggestion that he would make would meet all respect and consideration at my hands, and that so far as it was in my power to do so I would carry out his wishes with all energy and with all the means at my command.

In reply to this communication I received a letter from General McClellan, very general in terms, and proposing nothing towards the accomplishment of the purpose I had suggested to him. It became apparent that considering the situation in which the Army of the Potomac and the Army of Virginia were placed in relation to each other, and the absolute necessity of harmonious and prompt co-operation between them, some military superior, both of General McClellan and myself, should be called to Washington and placed in command of all the operations in Virginia.

In accordance with these views Major-General Halleck was called to Washington and placed in general command. Many circumstances which it is not necessary here to set forth induced me to express to the President, to the Secretary of War, and to General Halleck my desire to be relieved from the command of the Army of Virginia and to be returned to the western country. My services were, however, considered necessary in the projected campaign, and my wishes were not complied with. I accordingly took the field in Virginia with grave forebodings of the result, but with a determination to carry out the plans of the government with all the energy and with all the ability of which I was master.

On the 29th of July, 1862, he left Washington with the design to cover, as far as possible, the front of Washington, and make secure the Valley of the Shenandoah, and so operate upon the enemy's lines of communication to the west and northwest as to force him to make heavy detachments from his main force at Richmond, and thus enable the Army of the Potomac, without molestation, to withdraw from its position at Harrison's Landing, and take transports for Aquia Creek or Alexandria.

During these movements the battle of Cedar Creek was fought 9th August.

On the 16th he became apprised by an intercepted dispatch that General R. E. Lee, with the main portion of the Confederate army, intended to overwhelm him before the Army of the Potomac could come to his assistance. The fate of the country depended on his ability to hold his ground until re-enforced by that army, for if the capital had fallen it is highly probable the Confederate Government would have been recognized by foreign powers.

On the 14th August the Confederate Maj. Gen. T. J. Jackson had begun his march from Gordonsville. He had obtained permission from General Lee to make one of his characteristically bold and decisive moves in advance, and on the knowledge of this fact many subsequent events will become plain. The permission was incautiously given; soon, I have reason to believe, repented of. Even General Longstreet himself admits having remonstrated when he heard of it.

The movements of General Pope's army during these trying days are worth studying. Limited, as he was, by orders from Washington, he did all.that a courageous and able general could do.

As late as the 20th, he was ordered by the general-in-chief to hold the line of the Rappahannock, and on the 21st " to dispute every inch of ground, and fight like the devil until we can re-enforce you."

Meanwhile Jackson, covered by the Bull Run Mountain Range, was marching rapidly to Salem and Thoroughfare Gap, positively outflanking General Pope, who, confined by his imperative instructions, could do. but little. Jackson was now about three days ahead of the main body of the Confederate army.

General Pope's army had been re-enforced from the Army of the Potomac by the Army Corps of Major-General Heintzelman and much of Burnside's Ninth Corps, under Reno, and by the division of Maj. Gen. John F. Reynolds, of Pennsylvania Reserves.

On the 26th August, Jackson marched from White Plains through Thoroughfare Gap, by Haymarket and Gainesville, reached Bristoe Station at sunset, and the same night sent a detachment to seize Manassas Junction.

On the 25th General Pope's headquarters had been at Warrenton, and the 26th they were at Warrenton Junction.

On the morning of the 27th General Pope, having relinquished his former line of operations, which he had held later than his judgment dictated, under the orders he had, began his movement against Jackson, and on the evening of that day General Hooker's division of Heintzelman's corps having moved along the railroad from Warrenton Junction toward Manassas Junction, and meeting Ewell's division of Jackson's forces at Bristoe Station in the afternoon, after a sharp fight drove him out in the direction of Manassas Junction. General Pope made his headquarters with this division.

In his rear, at Warrenton Junction, was the petitioner's command, the gallant Fifth Corps of the Army of the Potomac.

General McDowell with his own and Sigel's corps, and Reynolds' division, were at Gainesville, interposed between Jackson and Thoroughfare Gap, while Reno, with his corps and Kearney's division of Heintzelman's corps, was at and near Greenwich, within supporting distance of McDowell. Jackson's main force was concentrated at Manassas Junction—a point, by the way, he would possibly never have reached if the promised re-enforcements had been sent from Alexandria to that point.

The New Jersey brigade under Brig. Gen. Geo. W. Taylor, of the Sixth Corps (Franklin's), got up to Manassas Junction in season from Alexandria, but unsupported, after a gallant fight were routed and their commander mortally wounded. Had the entire corps been there the subsequent days' battles might not have occurred (Board's Record, pp. 540, 750).

Two courses now remained open for Jackson, seeing that his line of retreat through Gainesville and Haymarket to Thoroughfare Gap was held by McDowell, viz, to retire through Centreville, which would carry him still farther from the main body of General Lee's army, or to mass his force and assault Hooker at Bristoe Station and turn his right.

If this last move should be made, daybreak was the time when it would be most likely to be carried into effect.

At this juncture General Hooker reported his ammunition nearly exhausted, and that he had but about five rounds per man left.

We now come to the charges in this case.

FIRST SPECIFICATION, FIRST CHARGE, CONSIDERED.

The petitioner was convicted of this specification, that he had received at Warrenton Junction, Virginia, on the evening of August 27, 1862, an order from General Pope, dated 6.30 p. m., from Bristoe Station, announcing a severe fight there between Hooker's division of Heintzelman's corps and the enemy (Jackson's forces, Ewell's division), and directing him to start at one o'clock at night and come forward with his whole corps, or such part of it as was with him, so as to be at Bristoe Station at daylight next morning, *as it was necessary on all accounts that he should be there* by daylight, and that if Morell's division of his corps had not joined him at Warrenton to send word to him to push forward immediately, and to send word to General Banks to hurry forward with his (Banks') corps at all speed to take the place of the accused at Warrenton, and that General Pope had sent an officer with this peremptory dispatch to the petitioner at Warrenton Junction.

Did Major-General Porter do what he was distinctly and explicitly ordered to do by Major-General Pope, namely, march with his corps at one a. m. of August 27th from Warrenton Junction? Or did he arrive at Bristoe Station at daylight as commanded? The answer is that he *neither started nor attempted to start at one a. m., nor did he arrive at daylight* at the point to which he was ordered. The court convicted him of that offense, and he has not produced before this Board a single particle of "newly-discovered evidence," or even a new excuse, as the Board will perceive by reference to the record of his court.

On his trial he claimed that the roads were blocked with wagons, that the night was dark, that his troops were fatigued, that he made great personal exertions *after* the march began, *after daylight*, to clear the road. It further appeared that Major-General Pope sent messages to him to expedite his movements (accused's defense, G. C. M. Record, p. 256). It is no answer to such a charge in military law to enter upon a collateral issue by way of justification or excuse in order to ascertain whether there was any real necessity for a punctual compliance with the exact terms of such an order, or even whether it could be fully complied with. On the commanding general of the Union Army of Virginia, who issued the order, rested the responsibility of the operations with which he was charged by his government, in the face of an active and enterprising enemy flushed with success, it having recently relieved Richmond from danger, and having put the gallant Army of the Potomac for the time being on the defensive, in a position at Harrison's Landing, where it could not prevent the Confederates from entering on offensive operations. When Major-General Pope issued a peremptory order and indicated a certain time when its execution should be commenced, the petitioner had no right whatever to set his will up in opposition, and to say that he would not start until a later hour.

The cumulative evidence presented here has exhibited some curious facts, and careful examination will possibly show that they leave the petitioner's case worse than before.

It appears that under this order, instead of arriving at daylight as directed, the petitioner did not arrive himself until between 10 and 11 o'clock in the morning at Bristoe Station. In examining the language of the order it would seem to be quite impossible to put it in terms more precise or imperative. It was dated late in the afternoon, and it shows on its face that it contemplated the possibility that Major-General Morell's division of the Fifth Corps, then under the petitioner's command, had not yet arrived at Warrenton Junction. That the petitioner should be informed of the state of affairs, the order with unusual minuteness placed before him the circumstances as they were then seen by the commanding general. The order positively directed that he should leave Warrenton Junction at a precise time—no discretion was allowed; and the commanding general, in order that there should be no mistake as to the execution of it, sent an officer of his own staff to conduct the accused to Bristoe, so that he should have the benefit not only of that officer's knowledge of the road, but also the *direct, immediate influence and authority of the commanding general himself in doing anything that might be necessary to further the objects of the order.* As a reason why he should start at one o'clock in the morning this strong language is used: "It is *necessary on all accounts* that you should be here by daylight."

There is no question that the order was a lawful order. General Pope, in his examination before the court-martial, explained the reasons for the urgency of the order (G. C. M. Record, p. 12). Captain De Kay, Fourteenth United States Infantry, who carried the order, swore, on the original trial, that he delivered it between nine and nine-thirty p. m. (G. C. M. Record, p. 43).

The assistant adjutant-general of the accused, Lieut. Col. Frederick T. Locke, said the order was received at very nearly ten o'clock p. m. (G. C. M. Record, p. 134).

The petitioner had two divisions in his corps—the Fifth Army Corps—then under his command, viz, Maj. Gen. George W. Morell's and Brig. Gen. George Sykes'.

Maj. Gen. George W. Morell, on the trial in 1862 (G. C. M. Record, p. 143) said, when called for the accused, as to the time of his arrival at Warrenton Junction:

I arrived there myself about the middle of the afternoon. I think my command—the last of it—did not arrive there until near sunset.

And before this Board he has said that most of his divisions were there before dark (Board's Record, p. 430).

As to Sykes' division, Capt. Drake De Kay, who had been in Warrenton Junction early in the day of the 27th, testified on accused's trial, 8th December, 1862 (G. C. M. Record, p. 44), that the regulars of Sykes' division were in camp there as early as ten a. m., because he visited several officers of his own regiment in camp there.

Brig. Gen. George Sykes, United States Volunteers (now colonel Twentieth United States Infantry), says before this Board that he thinks his command got into Warrenton Junction about one p. m. 27th August (Board's Record, p. 445). Therefore, as the petitioner in his opening statement before this Board has stated (p. 22) as one of his excuses for disobeying Major-General Pope's order, that General Sykes, when discussing it with him at the time, represented his men, "after a long fatiguing march extending into night, as in no condition to renew the march without some interval of rest," it is sufficient to refer to Sykes' sworn statement as to the time his division arrived in Warrenton Junction—confirmed as it is by other evidence—in order to lead to the conclusion that the latter never said anything of the sort.

Now, what did this petitioner do when he got the order? Did he direct his assistant adjutant-general, who has been so much and so often a witness in this case, to send out a detachment to clear the roads, or to stop any wagons passing through Warrenton Junction towards Bristoe?

Captain De Kay, at the time (G. C. M. Record, p. 43), told him of the condition of the road—that it was good—that there were a good many wagons on it, but that he had passed the last wagon a little beyond Catlett's Station moving slowly.

Thus was he apprised of what was necessary in order to perform the required duty; but, handing the order to one of his generals, he remarked, "Gentlemen, there is something for you to sleep on" (G. C. M. Record, p. 43).

This precise expression remains uncontradicted, and even the petitioner's witness on his trial, Brigadier-General Butterfield, the only one he seems to have cared to interrogate on the subject, said that petitioner remarked "there was a chance for a short nap, or something of that sort, I do not remember the exact words" (G. C. M. Record, p. 185).

Captain De Kay then spoke up and told him—

That the last thing General Pope said to me [him] on leaving Bristoe Station, was that I [he] should remain with General Porter and guide the column to Bristoe Station, leaving at one o'clock, and that General Pope expected him certainly to be there by daylight, or relied upon his being there by daylight.

The petitioner, however, determined not to start until daylight (G. C. M. Record, p. 44), and Captain De Kay had nothing to do but wait and accept the hospitalities of corps headquarters.

Thus did the petitioner set up his will against the lawful order of his commanding general—orders he had sworn to obey in accepting his commission—and a jury of his peers convicted him of the crime after a patient and laborious investigation of forty-five days.

It will always be impossible to know the exact thoughts which influenced this petitioner in his manifold acts of omission and commission during the few eventful days he was under Major-General Pope's immediate command. We can gather them only from his words and acts.

The order being an urgent as well as an imperative one, why did he not send word to General Pope of his determination not to move. His delay might possibly ruin any movement or combination contemplated by his commanding general. Did he hope for this, or was he merely using every means to interpose delays, so that his late commanding general should reach the front from Alexandria and assume command of the whole?

To say that the veteran division of regulars under Brigadier-General Sykes would have straggled or become disordered and disintegrated in the nine-mile march to Bristoe, is to assume a want of discipline and *esprit de corps* in that splendid division which few who ever knew it will concede. To say that it was fatigued and not able to march is contradicted by pointing to the hour at which it arrived in Warrenton Junction.

According to petitioner's own witnesses, General Sykes' division had been in camp nearly fourteen hours, from 12.30 p. m. of the 27th August, before it would have had to move at all under General Pope's order, and if the government evidence is to be relied on, given as it was when the recollection was vivid, the division had been quietly in camp fifteen hours.

It is further to be remembered that General Pope's order contemplated only the march at 1 a. m. of Sykes' division, leaving Morell to follow, as he did not know whether the latter had yet arrived at Warrenton Junction or not.

However, even Morell's entire division, according to petitioner's own witnesses, had been in camp at least six hours, from 7 p. m., before any march was required.

No pretense can be raised that the petitioner here did not fully know the intent and effect of the order, for one of his witnesses on his trial, Brig. Gen. *Daniel Butterfield* (G. C. M. Record, p. 185) said that the accused, at the time, stated—

Rather decidedly, there was the order; it must be obeyed. That those who gave the order knew whether the necessities of the case would warrant the exertions that had to be made to comply with it.

Did he make the exertions to comply with it?

The whole allegation of disobedience of orders in this specification finds the true principle of obedience enunciated by the petitioner at the time he made that remark.

So necessary did the commanding general seem to think it was that the petitioner's troops should be speedily at Bristoe, that, as was shown on the original trial, he sent messengers to him *en route,* and even vouchsafed as late as 6.05 o'clock on the morning of the 28th to inform petitioner that General Hooker reported his ammunition exhausted, and requested him to come forward at once with all possible speed (Board's Record, p. 1126).

Fortunately for the nation General Jackson did not know the condition General Hooker's division was in, and made a night march with his whole command—infantry, cavalry, and artillery—via Manassas Junction to Centreville and stone house, on the very night petitioner pleads that it was too dark for him to move Sykes' regulars.

General Pope need not have given any reason whatever why he desired petitioner to march at 1 a. m. or why he desired him to be at Bristoe at daylight. His courtesy was thrown away, but the fact that he did go fully into his reasons for issuing the order took from the petitioner any *possible opportunity for exercising any discretion whatever as to literal compliance.*

There is not a word in the whole order which shows that General Pope left him any discretion as to the *end* to be obtained, viz, "On all accounts to be in Bristoe at daylight."

Anxious hours they must have been to the commanding general from daylight until all certainty of Jackson's attacking had passed away.

However, as the commanding general was not bound to give any explanation of his order, none is needed in considering whether the petitioner obeyed or disobeyed it.

Those were perilous and critical times for the government, requiring great and unusual exertions on the part of that army, and so far as the field and line and rank and file were concerned, there can be no question that they were actuated by a desire to do their whole duty.

The petitioner here took counsel with some of his general officers what should be done as to General Pope's order, although he had no power to call a council of war in order to transfer responsibility.

As to what the petitioner actually did, reference to the testimony of some of the witnesses will afford some indication.

If there were wagons on the road between Warrenton Junction and Bristoe, it is plain that the first simple duty of a commanding officer who had to make a night march would be to get control of the road by sending a detachment in advance and parking such wagons on each side as might be found in the way.

The Board will recollect the evidence of Brevet Brigadier-General Taylor, First Pennsylvania Cavalry, who had been encamped in that country for some weeks, and been over it a number of times, in which he described what an immense plain it was, with roads, as we see in their evidence, running parallel to each other for operations on both sides of the track; it was all open country at that time, with very little, if any, woods, and those in but detached pieces (Board's Record, p. 910).

Now, what were the exertions of the petitioner of after he got the order between 9 and 10 p. m. to move precisely at 1 a. m.? It seems he stepped out from the light of his tent to look around, and concluded it was dark, and then decided to postpone marching until 3 a. m. instead of 1 (G. C. M. Record, p. 185).

The same witness to this fact says he sent two aides to investigate the condition of the road and to ask General Pope to have the road cleared so that they could come up.

In this there must be error, or more would have been produced on the subject; but as the petitioner's aides actually remained with him, as appears by their evidence, they evidently did not do anything of the sort.

However, if such messengers were sent to General Pope, it appears explicitly by the witness's evidence that they were sent before the petitioner decided to postpone the marching until 3 a. m., which the witness also had recommended. Therefore, assuming it true that the request was sent to General Pope, it would have led him to believe that the petitioner proposed to start at the time he himself had ordered.

If the petitioner did actually send any one to General Pope during that night, requesting the road cleared, it would show that he *knew what he should do before marching at his end of the line.*

When Lieut. Col. *Joseph P. Brinton,* of the Second Pennsylvania Cavalry, went (G. C. M. Record, p. 205), at ten o'clock at night, from Catlett's Station to Warrenton Junction, on this very road that petitioner was to march over, and saw the latter at midnight, the petitioner then asked him if he would not send out some men, when he got back, to have the road cleared. Colonel Brinton says that he sent some men to get the wagons out of the way, but didn't know the result.

This, it will be observed, was after midnight. Already had the petitioner, for upwards of two hours, the order in his possession.

Major General *Morell* says he himself received no orders from petitioner to send any of his command to clear the road to Bristoe (Board's Record, p. 430).

Had any been sent from General Sykes' division it would undoubtedly have been shown, but it has not been.

Capt. *Francis S. Earle,* General Morell's assistant adjutant-general, (Board's Record, p. 414,) knew of no orders being given the night before, or any effort made to clear the road from Warrenton Junction to Bristoe Station.

Lieut. *Stephen M. Weld,* petitioner's aide-de-camp, has stated before this board on his behalf that *after* daylight he found the road completely blocked from Warrenton Junction for the first three miles.

General *Sykes,* however, and other of his witnesses, testified on the court-martial, in December, 1862, that his division, which led the column, ran upon this train of wagons within two miles of camp (G. C. M. Record, p. 177). He says that they halted for fully an hour on the Bristoe side of the stream, two miles) from Bristoe, and arrived at that place at 10.30 o'clock. His division was then thrown into position a little in advance of that place.

Maj. *G. K. Warren,* Corps of Engineers, then Colonel Fifth New York Volunteers, commanding a brigade of Sykes' division, called by petitioner, says (Board's Record, p. 31), they arrived at Bristoe between 8 and 9 a. m., 28th August. He further says as follows (Board's Record, p. 30).

I think we were under arms at about 3 a. m. We stood there waiting to get our place in column until daylight. Never left our camp until it was light enough to see. * * * Saw wagons all over the plain, but we were enabled, at the time we marched, to avoid them. I don't remember now of being impeded by any of the wagons after we got daylight.

Petitioner's chief of staff, Lieut. Col. *Frederick T. Locke,* says (Board's Record, p. 296):

Question. How far did you get along before there was any relief from cavalry sent forward by General Pope to your aid?
Answer. My recollection is that we had got out into open ground, and were not far from Bristoe.
Question. Catlett Station, I think you said before?
Answer. I think that is the name of the place.
Question. Before the arrival of that regiment did you have any cavalry that were available to clear the road?
Answer. No, sir. We had three or four orderlies.
Question. Did you accompany General Porter and ride up with him to General Pope on arrival?
Answer. I did.
Question. What happened then?
Answer. We rode up to where General Pope was sitting on his horse, I think on the slope of a hill nearly opposite Bristoe Station. General Porter rode up and accosted him, and told him the difficulties we had met on the march, and asked that measures be taken in order that the trains might be parked so that his column could come through; that the cavalry had only just reported that had been sent to him, for which he had applied. I was immediately sent back with authority from General Pope to have this cavalry close up the trains and park them as rapidly as possible, which I did.

The cavalry here referred to was probably the First Maine, left at Catlett's Station, according to this witness's evidence on the court-martial (G. C. M. Record, p. 136), though he did not then say that General Pope sent them.

This witness's recollection, however, is shown in his evidence in this behalf to be faulty, for Capt. *George Montieth,* petitioner's aide-de-camp, and called by him on the trial 2d December, 1862, said (G. C. M. Record, p. 126):

Question by accused. What efforts were actually made, and how long were you in removing the wagons, if you removed them at all?
Answer. * * * We were also assisted by *some cavalry sent with us.* I think there were some half dozen mounted men. After General Porter sent us with the cavalrymen, he also sent Lieutenant-Colonel Locke with either a company or squadron of cavalry to labor in the same way.

That is, from the other end of the line.

This cavalry, it will be perceived, was that which the petitioner tem-

porarily had under Lieut. Col. Jacob S. Buchanan, Third Indiana Cav.
alry, at Warrenton Junction.

The fact that Lieutenant-Colonel Locke has a mistaken recollection on this interesting point will become of serious import in discussing later his recollection on other serious points.

As the column tardily approached Bristoe over the plains of Manassas, despite General Pope's urgent messages, "stumps" make their appearance in the road near that place, which shows that the column must have advanced on different parallel army roads over those extensive plains, as the main road had been in use probably a century.

As to when they arrived, Col. *Charles A. Johnston*, Fifteenth New York Volunteers, Martindale's brigade, Morell's division, a witness for petitioner, says, substantially (Board's Record, p. 84), his regiment did not leave Warrenton Junction until 6 a. m., and reached Bristoe at about 3 p. m. Was under arms at 2 a. m.; but as the roads were blocked with wagons, did not leave until 6.

This shows the character of petitioner's efforts to join General Pope, for a guard across the roads at Warrenton Junction would have compelled the wagons to take to the fields in order to get along.

His recollection, however, it will be perceived, is very different from General Warren's.

Maj. *George Hyland, jr.*, Thirteenth New York Volunteers, Martindale's brigade, Morell's division, called by petitioner (Board's Record, p. 114), says his regiment camped "that evening, I think, at Bristoe," 28th August.

Bvt. Brig. Gen. *Chauncey McKeever*, assistant adjutant-general United States Army, a witness for petitioner, and formerly chief of staff, Heintzelman's corps, has testified, on cross-examination, as follows (Board's Record, p. 151):

Question. If a peremptory order had been received at Warrenton Junction to move from that place to Bristoe at 1 a. m. on the night of the 27th and 28th of August, is it your opinion, as a military man, that the troops at Warrenton could have been put in motion on the road to Bristoe in order to comply with such a command?
Answer. They could have been put in motion, I presume. I know nothing to prevent their being put in motion.
Question. Do you recollect about what time it was daylight on the 28th of August?
Answer. I should think about four o'clock; may be a little later—not much.

Just here it is well to observe that while the petitioner thought it was too dark to move at one o'clock, he fixed the time for leaving at two hours later, when it would still be dark; in fact, at a time when, as we know, just before day, it is always the darkest.

Lieut. Col. *Robert Thompson*, One hundred and fifteenth Pennsylvania Volunteers, a witness for petitioner, said there were "stumps in the road," in one part, and then, on cross-examination, testified as follows (Board's Record, p. 239):

Question. Suppose part of your troops had several hours' rest on the day of the 27th, and you had received a peremptory order to march at one o'clock, with such troops as you could, with your command from Warrenton Junction to Bristoe, could you have done it that day?
Answer. If I could I would. I would have *tried* it.

Capt. *B. B. Fifield*, commissary of subsistence, called by the accused on the trial in 1862 (G. C. M. Record, p. 123), said that the wagons stretched along for three or four miles. He found them on the way from Warrenton Junction to Bristoe, between Warrenton and Kettle Run; that there was a jam between Warrenton Junction and Kettle Run; but when questioned by the court he stated the case as follows:

Examination by the Court:

Question. With one hundred efficient men, commencing at 10 o'clock that night, do you think you could have cleared the wagon-road so as to have rendered it passable for troops?

Answer. If I could have had command of the wagon-road and of sufficient force when the wagon-trains commenced their movement, I think I could have kept them from a jam.

Col. *Robert E. Clary,* called by the accused in 1862, answered, on cross-examination, as follows (G. C. M. Record, p. 121):

Question. In your opinion, could or could not General Porter, after the receipt of his order to move, which receipt was at 9.30 p. m. on the 27th of August, have cleared the road entirely of wagons by one or two o'clock that night, so that his march would not have been much impeded?

Answer. I think the troops could have passed over during the night had a sufficient force been sent in advance to have cleared that road of those obstructions, which, at the time I passed over it, extended only three miles, I think. When I passed over the road it was between two and three o'clock in the morning. What the obstructions had been previous to that time I am unable to say.

Question. Will you state whether at one o'clock the character of the night and the state of the road was such as, in your judgment, to render practicable the march of General Porter's troops to Bristoe Station, to arrive at or about daylight?

Answer. Not without the preliminary steps which I have previously stated ought to have been taken.

Question. Were or were not the first three or four miles of the road from Warrenton unobstructed?

Answer. They were, as I passed over them.

It will be remembered that the accused's witnesses corroborated exactly what Captain De Kay, the government witness, said as to the character of the road at that time of night, between Warrenton Junction and the run, for the first two or three miles; and also what General Sykes, a witness for the accused, stated to be the case next morning.

It is a curious fact that one of petitioner's then aide-de-camps, Lieut. George Monteith, was on the route from Warrenton Junction to Catlett's Station—this very road—having left the former place half an hour before sunset (G. C. M. Record, p. 126), and found some wagons stopped, and others moving along; but when he got back, although undoubtedly becoming aware of the order which Porter had received, he made no report as to the wagons. He had been ordered to find a road to Greenwich, where, under previous orders, Porter's corps was destined. Yet he did not consider it of sufficient importance to allude to the fact of wagons being on the road. The fact is it was too common a thing, and did not impress itself upon his mind as an insuperable obstacle to any movement. Next morning Porter sent him and Lieutenant Weld, with but about half a dozen cavalrymen, to clear the road of wagons, although he then had quite a strong detachment at his headquarters of cavalry. This was between 4 and 5 a. m.—*after* daylight—when he must have known that the wagoners were on the move again. Of course those that were in the park during the night by the side of the road, after daylight, taking an hour to feed, and so forth, being, as is seen, several miles beyond Warrenton, began to pull out into the road and move in the same direction as petitioner's troops. Of course, when his advance came up with them, he found the road quite full.

Lieutenant-Colonel *Locke,* assistant adjutant-general, already referred to, who was a witness for the accused in 1862 as well as before this Board on this subject, then swore that petitioner had a report of the condition of the road from Warrenton Junction to Bristoe at *about* 8 *p. m.* (G. C. M. Record, p. 139); that petitioner made great personal exertions to clear the way *after daylight,* and that his staff assisted, and that at Catlett's Station he got a detachment of the First Maine Regiment assigned to him (G. C. M. Record, p. 131). This witness stated what was undoubtedly the more prudent course in answer to the following question by the court:

Question. Upon a report of bad roads, would it be a reason for commencing the march before or after the time fixed in the order, if the time ought to be varied from at all?

Answer. If the time were to be varied from, it would be better to have it prior to the time fixed than after.

Corporal *Solomon Thomas*, Eighteenth Massachusetts Volunteers, Martindale's brigade, Morell's division, called for the government, corroborates Col. Charles A. Johnston and Major Hyland, petitioner's witnesses, as to the late hour Martindale's brigade arrived, though he puts the arrival of his own regiment at about 2 p. m. 28th August (Board's Record, p. 844); but, like General Warren, can recollect no obstacles to their march until near Bristoe, where they turned into a road where there were "stumps" (page 843, Board's Record).

It is not necessary to discuss a collateral issue, such, for example, as to whether there was any necessity, real or fancied, for the issuance of General Pope's order to the petitioner, because, as has just been remarked, he was not bound to give any reason for it.

However, departing in this instance from the straight path of argument as to what the petitioner did or failed to do under the specific charges of which he was convicted, it seems proper, in consequence of the unprecedented assault made by him on his former commanding general, to say, collaterally, that General Pope, on the original trial, explained to the court some of the reasons for the urgency of the order (G. C. M. Record, p. 12).

Petitioner, with an assumption of knowledge as to what was transpiring at Bristoe on the afternoon of the 27th, which was necessary in order to justify his departure from his orders, says that General Pope did not know that General Hooker's division was out of ammunition until an hour after he sent petitioner his orders at 6.30 p. m.

Not only did General Pope swear that he did know it (G. C. M. Record, p. 12), but General Heintzelman, General Hooker's corps commander, also has sworn (G. C. M. Record, p. 80) that he himself made known that fact to General Pope late in the afternoon of the 27th of August, so that General Pope had that information both from General Hooker and General Heintzelman.

Bvt. Maj. *Willard Bullard*, Seventy-fourth New York Volunteers, second brigade, Hooker's division, has said before this Board (Board's Record, p. 732) that, on the afternoon of the 27th of August, his regiment had pretty well exhausted its ammunition.

Lieut. *Charles Dwight*, A. D. C., says on this subject as follows (Board's Record, p. 722):

Question. Where were you on the evening of August 27, 1862?

Answer. I was on the field where the skirmish with the rear brigade occurred, at Bristoe Station, in Hooker's division, Excelsior brigade.

Question. When that action was over what was the condition of your command as to ammunition?

Answer. We were short of ammunition. I was sent by Colonel Taylor to General Hooker to ascertain what we should do in case we were attacked during the night, as there seemed to be some doubt as to whether it was a rear guard or whether there would be an attack made. General Hooker replied to me, nearly as I can recollect, "Tell Colonel Taylor that we have no ammunition, but that there has been communication had with General Pope, and General Pope has communicated to General Porter, and General Porter should be here now; he will be here in the morning certainly."

Question. What direction did you receive in case you were attacked?

Answer. To do the best we could and depend upon our bayonets.

The fact that when petitioner got to Bristoe Station the occasion for his presence had passed, had nothing to do with the question whether he had obeyed or disobeyed his orders.

Lieut. Col. Frederick Myer, chief quartermaster to Major-General McDowell's corps, was ordered just before dark by General Pope, in consequence of General Hooker's action ahead of him, to put all the trains in park.

He testified that he did so, "and gave directions to all the quartermasters to go into park," and that "the head of the train commenced moving just at daylight"; that the roads between Warrenton Junction and Bristoe were in "excellent condition at that time" (G. C. M. Record, p. 108). On cross-examination he said, "the trains were not unharnessed, but ready to move at a moment's notice." The head of the train was about a mile and a half from where General Hooker had his battle, and the wagons were coming into park nearly all night.

From this evidence it will be perceived that the time fixed for the petitioner's march to Bristoe was *just the time when the road would be least obstructed, and with the most ordinary and customary precautions, such as have been indicated, the petitioner could have obtained complete control of not only the road, but the fields on each side, if necessary.*

It is also to be noted that only precisely the same points are raised now as were presented to the court.

With reference to the exertions which the petitioner knew at the time he could have made to have prevented the slightest obstruction to his march, the testimony of Lieutenant-Colonel Buchanan is important. This gentleman, unexpectedly called for the government so far as he was concerned, and leaving his professional engagements in the courts with reluctance, came here and testified as follows:

Question. Have you any recollection of any movement of General Porter's Corps from Warrenton Junction toward Bristoe on the morning of the 28th?

Answer. If I have got the dates right, General Porter was there on the morning of the 29th. I was there when General Porter left in the morning of the day he started for Bristoe; my recollection is that it was on the morning of the 29th.

Question. What conversation had you with General Porter before he started off to Bristoe Station?

Answer. On the evening before he started somebody gave me an order to be in readiness to move at three o'clock in the morning. I was in front of General Porter's headquarters at three o'clock in the morning, but I saw no one until after the break of day. Then some one came to me and told me to let the men get their breakfasts and let the horses be fed; that was done, and I immediately went back to the place I occupied. Some time afterward, after sunrise, I saw General Porter. I wanted to go back to Fredericksburg to my regiment. I only had about ninety men with me, and I expected to go back the day before. I rode out with him in the woods, where he was in camp, until we got into an open field; he asked me to send a detachment of the command I had forward to clear the road toward Bristoe Station two or three miles; this was done. I waited some little time and the infantry began to move. About that time he handed me a letter, and directed me to give it to General Burnside, and told me I could go. I started toward Fredericksburg; he sent an aide after me and brought me back, and told me he was apprehensive that I might be captured. He told me to say to General Burnside—I cannot get his language—but the idea was that there was no disaster that was very threatening as yet, and he hoped for the best.

* * * * * * *

Question. You did not accompany any of your detachment toward Bristoe?

Answer. No, sir; I believe I waited until four or five of the men came back.

Question. When did you get this order from General Porter to send a detachment down there?

Answer. After I got out of the open woods into the field.

Question. What time of day would you say it was, having reference to daybreak?

Answer. The sun was probably an hour high.

Question. What troops were there with General Porter at that time?

Answer. I don't know. When I first went there General Pope was there; General Pope had left, and General Heintzelman commanded there. I do not think I saw any other general officer that I knew except those two.

Question. Do you know whether General Heintzelman's corps was there at that time?

Answer. I do not. I was camped in front of General Porter's headquarters, that is, toward the road. I came up probably a hundred and fifty yards, and a little to his left; and the troops were generally, I think, over south, and farther on toward Manassas. I did not move about any while I was there—but very little. I staid with my command. I was expecting every hour to get permission to return to my regiment at Fredericksburg. As to the roads, as we went up, I think, on Monday night, I feel pretty well satisfied that there was a little rain; but there was no mud that I recollect of. As we went back it was dry. I recollect the next night I was sent by General Burnside up over part of the road that I had gone down to see what there was up there, and I recollect that night as being very dusty.

Question. You say you were in front of General Porter; at what time?

Answer. Three o'clock in the morning I had got the order.

Question. Do you recollect anything moving along to the road?

Answer. No, sir; when I went there it was very quiet. I saw no light in his headquarters at all. I did not know whether he was there or not.

Question. During that night do you recollect whether there were troops or wagons or artillery moving?

Answer. I did not hear any. I slept but little; we had no tents, and I slept in blankets.

Question. Between three o'clock in the morning, the time you were in position in front of General Porter's headquarters, to the time the troops began to move, as you have stated, have you any recollection as to any forces or wagons or artillery passing down on the road toward Bristoe?

Answer. No, sir; not until after we went out in the open field, if my memory serves me correctly; very soon after we were there the infantry began to move, but they may have been moving before that and I not know it.

Cross-examination by Mr. Bullitt:

Question. When you say the infantry began to move at that time, you only mean to say that it is the first time you saw them moving.

Answer. Yes, sir.

Question. Might they not have been moving for an hour or two before and you not know it.

Answer. Yes, sir.

Question. Two or three hours before?

Answer. Yes; might have been moving all night if they were not near enough to me for me to hear it.

*　　　*　　　*　　　*　　　*　　　*

Question. Did you see the head of the column?

Answer. No, sir. We went right back of General Porter's headquarters, out of the woods, on the road toward Bristoe Station; when I got out into the open field, probably a hundred yards, General Porter halted, and there is where he directed me to send a detachment to clear the road.

Question. How long were the cavalry gone?

Answer. They caught up with me—I don't know how far—after I was on the road home.

Question. Did General Porter, when he gave you the direction to clear the road, leave you and go on?

Answer. No, sir; he remained with me.

Question. About how long?

Answer. Not very long.

Question. According to your present recollection?

Answer. I cannot tell you.

Question. An hour?

Answer. O, no, sir.

Question. Half an hour?

Answer. Well, yes; it may have been longer; it may have been shorter.

Question. You say the sun, you think, was about an hour high at that time?

Answer. Yes, sir.

Question. Did you see any of General Porter's troops moving at that time?

Answer. I did not see any troops moving until after I had got out into the open field, until the detachment had been forwarded to clear the road, and then I saw the infantry moving.

*　　　*　　　*　　　*　　　*　　　*

Question. But you saw nothing to indicate a movement until about that time. What time was it when you first heard these indications of life?

Answer. The day had broken—the sun was not up—pretty near after daybreak.

Question. How long after that before you saw General Porter?

Answer. I did not see him until after sunrise.

Question. How did you come to see him then?
Answer. He was on his horse.
Question. How did you happen to see him?
Answer. I was directed to report back in the same position after the horses were fed and the men had their breakfasts, so I went back and halted in front of headquarters.
Question. That was after the men had their breakfasts?
Answer. Yes; after sunrise.
Question. How long after?
Answer. I cannot tell; it was not very long after sunrise. It may have been half an hour, may be an hour. It is a good while ago.
Question. Did General Porter say anything to you about the fact that he was in want of cavalry?
Answer. Yes, sir.
Question. Did he say to you that he wanted to detain you there?
Answer. Yes, sir.
Question. Why did he not detain you?
Answer. He did detain me two days, using my men for orderlies.
Question. How did he come to let you go?
Answer. I don't know.
Question. How many men did he use for the purpose of orderlies?
Answer. Pretty hard to tell; sometimes more, sometimes less. * * *

Question. Where was your cavalry in camp?
Answer. About 125 or 150 yards nearly in front of General Porter's headquarters.
Question. Were they all there?
Answer. When they were not out acting as messengers.
Question. They were there during these three nights and two days of which you speak, except when they were out on duty?
Answer. O, yes.

It will be perceived that Colonel Buchanan has placed the departure of the petitioner a day later than the fact, but at the same time he attempted to make it plain that he was not positive as to the dates, because he repeated during his evidence the remark, indicative of doubt whether he was "correct as to dates." The substance of his evidence shows that he was with the petitioner when the latter received from General Pope the orders to move at 1 a. m., for he himself was required by petitioner to get his detachment under arms in front of petitioner's tent at 3 a. m. He saw the troops move towards Bristoe *after* daylight and then gave a small detachment, by petitioner's personal orders, to clear the road towards Bristoe. He was probably detained as long as he was at Warrenton Junction in consequence of petitioner's desire for cavalry which he had expressed to General Burnside in a dispatch two days before (*vide* accused's Exhibit A, G. C. M. Record, p. 228), in which he said, "I want cavalry to remain with me for a few days."

When a witness states a fact as having positively occurred on a particular date, it places his evidence under a different form of inspection from that of the witness who states facts as having occurred on or about a particular time, and does not pretend to be precise as to dates.

That Colonel Buchanan's detachment was at Warrenton Junction at daylight on the 28th of August, 1862, is apparent from Captain Montieth's evidence just given. The orders to him of the petitioner show that the latter knew perfectly what was necessary in order to comply with General Pope's order.

CHARACTER OF THE NIGHT—FORCES MARCHING.

In comparing the evidence of witnesses on this point considerable discrepancy is observed, which is to be expected after the lapse of sixteen years, and the only way to determine what the night really was as to darkness is by ascertaining what was actually done by persons during the night.

During the day's actions to which our attention is directed I recollect having been sent up the Shenandoah Valley from near Harper's Ferry to Winchester, on special service, in command of my own company and of three hundred men of another regiment; but although the duty involved possible contact with the enemy, and my responsibility was considerable, I find I cannot say without reference to my papers whether I made that movement on the 29th or 30th of August, 1862, or whether there was a moon at night or clouds, although I was up nearly all of two nights, at that time, from anxiety for the safety of my command in the position I was placed in.

Probably the description by some of the witnesses that the night of the 27th August, 1862, was a "dark starlight·night" will explain it. This is what Capt. William W. Macy, Nineteenth Indiana Volunteers, Gibbon's brigade, King's division, McDowell's corps, terms it. This witness (for government) says his regiment was on the march most of the day from Sulphur Springs until 10 or 10½ p. m. (Board's Record, p. 583); that the night "was most too dark to march pleasantly. We marched (says he) some nights that were a good deal darker than it was that night. We were on the march, but, of course, it is unpleasant marching after night." He further remarked that the regiment kept its ranks (p. 584) and that the roads were dusty, and then referred to obstructions as follows:

I think that the wagon-trains and artillery had the road a good part of the time, and we had the side of the road off through the fields.

Question. Did you find any difficulty in marching through the fields up to 10 o'clock at night?

Answer. No, sir; not that I recollect.

Private *William E. Murray*, Company C, Nineteenth Indiana Volunteers, Gibbon's brigade, King's division, McDowell's corps (for government), who kept a diary and noted the time by his watch, corroborates this last-named witness in the facts noted, and says they marched up to 10 p. m.; that he did not lie down until midnight; and was in line at 4 a. m. There were peculiar circumstances of a dramatic nature narrated by him, which indelibly impressed that night on his memory.

The next evening (28th August) he was wounded in King's action with Jackson on the Warrenton pike, and was carried to Manassas Junction—to the Weir house. There he recorded in his diary for the 29th August, 1862 (p. 589): "News from the field communicates very hard fighting all day; heavy cannonading."

Private *Samuel G. Hill*, of the same company and regiment as the last witness (government witness), says the night of the 27th was a clear night, as he and some of his companions were out foraging for poultry and cooking their suppers until 3 a. m. (Board's Record, p. 592). He was badly wounded the next evening.

Capt. *William M. Campbell*, Company I, same regiment as the last witness, corroborates the other witnesses for government from that regiment by other incidents which fixed the character of the night in his recollection. (Board's Record, p. 594).

Private *J. H. Stein*, of Company C, of the same regiment, while corroborating the others (p. 597), remarked that from eight to eleven it was not so light as afterwards. He was badly wounded the next evening, 28th August. This statement of Mr. Stein is in harmony with the statements of some others, as for example, Brig. Gen. *Gilman Marston*, then colonel Second New Hampshire Volunteers (government witness), whose recollection is that the night, at the place where he was, some miles distant, was from 9 to 10 o'clock misty and rainy and quite dark. Afterwards he thinks it was not rainy (Board's Record, p. 860).

Bvt. Brig. Gen. *Rufus Dawes*, colonel Sixth Wisconsin (then its major), Gibbon's brigade, King's division, McDowell's corps, says that on the 27th they marched to a camp near Buckland's Mills, and got there after dark, and marched again before daylight (Board's Record, p. 835).

Bvt. Brig. Gen. *Thos. F. McCoy*, colonel commanding One hundred and seventh Pennsylvania Volunteers, Duryea's brigade, Ricketts' division, McDowell's corps, kept a diary and noted time from his watch, and says his regiment marched all night on the 27th until 1 a. m. of the 28th, and he then understood, as his regiment had the rear, that all of the division also marched during the same time (Board's Record, p. 640).

Bvt. Maj. Gen. *Wm. Birney*, commanding Fifty-seventh Pennsylvania Volunteers, Kearney's division, Heintzelman's corps, says that his regiment marched that night (27th August), some time before daybreak, in the direction of Bristoe Station (Board's Record, p. 680); that they arrived there at a very early hour, an hour after daybreak, and that he was in the rear of the column as his brigade (Kearney's division) had gone before he marched, and his movement was then impeded by other troops for whom he waited until they passed (p. 683). He thought it was a dark night.

Brig. Gen. *I. H. Duvall*, United States Volunteers, then major First West Virginia Volunteers, Ricketts' division, McDowell's corps, has given some interesting testimony as to the road he took for a portion of the way, on the night of the 27th August, which was the identical road petitioner was required by Major-General Pope's orders to march upon from Warrenton Junction to Bristoe Station via Catlett's Station. His statement as to that road shows what petitioner might have done had he *loyally* undertaken to comply with his orders.

Brigadier-General *Duvall* testified as follows (Board's Record, pp. 860 and 862):

Answer. On the evening of August 27 I was with my brigade; we were about four miles, I think, northwest of Warrenton at that time, north or northwest, and I was directed by my colonel to carry a letter that he handed to me from General Ricketts to General Pope.

Question. To what point?

Answer. It was supposed to be somewhere near Centreville; that was my order.

Question. What did you then do?

Answer. I started and made the trip and delivered the letter.

Question. You left the camp about what time?

Answer. Nearly dark; it was after sundown.

Question. What road did you take?

Answer. I came back to Warrenton, and I followed then the road running from Warrenton in the direction of Catlett Station. I was directed to go that way and keep out of the way of the enemy.

Question. Did you pass through Warrenton Junction?

Answer. No, sir; I struck the road at Catlett's.

Question. What direction did you then take?

Answer. I took the road leading from Catlett Station to Manassas Junction, by the way of Bristoe.

Question. Where did you find General Pope?

Answer. I found General Pope near Manassas Junction.

Question. What was the character of that night?

Answer. I don't know that I recollect distinctly in regard to that; I rode all night, though, until about three o'clock in the morning, when I took a little rest; I had no particular difficulty in finding the way.

Question. From Catlett Station to Bristoe did you meet with any obstruction to your movements?

Answer. There were a great many wagons along the line; there were some troops, but I went along without any particular obstruction. There were no obstacles that kept me from going.

*   *   *   *   *   *   *

Question. In your movements on the night of the 27th and morning of the 28th from Warrenton to Catlett Station and Bristoe, did you find these wagons that you speak of an obstruction to the movement of troops?

Answer. I had no troops. I was on horseback; I rode along and occasionally I would have to ride around some wagons in the road; but I kept going; I didn't stop for them.

Question. What was your opinion as to whether troops could have been moved, a column or a brigade for example, from Catlett Station to Bristoe on that road that you went over at that time?

*   *   *   *   *   *   *

Answer. I think troops could have marched; there were places where they could not have marched in regular order; they would have had to go around wagons in some way, but there would have been no difficulty in discovering the road; troops could not have marched in regular order of marching; they could have, broken file, perhaps.

Lieut. *E. P. Brooks*, acting adjutant Sixth Wisconsin Volunteers, with a detachment of sixteen cavalrymen from the Sixth New York Volunteer Cavalry, that same night carried orders from Major-General Pope to Major-General Reno and Maj.-Gen. Phil. Kearney, received, respectively, at 12.20 a. m. and 1 a. m.

The petitioner has seen fit to criticise these orders and introduced one, against objection, on cross-examination, in order to make "comparisons" (Board's Record, p. 1025).

A discussion of these mere *collateral* questions will be avoided in this argument for the government as much as is consistent with reasonable regard for the rights of others, not parties plaintiff or defendant, but whose reputations are assailed with no opportunity to them to defend themselves.

The record of the trial in 1862 shows that the character of the night, obstacles on the road, and efforts to remove them, were very fully inquired into.

The character of the night of the 27th August, 1862, was passed upon by the court.

The petitioner did not march his troops during that night—this is a fact which is too thoroughly fixed to require argument—while numerous other troops did march. Indeed, it is safe to say that it is a single instance where orders to march that night in both armies at any time that night were not complied with.

During the whole four and a half years of the war of the rebellion, the national troops, when occasion required them to march, permitted no such plea as darkness in an August night to interfere with the movement.

History is full of illustrations of immense difficulties surmounted by armies and corps in the effort to comply with orders.

Several recur, but whoever hears or reads this argument will be able to give illustrations for themselves.

During the "Wilderness" campaign, under General Grant, the Army of the Potomac surmounted difficulties in comparison to which the pleas in the way of excuse by the petitioner appear puerile.

JACKSON'S COMMAND MOVING NIGHT 27TH AUGUST.

On this same night in August when the petitioner would not march, Maj-Gen. T. J. Jackson, commanding the Confederate forces then operating against Major-General Pope, was marching his entire army, some from near Bristoe and the remainder from Manassas Junction to Centreville or stone house, on the Gainesville and Centreville turnpike.

On this subject Major *Henry Kyd Douglas*, of his staff, government witness, testified as follows (Board's Record, page 707):

Question. Were you at Manassas Junction during that month before this time?
Answer. I was at Manassas Junction on the 27th.
Question. At what time did you leave there; or rather, at what time did the entire command of General Jackson leave there?
Answer. After dark some time, when the troops had been supplied with as many stores as they could well carry—you know there were a quantity of them captured there—they were marched off along through the night. With some of them it may have been between midnight and morning before the last of them got away. The leading division of A. P. Hill's was Taliaferro's. I dont know whether he went up by Dawkins' Branch or whether he went up this way [Manassas Junction to Groveton]. Ewell went on the Manassas and Sudley road up toward Sudley Church. A. P. Hill went to Centreville. Lawton went up toward the Warrenton, Alexandria and Washington road.
Question. Then all of General Jackson's command were moved in the night-time from Manassas Junction up to that line between Centreville and Groveton?
Answer. Yes; some of them may have started out before night, and those that were there moved away from Centreville on the night of the 27th.

Jubal A. Early, a government witness, who was a Confederate brigadier-general during this campaign in Ewell's division of Jackson's command, says (Board's Record, p. 852) that Jackson's forces marched the night of the 27th and that his brigade "covered the withdrawal." He further testified as follows:

Question. Did you experience any difficulty in marching that night?
Answer. O, no; that was an open country there; it was very familiar to us; we had been there the year before.

This evidence is but confirmatory of the Confederate reports which have been submitted here on the subject and which I read from in my opening argument.

Thus it is apparent that during the night the 27th August, 1862, very nearly all the contending forces operating in the vicinity of the Bull Run battle-fields were in motion to take up new positions.

The evidence of Lieutenant-Colonel Buchanan has afforded the opportunity to contrast the movements that night of the commanding general of the Army of Virginia and the subordinate corps commanders, who had but that 27th August come under his orders.

The former at the front is with Hooker when he makes his gallant little fight against Ewell, and, loyally desirous to carry out the wishes of the General-in-Chief and President "to fight like the devil," and to open the road then barred to the National Capital, spends much of this night in writing dispatches and making combinations to destroy the over-confident enemy, who had pushed three days ahead of his supports.

The latter, the petitioner, receiving a peremptory and imperative order to march at 1 a. m., tells his sympathetic division and brigade commanders that it is something for them to sleep on, and proceeds to follow his own advice, for, says Colonel Buchanan, "the first indication of life that I saw about the headquarters was some one came to me after break of day and directed me to have the men get their breakfasts" (Board's Record, p. 608). He had been patiently sitting on his horse with his cavalry detachment in front of petitioner's quarters from 3 a. m. until daylight and never saw the petitioner until "after sunrise."

Meanwhile, the commanding general of the army, sanguine of his ability to overwhelm Jackson if loyally and understandingly supported, and anxious to deliver an effective blow in the cause of his country, waits, and waits in vain, for the presence of petitioner's corps—the finest body of troops in his command—a portion of which did not reach camp until late in the day.

4 G

One curious circumstance is to be noted in connection with the petitioner's excuses as to the enormous number of wagons on Manassas Plains between Warrenton Junction and Bristoe, that a detachment started with ambulances from Bristoe on the same road for Warrenton on the morning of the 28th.

The testimony on this subject by Capt. James Haddow, Thirty-Sixth Ohio Volunteers, confirmed as it was in essential particulars by that of Lieut. A. F. Tiffany and Private N. P. Beach (Board's Rec., pp. 874, 877, 878), is as follows:

Question. Where were you at sunset on the 27th of August, 1862—about that time?
Answer. We were on the road between Catlett Station and Bristoe.

Question. Did you after that go toward Catlett Station; if so, at what time and under what circumstances?
Answer. We marched that night to Bristoe, arriving at Bristoe Station after dark some time; we remained there that night; on the following morning the regiment went on in the direction of Manassas; the company of which I was a member was detached and put in charge of a major of the medical department to go back in the direction of Warrenton with ambulances and obtain medical supplies; we returned to somewhere near Warrenton, passing Catlett Station at some distance on the morning of the 28th; we returned to Bristoe on the evening of the 28th.

Question. At what time did you set out from Bristoe Station to go in the direction of Catlett Station?
Answer. I could not give the hour, but pretty early in the morning—as soon as we got up and got breakfast.

Question. Did you during that day see General Porter's corps?
Answer. We met troops (it was a frequent habit to ask soldiers what troops they were), and they said they were General Porter's troops. Porter's troops lay at Warrenton Junction on the afternoon of the 27th when we left there.

Question. What difficulty, if any, did you experience on the morning of the 28th in taking this ambulance train from Bristoe Station to Catlett Station?
Answer. I don't think we had any material difficulty in getting through; we must have had at least three ambulances; we passed through trains and passed troops; we must undoubtedly have made a march that day of 16 miles; we could not have met with serious obstructions.

Questions. Do you know what troops you met?
Answer. They said they were General Porter's; we inquired frequently; of course I was not acquainted with General Porter's corps, we had just reached the East from the West, and all troops were strange to me.

That the order to petitioner to march at 1 a. m. was urgent and imperative in its terms is beyond question. That it was disobeyed is clearly proved. The petitioner proffers excuses for this disobedience, and by this proffer admits the disobedience, giving his reasons for non-compliance with the terms of the order. These excuses are presented by him as coming under four heads:

First. Darkness of the night.

Second. Obstructions on the road.

Third. The fatigue of his troops.

Fourth. The counsel of his subordinate generals.

1. The plea of darkness is conclusively answered by the fact, fully proved, that bodies of troops, both of our own army and of the enemy, were marching on that very night, both north and east of petitioner, and at no such distance from him as could have made any difference in the character of the night.

2. If the road was obstructed, this was a reason for the greater promptness in beginning his march promptly and for urging it forward. If he had no cavalry to clear the road, it was also the more imperative to start early. This was but a reason for sending a detachment of infantry forward in advance of the time at which he was ordered to march, in order to give notice of his coming and to explore the roads and clear the way as far as possible. It was no reason for foregoing such preparations or for deferring *the time* to begin his march.

But the obstructions were sure to be less than at any hours of the twenty-four if his march began at one o'clock. By that hour most, if not all, of the wagons would be likely to be parked or halted for the night. The time to which he adjourned his march was the very time at which they would again be taking the road.

3. The fact that he was ordered to march with one division of his troops only, if the others were not up, shows that no discretion was left him such as he claims, because of the late arrival and fatigue of his rearmost division. It was a plain implication that one division would be very nearly behind or immediately following.

· The divisions were in no way detached from each other. The corps was marching as a whole, yet his commanding general orders him to march with one division, even if the other had not arrived. How much interval of rest for the leading division did these terms allow? Plainly no discretion in this respect was allowed. The requirement of the order was absolute.

4. What was the counsel of his generals? Their own evidence, as given in 1862, though cited at his instance and as his witnesses, paints the line of proceeding he adopted in this council of his officers in too condemnatory colors to be obliterated or lost sight of by any ingenuity before this board.

He did not utter or make known to them anything but the single fact that he was directed to march at one o'clock. He named the hour and invited their counsel, but said nothing of the urgency, and he encouraged them to the counsel he wished by adding to his mention of the hour the sneering or indifferent remark, "There is something for you to sleep on." He handed the order to the one of his generals with whom he was most intimate with this remark; and the result was that the one who received it, if he looked at it at all, glanced at it so slightly that he remained unacquainted with its terms.

General Sykes said (p. 176, G. C. M. Rec.):

General Porter informed me that he had received an order * * * directing his corps to march at one o'clock.

(P. 178):

Question by the Judge-Advocate. Do you remember whether you were made acquainted with the urgent language of the order stating that by all means General Porter must be at Bristoe Station by daylight the next morning?

Answer. No, sir; I did not; for I am satisfied that if the urgency had been made known to us we would have moved at the hour prescribed.

General Sykes subsequently attempted to modify this opinion so far as to claim a certain discretion on the part of a corps commander; but I am content to let this, the opinion which as a soldier he gave at once, when the matter was first clearly presented to him, answer.

General Butterfield said (p. 185):

Question by the accused. Will you state what was said by General Porter in relation to that order and what the order was?

Answer. The order, I believe, was for General Porter to move his forces at 1 o'clock in the morning to Bristoe.

(P. 187):

Question by the Judge Advocate. Did you see the order, the 27th, from General Pope, or know anything about the urgency of its terms?

Answer. I did not read it.

General Morell says, in answer to the question as to "what occurred":

(P. 145):

General Porter said to us that he had received this order to march at one o'clock that night; we immediately spoke of the condition of our troops—they being very much fatigued, and the darkness of the night, and said that we did not believe we could make any better progress attempting to start at that hour than had we waited until daylight. After some little conversation General Porter said, "Well, we will start at three o'clock—get ready." I immediately left his tent, &c.

Such was this council of generals, and such the way that petitioner directed its counsels on this *first* occasion in which he was called on to act in support of the general under whose unwelcome command he had newly come.

When the pleas of the night being too dark, troops fatigued, and the road obstructed with stumps by way of excuse were gravely advanced here as insuperable obstacles to any movement whatever, the history of the regular American Army suggested a striking example as applicable to this case.

On the 2d January, 1777, General Washington found himself in Trenton, N. J., with the Delaware behind him impassable from the ice and the enemy in full force before him under Lieut. Gen. Earl Cornwallis, and separated from him only by the narrow Assunpink Creek. The question of the existence of this nation as an independent republic hung upon the events of that night. The night before, two of his brigades, under General Washington's order, had made a night march through mud, snow, and water, over rough roads, to join him, and that day were in action. Ill-clad and suffering, the whole army was on this 2d January called upon for another night march, and proceeding around the left flank of Cornwallis' forces by a wood road filled with stumps from two to five inches high, they approached towards morning the town of Princeton, were in action that day also, and marched until between ten and eleven o'clock that night to Somerset Court-House.

The darkness of those nights, the roughness of the roads, the severe inclemency of the weather, or the want of shoes and proper clothing, did not deter those patriots who were loyal to the orders of their general from making a night march; and the nation was saved.

The first specification to the first charge has now been considered. It is particularly significant, as showing the first in a series of disobediences to orders all having one object, disloyalty to the orders of the commanding general, and a determination to do nothing until the commanding general of the Army of the Potomac should arrive from Alexandria and assume command under the sixty-second article of war.

Comparisons are never agreeable, and for Major-General Pope to have been hailed as the saviour of the national capital would probably never have met the petitioner's preferences.

General Washington early laid down the rule of obedience to orders, as understood in the British army, from whence came the American articles of war and customs of the service. Said he:

It is not for every officer to know the principles upon which every order is issued and to judge how they may or may not be dispensed with or suspended, but their duty is to carry them into execution with the utmost punctuality and exactness. They are to consider that military movements are like the working of a clock, and they will go quickly, regularly, and easily if every officer does his duty; but without it be as easily disordered, because neglect from any one, like the stopping of a wheel, disorders the whole.
The general, therefore, expects that every officer will duly consider the importance of the observation, their own reputation, and the duty they owe to their country. He claims it of them and earnestly calls upon them to do it. (General Orders, Army Headquarters, Toamensing, Penn., October 10, 1777.)

When one of petitioner's general officers, who advised him not to march at 1 a. m., said in the original trial that "the movement would not have been impracticable, but * * * would have been a false military movement" (G. C. M. Record, p. 179), he made an unfortunate commentary upon the language of Washington, which requires no remark.

The rule thus enunciated by the great patriot was well known in both armies.

Mr. *Samuel*, in his "Historical Account of the British Army and of the Law Military" (London edition, 1816, page 285), in discussing the British article of war, which is identical with the American, as to "disobedience of orders," first adverted to mere neglects, which in that service, as in our own, are chargeable only as conduct "to the prejudice of good order and military discipline," and then proceeded to discuss and define the meaning of the article under which the petitioner in this case was tried on the first charge. Said he:

In the *second*, the absolute resistance of, or refusal of obedience to, a present and urgent command, conveyed either orally or in writing, by the non-compliance with which some immediate act necessary to be done might be impeded or defeated, as high an offense is discoverable as can well be contemplated by a military mind; inasmuch as the principle which it holds out would, if encouraged, or not suppressed by some heavy penalty, forbid or preclude a reliance on the execution of any military measure.

It is this *positive* disobedience, therefore, evincing a refractory spirit in the inferior, an active opposition to the commands of a superior, against which, it must be supposed, that the severe penalty of the article is principally directed. This highly criminal disobedience may arise, either out of the refusal of the officer or soldier to act as he is ordered—to march, for instance, whither he is bidden—or to desist from any act or purpose which he is prohibited by a direct command from pursuing; for it would in many circumstances, which may easily be imagined, be as dangerous to persist in a forbidden course, as to decline or recede from one that is commanded.

Whether the orders of the superior enjoin an active or a passive conduct, the officer or soldier subject to them is equally obliged to obey. Otherwise, every military operation or enterprise would be made to depend, not on the prudence or counsel of the commander, but the will or caprice of the soldiery, either for the furtherance or obstruction of its object.

Prompt, ready, unhesitating obedience in soldiers, to those who are set over them, is so necessary to the military state, and to the success of every military achievement, that it would be pernicious to have it understood that military disobedience, in any instance, may go unquestioned.

It is not to be overlooked, notwithstanding the construction or modification which the *disobedience*, contemplated in the article, may appear to be capable of—and which favorable sense is often put on the severe terms of its letter by the lenient sentences pronounced by courts-martial on cases of a *negative* character, or of minor consequence—that the fifth article, in fact, makes no distinction between one act of disobedience or another. And that when any is to be made, it must always depend on the view which a court-martial may take of the circumstances submitted to it, with their contemplation of the spirit of the article, or the mutiny act; and that wherever it is made, it will be, not in relaxation of the principle of implicit obedience inculcated by the article, but in the exercise of a discretion, lawfully resident in the court, to mitigate, according to circumstances, the rigor and severity of the law.

Except in the solitary instance where the illegality of an order is glaringly apparent on the face of it, a military subordinate is compelled to a complete and undeviating obedience to the very letter of the command received. The most important consequences may often rest on the precise mechanical execution of an order which in appearance to the military inferior may have a substantive and a sole object in its view, while in the design of the commander it may be combined with a vast and various machinery, and a deviation from it, even with the best intentions and the best success, separately considered, might defeat the grand end of the meditated enterprise. Hence it is scarcely possible to imagine a case when a subordinate officer would be at liberty to depart from the positive command of his superior. The justice of the Roman father who put his brave and successful son to death for disobedience to his commands, has never been called in question; though many have wished that the feelings of the father had softened, in that particular case, the stern severity of the judge.

None, however, will quarrel with the precept, though they may incline not to imitate the example. But even a mild and Christian philosopher, sitting in his own closet and studying an excuse for the breach of a military command, was after all obliged to content himself with an apology, in a possible but single case; or rather, his ingenuity being tasked, was unable to suggest anything more than an expedient, and that perhaps not altogether unexceptionable, which might plead for a suspension in the execution, not in the supersession of a military order.

To use the words of *Archdeacon Paley*: "If the commander-in-chief of an army detach an officer under him upon a particular service, which service turns out more difficult or less expedient than was supposed, insomuch that the officer is convinced that his commander, if he were acquainted with the true state in which the affair is found, would recall his orders, yet must this officer, if he cannot wait for *fresh directions* without prejudice to the expedition he is sent upon, pursue, at all hazards, those which he brought out with him."

The impression of this passage might be broken, but could not apparently be strengthened, by any comment.

SECOND SPECIFICATION, FIRST CHARGE.

The second specification under the first charge of disobedience of orders is next to be considered. That specification was based on the following order:

[General Order No. 5.]

HEADQUARTERS ARMY OF VIRGINIA,
Centreville, August 30, 1862.

Gens. McDOWELL and PORTER: You will please move forward with your joint commands towards Gainesville I sent General Porter written orders to that effect an hour and a half ago. Heintzelman, Sigel, and Reno are moving on the Warrenton turnpike, and must now be not far from Gainesville. I desire that, as soon as communication is established between this force and your own, the whole command shall halt. It may be necessary to fall back behind Bull Run, at Centreville, to-night. I presume it will be so on account of our supplies. I have sent no orders of any description to Ricketts, and none to interfere in any way with the movements of McDowell's troops, except what I sent by his aide-de-camp last night, which were to hold his position on the Warrenton pike until the troops from here should fall upon the enemy's flank and rear. I do not even know Ricketts' position, as I have not been able to find out where General McDowell was until a late hour this morning. General McDowell will take immediate steps to communicate with General Ricketts, and instruct him to rejoin the other divisions of his corps as soon as practicable. If any considerable advantages are to be gained by departing from this order, it will not be strictly carried out. One thing must be had in view, that the troops must occupy a position from which they can reach Bull Run to-night or by morning. The indications are that the whole force of the enemy is moving in this direction at a pace that will bring them here by to-morrow night or next day. My own headquarters will be, for the present, with Heintzelman's corps or at this place.

JOHN POPE,
Major-General Commanding.

To understand the condition of affairs at this time, a little explanation, in order to make a connected narrative, is desirable. We have seen that on the 27th of August General McDowell with his corps and Reynolds' division and Sigel's corps were interposed between Jackson and Thoroughfare Gap, and that Jackson's supports were beyond that range of mountains, pushing forward with all their might lest he should be captured, and that Heintzelman's corps, comprising Hooker's and Kearney's divisions and General Reno's detachment of the Ninth Army Corps, were within easy striking distance, and petitioner's corps was but a few miles away between Manassas Junction and Bristoe, while Banks' corps was behind petitioner's in charge of the trains. In order to envelop Jackson, Kearney's division of Heintzelman's corps and Reno's detachment on the same night received orders which brought them, one to Bristoe and the other to Manassas Junction; but as Jackson had retired to Centreville, these forces and Hooker's division of Heintzelman's corps were pushed up toward the stone house and Centreville. It is not necessary to discuss here the curious concatenation of circumstances by which in the movement of McDowell's and Sigel's corps from the neighborhood of Gainesville east between the Warrenton pike and the Manassas and Gainesville road on the 28th they became separated, Sigel moving to Manassas Junction, Ricketts' division of McDowell's corps being sent back to hold

Thoroughfare Gap, arriving too late to make it effectual, King's division of McDowell's corps pursuing the Warrenton, Gainesville, Groveton, and Centreville pike toward Groveton, running into Jackson, who had abandoned Centreville, taken up a concealed defensive position just north of Groveton within a few hundred yards of the Independent line of the Manassas Gap Railroad, having a fight there on the night of the 28th, then, without, seemingly, the best of reasons, King's division quitting that pike and moving down to Manassas Junction by the very road by which petitioner was next day, in view of this falling back, ordered to advance; Reynolds' division meanwhile having come down between Sigel and King partially across the country and down to Bethlehem Church and then up the Sudley Springs' road and out to the left, south of the Warrenton road. General Reynolds, we have seen, was within supporting distance of King on the night of the 28th, because he testified he rode over across the country from Newmarket to the Warrenton pike near Groveton and then westward to General King's position along the Warrenton pike (G. C. M. Record, p. 170). His troops followed him, as is plain from Bvt. Brig. Gen. Charles Barnes' evidence (Board's Record, p. 660). The fight of the 28th has nothing to do with this case; but on the morning of the 29th, when it was found by the commanding general, Pope, that King's division, one of the finest in the Army, had left its position of the night before, where it was interposed between General Jackson and Thoroughfare Gap (General King himself being ill at the time), and had come down to Manassas Junction and left the door open, he undertook to close that door by sending petitioner's corps, a fresh body of troops, right out on that road with the greatest expedition.

On the morning of the 29th of August at 5.30 o'clock the petitioner had received an order from General Pope, dated 3 a. m. near Bull Run, " to move upon Centreville at the first dawn of day with your [his] whole command, leaving your train to follow. It is very important that you should be here at a very early hour in the morning. A severe engagement is likely to take place and your presence is necessary." (Accused's Ex. No. 4, G. C. M. Record, p. 235.)

It has been sought on behalf of the petitioner to put the receipt of this order at a later time for the reason that in a communication which he dated 6 a. m. to General Burnside he said he had just received the order, and also to put the time of his departure from Bristoe towards Manassas Junction at half past six o'clock because the petitioner in the same dispatch to General Burnside said, " I shall be off in half an hour." As to the time of the receipt of the order it is sufficient to say that his own exhibit presented to the general court-martial on his trial shows the hour of receipt to be at 5.30 a. m. His own witness, General Morell, on that trial (G. C. M. Record, p. 146) said the dispatch was received between daylight and sunrise, not *after* sunrise as narrated in the petitioner's opening statement, and that the leading division (Sykes') did not march until seven o'clock, and his own division followed immediately.

The fact remains, therefore, even on the petitioner's own showing in evidence that the first order he received on the 29th of August, 1862, was not promptly obeyed. At the hour of its receipt as the troops were merely in bivouac it seems quite plain that they were prepared for immediate movement and had already their breakfasts.

The petitioner has said in his opening statement that this order surprised him; that no severe engagement could take place near Centreville; that Jackson's army had not gone there. Of this he could know nothing, for he was not at the front. But the statement is gravely made, nevertheless; and at once he sets his judgment up against that of his commander—settles it to suit himself. Fully apprised that a severe engagement was likely to take place and that his presence was necessary, we perceive that he did not instantly and vigorously push forward, although his troops were now fresh.

Bvt. Brig. Gen. *Horace Bouton,* formerly of the Thirteenth New York, Martindale's brigade, Morell's division, says his regiment was encamped half a mile toward Manassas. The distance from Bristoe, Station to Manassas Station was about four miles. (Board's Record, p. 51.)

According to Capt. *George Monteith,* formerly aid-de-camp of the petitioner, and called by him as a witness (Board's Record, p. 310), the head of the column [Sykes'] was halted when it had gone a quarter to a half mile beyond Manassas Junction; and that Major-General McDowell came up a very few minutes after their arrival, and after the arrival of Brigadier-General Gibbon. He also said (Board's Record, p. 315) that the petitioner's troops turned to go to Gainesville, about 9. a. m. He also testifies, he being with petitioner, that General Gibbon told them of the action of the night before of King's division upon the Warrenton turnpike, between Groveton and Gainesville. There is a distinction, not, however, of much importance to be made between Manassas "Station" and Manassas "Junction"; Manassas Junction being according to the testimony of Capt. *J. A. Judson,* called by the petitioner (Board's Record, p. 110), where the Orange and Alexandria Railroad joins the Manassas Gap Railroad; and according to General *G. K. Warren* (Board's Record, p. 51), if you wanted "to shorten the distance from Bristoe by turning off towards Gainesville where the roads separated at a very small angle, there would be a variation of a mile," which would be gained in moving off at Manassas Junction towards Gainesville on the Manassas and Gainesville road, instead of coming up at Manassas Station.

As to how far Sykes' division got on the road towards Centreville, under the pressing order the petitioner had received at 5.30 a. m., General *Warren* has said (Board's Record, p. 17):

While our corps was passing Manassas Junction the order came for us to move towards Gainesville. General Sykes' division had already passed the junction towards Centreville, and my brigade was at the rear of it. I suppose to avoid delay, and without any delay, Morell's division, which was following, turned off on this road towards Gainesville; as soon as it cleared the road our division faced about, which brought my brigade in advance in Sykes' division.

He further said (Board's Record, p. 33):

My brigade just got past the road at the junction which leads up to Gainesville, * * * General Morell's division moved at once upon the Gainesville road.

So that Morell's division did not go to Manassas Station according to General Warren, but struck off where that small angle is made at Manassas Junction.

Private *John S. Slater,* Thirteenth New York Volunteers, called for the government, Martindale's brigade, Morell's division, said (Board's Record, p. 324) that they marched towards Manassas from Bristoe, and then cut across the country.

This is further confirmed by the evidence of Maj. *Geo. Hyland, jr.,* of the Thirteenth New York Volunteers, called for the petitioner (Board's Record, p. 115), who says that from near Manassas Junction they went toward Gainesville.

Sergeant *Ferdinand Mohle,* who belonged to the same regiment in Morell's division, a government witness (Board's Record, p. 675), says that they got not quite up to Manassas Junction when they countermarched.

It is confirmed also by the testimony of Brevet Lieut. Col. Joseph P.

Clary of the same regiment, a government witness (Board's Record, p. 672), who says the same thing substantially.

The petitioner has said (p. 26 of his opening statement), that hastening in advance of his command to join General Pope he met verbal orders to March to Gainesville and take King with him; that this verbal order required him to reverse his march and move back through Manassas Junction and along the Gainesville road past Bethlehem Church to Gainesville; that because it was a verbal order he sent one of his staff, Dr. Abbott, to General Pope in order to procure a written order.

For some occult purpose Capt. *John H. Piatt*, an aide-de-camp of General Pope, has been introduced into this case by the petitioner. In his testimony he stated substantially that after General Pope reached Centreville on the morning of the 29th, *he* was sent back with an order to General *McDowell* which was to direct General *Porter* to take General *King* and advance towards Gainesville; and that he met the petitioner near Bull Run Creek on the west side of the creek, and also his troops, about nine o'clock, moving up towards Centreville in marching order (Board's Record, pp. 1142, 3, 4, 5); that he gave the purport of the order to the petitioner who told him where he would probably find General McDowell; that he rode on and found General McDowell about or near Manassas Junction and gave him the order; and that General McDowell told him "to say to General Pope that he had received his order and he had directed Porter to put King upon his right so he could have him if he wanted him—that is, if General Pope said so."

Unfortunately for the credibility of this evidence, Captain *Monteith*, as we have seen, had made a different statement. If General McDowell had directed General Porter to do that which he told Captain Piatt he had directed him to do, it is hardly conceivable that petitioner would have presumed to continue his march towards Centreville in defiance of such an order. But everything points to the conclusion, from the petitioner's own statement, that the verbal order he received was addressed to himself and followed almost immediately by a written order from General Pope through General Gibbon; and certainly before he had seen General McDowell at all, because General Gibbon's order was in his possession before General McDowell appeared, according to his own evidence.

It is further evidenced by the joint order which forms the basis of this specification in which General Pope mentions that he did not know General McDowell's position until a late hour in the morning.

Major-General *Morell*, also a witness for the petitioner, says (Board's Record, p. 421), that General Sykes' division was at Manassas Junction at 8.30 a. m., as appears by the dispatch of Sykes to Morell.

Also by dispatch which he produced, of the petitioner's assistant adjutant-general, that the head of the column was halted beyond the junction.

Lieut. *S. M. Weld*, another former aid-de-camp of the petitioner and a witness on his behalf, has stated (Board's Record, p. 262) his impression that the head of the column did not get over half a mile beyond Manassas Junction, though the petitioner himself went beyond towards Centreville; and that they turned towards Gainesville about 9 a. m.

Assistant Adjutant-General Locke has said in his evidence on this subject as follows:

Question. How far did you and General Porter, being in advance of the troops, get beyond Manassas Junction towards Centreville?
Answer. We got to the brick house called a warehouse (Weir house), which was a little below the junction. There we stopped for some little time, and General Porter held a conference with General McDowell.

Question. In that house?

Answer. The outside of the house. After this conversation closed, the general and myself rode on probably a quarter of a mile towards Centreville. There we were met by an officer from General Pope, who gave General Porter a verbal order to the effect that that march was to be changed to the direction of Gainesville, and then immediately sent me back to halt the column for fear that it should get too far and they would have to retrace their steps.

So that this witness did not pass all of General Porter's corps, or pass any of it.

Question. Did not he accompany you?
Answer. Not just then. I left him in conversation with this officer.
Question. How soon did he come up?
Answer. Very soon after.
Question. And joined you at Manassas?
Answer. Yes, sir.
Question. You having halted the column as you passed up?
Answer. Yes. I met the head of the column as I got up just near where we turned to go up the Gainesville road.
Question. Did you know Dr. Abbott on the staff of General Porter at that time?
Answer. Yes, sir.
Question. Do you know of his having that morning gone to General Pope and brought back an order or a message?
Answer. I think I recollect the circumstance.
Question. When you got back to Manassas Junction, what happened?
Answer. As I halted the head of the column, General Gibbon rode up with an order to General Porter from General Pope in writing. He gave me the order and I think I read it before General Porter joined us. He came up almost immediately. The order was signed by General Pope himself.

As the column was halted at Manassas Junction at 8.30 a. m. (Sykes' division), according to Sykes' own dispatch, it is plain that the verbal order which the petitioner received to move toward Gainesville must have come into his possession before the column had halted. While there they were taking ammunition from their train, which, according to General Morell (Board's Record, p. 422), took only half or three-quarters of an hour; and according to Assistant Adjutant-General Francis S. Earle, a witness for the petitioner (Board's Record, p. 409), detained them only about half an hour. He also says (Board's Record, p. 414) that they left Bristoe that morning about 7 a. m. for Manassas Junction. As Capt. George Monteith, petitioner's former aide-de-camp, has said (G. C. M. Record, p. 127), in 1862, that they found their ammunition train going into Manassas Junction when they got there, and as it took half an hour for them to obtain it from the wagons before countermarching partially toward Gainesville (Sykes' division being the only one that had to face about, the head of Morell's division not having gone beyond the junction, where the roads, according to General Warren, made a very small angle), it is apparent, even on the petitioner's own statements, that nine o'clock is about the time, at the outside, the head of Morell's division moved to the left toward Bethlehem Church and Gainesville, followed thereafter by Sykes, who, from being on the right, had now become the left division.

Much has been said of an interview at the Weir house between Major-General McDowell and the petitioner, near Manassas Junction, on that morning. It will be noticed that Captain Piatt, the officer or aide-de-camp of General Pope, who had met the petitioner on the road between Manassas Junction and Centreville, had quite a long conversation with him there, according to Colonel Locke. Therefore, when the petitioner met General McDowell at the Weir house, it is apparent that he must have had the latest information from General Pope of what was going on and what was to be done. That should be contrasted with his opening statement that he looked to McDowell as the man above all others to give him that information.

Brigadier-General *Gibbon*, of King's division, after the night march of the 28th August down from the Warrenton pike to Manassas Junction, started just as the day was breaking (Board's Record, p. 243) to find General Pope in order to notify him of the fact that General King's division had retired from the Warrenton pike and was no longer interposed between Jackson, who was north of Groveton, and Thoroughfare Gap. Finding General Pope at Centreville, having ridden there as rapidly as he could, a distance of six miles, he gave him information, and immediately received a written dispatch to petitioner, was furnished with a fresh horse, and started back, meeting the petitioner at the junction. He says when he arrived back he found petitioner's troops stationary. Almost immediately afterward, while the petitioner had the order in his hand, General McDowell came up and the petitioner gave it to him. Brigadier-General Gibbon says (Board's Record, p. 245):

General McDowell requested General Porter, when he formed his line of *battle*, which it was supposed he would form in the direction of Gainesville, that he would place King's division on his right, so that he (McDowell) could have his command together, it being known at the time that Reynolds' division, a portion of McDowell's command, was out in that direction somewhere, supposably on the right of what would be Porter's line.

At that time General Gibbon says that General McDowell did not assume command over the petitioner, hence the request. That order which the petitioner received at the hands of General Gibbon was as follows:

HEADQUARTERS ARMY OF VIRGINIA,
Centreville, Aug. 29, 1862.

Push forward with your corps and King's division, which you will take with you, upon Gainesville. I am following the enemy down the Warrenton turnpike. Be expeditious, or we will lose much.

JOHN POPE,
Maj. Genl. Commanding.

Certainly language could not be plainer in order to apprise the petitioner what the commanding general proposed to do, and General Gibbon's own testimony, which I have thus cited, shows the intent to form a line of battle.

Gainesville may be assumed, for the consideration of the geographical features of this case, to be the apex of an equilateral triangle to the westward, with Manassas Junction at the angle to the south and Centreville at the angle to the north, the base line being between Centreville and Manassas Junction. It is apparent, therefore, that by rapidly moving up what is known as the Manassas and Gainesville road toward Gainesville on one side of the triangle, and Major-General Pope's forces moving up on the Gainesville, Warrenton, and Centreville pike ("Warrenton pike") from Centreville on the other side of the triangle, the two separated portions of General Pope's army would rapidly converge upon the same point. If General Pope's forces were following the enemy down the Warrenton pike and petitioner's forces on an unobstructed road could move with expedition, it would place them on the flank and possibly on the rear of the enemy.

ROUTE OF MARCH TO GAINESVILLE.

At 9 a. m., which is the hour also put by Brig. Gen. *Charles Griffin*, a witness for the accused on his original trial (G. C. M. Record, p. 162) as the time when they started out, Morell's division of the petitioner's corps moved toward Bethlehem Church and Gainesville.

The petitioner puts the arrival of his command at Dawkins' Branch, beyond which it did not collectively go, at 11.30 a. m.

According to the petitioner's witnesses Major Warren and Mr. Judson, the distance from Manassas Junction to Bethlehem Church is three miles, and from Bethlehem Church to Dawkins' Branch, the point at which petitioner's head of column halted for the day, is two miles—in all five miles. (Board's Record, pp. 51, 109.)

Brigadier-General Gibbon says (Board's Record, p. 253) that he accompanied the head of the column to pilot it into the Manassas and Gainesville road, which he had just passed over the night before; and says, further:

I accompanied General Morell, my impression is, until I approached the position where I had left my brigade in the morning. I cannot tell where that was. I don't know how far from the junction that was. When I got to that position, probably before, I left the column of the Fifth Corps, and resumed command of my own brigade.

His brigade of King's division, to which belonged the Sixth Wisconsin Volunteers, was lying between Bethlehem Church and Manassas Junction, where he rejoined it when he ceased to pilot Morell's division on the road he had been on during the night. On cross-examination, with reference to this interview between the petitioner and General McDowell, Gibbon said (p. 254):

Question. General McDowell said he wanted to have you so place your division that you could come in on the left of Reynolds?
Answer. That was not the way he put it. It was to go in on Porter's right; that was the way he said it; that is what he meant according to what I understood; on the left of Reynolds, but he didn't put it that way.

Lieut. *E. P. Brooks*, adjutant of the Sixth Wisconsin, appears to have been detailed to show Morell's division the road. His testimony is as follows (Board's Record, p. 1022):

Question. Where were you on the morning of Friday, August 29, 1862?
Answer. On the morning of the 29th I came with King's division from the battle-field of the night of the 28th back to Manassas Junction.
Question. What orders, if any, did you receive that morning?
Answer. I received an order to go with Morell's division of Porter's corps back to the battle-field where King had fought the night before.
Question. Did you do so?
Answer. I went back to a point where I presumed General Morell would have no difficulty in finding his way to the turnpike, and then I returned to King's division.
Question. Could you, by looking at the map, indicate the point to which you went with Morell's division [Duffee map shown witness]?
Answer. We moved out on the Gainesville road. I do not think this map is quite complete.
Question. State in what respect.
Answer. There is a road running from somewhere in this vicinity across in that direction [across to Lewis lane No. 1].
Question. From whose place and to what point?
Answer. I could not say. I merely know from the general direction that I carried Morell's division; I rode with Morell at the head of the division until we reached this point. My impression is that we crossed Dawkins' Branch, but I am not positive about that. We certainly got so near here that I could point out to him the direction of the battle-field of the night before.
Question. Which road had you come down the night before from Gibbon's battle-field?
Answer. The battle-field of the night before, the line of battle ran across there [near the Douglass and Brewer houses]. There were two regiments of Gibbon's brigade engaged on the east of the woods. When we fell back that night we fell back directly across the Warrenton turnpike, and struck the lane about there [about near the word "lane" of Lewis lane No. 2]. Colonel Bragg and myself were at the head of the column; and we marched down this way until we reached this road here [not indicated], and this road [road marked in ink on the map "E. P. B."]. Then we followed down the Manassas and Gainesville road to the junction. When we got there, as I say, in the morning, I went back with Morell's division to this point. [Witness indicates a point near Dawkins' Branch.]

The general concurrent testimony of the witnesses puts the arrival somewhere at about 11 a. m.

Capt. *Augustus P. Martin*, chief of artillery to the petitioner, and called as a witness for him, both on the original trial and now (Board's Record, p. 1128), puts the arrival of of the column at Dawkins' Branch at about 11 a. m. That would make its rate of march 2½ miles an hour; King's division following behind; and Major-General McDowell being with it, he being the senior to the petitioner in rank, but not at first apparently assuming any command.

From the fact that General Gibbon brought the order from General Pope, and Lieutenant Brooks was detailed from his [Gibbon's] brigade to act as pilot the remainder of the distance, it seems to be manifest that when General Pope ordered the petitioner to push forward upon Gainesville he intended that they should take the very road that King's division had come down upon the night before, which ran into the Warrenton Pike a little easterly of Gainesville.

It is to be noted here that the road leading from Deats', just south of Dawkins' Branch at its junction with the Manassas and Gainesville dirtroad, up to Lewis lane No. 1, is not indicated on this map, although testified to by Lieutenant Brooks as a road then in existence. It was presumably an army road, like one of the many made through that portion of the country during the years 1861–'62, while the Union and Confederate armies were respectively encamped there. I find by my notes made during a personal inspection of the ground last August that the inhabitants of that locality pointed out to me the location of this very road, the traces of which are still visible, and that I put it down at the time upon my map not knowing of the positive evidence Lieutenant Brooks has since given as to its former existence. In looking at the official map it is apparent that that would be the shortest route, from Milford and Bristoe up through Deats' past Thomas Nealon's, a little to the eastward of his residence, and so on up to Lewis lane No. 1, where it strikes the *old* Warrenton, Alexandria and Washington road, and thus through Groveton, to Sudley Church, and Aldie. The fact, therefore, of the existence of that road in 1862 does not merely depend upon the notes of my own inspection, but is supported by the evidence of a material witness. But one witness has given a different route for King's division in coming down from the Warrenton pike to Manassas Junction during the previous night, and that is Captain Judson (Board Record, p 108); but on cross-examination (p. 109) he said, "I have no recollection of the march at all."

Brig. Gen. *Marcenus R. Patrick*, another witness for the petitioner, who was in the fight of King's division on the 28th, said they "struck south" (Board's Record, p. 185); and on page 187 Board's Record he said (after mentioning their position next morning near Bethlehem Church):

Question by petitioner. *What happened next after King's departure for Centreville?*
Answer. I was ordered I think by McDowell in person, to move as soon as I could in the rear of General Porter; Porter having just passed through, or passing through nearer Manassas Junction, to go back to the scene of our fight the night previous.

From this it will be perceived incidentally that Brig. Gen. Rufus King, who commanded the particular division of General McDowell's corps, *had at this very time departed for Centreville from Manassas Junction.* On cross-examination this same witness, referring to this movement of the petitioner's corps towards Gainesville, and past the place where King's division was lying in the road, quotes from his diary as follows:

At about ten o'clock Porter's corps having passed on towards our lines of yesterday we were ordered to follow him, and did so.

Further on the witness said (Board's Record, p. 196):

(Cross-examined by RECORDER:)

Question. Did you know at the time what orders they had ?

Answer. No, sir; I don't think I did; but I knew that Porter was ordered forward to the scene of yesterday's operations, because McDowell told me that.

Question. Where was the scene of the previous operations ?

Answer. Where we had the fight before.

Question. On the Warrenton pike ?

Answer. My inference was, from what McDowell said to me, that he wanted me to go in there, because I could pilot Porter.

Question. On the Warrenton pike ?

Answer. Our fight was up where Gibbon was [northwest of Groveton].

Question. Was that fight reported as being at Gainesville, rather than at Groveton, of the night before ?

Mr. CHOATE. Reported by whom ?

Question. Well, by anybody. By King.

Answer. It had not taken form yet. I don't know that many people knew about it. I don't know that Porter knew about the fight much until I told him. I don't remember whether it was called Gainesville or Groveton.

* * * * * *

Question. How did this conversation between you and McDowell arise, in which you have said that he made some remarks in reference to General Porter's position on that road ?

Answer. Do you mean when he met me to turn me back ?

Question. Yes.

Answer. It was because he had ordered me to tell General Porter to keep with me and to pilot him back to the scene of last night's operations. I think the language was that I was to go with Porter back to the scene of last night's operations.

Question. When he spoke of General Porter's position when he came and took you up the Sudley road, do you recollect his language ?

Answer. I do not.

* * * * * *

Question. How rapidly did you march that morning on that road from Manassas Junction towards and beyond Bethlehem Church ? .

Answer. I think Porter's rear had got along some little distance before I joined, and that I marched rather rapidly until I got up with him.

Thus it is apparent that at the time Lieutenant Brooks was piloting the petitioner's corps under the order that Brigadier-General Gibbon had brought from Major-General Pope, the *purport and intention of that order was that petitioner's corps should move up to the lines occupied in the fight of the evening before by King's division on the Warrenton pike just south of the Browner-Douglass place* delineated on the map which has been used in this case.

Major *G. K. Warren*, the petitioner's witness says (Board's Record, p. 18) that arriving at Dawkins' Branch he "found that General Morell's division had moved off to the right towards the Manassas Gap Railroad, * * * say a quarter of a mile"; that General McDowell has been at Manassas Junction that morning with the petitioner. At the last-named place the petitioner was not under his [McDowell's] command and had received the latest information from Major-General Pope. Whatever information Major-General McDowell could furnish him at that time relative to the actual situation of affairs from the limited knowledge he [McDowell] *then* had might be and possibly was serviceable, but it would have had no effect whatever so far as the petitioner's order was concerned which he [petitioner] had received at that time from General Pope to move "at once towards Gainesville and be expeditious or we should lose much." That was the order which controlled and governed petitioner's action at that time, and neither Major-General McDowell nor any one else could rightfully have influenced him in delaying to obey that order.

That General McDowell was anxious to furnish him with all the information possible is manifested in the fact that he gave him his own map of that part of the country, which, as it turns out, was the only map they had at that time.

About the time the column halted at Dawkins' Branch, on the Manassas and Gainesville road, Dr. Abbott, of the petitioner's staff, returned from General Pope's headquarters with the *written* response that the petitioner had requested in the morning when he first received a *verbal* order from General Pope to move in that direction, this written order by Dr. Abbott's hands being supplementary to a written order which had been sent intermediately to the petitioner by the hands of Brigadier-General Gibbon. (G. C. M. Record, p. 65.)

For disobedience to the joint order the petitioner was tried under the specification we are now considering. He has shown in his opening statement, page 31, that he knew what the objects were to be accomplished under this joint order, namely:

1st. To move towards Gainesville;

2d. To establish communication with General Pope's forces on the right; and

3d. When this communication was established to halt.

He says that there was nothing in this order that contemplated a battle; but *in the light of previous orders that he had received that day, and of the orders he had received on previous days*, it seems quite clear that this last statement of the petitioner is one that cannot be sustained. The very first order he received from General Pope that morning said:

A severe engagement is likely to take place, and your presence is necessary.

Two days before, on the 27th of August, he had received a communication from General Pope, through the chief of staff of the Army of Virginia (see page 88, petitioner's opening statement), in which he was told that the army would probably move to attack the enemy next day in the neighborhood of Gainesville. And on the day before that, the 26th of August, General Pope in person wrote him a communication (see petitioner's opening statement, page 87), in which he said:

I do not see how a general engagement can be postponed more than a day or two.

The second order from General Pope that the petitioner received, at the hands of General Gibbon, that morning, the 29th August, at Manassas Junction to push forward with his corps and King's division on Gainesville, and "be expeditious," showed that the purpose of General Pope was to attack the enemy before he could receive re-enforcements, and, if possible, overwhelm and destroy him. And from the fact that General Gibbon had delivered the order to petitioner in person, and told him all about the operations of the night before, and of his [Gibbon] proceeding of his own accord to see General Pope in order to have troops sent out in this very direction to intervene between Jackson and anything that might be coming through Thoroughfare Gap, for the express purpose of overwhelming Jackson, if possible, it is apparent that at the moment the petitioner received this joint order from General Pope at the hands of Dr. Abbott, of his staff, *he knew that the movement on Gainesville was for the express purpose of engaging the enemy.* Otherwise, no reasonable explanation could be given of the order which he had received from General Gibbon, that as General Pope's army was following the enemy down the Warrenton pike, he, the petitioner, was to "be expeditious" in getting up towards Gainesville, or we should "lose much." It must be noted, also, that in this joint order the previous order received at the hands of General Gibbon is taken as expressive of the intention of the commanding general with reference to the joint order itself, for he says, in the joint order:

I sent General Porter written orders to that effect an hour and a half ago.

Namely, to move forward on Gainesville.

But General Pope also stated what troops were moving down the Warrenton pike or that vicinity; that they could not be very far from Gainesville, and that *as soon as communication was established between that force and the petitioner's and General McDowell's,* the whole command should halt. The accidental fact mentioned that it might be necessary to fall back behind Bull Run at Centreville that night was, as General Pope presumed, "on account of his supplies." General McDowell, by the joint order, was directed to take immediate steps to communicate with his other division commander, Brigadier-General Ricketts, so as to instruct him to rejoin the other divisions of his corps as soon as practicable. Now, one of the divisions attached to General McDowell's corps at that time was Brigadier-General Reynolds' division, which was placed on the left of Maj. Gen. Franz Sigel at daylight by General McDowell's personal orders, having reference to an offensive movement which General Sigel had been directed to make by General Pope against the enemy. The petitioner *was aware of this,* and yet he says there was nothing in this order that contemplated a battle. The "joint order" itself was merely the result of petitioner sending Dr. Abbott of his staff to General Pope for written orders when he received between 8 and 9 a. m. verbal orders—he not then knowing that written orders were coming intermediately to him from General Pope, at General Gibbon's hands.

The moment General McDowell received *his* copy of the joint order, he rode forward to the head of the petitioner's column from the position he himself had taken on the Manassas and Gainesville road near Sudley road, to await General Ricketts' arrival from Bristoe Station.

We know from the testimony of a number of witnesses that even while petitioner was at Manassas Junction in consultation with General McDowell, Sigel's artillery was heard in action; and that when the petitioner's head of column reached Dawkins' Branch the noise of the contest obliquely on his right and rear was plainly perceptible. In other words, the main column, under General Pope, had met the enemy east of Gainesville, between it and Groveton, and had become engaged with it. For the petitioner, therefore, to continue his march towards Gainesville on the road to the left and southwest of Thomas Nealon's was to march away from the place of action and separate still more widely the two flanks of the army.

In order to carry out the requirements of the joint order that the army should not be in this unmilitary shape, it was absolutely necessary that the Fifth Corps should be taken directly over to the north and right, in order to form connection with Brigadier-General Reynolds' division, which was on the left of General Sigel's corps of General Pope's army.

There were three ways of doing this:

1st. Of moving directly by the Army road (which Lieutenant Brooks had shown General Morell as being the one which King's division had come down that night) due north to Groveton from Dawkins' Branch.

2d. By directing the head of the regular division, under General Sykes, to take the Milford road from Milford and Bristoe which went up through Five Forks to Compton's lane.

3d. To take the road known as the Manassas and Sudley road to the rear of the line of battle, which would have made it necessary that the divisions of the petitioner's corps should countermarch for that purpose; the forks of the Manassas and Sudley and the Manassas and Gainesville road being distant 2¾ miles from the head of petitioner's column at Dawkins' Branch.

But in this connection it should be noted under this third head, that as the country was quite open midway between those two points, troops could be carried right across the country to that road, just as General McDowell carried, according to General Patrick's evidence, the latter's brigade of King's division to the Manassas and Sudley road in order to apply it and put it in action soonest in the manner which had been suggested by petitioner himself to McDowell just before.

No explanation has been given why the petitioner made no effort during all that long 29th day of August, 1862, to push his corps up into conjunction with General Pope's army by means of the roads passing through Five Forks. If north of the Manassas Gap Railroad the woods had been as impenetrable as he would have us believe, it is plain that in passing through those roads in order to take position to the left rear of our army, under General Pope, his troops would have been protected from any flank attack which he would have appear as so much to have been dreaded while making the movement.

John T. Leachman, one of the petitioner's witnesses, a resident of that vicinity, whose evidence is yet to be commented upon, said, however (Board's Record, p. 123), that in 1861 and 1862 the Confederate forces encamped not far from Bethlehem Church; and on page 125, that sometimes wagons for country purposes are driven along these very roads through Five Forks; this evidence of the witness having reference to the road as it was in August, 1862.

Major *Warren*, the petitioner's witness (Board's Record, p. 17), said that no prudent man having anything at stake would march his men through there unless he had possession of the outskirts; if he had possession of the outskirts he could march a column through there very well. This evidence he qualified further (Board's Record, p. 39) by saying:

It is always possible where a man can go afoot to take an army.

By examining the record it will be seen that no effort whatever was at any time made by the petitioner during that day to ascertain the character of the roads through "Five Forks" up to the left and rear of General Pope's army. He does not seem to have sent any staff officers up there, nor any orderlies, nor anybody, and his failure to do so can then only be explained on the supposition that he did not care as to what was being done on the right.

We know from the testimony of two government witnesses, Captain *McEldowney*, of the Twenty-seventh Confederate Virginia Infantry, and Lieut. *B. T. Bowers*, First Ohio Battery (Board's Record, pp. 952, 953, 956), that the roads through Five Forks from the Manassas and Gainesville road up to the old Warrenton, Alexandria and Washington road at Compton's lane are good and that they drove through that very road at a trot in a two-horse wagon.

When the petitioner's corps came to a halt, the head of the column at or near Dawkins' Branch, which, by the way, in the month of August is nothing but a dry ditch or ravine, General McDowell, who was with King's division on the rear of the road awaiting the arrival of General Ricketts' division from Bristoe, received his copy of the joint order, and immediately moved to the front in order to communicate with petitioner and assume command for the time being under its requirements.

Major-General *Morell*, petitioner's witness, who was at the head of the column, says (Board's Record, p. 432,) that they met a mounted man before reports came from the skirmishers. In his original evidence before the court-martial he said as follows (G. C. M. Record, p. 146):

We had gone up the road towards Gainesville, perhaps about three miles, when I met a mounted man coming towards us. I stopped him and asked him the road to

Gainesville and also the news from the front. He said he had just come from Gainesville, and that the enemy's skirmishers were then there to the number of about 400
and their main body was not far behind them. I then moved up the road, and in a
short time our own skirmishers reported that they had discovered the enemy's skirmishers in their front. The column was then halted by General Porter, who was with
me.

This mounted man to whom this witness refers was evidently one of
General Buford's cavalry; because he would otherwise have held him
in custody as a suspicious character. And as this argument progresses
in reference to the evidence in this case it will be perceived that on that
very road had come down that morning and was then with General
Morell a squadron of this very cavalry under Capt. John P. Taylor.
Therefore, if there were any of the enemy's skirmishers on that road at
that time they were just arriving there; and it remains to be considered
what skirmishers they were and where they came from.
It seems that the Sixty-second Pennsylvania held the infantry advance
on this road; and when it was fired upon by the skirmishers, the columns halted by the petitioner's orders. Two companies of that regiment
were in the advance; immediately the other eight companies were sent
out. What was done at that time is best described by Brig. Gen. Charles
Griffin, who testified for the accused on the original trial, and whose
evidence is given in brief at page 497, Board's Record:

Page 161 G. C. M. Record: The halt at Manassas Junction was for half an hour.
Page 162: Left Manassas at 9. The skirmishers, Sixty-second Pennsylvania, commenced firing with the enemy's pickets possibly five miles from Manassas. Porter rode
up and column halted. The other eight companies Sixty-second sent out. Porter
then read Pope's communication (the one jointly to Porter and McDowell) to himself,
Morell, and Butterfield, all dismounted. We then went back to the rear on a hill, say
three hundred yards. A battery, I believe, was placed in position there. We were
there some time when McDowell rode up. Pickets of the Sixty-second were recalled
by Griffin by order. P. 162: I received an order almost directly after General
McDowell had left, to recall my pickets and orders to move my command to the right.
I attempted to go to the right and moved probably 600 yards until with the head of
my column I crossed a railroad said to run to Gainesville. Here we met with obstructions which we could not get through. It was reported by somebody, I cannot say
who, "You can't get through there." We then faced about and moved back to the
hill. * * * My brigade was then placed in position. It was a very good
position to repel an attack. P. 165: When my brigade moved to the right across the
railroad we ran into some little, thick, pine bushes; halted until ordered to move
back again; made no reconnaissance whatever. P. 169: Merely obeyed orders. P.
162: During the day large clouds of dust were going to our front and to our left
from a point stated to us then to be passing through Thoroughfare Gap. There were
large clouds of dust all that afternoon, in fact nearly all day, as I can recollect,
coming from a point said to us to be Thoroughfare Gap. I should say it was three
or four miles from where I was; fully that. I except, of course, these batteries that
opened on us about 10 o'clock; they were nearer. They were within 1,200 or 1,500
yards. We saw scattering groups of horsemen or of infantry. *In fact, there is not a
doubt, if that point was Thoroughfare Gap, that the enemy was coming through there all
day.* P. 163: When Morell got his orders near sundown to attack "we had started
back towards Manassas Junction."

The skirmishers from the Sixty-second Pennsylvania, which crossed
Dawkins' Branch, appear to have been almost immediately withdrawn
and the Thirteenth New York Volunteer Infantry, under Col. E. G.
Marshall of the Regular Army (now colonel United States Army, retired), sent out in its stead.
Lieut. *Walter S. Davis*, Twenty-second Massachusetts Volunteers,
petitioner's witness, says (Board's Record, p. 398), that Colonel Marshall
was sent out *before* General McDowell arrived.
Assistant Adjutant-General *Francis S. Earle*, petitioner's witness
(Board's Record, p. 415), says that Marshall was thrown out as soon as
they began to deploy, which was immediately, and that General McDowell

came up *afterwards* (Board's Record, p. 416); also that General Morell that day said he had about 6,000 men in his division.

Capt. *George Monteith*, aid-de-camp of the petitioner, called for him (Board's Record, p. 311,) says General Morell detailed Colonel Marshall to move out *before* General McDowell came up.

Private *John S. Slater*, Thirteenth New York Volunteers, now a lawyer, a government witness, says that petitioner detailed Colonel Marshall for this duty. (Board's Record, p. 325.)

Major-General *Morell* himself, petitioner's witness, said (Board's Record, p. 432) that Colonel Marshall was sent out as soon as the division halted at Dawkins' Branch.

Lieut. *James H. Wilson*, Thirteenth New York Volunteers (Board's Record, p. 370), called by the government, says that his regiment, under Colonel Marshall, was immediately deployed. He answered further as follows:

> By the RECORDER:
>
> Question. Did you see the enemy that day?
> Answer. I don't recollect that I did. I do not have any recollection now of seeing any of them.

We know the direction in which Colonel Marshall's regiment was deployed, from his own evidence as well as the evidence of others not disputed; they were thrown out in the space directly to the front between a ravine just northeast of Thomas Nealon's and the Manassas and Gainesville road where it took a turn towards the left from Dawkins' Branch and westerly to the woods in front. A continuation of that road, which led somewhat to the left from Dawkins' Branch, would have carried the petitioner's corps still further away at every step he would have taken from General Pope's army, which at this time, from the sound of cannonading, was northeast of him, to the right and a little to the rear.

At this juncture Major-General McDowell rides up with a copy of the joint order in his hand.

It was testified to in the original trial by Assistant Adjutant-General Locke, for the defense (G. C. M. Record, p. 135), that General McDowell said:

> Porter, you are too far out already. This is no place to fight a battle.

That portion of the remark, that it was no place to fight a battle, General McDowell explicitly denied in his evidence, because it was a very good place in which to fight a battle.

There were, however, other considerations to come in there, namely, whether it was a good place to fight a battle in when he did not believe the enemy to be on his immediate front in force, and when by remaining there the left wing of the army would be separated from the right, contrary to all military principles, a distance from a mile and a half to two miles; so that if any enemy did come down in their front they would be enabled to interpose and destroy them in detail. General McDowell said on the original trial on cross-examination as follows (G. C. M. Record, p. 87):

> I have no recollection about that place not being the one in which to fight a battle. Something may have been said about not going further toward Gainesville in reference to falling behind Bull Run that night.
>
> Question. If anything was said in relation to the facility of getting back to Bull Run that night, do you remember whether it was that the accused was too far in the front or would be too far in the front if he moved further on?
>
> Answer. It was hardly a question of going further on; it was more a question of turning to the right and going against the enemy then passing down the Warrenton pike.

With reference to the remark testified to by Assistant Adjutant-General Locke, and which has been repeated in other forms by other witnesses for the accused before this Board, General McDowell in the original trial further said (G. C. M. Record, p. 218): '

I cannot recollect precisely what occurred between General Porter and myself, or what conversation and what words passed between us at that time. The subject of our conversation, as near as I can recall it to mind, was the order which we, each of us, had received from General Pope, and particularly that part of it which referred to our not going so far forward that we should not be able to get behind Bull Run that night or before morning. I cannot say what language I used or how it may have been understood whilst talking on that point. As to that particular speech, that the ground, so far as topography was concerned, not being a place to fight a battle, I have no recollection of having said anything to the effect that it was not a good place to fight on. It was about as good a place, so far as topography was concerned, as any other in that part of the country. I think our conversation was chiefly upon the subject of not putting ourselves in a position to be unable to fulfill the requirements of the order about retiring behind Bull Run, and about not going so far towards Gainesville, or going to Gainesville, *that this could not be done.* Without being able to say what was said either by him or me, I think, so far as my best recollection goes, that the object and purpose of our conversation at that time was in relation to that point.

As the principal purpose in that movement towards Gainesville, after it became evident by the cannonading that General Pope's right was engaged, was that the two wings should unite, the remark attributed to General McDowell by these persons is the one that he would most naturally have made under the circumstances, that the petitioner was too far out, too much to the left, at too great distance from the other wing of the army to render it any service under the circumstances as they then existed. The presence of two regiments thrown forward as skirmishers beyond Dawkins' Branch, principally to the left of Nealon's, showed that a continuation of the movement in that direction was improper and faulty. Major-General McDowell was then in command under the (old) sixty-second article of war by reason of the joint order. It was his duty to decide upon the circumstances of the case and determine what should be done in order to comply with the wishes of the commanding general. The order itself specifically gave him a discretion to vary its mode of execution to suit the circumstances. Had no discretion been given his action might have been different. The discretion being given him, his decision was conclusive, and formed part of the joint order itself as communicated by him at the time to the petitioner, who was the other corps commander, and who himself suggested the variation.

General McDowell made the decision, and we shall see what was required to be done under it. In point of fact, that which General McDowell directed under the joint order was precisely that which the order previously received by the petitioner at the hand of General Gibbon from General Pope required, namely, *to go to the right from Dawkins' Branch, so as to strike the Gainesville and Warrenton turnpike at the point where King's division had been in action the night before,* and not to take the road, still in use, to the left of Thomas Nealon's house, just beyond Dawkins' Branch, but the "army road," running from Dawkins' Branch due north to Lewis Lane No. 1.

Bvt. Maj. Gen. John Gibbon, U. S. A., King's division, McDowell's corps, a witness for petitioner, referring to his interview with Major-General Pope early that morning at Centreville, when he went to apprise him of the withdrawal of King's division the night before, said (Board's Record, p. 259):

Question. Did he explain to you the purpose of that order?
Answer. Well, the fact is that the purpose of the order was rather dictated by myself, because I told him I had ridden that distance to give him this information, deeming it important, supposing if he had any available troops he would send them out on

the road. At that he turned around to Colonel Ruggles and told him to write the order in pretty much the terms I have seen it, directing General Porter to move out on the road, and take King's division with him.

Question. Was that order intended to be the substance of what you had communicated?

Answer. I think so.

Question. Towards what point did that order direct the march?

Answer. *I understood right out on the road we had come in.*

Question. Where you were the night before?

Answer. Yes; if he could get there for the purpose of interposing a force between Jackson's detached force and Lee's main army.

Question. Was it not Lientenant Brooks who acted as guide on that occasion?

Answer. I recollect an officer by that name who was reported to me as having been over a portion of the ground, and I think it more than likely that he is the officer.

*   *   *   *   *   *   *

(Board's Record, p. 245.) He further answered as follows [after he returned to Manassas Junction] :

Question. What did you then do?

Answer. I think, at the request of General Porter—at any rate, at the request of some one—I passed to the head of his column, and accompanied General Morell, the commanding officer of the leading division, into the road leading towards Gainesville, and rode along with General Morell until we reached the position where I had left my brigade in the morning, and then joined that, and the troops passed on in the direction of Gainesville.

Question. Then had General Morell passed the point with his division where your troops were lying in the morning?

Answer. Yes; not only General Morell, but I presume the whole corps.

Question. That is, they had gone on the road towards Centreville?

Answer. They had passed where the Gainesville road came into the Gordonsville railroad.

Question. They were going in the direction of Centreville when you delivered this order?

Answer. Yes. I don't think, however, the head of the column was very far ahead of it.

*   *   *   *   *   *   *

Question. You took an order by which they were to return and go towards Gainesville?

Answer. They were stationary when I saw them.

Question. Do you know how long they had been stationary?

Answer. No, sir.

Question. You went back with General Morell?

Answer. My impression is I accompanied him until I got to my position.

Question. They were marching toward Centreville?

Answer. Yes, sir.

Answer. I didn't know where General Reynolds was.

Question. You overheard a conversation previous to that between General Porter and General McDowell, did you not?

Answer. Previous to what?

Question. Previous to being taken off up the Sudley pike.

Answer. Yes; in the morning when I delivered this order.

Question. General McDowell said he wanted to have you so place your division [King's] so that you could come in on the left of Reynolds?

Answer. That was not the way he put it. It was to go in on Porter's right; that was the way he said it; that is what he meant according to what I understood; on the left of Reynolds, but he didn't put it that way.

From this evidence it is plain that petitioner knew from General Gibbon before he [petitioner] left Manassas Junction towards Gainesville, on the morning of the 29th, that General Pope's order required him to march just in the direction subsequently indicated by General McDowell.

Col. *Timothy Sullivan*, of the Twenty-fourth New York Volunteers, King's division, McDowell's corps, a witness for the petitioner, said (Board's Record, p. 98), when referring to the fact of his division lying along the road between Bethlehem Church and Manassas Junction, on the morning of the 29th, that petitioner's corps passed them going back on the road that they had come down on.

Bvt. Brig. Gen. *Edward D. Fowler*, commanding at that time the Four-teenth New York Volunteers, the well known "Brooklyn" regiment, Hatch's brigade, King's division, McDowell's corps (a witness for the government), testified (Board's Record, p, 548) that Porter's corps passed them at Manassas Junction from half past 8 to 9 a. m., and they followed some distance. Said he:

It was expected we would go up and go in at the same place we were in at the night before; but the story was then that somebody over on the right was pressed—Sigel or some one else—and we were turned off in this direction [north], on the Sudley Ford road to there. We marched in this direction and then on the Sudley Ford road to the vicinity of the old battle-field of Bull Run; I recognized it because I was there, the appearance of the ground, stunted pines, and the nearness of the Warren-ton pike. We arrived at that place perhaps at two o'clock in the afternoon—any-where from one to three o'clock in the afternoon. I was very anxious, and expected even before we halted there to hear, on what was our front and left, the guns of Porter's division. I had an idea that we had Jackson rather in a trap. We remained at that place near the battle-field of Bull Run, near the stunted pines and cedars, on an eleva-tion where we could see the battle going on—not the battle, but the smoke of the battle, because there was a ridge that intervened between us and where the battle was. We could hear artillery and infantry firing, and cheers and shouts beyond this place. We remained there until perhaps five o'clock in the afternoon, maybe half past five, when we had orders to go down on the Warrenton pike and move on the enemy. The impression I had then was that the enemy were falling back.

Petitioner himself, as a witness before Major-General McDowell's court of inquiry, admitted that from information received from Brigadier-General Gibbon he knew that the—

Object was to strike the turnpike before the advancing enemy should arrive. The sooner we arrived there the more effective would be our action. (Board's Record, p. 1009.)

The fact being substantiated that it was expected that the petitioner's corps should go *directly* to the right at Dawkins' Branch, at right angles to the road he was then on (the Manassas and Gainesville road), the next point to be considered is, what was done while General McDowell was in command of the joint corps? Whether the command of the peti-tioner moved up with expedition to Dawkins' Branch, or not, from Man-assas Junction, under the very urgent orders he received, is of compar-atively little importance. If he left Manassas Junction at 9 o'clock and arrived at Dawkins' Branch at eleven, we find that he marched at the rate of 2½ miles an hour. He would have been careful, under those im-perative orders, to have done as much at that time, for the reason that Major-General McDowell knew his orders and was directly behind him and was witnessing his movements, and there was no possibility, so long as Major-General McDowell was there, for any evasion.

GENERAL M'DOWELL'S ORDERS TO PETITIONER.

It is a singular and important fact, in the consideration of this case, that the petitioner himself has, on several different occasions, deliber-ately made statements concerning the movements that we are now con-sidering which cannot be reconciled under any possible state of facts. What the petitioner has said as to the interview he had at the front with Major-General McDowell will be found to contain many contradic-tions. General *McDowell's* evidence on that subject before the court which tried the petitioner is as follows (G. C. M. Record, p. 84):

Question. Will you state fully what occurred in that conference? [The one above referred to.]
Answer. On passing the head of General Porter's column, which was on the road I have before mentioned, General Porter was in advance of the head of his column—I think on a slight eminence, some of his staff near him. I rode up to him, and saw

that he had the same order as myself—the joint order. Soon after my attention was directed to some skirmishing—I think some dropping shots in front of us. The country, in front of the position where General Porter was when I joined him, was open for several hundred yards, and was, as I supposed, by seeing the dust coming up above the trees, [near] the Warrenton turnpike, which was covered from view by woods. How deep those woods were I do not know. It did not seem at that time to be a great distance to that road—the Warrenton turnpike. I had an impression at the time that these skirmishers were engaged with some of the enemy near that road.

I rode with General Porter from the position he occupied eastward to the right. That is, the column being somewhat west of north, and I going east, made an angle with the line of troops on the road. The joint order of General Pope was discussed between us; the point to be held in view, of not going so far that we should not be able to get beyond Bull Run that night; that was one point. The road being blocked with General Porter's troops from where the head of his column was back to Bethlehem Church; the sound of battle, which seemed to be at its height on our [the] road to Groveton; the note of General Buford indicating the force that had passed through Gainesville, and, as he said, was moving towards Groveton, where the battle was going on, the dust ascending above the trees seeming to indicate that force to be not a great distance from the head of General Porter's column. I am speaking now of that force of the enemy referred to by General Buford as passing down the Warrenton turnpike towards Groveton. I understand this note of General Buford to refer to a force of the enemy.

The question with me was how, soonest, within the limit fixed by General Pope, this force of ours could be applied against the enemy. General Porter made a remark to me which showed me that he had no question but that the enemy was in his immediate front. I said to him: "*You put your force in here, and I will take mine up to the Sudley Springs road, on the left of the troops engaged at that point with the enemy,*" or words to that effect. I left General Porter with the belief and understanding that he would put his force in at that point. I moved back by the shortest road I could find to the head of my own troops, near Bethlehem Church, and immediately turned them up north on the Sudley Springs road to join General Reynolds' division, which belonged to my command, and which I had directed to co-operate with General Sigel in the movements he (General Sigel) was making at the time I left him in the morning.

* * * * * * *

Question. You have said that the accused made an observation to you which showed that he was satisfied that the enemy was in his immediate front; will you state what that observation was?

Answer. I do not know that I can repeat it exactly, and I do not know that the accused meant exactly what the remark might seem to imply. The observation was to this effect—putting his hand in the direction of the dust rising above the trees— "We cannot go in there anywhere without getting into a fight."

Question. What reply did you make to that remark?

Answer. I think to this effect: "That is what we came here for."

Question. Was or not the battle raging at that time?

Answer. The battle was raging on our right; that is, if you regard the line of the road from Bethlehem Church to Gainesville to be substantially northwest; the battle was raging to the right and east of that line at Groveton.

The expression which General McDowell testifies to as used by the petitioner as indicative of a reluctance to fight at that time is uncontradicted. We shall see, as we proceed in the consideration of the evidence adduced before this board and before the court originally, that this significant expression was but the continuation of a remark that he had really made but a few minutes before to Colonel Marshall, when he sent him out in command of the skirmish line. The dust rising over the trees to their right and front, in the direction of Meadowville Lane, to which both the petitioner and General McDowell referred, we shall see was the dust then being raised by the hundred troopers of Col. T. L. Rosser's Fifth Virginia Cavalry of Maj. Gen. J. E. B. Stuart's cavalry division of Jackson's command, in order to delude and retard the advance of the petitioner's corps.

Capt. Mark J. Bunnell, then lieutenant of the Thirteenth New York Volunteer Infantry, Col. E. G. Marshall, says (Board's Record, p. 678) as follows [his regiment being the one petitioner deployed as skirmishers at Dawkins' Branch]:

Question. Do you know what the orders were under which they were deployed?

Answer. My recollection is that the regiment was halted there; I was lying on the grass at the time, and General Porter rode up and asked where the commander of the regiment was. I stated that he was a short distance from there, with a group of officers. He wanted to see him, and I think I called to an orderly and stated to him what I wanted. He called Colonel Marshall, and they came down within a few paces of where I was, and Colonel Marshall then received his orders to deploy his regiment as skirmishers in front.

Question. Did you hear the order?

Answer. I stood right there so I could hear.

Question. What were the orders that General Porter gave Colonel Marshall?

Answer. I could not hear all the conversation, but to deploy his regiment as skirmishers, as we were about ready to move out; *not to bring on a general engagement*, but the idea was that we had to do duty only as skirmishers.

* * * * * * *

Question. What could you see and hear during that day?

Answer. I saw some skirmishers from the opposite side—two or three cavalrymen I saw come out in a cornfield in front a little to the right—and heard firing.

Question. In which direction?

Answer. Soon after we were in position there was some firing in front, and a little to the right of the front.

Question. Artillery or infantry?

Answer. Artillery and some carbine firing—cavalry. That was the skirmish line, I judge.

Question. Could you see any enemy in your front?

Answer. Only those few cavalrymen that came out there.

Question. Do you know whether the enemy came down in force in your front that day; if so, when?

Answer. The impression was that there was some force there in the *latter part of the afternoon*. I did not see them; I could not see them.

Question. Was there any contest of any description in any other direction than directly in your front and right?

Answer. Judging from the firing, there was at the right.

Question. What was it; infantry, or artillery, or both?

Answer. Both.

Question. How near were you to that contest?

Answer. It would be almost impossible to tell.

Question. You could hear musketry distinctly?

Answer. Yes; very distinctly.

Question. Could you hear anything else indicating a contest or battle?

Answer. Late in the afternoon we could hear the huzzas and howling of the soldiers, apparently as though they were charging, and going backwards and forwards a number of times.

Question. How early in the afternoon did you hear those sounds of cheering, &c.?

Answer. I cannot tell you the time. I should judge it must have been towards five or six o'clock, and perhaps later, because the firing was kept up after dark.

Question. Relative to sunset, when did you first begin to hear those indications?

Answer. I should judge about sundown.

Question. Before that time could you hear any infantry and artillery firing; if so, when; before you heard the cheers?

Answer. Yes; there was some firing to our left [right?], but not to any great extent.

Question. How early in the day was that?

Answer. Along in the afternoon.

Question. The artillery firing?

Answer. Yes; some artillery firing soon after we took our position as skirmishers from perhaps one battery off a little to our right in front.

Question. Any other artillery firing in the distance?

Answer. Yes; to the right.

Cross-examination by Mr. CHOATE:

Question. How near were you to Colonel Marshall and General Porter when General Porter was giving to Marshall his orders?

Answer. About as near as I am to you.

Question. Did you hear in that position?

Answer. I think so; but perhaps not all.

Question. Do you recollect all the conversation?

Answer. I don't know as I do recollect all that passed, because I may not have heard all that passed.

* * * * * * *

· Question. Did you see any captured scouts brought in?

Answer. No, sir.

By the RECORDER:

Question. What was it that transpired that time when General Porter gave that command that especially impresses it upon your recollection?

Answer. It was this: That we were going to have, we supposed, a pretty hard battle; had talked of it from the time we were countermarched from Manassas Junction, as soldiers naturally will; and I remarked to some of the men afterwards what I heard as we were going down on the skirmish line; I remarked it because it was a sort of relief to me; like a great many soldiers, I did not care to go into a fight unless it was really necessary. That is why it impressed my memory.

By the PRESIDENT OF THE BOARD:
· Question. You were shot the next day, I understand?
Answer. Yes, and laid on the field nine days.

From this uncontradicted evidence of a witness who heard the petitioner give these orders to Colonel Marshall not to bring on a general engagement, possibly within five, certainly not more than ten or fifteen minutes before the conversation of the petitioner with General McDowell, it is evident that the same thought was then running in his mind, of an intention or desire not to fight at that time under Major-General Pope. Major-General McDowell, *loyal* to the orders of his superior, anxious to see a union effected between the then separated wings of the army as soon as possible in consequence of the contest then going on to the right, after giving his orders to the petitioner, under the discretion given him by the joint order, moved immediately by the shortest line, as will be perceived on looking on the map, down to the location of his own corps, one division of which (King's under General Hatch) was between Bethlehem Church and the Sudley Springs road, on the Manassas and Gainesville road. Had the Manassas Gap Railroad from near Dawkins' Branch, where Major-General McDowell and the petitioner had made their observations, down to Bethlehem Church been rendered impassable by the open culverts which the petitioner's witness, Leachman, seemed to think would prevent infantry moving along (Board's Record, p. 141), and if the woods at that place had been so dense and impenetrable for foot-troops as the petitioner would have us believe, it would have been impossible for Major-General McDowell to have moved down there on the shortest line on horseback at a gallop or so rapidly as to leave his staff behind. The speed at which he moved, after a determination had been reached as to the next military movement, shows the anxiety he had to unite the two wings of the army as speedily as possible. Himself zealous and unsuspicious, he did not, at the time, attach to the remark of the petitioner, that by putting his forces in at the right he would get into a fight, that significance which, in view of its repetition in various forms, previous and subsequent, should properly be attached to it.

King's division, it will be noticed, was at this time quite 2½ miles from the head of the petitioner's column, then at Dawkins' Branch. To have deployed it to the left and brought it to the front there in line of battle would have been to separate the wings of the army still further, with less possibility of their being united. As the Sudley Springs road was the nearest for that division to move upon in order to come the quickest into position on the right of petitioner's corps, so as to be joined to the other divisions of Major-General McDowell's proper command, the quickest way to apply it in the contest then raging was by moving it in the very direction that Major-General McDowell took it.

As there had been much misrepresentation in the press and considerable misunderstanding in the public mind as to the responsibility for the various disasters in that campaign, and as General McDowell had been a prominent actor in it, he asked President Lincoln, after its conclusion, for a court of inquiry under the statute to examine into his entire conduct from its very beginning, and at the same time he invited all who knew anything of the transactions of that campaign in which his corps or command was concerned to come forward and give evidence on the subject.

This court sat a long time in Washington, in the same building and contemporaneously with the general court-martial that tried the petitioner. Major-General McDowell gave evidence in the case of the petitioner, because he was subpœnaed as a witness and had to do so. The petitioner volunteered evidence in the case of Major-General McDowell before the latter's court of inquiry, because General McDowell had given a general invitation to all to come forward. The petitioner having been duly sworn as a witness before General McDowell's court of inquiry, testified, and the following are extracts from his evidence:

PETITIONER'S TESTIMONY BEFORE GENERAL M'DOWELL'S COURT OF INQUIRY.

* * * * * * *

Question by Court. What order did General McDowell give, or what authority did he exercise over you, and in virtue of whose order? State fully and particularly.

Answer. General McDowell exercised authority over me in obedience to an order of General Pope's addressed jointly to General McDowell and me, and which I presume is in possession of the court. I have no copy of it. Our commands being united he necessarily came into the command under the Articles of War.

* * * * * * *

* * * General McDowell on arriving showed me the joint order, a copy of which I acknowledged having in my possession. An expression of opinion then given by him to the effect that that was no place to fight a battle and that I was too far out, which, taken in connection with the conversation, I considered an order, and stopped further progress towards Gainesville for a short time. General McDowell and I went to the right, which was rather to the north, with the view of seeing the character of the country, and with the idea of connecting, as that joint order required, with the troops on my right. But very few words passed between us, and I suggested, from the character of the country, that he should take King's division with him and form connection on the right of the timber, which was then on the left of Reynolds, or presumed to be Reynolds. He left me suddenly, not replying to a call from me to the effect, "What should I do?" and with no understanding on my part how I should be governed, I immediately returned to my command. On the way back, seeing the enemy gathering in my front, I sent an officer, Lieutenant-Colonel Locke, my chief of staff, to King's division, directing it to remain where it was for the present, and commenced moving my command towards Gainesville and one division to the right, or north of the road. I received an answer from General McDowell to remain where I was; he was going to the right and would take King with him. He did go, taking King's division, as I presumed, to take position on the left of Reynolds. I remained where I was. When General McDowell left me I did not know where he had gone. No troops were in sight, and I knew of the position of Reynolds and Sigel, who were on our right, merely by the sound of Sigel's cannon, and from information that day that Reynolds was in the vicinity of Groveton. The head of my corps was on the first stream after leaving Manassas Junction on the road to Gainesville, one division in the line of battle, or the most of it.

Question. Did you consider the expression of General McDowell, as stated by you, that you were too far to the front, and that this was no place to fight a battle, in the light of an order not to advance, but to resume your original position?

Answer. I did when King's division was taken from me, and as countermanding the first order of General Pope, under the authority given him by that joint order.

* * * * * * *

Question by Court. State, as far as you know, what followed, so far as the movements of General McDowell's troops and your own were concerned, and what orders you subsequently received from General McDowell.

Answer. General McDowell took King off to the right. I knew nothing further of his movements. I remained where I was until three o'clock next morning. A portion of the command left at daybreak. I received no orders whatever from General McDowell.

* * * * * * *

Question by General McDowell. What did you understand to be the effect of General McDowell's conversation? Was it that you were to go no further in the direction of Gainesville than you then were?

Answer. The conversation was in connection with moving over to the right, which necessarily would prevent an advance.

* * * * * * *

Question by General McDowell. Witness speaks of the effect of General McDowell's message (as brought by Colonel Locke) to have been to cause him to remain in position at the place where General McDowell first saw him. How long did witness' troops continue in this position?

Answer. A portion of the command remained there till daybreak the following morning, and some till after daybreak. The most of Morell's division was on or near that ground all day.

Question by General McDowell. Did witness conceive himself prohibited from marching or attempting to make any movement to the front, or to the right, or to the front and right?

Answer. By that direction or order, taken in connection with the joint order, I considered myself checked in advancing, especially taken in connection with the removal of King's division. I did not consider that I could move to the right, and I considered that General McDowell took King's division to form a connection on the right or to go to the right and form such a connection as was possible. I add further that I considered it impracticable to go to the right.

Question by General McDowell. Did witness *attempt* to make any movement in either of the directions above named?

Answer. Not directly to the right. I did to the right and front, and when I received the last message from General McDowell to remain where I was I recalled it.

Question by General McDowell. Did you make no attempt to go to the right or to the right and front after that message?

Answer. I made no attempt with any body of troops. I sent messengers through there to go to General Pope and to get information from the troops on the righ..

Question by General McDowell. After General McDowell left the witness, did the witness not know he was expected by General McDowell to move to the right or to the right and front?

Answer. I did not.

Question by General McDowell. Witness speaks of having reported to General Pope. When did witness conceive himself as no longer under General McDowell?

Answer. My messages were addressed to General McDowell, I think, all of them. The messengers were directed to deliver them to General Pope if they saw or met him. I considered myself as limited in my operations under General McDowell's orders until I should receive directions from General Pope.

Question by General McDowell. How long was witness and General McDowell together before they moved to the right with a view of seeing the character of the country?

Answer. I do not think that we were together more than four or five minutes; though I have no distinct recollection.

Question by General McDowell. How long were they together after moving to the right?

Answer. It may have been ten or twelve minutes, perhaps longer.

Question by General McDowell. Witness refers to some conversation between himself and General McDowell when they first met, which, taken in connection with an expression of opinion by General McDowell, witness considered an order. Can the witness state what that conversation was?

Answer. I only recollect the impression left upon my mind at the time, and merely a reference to the artillery contest going on far to our right.

Question by General McDowell. Was not the joint order referred to, in that conversation?

Answer. I have no recollection of it. It may have been referred to, because we went to the right, my belief is, to look at the country; but I do not recollect anything at all of the order being referred to.

Question by General McDowell. Were not the remarks witness here states to have been made by General McDowell made with reference to the point in the joint order which required the troops not to go to a point from which they could not get behind Bull Run that night?

Answer. I think I have replied to that question by stating I do not recollect.

Question by General McDowell. Does not the witness recollect asking General McDowell if he knew of any roads leading to the right or right and front of the head of witness' column?

Answer. I do not. Early in the day General McDowell loaned me a map and may have given more explanation with it. This is all the information I recollect of receiving, or having in my possession, of the country.

Question by General McDowell. Does not the witness recollect of being made acquainted by General McDowell with information received by him from General Buford as to the force of the enemy which had passed through Gainesville?

Answer. I do.

Question by General McDowell. When the witness and General McDowell moved to the right, "with a view of seeing the character of the country," what were the few words which witness states passed between them?

Answer. I have given some of the words already; that was, my suggestion to take King's division to the right. I have no recollection of any conversation or any words being used by me or him, except when reaching the railroad, remarking that the railroad was an obstacle—we having some little difficulty in getting over it with our horses.

Question by General McDowell. Does the witness recollect nothing of what was said by General McDowell on that occasion, and of his telling the witness to take his troops across to the Warrenton road, and of General McDowell's intention to go back to take his troops up the Sudley Springs road?

Answer. To the best of my recollection nothing of the kind was conveyed to my mind.

From the petitioner's own statements made at this time, it is apparent that he perfectly understood what was meant by General McDowell when he arrived at the head of petitioner's column at Dawkins' Branch, and conversed with him about his position.

Two superserviceable witnesses, Walter S. Davis (Board's Record, p. 391) and Francis S. Earle (Board's Record, p. 410), appeared before this Board on petitioner's behalf. Davis says that General McDowell remarked to the petitioner when he arrived up the Manassas and Gainesville road at Dawkins' Branch, "Porter, you are too far out; move your troops back into these woods"; and Francis S. Earle says that he heard General McDowell say, "Porter, you are too far out," and make a motion with his hand back, and heard the word "back"; he did not hear him say "move your command further back." The latter witness, however, on the cross-examination (Board's Record, p. 416), said he did not see the enemy's skirmishers, even during the day; consequently, if he did not see any skirmishers during the day, he could not have understood at the time any remark that General McDowell might have made relative to the then position of the troops as having any reference to a battle directly in their front.

But whether or not Major-General McDowell said anything then as to their position to the petitioner, whatever he did say, as understood by the petitioner, appears to correspond exactly with the general plan of operations from the moment the "Gibbon" order was received in the morning; for on the question by General McDowell on his Court of Inquiry to the petitioner:

Question. What did you understand to be the effect of General McDowell's conversation; was it that you were to go no further in the direction of Gainesville than you then were?

Answer. The conversation was in connection with moving over to the right, which necessarily would prevent an advance. (Board's Record, p. 1011.)

The petitioner, therefore, perfectly understood whatever remark General McDowell made at the time, as appears by his own evidence; and that to pursue a march to the left of Thomas Nealon's with two regiments of skirmishers thrown out along the Manassas and Gainesville road, was not the movement to the *right* which General Pope intended they should make.

From the extracts just given from petitioner's evidence on General McDowell's Court of Inquiry, it will be seen that he then claimed:

1. That General McDowell exercised authority over him in obedience to an order of General Pope's addressed jointly to General McDowell and himself; and, further, that " our commands being united, he necessarily came into the command under the Articles of War."

2. That he considered himself limited in his operations under Gen-

eral McDowell's orders until he should receive directions from General Pope.

3. That General McDowell gave him no orders to take his troops to the right over to the Warrenton road—none to move to the front or right, or the right and front—but that he was checked by General McDowell in his intention to advance. And yet, as has just been noted, it was apparent when General McDowell got up to Dawkins' Branch it was understood by McDowell's own conversation with him that it was desired that the petitioner should go to the right and no longer make an advance.

4. He, therefore, claims to have been reduced to a state of inaction, so far as any order, direction, or instruction of General McDowell was concerned; and that this condition of enforced inaction continued till he should receive directions from General Pope.

We have seen, however, by Brigadier-General Griffin's testimony already cited, that while General McDowell was with petitioner at the front, the latter made a sort of effort to move to the right as directed.

PETITIONER'S REPLY OF MARCH, 1870, TO HON. Z. CHANDLER'S SPEECH IN THE UNITED STATES SENATE, FEBRUARY 21, 1870.

In this he said:

I have asserted, and ever shall assert, that General McDowell's order to me was to remain where I then was, while he would place King's division on my right and form the connection enjoined in the joint order.   *   *   *   *   *

He further says in that reply:

*   *   *   An immediate examination by us of the country towards Groveton showed the impracticability of doing *directly* what he desired, "placing King on my right and thus forming connection with the troops near Groveton;" and General McDowell left me without further instructions, but with the understanding that he would, by going *around* behind the woods separating us from Groveton, take King and Ricketts with him to join his command (Reynolds and Sigel), then at Groveton. *   *   *   *   *

As General McDowell's order to me at that time alone prevented an immediate engagement of my troops, and resulted in prolonging the "inaction" which you condemn in me, I deem it proper to state these facts fully.   *   *   *   *   *

I have shown that my "inaction" up to the afternoon of the 29th was in strict obedience to orders.

I now meet your charge of inaction up to a later hour in that day.

After General McDowell left me (early afternoon 29th), and up to the time of General Pope's positive order of 4.30 p. m. (29th), reaching me 6.30 p. m., I was certainly as free to exercise my "discretion" under Pope's "joint order" as McDowell was.

Under the "joint order" he elected to divide our forces and march to another field, where it seems he arrived too late for his troops to be successfully used. Under it I elected to hold my position, neutralize double my force, and, in the enemy's opinion, saved by my action both Pope and McDowell from capture or total rout.   *   *   *

He further adds:

To show that my views are in no wise changed, and that I now raise no new issue, I quote from my defense before the court:
*   *   *   *   *   *
It is well that this alleged order, "put your troops in there," to me by General McDowell, does not so appear charged as specified, for now I will demonstrate that he did not then give me, and cannot be believed to have given me, any such order.   *   *   *   It would have been proclaimed forthwith at the headquarters of General Pope: it would have been blazoned among the charges and specifications side by side with the order itself, and, if true, it ought to have made the words of exculpation which General Pope uttered to me at Fairfax Court House on the 2d September, four days afterwards, choke him as he spoke. But it is not true that General McDowell then, or at any time in that day, gave me any such orders, "to put my troops in there," or to do anything of the kind; and fortunate is it for General McDowell that it is not true, for if he had given me any such mandate to thrust my corps in one [over?] that broken ground between Jackson's right and the separate enemy massing in my front, the danger and disaster of such a

movement would have been then and now upon his hands. I am glad that I can say that General McDowell is utterly in error upon this point, and is no way chargeable with such military blunder.

* * * * * * *

This narrative covers the period of time between noon of the 29th and the hour of Pope's order of 4.30 p. m. * * * * *

PETITIONER'S STATEMENT TO PRESIDENT GRANT.

In the petitioner's appeal to the President, in June, 1869, "for a re-examination of the proceedings of the general court-martial in his case," he undertook to answer a statement which had been made to the express effect that he "did not even try to pass over the ground between him and the enemy on the 29th August, which he claimed as impassable, and also occupied by the right wing of the enemy."

Said he:

I shall show that the movement to pass over that ground was thwarted by General McDowell's orders to me, and fortunately it was so.

And also:

That even an effort to communicate by messengers failed from the nature of the country and the occupation of it by the enemy.

Reference to petitioner's "illustrative" maps in these closing arguments will show that over this alleged "broken ground" and impracticable or impassable country Longstreet subsequently moved his divisions in line of battle.

PETITIONER'S STATEMENT BEFORE THIS BOARD.

Again, before *this* Board, he has said (p. 31 statement):

The three objects to be accomplished under the joint order were: 1. To move towards Gainesville. 2. To establish communication with Heintzelman, Sigel, and Reno. 3. When this communication was established to halt.

But the troops should occupy a position from which they could reach Bull Run by night or the next morning. There was nothing in this order that contemplated a battle.

On the contrary, the command being to halt when communications were established, implied the contrary.

The joint order had been fulfilled as far as it could be complied with, when General McDowell rendered it impossible to move any further towards Gainesville with our joint forces by taking King's division with him.

After he left me, I was not only authorized but bound to exercise the discretion authorized in the joint order, holding in view "that the troops must occupy a position from which they can reach Bull Run to-night or by morning." The corps had already marched ten miles, and was then about eight miles from Bull Run.

* * * * *

While returning to my command, I saw the enemy's infantry coming to the railroad, and artillery moving to a slight elevation north of it.

Impressed as I was with the strength of the force in my front, I yet determined to make the effort to move towards Gainesville if it was at all feasible to do so.

Believing that then, if ever, before the enemy formed in too great strength so close to us, was the time to strike with our united forces, I determined, General McDowell having left me, to take the responsibility, and directing Morell to continue the deployment for an advance, sent my chief of staff, Colonel Locke, to instruct King not to go away. Sykes was coming up as rapidly as Morell's deployment permitted.

Colonel Locke soon returned and gave me the following message from General McDowell, whom he had found with King's division: "Give my compliments to General Porter, and say I am going to the right, and shall take King with me. He had better remain where he is, but, if necessary, to fall back, he can do so on my left." (G. C. M. Record, p. 135.)

This message decided my course. Not that I regarded it as an order obligatory upon me—for I was now independent of General McDowell—but, in face of what we had the best reason to believe was a largely superior force to mine, General McDowell's moving away with King's force beyond all possible assistance to me, left me no alternative but to conform to the course he had adopted, because I was too weak to make an effective attack.

These deliberate statements of petitioner, it will be perceived, are irreconcilable, for in one he says substantially that after McDowell left him and up to receipt of the 4.30 p. m. order he was certainly as free to exercise his discretion under Pope's joint order as McDowell was, and that he *did do so;* in the other he says that a movement to the right was thwarted by General McDowell's orders; and yet it appears he felt it incumbent on him during that day to report to McDowell that he had undertaken to do the very thing he says McDowell thwarted. (See dispatches Nos. 28 and 29, in petitioner's opening statement.)

[Dispatch No. 28.]

[Original not dated.] AUGUST 29, 1862.

Gen. MORELL: Push over to the aid of Sigel and strike in his rear. If you reach a road up which King is moving, and he has got ahead of you, let him pass, but see if you cannot give help to Sigel.

If you find him retiring, move back towards Manassas, and should necessity require it, and you do not hear from me, push to Centreville. If you find the direct road filled, take the one via Union Mills, which is to the right as you return.

F. J. PORTER,
Maj. Genl.

Look to the points of the compass for Manassas.

Of course, if the petitioner had been up to the front himself with Major-General Morell at that time instead of 2⅝ miles to the rear at the forks of the Manassas and Gainesville and Sudley Springs road, no *written* order would have been necessary. That written order was evidently sent after petitioner had retired to the rear, and after General McDowell had gone, Morell being left at the front near Dawkins' Branch. This petitioner has stated that he himself previously sent Lieutenant-Colonel Locke, his adjutant-general, back to General McDowell on the road (that is before he himself went back beyond Bethlehem Church), and General McDowell sent him up word that he was going to take King's division away, and for him to remain where he was. Nevertheless, we see that this petitioner *did* send Morell an order to "push over to the aid of Sigel and strike in his rear"—the very route and direction that he has attempted to make us believe was so impracticable. If, when he was with General McDowell to the right of the "Manassas and Gainesville" dirt road near Dawkins' Branch, he discovered, as he says he did, that the route over towards the Warrenton pike was impracticable (petitioner's opening statement, p. 31), why did he, from his field headquarters 2⅝ miles to the rear of Dawkins' Branch, if he had any orders from General McDowell to remain where he was, send that order to Morell to go over to the aid of Sigel, who was then out on this line north of the latter in the vicinity of Groveton?

[Dispatch No. 29.]

AUGUST 29, 1862.

Generals McDOWELL AND KING:

I found it impossible to communicate by crossing the woods to Groveton. The enemy are in strong force on this road, and as they appear to have driven our forces back, the firing of the enemy having advanced and ours retired, I have determined to withdraw to Manassas. I have attempted to communicate with McDowell and Sigel, but my messengers have run into the enemy. They have gathered artillery and cavalry and infantry, and the advancing masses of dust show the enemy coming in force.

I am now going to the head of the column to see what is passing and how affairs are going. Had you not better send your train back? I will communicate with you.

F. J. PORTER,
Maj. Genl.

RELATIONS OF THE PETITIONER TO GENERAL M'DOWELL AS TO COM-
MAND ON THE 29TH AUGUST.

It will be of interest to note petitioner's several statements touching
the relations as to command, and as to his responsibility, in connection
with General McDowell.

In his first statement, made under oath before the court of inquiry
within a few weeks after the occurrences in question, being asked:

When did he conceive himself no longer under General McDowell ?

Said:

My messages were addressed to General McDowell, I think all of them. The messengers were directed to deliver them to General Pope, if they saw or met him. I
considered myself as limited in my operations under General McDowell's orders until
I should receive directions from General Pope.

Seven years after, in his appeal to the President, he speaks of having
recalled Morell's division to its former position under McDowell's "re-
iterated order"—an order he claims to have received *after McDowell had
left him.*

A year later, his view of his relations to General McDowell were that—

After General McDowell left me (early afternoon, 29th), and up to the time of General Pope's positive order of 4.30 p. m. (29th), reaching me 6.30 p. m., I was certainly
as free to exercise my "discretion" under Pope's "joint order" as McDowell was.

Under the "joint order" he elected to divide our forces and march to another field.

*   *   *   *   *   *

Under it I elected to hold my position.

(Yet, with strange inconsistency, he speaks of receiving a message
from McDowell, after the latter had left him, as one not to be disregarded,
and which he claims to have obeyed.)

And (after the lapse of another eight years) in his late statement before this Board he states, in reference to the message he says he received,
that McDowell was going to the right with King:

This message decided my course. *Not that I regarded it as an order obligatory on me,
for I was now independent of General McDowell.*

So it appears that, in 1862–'63, he prefers that it should be held that
the acts and omissions of the 29th were due to McDowell's orders to him.
But in 1870 and 1878, having in the mean time seen that this position was
not tenable—not tenable from the fact that it had been shown he had,
during the day, given abundant proof he did not feel himself forced to
a state of inaction—he shifts his ground. He no longer claims that it
was General McDowell's *orders* to him, for after McDowell left him he
had been free to act—was *independent of him.* He now holds that it was
McDowell's *act* in taking King to the right which restrained him. This
act having prevented his doing what he claimed he desired to do—engage
the enemy in the direction of Gainesville; or do, even had the ground
permitted it, as McDowell swears he had directed him to do, engage the
enemy in the direction of Groveton, viz, to the right and front of that
place.

But this very act, which petitioner alleges as the cause of paralysis on
his part, and which he and his defenders have condemned as unwise, is
one he states in 1862–'63, under oath, to *have been done at his own suggestion.*

It will be seen from his testimony before the court of inquiry that, in
recounting what passed between McDowell and himself, after the second
meeting at the head of his column, petitioner testified as follows:

General McDowell and I went to the right, which was rather to the north, with the
view of seeing the character of the country, and with the idea of connecting, as that

joint order required, with the troops on my right. But very few words passed between us, and *I suggested*, from the character of the country, *that he should take King's division with him and form connection on the right* of the timber, which was then on the left of Reynolds, or presumed to be Reynolds.

And in his reply to Hon. Zachariah Chandler, he says:

* * * And General McDowell left me without further instructions, but *with the understanding* that he would, by going *around* behind the woods separating us from Groveton, take King and Ricketts with him to join his command (Reynolds and Sigel) at Groveton.

In connection with this march of King's division, and in view of petitioner's claim that while McDowell was with him he was subject to his orders, and after he left him he was independent of him, it is unaccountable that—after McDowell had left him with, as petitioner says, the understanding that he was to take King and Ricketts around behind the woods · to join the troops at Groveton—petitioner should almost immediately have sent *direct* to a division, under McDowell's immediate command, orders in contravention of those he admits he knew McDowell himself was to give it!

PETITIONER'S SWORN STATEMENT AND DISPATCHES CONTRASTED IN RELATION TO GENERAL M'DOWELL'S ORDER.

If there is one thing more than another which the petitioner here claims with constant and unvarying pertinacity and vehemence, it is that when General McDowell left him he had given him no orders to go into action with his troops, and thereafter that he gave him none. He was asked, when a witness, among other questions to the same end:

If he did attempt to make any movement in either of the directions named? ["To the front or right, or to the front and right."]

He said:

Not directly to the right; I did to the right and front, and when I received the last message from General McDowell to remain where I was, I recalled it.

He was then asked:

Did you make no attempt to go to the front, or to the right and front, after that message?

And said:

I made no attempt with any body of troops.

He was further asked:

After General McDowell left the witness did the witness not know he was expected by General McDowell to move to the right, or right and front?

And said:

I did not.

In his defense before his own court-martial he is still more emphatic, and in speaking of the period of time from noon on the 29th to the hour of General Pope's order of 4.30 p. m., says:

But it is not true that General McDowell then, or at any time during that day, gave me any such orders "to put my troops in there" or to do anything of the kind; and fortunate is it for General McDowell that it is not true, for if he had given me any such mandate to thrust my corps in over that broken ground, between Jackson's right and the separate enemy massing in my front, the danger and disaster of such a movement would have been then and now upon his hands. I am glad that General McDowell is utterly in error upon this point, and is in no way chargeable with such fatal military blunder.

6 G

But in his statement before this Board the petitioner publishes two
of his dispatches of the 29th (p. 35), numbered Nos. 28 and 29. In the
first he orders General Morell (commanding the advanced division of his
corps) to—

Push over to the aid of Sigel and strike in his rear.

In the second, addressed to Generals McDowell and King, he says:

I found it impossible to communicate by crossing the woods to Groveton. * * *

Communication, we must recollect, was by the joint order directed to
be established by General Pope between Generals Porter and McDowell
and the left of the main army, where Brig. Gen. John F. Reynolds was.

RECENTLY DISCOVERED DISPATCHES.

General McDowell swore he ordered petitioner "to put his troops in
there." The latter denied it, but these dispatches just cited show, even
in petitioner's own statement to this Board, *that he knew it was expected
of him by McDowell;* and now we come to the consideration of the *newly-
discovered dispatches,* on the same subject, of great importance, viz, one
addressed to General McDowell dated 29th August, 6 p. m., which says:

Failed in getting Morell over to you. After wandering about the woods for time I
withdrew him, and while doing so artillery opened on us. * * * *

Another, addressed to General McDowell or King, says:

I have been wandering over the woods and failed to get a communication to you.
* . * * * *

In the third, addressed to General McDowell, he says:

The firing on my right has so far retired that, as I cannot advance and *have failed to
get over to you except by the route taken by King,* I shall withdraw to Manassas. * * *.

It will be seen from some of the foregoing extracts, taken in connection with the "sketch of 2d Manassas, August 29, 1862," published in
petitioner's statement before this Board, that petitioner, after receiving
McDowell's last message, deliberately reported that he had made an
attempt, or attempts, of some kind or other, to move some of his troops
over the country to the United States forces at or near Groveton; though,
when especially interrogated with respect thereto by General McDowell,
while on the witness-stand, he denied having done so.

They show, as before stated, that he did not feel himself held to a
state of *inaction* by any order General McDowell gave him; and they
also show that what he says he attempted was in the exact direction of
what McDowell states he ordered him to do, to wit:

To put his troops in there. [In the direction of the Warrenton pike and Meadowville Lane.]

In view of petitioner's claim, that as this attempt to move Morell over
to the Warrenton pike, "to aid Sigel," or "over to McDowell," was
made after the latter had left him, he had then become independent of
McDowell, "free to exercise his own discretion," and, in view of petitioner's most emphatic declaration, made in his defense before his court
in 1863, and repeated as emphatically in 1870, that any such movement
would, in his judgment, have been a "fatal military blunder," involving
disaster, *it is not only an obvious inference but an inevitable conclusion, that
he must have been acting under the constraint of some superior authority;
that he would not merely of his own motion have involved his troops in the
consequences of, as he states it,* "a fatal military blunder."

And as, during this time, there was no authority acting upon him but that of Pope, and McDowell, during the time the latter was with him, and as he then received no orders from Pope, *he must have acted, in the particular in question, under the order McDowell gave him before they parted and while he was still subject to his control.*

Therefore, in the assertion by General McDowell, that before he left petitioner for the last time on the 29th August, he did order him *to put his troops in there* [in the direction of Warrenton pike], where the dust was rising, and in the denial by petitioner that McDowell gave him any such order, it is petitioner's memory which is in fault.

There are some interesting bits of confirmatory evidence to Major-General McDowell's as to the orders he gave petitioner at the Manassas Gap Railroad from petitioner's own witnesses.

Thus when the latter during the afternoon sent a dispatch from his remote headquarters 2⅜ miles to the rear to General Morell (dispatch No. 31.) to put his division back in the bushes, Morell swears (Board's Record, p. 422) that he had two brigades deployed on the ridge facing Dawkins' Branch in front of the bushes, and that they were not put back until the receipt of that dispatch.

It is thus plain that General McDowell when he arrived at Dawkins' Branch, before riding to the right, never gave any such order "to put the division back in the woods" as testified to by the witnesses Earle and Davis, or the petitioner would have done it then and there instead of deploying on the ridge.

This witness's testimony is noticeable (Board's Record, p. 425):

Question. In your former testimony, as well as in that of many other witnesses, there are descriptions of movements, of operations of your troops that day to and fro, backwards and forwards, on the ground in the neighborhood of Dawkins' Branch; you recollect that?

Answer. Yes, sir.

Question. Will you please state to the Board what was the general object of such movement?

Answer. Do you mean from the time we first arrived there?

Question. Yes; not in detail, but general.

Answer. While we were getting into line, General McDowell joined General Porter, and very soon they rode off to the right. General Porter returned and directed me to move my command to the right. McDowell and Porter went off in this direction [east] and passed over a corn-field until they came to heavy timbered land. We followed close behind them; they seemed to have examined the timber and found that it was impracticable. It looked so to me, also. General Porter returned, and ordered me to return to my former position.

Question. Returned from his ride with General McDowell?

Answer. Yes, sir; about off in this direction [near Five Forks].

Question. Across the railroad?

Answer. Across the railroad. Part of my command then came back and immediately resumed position on the ridge. I did not go far enough to extend my whole division. Hazlett's battery did not move at all. As we were coming back, moving by the flank, and were passing by Hazlett's battery, a section of the enemy's artillery opened fire. As soon as the infantry cleared the battery, Hazlett replied; then this section of artillery moved off some distance to the right on higher ground and commenced firing again. We then remained in that position until I received an order from General Porter to put the men under cover. Then I put them in the pine bushes.

This witness in his eagerness assumes that both General McDowell and the petitioner examined the timber to their right rear, at their backs, towards *Five Forks*, and found it impracticable. Apparently *retreat* instead of advance was what was in his mind, for he did not know that McDowell in the few minutes' conversation there with petitioner was discussing how to move to the right and front the quickest in order to apply where the dust was rising the full force at their joint disposal.

Capt. *George Monteith*, petitioner's then aide-de-camp, who was with him, saw this "heavy cloud of dust that was rising on the Warrenton pike." (Board's Record, p. 312.)

Lieut. *Stephen M. Weld*, another of petitioner's then aides-de-camp, says (Board's Record, p. 263) that after General McDowell and petitioner had been there a very short time, off to the right of the railroad, General McDowell—

turned off to the left and went to Bethlehem Church, and General Porter came back the same way he came in, recrossed the railroad, and joined his corps.

It is plain that petitioner's staff knew where McDowell went, as the railroad was a short cut to Bethlehem Church. If the woods were as impenetrable as Morell then says he thought them to be, McDowell could not go on horseback down that railroad to any point but Bethlehem Church.

Nevertheless, we find petitioner, when a witness before McDowell's court of inquiry, swearing as follows: "When General McDowell left me I did not know where he had gone." In his opening statement, however, before this Board he has said (p. 31):

General McDowell decided to take his divisions then on the road immediately in my rear and to turn back and go by the Sudley Springs road to Groveton to place them on the left of the troops at that place. * * * After he left me, &c.

It is here apparent that a decision *was* reached at the Manassas Gap Railroad and that McDowell moved off by the shortest road to do his part.

Which is to be believed, Weld or petitioner, as to the fact cited, is for those who read or hear this argument to determine for themselves.

Petitioner's evidence as a witness, when he appears against McDowell, is opposed to his own witnesses and own knowledge in his own case as to McDowell's intentions and movements, for in the first he swore that when General McDowell left him he, petitioner, "did not know where he had gone," while in his reply to the Hon. Zachariah Chandler he, petitioner, admits that General McDowell left him only after an explicit "understanding" that he, McDowell, should do the very thing he did do. Petitioner also, in his opening statement before this Board, further admits, as we have seen, that while he and General McDowell were together at the railroad, the latter came to a *decision* as to the mode of putting their corps in.

Another confirmatory bit of evidence as to what McDowell said when at the front of petitioner's column is found in that of Brigadier-General *Butterfield*, another of accused's witnesses.

Petitioner had ordered him with his brigade (Board's Record, p. 462) to cross the railroad and strike between Groveton and Gainesville so as to cover the dirt road which ran to the latter place to the left of Thomas Nealon's.

This, it will be observed, was a continuation of the march in a direction from Dawkins' Branch not contemplated by petitioner's orders, which were to go up by the road to the right which King came down on.

While going out on this movement General McDowell, having arrived at Dawkins' Branch, witnessed the movement, and then, having ridden towards the Manassas Gap Railroad with petitioner, Butterfield's brigade was withdrawn, and the latter significantly says: "*We were then moved a little farther to the right;* then returned to the left."

So long as General McDowell was on the ground, in actual command for the time being, the petitioner had to make pretense of obeying; but the moment McDowell departed, his reluctant brigadiers find a few pine bushes in their movement to the right (see Griffin's testimony, G. C. M. Record, p. 165), halt, make "*no reconnaissance whatever*," and are ordered by petitioner to move back again.

Thus, through this long summer afternoon, with the sound of the battle in his cars, and while thousands were offering themselves willing sacrifices to their country's cause, the petitioner, with his headquarters placed 2⅔ miles to the rear of his column (see his opening statement, p. 40), where he cannot possibly take instant advantage of any opportunity either for connecting with the right or for moving into action, remains inactive, and holds his gallant corps from going to the aid of their comrades.

If, indeed, overwhelming numbers had been on his front ready and eager to attack, as he now pretends, the indifference which would have permitted him to remain continuously so far to the rear is nothing short of criminal.

If, as has been shown, he knew that Reynolds' division, of three brigades, comprising thirteen regiments and four batteries, was operating on his (petitioner's) right (petitioner's opening statement, p. 31), and on petitioner's assumption of locations operating *directly* against Longstreet, facing him, then no assumed 25,000 men in that Confederate general's command should have prevented petitioner from pushing in with what he terms his own 9,000 (?) men on the right flank of that Confederate force. We will see that the petitioner's own forces were very much larger, by the official record, than what he undertakes in his opening statement to put them.

Had petitioner *pushed into action*, as he should have done, even on his own assumptions of positions and force under Longstreet, his own corps and Reynolds' division, with Schenck's division (Stahel's and McLean's brigades) of Sigel's corps and Stevens's brigade (Reno's division of Burnside's corps,) all of which were deployed in line on Reynold's right *south* of the turnpike, would have, without the assistance of King or Ricketts, quite equaled the whole rebel co-operating force, and left Jackson's exhausted and anxious troops to contend alone against the remainder of General Pope's army.

This is even on petitioner's present assumption that Longstreet had 25,000 men, at that time, present on the field.

According to the latter's statements here, two brigades (of Hood's division) were always *north* of the turnpike, and for most of the time Wilcox's division also.

NATURE AND EXTENT OF PETITIONER'S OPERATIONS AFTER GENERAL M'DOWELL LEFT HIM.

Petitioner having received an order from General McDowell modifying the mode of execution of the joint order given by General Pope when McDowell was with him, and clothed with the necessary authority to give him a valid order, this order did not lose its force and validity after they parted, but was one which imposed duties on petitioner, for the due discharge of which he is to be held responsible till he can show it was either countermanded by superior authority, or that its execution was, or became, impossible.

As to the nature and extent of what was done by petitioner after McDowell left him, it is significant of how feeble and inconsequential it must have been, that, within a very short time afterward, *even the memory had passed away from his mind*, and he could not recollect under oath:

(1.) That he had ordered his leading division commander *to push on to the aid of Sigel;*

(2.) That he had informed McDowell at 6. p. m. that he had "*failed in getting Morell over*" to him;

(3.) That he had (at six o'clock) ordered Morell "*to push up two regiments, supported by two others, preceded by skirmishers, the regiments at intervals of two hundred yards, and* ATTACK *the party with the section of artillery opposed to you (him).*"

For, when a witness on the court of inquiry being asked if, after the alleged return of Colonel Locke, he *attempted* even to make any movement " to the front or to the right, or to the front and right," he denied having done so; and, according to his version of the case in 1863, he simply continued in a state of inaction after McDowell left him.

To judge from his most recent statement, his principal object was not to make any attack on the enemy at all, but to conceal himself from him —to put everything out of sight—for he says to Morell (dispatch 30):

Come the same game over them they do over us, and *get your men out of sight.*

So it appears that it was more a game of hide and seek than one of attack that was contemplated or that was carried out. Petitioner had established himself personally near the forks of the Sudley Church and the Manassas and Gainesville road, which is, according to the map made up from the survey of last June, two miles and five-eighths behind the place where he was when joined by McDowell the second time, and where he had commenced deploying his leading division, with alleged thick woods between him and the head of his column or his partly deployed line. And it was from this place, so retired from the possible field of action, and from any chance of his knowing anything from his own observation, that he received Morell's reports and sent to him and to McDowell the dispatches heretofore referred to.

We shall see a little later in this argument that some of these reports of the petitioner to General McDowell that day had no foundation in fact.

PETITIONER'S RECOLLECTION IN 1863 OF HIS SECOND MEETING WITH GENERAL MCDOWELL AND HIS SUBSEQUENT STATEMENTS.

The petitioner has claimed in his opening statement here that he and General McDowell at their second meeting on the 29th at Dawkins' Branch discussed the joint order, conversed on the subject of the force reported * by Buford as belonging to Longstreet, yet his own testimony given immediately after his trial, when a witness on General McDowell's court of inquiry, is inconsistent with this modern recollection of their intercourse at that time.

Then he said as follows:

Question by General McDowell. Witness refers to some conversation between himself and General McDowell when they first met which, taken in connection with an expression of opinion by General McDowell, witness considered an order; can the witness state what that conversation was?

Answer. I only recollect the impression left upon my mind at *the time, and merely a reference to the artillery contest going on* FAR TO OUR RIGHT.

Question. Was not the joint order referred to in that conversation?

Answer. *I have no recollection of it. It may have been referred to, because we went to the right, my belief is to look at the country, but I do not recollect anything at all of the order being referred to.*

---

* A reference to this report, which is below, will show that Buford did not state Longstreet's arrival, but merely mentioned that a certain force had passed Gainesville, without saying who commanded it or to whom it belonged.

" HEADQUARTERS CAVALRY BRIGADE—9.30 a. m.

"GENERAL RICKETTS: Seventeen regiments, one battery, 550 cavalry, passed through Gainesville three-quarters of an hour ago on the Centreville road. I think this division should join our forces now engaged, at once.

"JOHN BUFORD,
" *Brig. General.*

" Please forward this."

This is the dispatch General McDowell showed to petitioner at Dawkins' Branch. (G. C. M. Record, p. 84.)

Question by General McDowell. Were not the remarks witness here states to have been made by General McDowell made with reference to the point in the joint order which required the troops not to go to a point from which they could not get behind Bull Run that night?

Answer. I think I have replied to the question by stating I do not recollect.

And with reference to their conversation when they rode to the right the petitioner testified that—

But very few words passed between us, and I suggested, from the character of the country, that he should take King's division with him and form connection on the right of the timber, which was then on the left of Reynolds, or presumed to be Reynolds.

* * *

It is evident, as just shown, that the petitioner knew he had been told by General McDowell to *act*, and act in support of the very movement he was making to come up on the left of Reynolds.

And it is also evident that this petitioner's failure to get over to aid Sigel, or march over to McDowell, was not because he met with any obstacle in his march or any restraint from the enemy. He failed to get over, that is true. It is also true, and he himself furnished all the evidence, that he *failed to start*, while from the dispatches which have been introduced for the government he would have it inferred that he had attempted to do as it is claimed he was ordered to do.

He equally defends his not having acted at all. *In other words, the petitioner gives evidence of knowing he was to act, and of his determining not to act.*

ROUTE TAKEN BY GENERAL M'DOWELL· AND PETITIONER TO THE RIGHT FROM THE MANASSAS AND GAINESVILLE ROAD.

Just here it is proper to indicate the direction taken by Major-General McDowell and petitioner when they moved to the right from the head of the latter's column after it halted on the Manassas and Gainesville road at Dawkins' Branch.

My belief is, from having been on the ground myself and from having examined it carefully last August, that those two corps commanders followed the direction of the branch—on its easterly side, not exactly where a road is delineated on the map, but quite near it on the 180 contour, where there is a sort of road—just in front of the then bushes which are now woods.

On the westerly side of the branch the ground gradually rises, and Nealon's, Carrico's, and Britt's are easily seen from the 180 contour near the branch and just in front of the timber or bushes marked upon the map.

If General McDowell and the petitioner had ridden northerly towards the railroad on the 200 contour, as the latter would have us believe, they would have been in thick bushes and unable to have seen the open country to the west and northwest.

As the two watered their horses in a little stream, and as even Dawkins' Branch at that season of the year is so dry as to consist of but a few pools, the only point where they could readily have done so would have been between the railroad and James Nickerson's house, and more than likely in the branch itself, whose name was not then known to them.

Griffin's brigade was deployed on the ridge, and also moved along it across the railroad until some "little, thick, pine bushes" brought them to a halt.

Had they deployed or moved on the 200 contour, they would, from the first, have been concealed, if any credence whatever is to be given to the map used in this case, and petitioner's subsequent order to Morell to post all the head of his column in he bushes (opening statement, p. 95, No. 31) would have been needless.

74

EXCUSES FOR PETITIONER'S INACTION CONSIDERED.

There are but two points in the petitioner's case as to the 29th of
August, which, despite the collateral issues raised in order to withdraw
attention from the main facts, are really material.

The first is, whether he got any orders from General McDowell which
held him to a state of inaction on the 29th of August, 1862.

The second, whether he ever received any order from Major-General
Pope, later in the day, to move into action (4.30 order).

The last point will be discussed by itself.

It was testified to upon the original trial by Assistant Adjutant-General Locke, chief of staff (G. C. M. Record, p. 135), that immediately after
General McDowell had left the petitioner over by the Manassas Gap Railroad, and the petitioner had returned to the head of his column on Dawkins' Branch, the latter sent him, Locke, to General *King* with directions
to him, *King*, to remain where he was; and that he brought back orders
from General McDowell to the petitioner for the petitioner to remain where
he was. The court-martial that tried and convicted the petitioner had
before it the full evidence of Lieutenant-Colonel Locke upon the subject,
and undoubtedly gave it all the weight that it was justly entitled to.
In the investigation before this Board an additional witness has been
introduced upon this subject in the person of an orderly named Leipoldt
(Board's Record, p. 56), who went to the Bethlehem Church with
Colonel Locke after the petitioner got back to the head of Dawkins'
Branch from the reconnaissance he and General McDowell had made
to the right. When Major-General McDowell and the petitioner separated after the final interview near the Manassas Gap Railroad, it
was in the belief and understanding on Major-General McDowell's
part that the petitioner would, as soon as practicable, carry out his
part of the programme agreed upon between them, and put his
forces "in there," in the direction of the enemy on his right front
towards the Warrenton pike where the dust was rising at the time
in heavy columns (Colonel Rosser's brush-dragging). It will be
observed, by reference to the map, that the point to which General
McDowell rode with the petitioner from Dawkins' Branch on the Manassas Gap Railroad was the best point from which to ascertain any possible
movement of the enemy; and that the nearer a person approached to
where the head of the petitioner's column was, on the Manassas and
Gainesville road, the less opportunity there was, on account of rising
ground in front and trees, to determine where the enemy could be. In
point of fact, at that time the two regiments, the Sixty-second Pennsylvania and Thirteenth New York, were shoved into the trees which lined
the left-hand road towards Gainesville. The distance from the Manassas Gap Railroad to Dawkins' Branch and the Gainesville road is about
half a mile and perfectly level on the ground over which the two general officers had moved with rapidity. The petitioner, as appears by his
own sworn evidence in the McDowell court of inquiry, had suggested,
at the time he and General McDowell were at the Manassas Gap Railroad, that the best means of carrying out the joint order and the
quickest way to apply King's division in the action then going on,
would be for General McDowell to take it up around by the Manassas
and Sudley road, and come in with it north of the old Warrenton, Alexandria, and Washington road, on the left of Reynolds' division, then
attached to McDowell's command and operating with Sigel. Therefore, General McDowell was galloping by a short cut down the Manassas Gap Railroad to Bethlehem Church, leaving his staff behind him

from the rapidity of his movements, in consequence of his haste to perform his share in the operations and help General Pope's army, then fighting Jackson. The petitioner says that, in the five or six minutes' time it must have taken him to gallop back to the head of his own column, at Dawkins' Branch, on the Manassas and Gainesville road, he saw the enemy gathering in his front, which induced him to send Lieutenant-Colonel Locke with the remarkable message to which I have just referred. This statement that, in this brief and hasty ride back to his corps, he saw the enemy gathering in his front in such force as to induce him to attempt to change the whole plan of operations that had been agreed upon not five minutes before, will be found, on considering the evidence of his own witnesses, to be based upon assumptions, not sustained by facts. Had he seen any enemy gathering upon his front from any quarter whatever, he would have brought, undoubtedly, some of his staff who were with him when he went with General McDowell, to testify as to the circumstances; and we know that that staff have been brought here, as well as before the original court that tried him, several times to give evidence on other points. They were, possibly, as much interested as he in knowing whether there was an enemy gathering in their front at the time. Certainly, if he had perceived any such thing he would have indicated it to them in some way. Riding with his back to the point from whence the dust was rising above the trees and with but a limited view on his right as he returned, in consequence of the woods where his own skirmishers were, it is apparent that he could not see that which he has asserted he did see. A glance at the map will show this.

There are some significant facts connected with this pretended message which must be referred to.

The division commanded by Brig. Gen. Rufus King, which had that morning been temporarily attached to the petitioner's command by General Pope's order, through Gibbon, comprised the brigades of Hatch, Gibbon, Doubleday, and Patrick; Brigadier-General Hatch being the ranking officer under the division commander.

On the evening before, in the action of that division on the Warrenton pike between Gainesville and Groveton with Jackson's command, it appears that Brigadier-General King was, according to the evidence of his assistant adjutant-general, *John A. Judson,* petitioner's witness (Board's Record, p. 103), in an ambulance sick; and that General Hatch was "practically in command." We have seen that on that morning of the 29th General Gibbon had given the petitioner an account of the action the night before. Now, when the petitioner's corps came along on the Manassas and Gainesville road, past the place where King's division was lying, the following took place, according to the evidence of the same witness, (Judson), the petitioner at the time being at the head of the column, and Captain Judson, assistant adjutant-general, with his own division there stationary:

Question. Did you have any conversation with him (petitioner)?
Answer. I did.
Question. State what.
Answer. General Porter asked me where the commanding officer of those troops was. *I conducted him to General Hatch.*
Question. Had General McDowell at that time made his appearance?
Answer. I have no recollection of seeing General McDowell since the day before up until that time.
Question. Did you learn from General Porter or General Hatch, after their interview, what was to be done?
Answer. I learned from some source that "King's division" was to follow in the rear of General Porter's column.

Thus it is apparent that petitioner gave his orders to Brigadier-General Hatch as commanding officer of King's division.

From further evidence of the witness (Board's Record, p. 105) it appears that General Hatch remained in command of the division all that day.

From the evidence of Brig. Gen. M. R. Patrick, another of the petitioner's witnesses (Board's Record, p. 187), we learn the following:

Question. Your brigade went alone when you got there? Had the other brigades got to Manassas Junction?
Answer. I cannot answer that, for it was quite a length of time before I saw the brigades or any other officer. I think General King was the first whom I saw. It was somewhere about eight or nine o'clock, while my commissariat and personal staff were hunting up supplies, &c. *General King rode over to my headquarters, and told me that he was not fit to be in command; that he was going to Centreville, and came over to bid me good-by.* I think Colonel Chandler, his adjutant-general, and I do not recollect who else, were with him at the time; he came to say good-by, and I do not know that I saw him after that. * * *
Question. (By petitioner.) *What happened next after King's departure for Centreville?*
Answer. I was ordered, I think, by McDowell in person to move as soon as I could in the rear of General Porter, Porter having just passed through, or passing through nearer Manassas Junction, to go back to the scene of our fight the night previous.

Captain *Judson* (Board's Record, p. 113), in speaking of the precarious health of General King at that time, said that he rode in an ambulance from the Rappahannock up, that he did not see him on horseback, to his recollection, and that he was constantly attended by Dr. Pineo, his medical director. Therefore, when this petitioner got to Dawkins' Branch before General McDowell joined him, he was thoroughly and fully apprised of the fact that Brigadier-General Hatch was in command of King's division, and that General King had left for Manassas Junction and Centreville.

On the trial in 1862 we find the following testimony (by Lieutenant-Colonel *Locke*, petitioner's chief of staff, p. 133):

I was sent by General Porter with a message to General King. On finding General King, General McDowell was with him. I stated my message to General King, and General McDowell answered: "Give my compliments to General Porter, and say to him I am going to the right, and will take General King with me. I think he (General Porter) had better remain where he is, but if it is necessary for him to fall back, he can do so upon my left."

This must have been after twelve o'clock, because it was after General McDowell had left him for the last time at the front.

Question. What was the message you carried from General Porter to General King?
Answer. For him to remain where he was until further orders.
Question. Did you understand that General King was under the orders of General Porter?
Answer. I did.
Question. Did you deliver the message that General McDowell gave you for General Porter, to the general?
Answer. Yes, sir.

General *McDowell* testified as follows (G. C. M. Record, p. 87):

Question. Have you any recollection that after you left the accused on the 29th and took with you King's division, the accused sent a message to you requesting that the division should be permitted to stay with his command?
Answer. *I received no such message.*
Question. Will you say in consequence of a message or otherwise, you sent a message to the accused with your compliments, telling him that you were going to the right and should take King with you, and that he (the accused) should remain where he was for the present, and if he had to fall back to do so on your left?
Answer. I do not recollect.
Question. Are you able to say that you are certain that you did not send such a message?
Answer. That is my impression, that I did not.

Brig. Gen. *Rufus King* testified as follows (G. C. M. Record, p. 212):

Question. You will remember it has been testified here that on the afternoon of the 29th August a message was borne from General Porter to you by one of his staff officers directing that your division should remain where it was, and that this message was communicated to you in the presence of General McDowell who made a response to it. The question I wish you to answer is whether you remember any such message to have been sent to you?

Answer. I do not

Question. Do you remember to have been with General McDowell on the afternoon of that day?

Answer. No, sir.

Question. It was also testified by the same witness, if you will remember, that in reply to the message General McDowell said: "I will take General Porter's division with me. Give my compliments to General Porter, and say to him that I think he better remain where he is." Do you remember to have heard any such message as that from General McDowell?

Answer. No, sir; I do not remember any circumstance of that kind to have taken place on *any* day.

Question. Do you think it possible that an interview of that kind between yourself and General McDowell, with a message of that kind communicated to you, and a response of that kind from General McDowell could possibly have occurred, and have now totally escaped your recollection?

Answer. I do not.

It is to be carefully noticed that Locke in his evidence distinctly and deliberately said that he had seen General King and handed the message to General King, and so forth.

Now, it is incredible that if any such message had ever been delivered to General *King*, and such response sent to it by General McDowell in the presence of General *King*, that neither of these gentlemen remembered it. The court-martial proceedings in the case of petitioner took place in December, 1862, not quite four months after this alleged occurrence, and while the memories of the witnesses to the events of the 29th and 30th of the preceding August were still unimpaired. This message and the response to it would have been highly calculated to have made a deep impression on all the persons concerned in it, involving, as it would have done, a total change in the movements just agreed upon between the petitioner and McDowell.

General McDowell had just left petitioner, having given him an important order, which, if it had been obeyed, would have brought his forces in a brief time into collision with the enemy. When he left petitioner he (petitioner) was in the act of deploying a portion of his command with the apparent intention of moving forward to the attack. General McDowell had witnessed part of this movement, and had left the field with the understanding that his order to "put his force in there" would be obeyed. Before leaving, however, it was agreed between them that General McDowell should take King's division with him in his movement with his corps up the Sudley road, and had he, in so short a time as is alleged, heard the request made to General King "to remain where he was" it must have caused him considerable astonishment, and made on the instant an unpleasant impression on his mind. It would have suggested at once the complete disruption of his plans—plans which were made with the sound of battle in his ears. Is it credible, therefore, that he could have sent such a response to such a message when he must have thought petitioner should be at the time alleged in actual movement towards the enemy?

The orderly, Leipold (Board's Record, p. 56), testified as follows:

Question. When next did you see General McDowell?

Answer. I saw him later in the day.

Question. You did see him afterwards?

Answer. Yes. Later in the day General Locke asked me to accompany him. We went back on the same road we came in the morning, probably a mile or two. I saw General McDowell and some other person. They were standing at the side of the road, dismounted.

Question. About where were they?

Answer. I think near a church.

If that was all down, and there was nothing of it but a pile of bricks, as at the last minute has been sought to be shown here by the petitioner's witnesses, they could not have been standing near a "church."

Question. Near Bethlehem church?

Answer. I was under the impression there was some other name to the church.

* * * * * * *

Question. Did you see General Locke deliver him any message?

Answer. *I don't remember.* General Locke dismounted and I took his horse. He went over and *conversed* with the officers.

Question. Did you see General McDowell after that?

Answer. I don't think I saw him after that that day.

It will be perceived that this witness does not remember of any message being delivered by Colonel Locke to General McDowell; he merely went over and *conversed* with the officers.

Some unpleasant inquiries suggest themselves concerning the question whether there was any such message. We have seen that the petitioner knew that General King had gone to Centreville, and that Brigadier-General Hatch was in command of the division. Why, then, should he have sent his assistant adjutant-general *to General King when he knew General King was no longer in command and sick?* Again, his assistant adjutant-general says positively that he found General King with General McDowell; and yet the petitioner's own witness, in conjunction with General King's evidence, shows that he was not there near Bethlehem church, but had already gone to Centreville. Again, if the enemy were gathering in his front, as he asserts, in such force as within five minutes after General McDowell left him it became necessary to change the entire plans that had been agreed upon, and it was desirable that he should move with his own corps and King's division instantly to the front, is it conceivable that his assistant adjutant general would have dismounted, given his horse to an orderly, and walked over to converse with these officers?

There is another curious circumstance connected with this that requires to be noticed, and that is that Brig. Gen. M. R. Patrick in his evidence says that when General McDowell came back down this Manassas Gap Railroad, out *here,* and met Patrick, he had a conversation with him and told him that he was obliged to take him back—Patrick's being the nearest brigade of King's division towards Dawkins' Branch and nearest to petitioner's corps; and that General McDowell took Patrick's division across the country to the Sudley road. So that, if General Patrick is to be believed, General McDowell, having taken the last of his own brigades right over below F. M. Lewis' house in a northeasterly direction and moved north up to the Sudley Springs road, could not have been at Bethlehem church as testified to by Lieutenant-Colonel Locke, he, McDowell, having started off apparently *immediately* with Patrick's brigade. (Board's Record, p. 189.)

There is another curious circumstance connected with this which also requires to be noticed. Col. Edmund Schriver, brevet major-general, and inspector-general, U. S. A., was then colonel and chief of staff to the corps commanded by Major-General McDowell. For all who were under the command of that general officer, he was the official organ of communication; and if the petitioner, while General McDowell was exercising command over the two corps, had anything to communicate to

General McDowell, that communication, according to the regulations governing the Army of the United States, would necessarily have passed through the hands of Colonel Schriver.

Colonel Schriver went up to Dawkins' Branch on the Manassas and Gainesville road with General McDowell, and rode to the right with him and the petitioner to the Manassas Gap Railroad, taking a few mounted orderlies with them. After the conversation between the petitioner and General McDowell and the latter had decided, as petitioner says in his opening statement, to act on the suggestion of the petitioner and take King's division, under Hatch, to the right, and had moved rapidly, at a gallop, down the Manassas Gap Railroad, Colonel Schriver was left with the escort and staff, and testifies as to his own future movements as follows (Board's Record, p. 832):

Question. State your rank in the Army.
Answer. Inspector-general and brevet major-general.
Question. What position did you hold on the 29th of August, 1862?
Answer. I was then on General McDowell's staff, when he commanded the Third Corps of the army of Virginia.
Question. Do you recollect being with him on the 29th of August, at the head of General Porter's column, in the neighborhood of Dawkins' Branch?
Answer. I do.
Question. Where did you go then?
Answer. Went out to the right with the generals, whose object was, I believe, to make some observations, and then returned to the place whence we started.
Question. Where did General McDowell leave you, or did he not leave you?
Answer. He left somewhere to the east or to his right looking out toward the railroad, my recollection is.
Question. Which direction did he take when he left?
Answer. I think he went in a southterly direction, off to where his divisions were.
Question. Did you go with him?
Answer. No.
Question. Which direction did you take?
Answer. I came a little to the left and went by General Porter's headquarters, and then came down, if I recollect rightly, the road General McDowell went, through the woods; I did not go with him.
Question. You went down the Gainesville road, then?
Answer. Yes, sir.
Question. Did you go back with General Porter, or did you follow him?
Answer. I really cannot recollect that; I know we met again.
Question. What transpired at that time when you met him there?
Answer. I had a little conversation; I cannot exactly recollect what it was, except the general said or expressed the belief that he might become engaged with the enemy, and that he had no cavalrymen; he either then proposed, or I proposed, or at any rate the arrangement was made, that he should have half of General McDowell's escort that was with me; it was turned over, and I left. He wanted them to send messages.
Question. At that time where were the enemy?
Answer. I am sure I do not know.
Question. Did you notice any?
Answer. No; I did not look for any; it was not my business.
No cross-examination.

It is apparent from this evidence of Colonel Schriver that the petitioner must, immediately after General McDowell's departure, have galloped back to his column near Dawkins' Branch on the Manassas and Gainesville road, at a speed certainly that would have prevented him making any special observation in any direction; because Colonel Schriver follows immediately afterward, and has a conversation with him there.

It is to be noted from that conversation that the petitioner said he might become engaged with the enemy, and that he had no cavalrymen for messengers or orderlies; and Colonel Schriver leaves half of those of General McDowell that he had with him. The expression that he *might* become engaged with the enemy was something for the possible future—not an immediate engagement with the enemy that had been "gathering in his front" within five minutes. His remark evidently contemplated the carrying out of General McDowell's orders, because he borrows these cavalrymen for the express purpose of sending messages to General McDowell; and we shall see as we go along that he sent several to him during the day. Had he at that time found it necessary to change the plan that had been agreed upon by which he was to put his force "in there" to the right front where the dust was in consequence of the enemy "gathering in his front," *why did he not tell Colonel Schrirer, who was the official organ of communication between him and General McDowell?* Why did he not call his attention to that which was, on his assumed state of facts, going to change the arrangement which General McDowell had just made at his own suggestion? As Colonel Schriver was going right down to where King's division was, if it had been necessary for that division to remain, Colonel Schriver would have been the proper party for the petitioner to make the request to for it to remain. He did not do so; and it is significant, further, that General Schriver did not notice any enemy "gathering" in the front. If there had been any serious demonstration in that direction he could not have failed to notice it. As it was, he did not. It is more than likely, in fact it has appeared in evidence in one form and another, that Lieutenant Colonel Locke, the petitioner's assistant adjutant-general and chief of staff, went backwards and forwards a number of times that day from Dawkins' Branch to Bethlehem church and the Sudley road (Board's Record, p. 299). He says so himself. The strength of his recollection has been exhibited between himself and other members of the petitioner's staff, relative to the efforts he himself made to remove obstructions on the road between Warrenton Junction and Bristoe on the morning of August 28, 1862. On cross-examination (Board's Record, p. 1042) he said his feelings are very strongly enlisted in behalf of the petitioner. That, of itself, whether enlisted in favor of him or against him, should have no special effect in uncontradicted evidence. Assuming for the sake of argument that General McDowell sent this message:

Give my compliments to General Porter and say that I am going to the right and will take General King's division with me, and that he had better remain where he is; if he has to fall back, to do so on my left.

It is inconceivable that, after having made an entire plan of proceeding in which the petitioner's corps was have been put into action, he should direct him to remain inactive. There is nothing to show that Lieutenant-Colonel Locke saw any enemy "gathering" on petitioner's front in the five minutes' ride from the railroad to the head of the column, or that the petitioner ordered him to communicate any such fact to General King, or anything more than a direction to General King, who was then on his way to Centreville in an ambulance, to remain where he was, assuming him to have been in command of the division for the sake of the argument. On such a supposition to assert that General McDowell should order the petitioner to remain where he was and not do anything when a contest was actually taking place on the right, is an absurdity of which no one who knows that distinguished officer would ever believe him capable.

When General McDowell left the petitioner on the Manassas Gap Railroad, after having amended the joint order so far as he was concerned, as to the manner of execution under the discretion which had been given him by the major-general commanding the whole army, it may be assumed that he left the petitioner in absolute command of his own corps, and had no further power or authority to order his movements in any direction. He only commanded the petitioner's corps by virtue of his seniority under the (old) sixty-second article of war, and while actually joined for and doing duty with them, and any direction or order which he might give from a distance, he not being in command of the army, and only a corps commander, would have amounted to nothing, and required no obedience, which the petitioner well knew from his own long service in the Army. Such a message as the petitioner on the original trial assumed was finally delivered to him from General McDowell, in the light of his, petitioner's, previous instructions to Colonel Marshall, not to bring on an engagement; and his remark to General McDowell, when the latter was on the Manassas Gap Railroad with him, that if he moved where McDowell ordered him he would get into a fight, would have well suited his views. *The court which tried him evidently believed that there was no such message and no such response.*

The petitioner himself has for another purpose said here that "the only positive order received by me [him] on the 29th I [he] tried to execute, but it was received too late for any result to be obtained" (page 62, Petitioner's opening statement).

It is particularly to be noticed from the evidence of General McDowell on the trial, which has been cited, that the petitioner claimed originally that the enemy was in his immediate front, and that General McDowell made up his mind upon such reports as the petitioner made to him at the time and upon what he himself could see from the best available point of observation, namely, near the Manassas Gap Railroad.

Several witnesses for the petitioner on the trial and before this Board have mentioned the fact of the capture of two or three scouts, so called—possible scouts—cavalrymen, by our cavalry. It has been sought on behalf of the petitioner to show that he was apprised of the presence of the divisions commanded by Major-General Longstreet in his front, because of the capture of these scouts, so called.

Lieutenant-Colonel *Locke*, chief of the staff of the petitioner, has undertaken to explain this with the same degree of recollection as in the other portions of his evidence, as follows (Board's Record, p. 301):

Direct examination:

Question. Were you present when two or three rebel scouts were brought in in the morning, after you got up to Dawkins' Branch?
Answer. I was.
Question. Did you know or hear, at that time, whose men they were?
Answer. I know what one of them said.
Question. What was it?
Answer. He said they were Longstreet's men.
Question. Do you know what cavalry there were in General Porter's command on the 29th, or what were these cavalry that brought in the scouts, and where he got them?
Answer. *We picked them up on the road;* there were but few that we had. We were very short of cavalry.

It is to be noticed here incidentally, in reference to a matter hereafter to be discussed, that this witness admits that they had picked up cavalry on the road, namely, the Manassas and Gainesville road, and we shall see from the evidence of Capt. John P. Taylor that that cavalry which the petitioner had there was a squadron of the First Pennsylvania under Taylor that had come down on that very road from Gainesville that morning, reported to Morell, and was leading the division back again towards Gainesville. Had it been known or surmised by the petitioner that Captain Taylor and some of his men were to be brought here on behalf of the government for another purpose the question he asked his chief of staff would probably have been omitted, because it appears that since the evidence here of those who belonged to that squadron, the petitioner has sought to prove that there were no cavalry there,

First, by Major-General Morell, recalled (Board's Record, p. 968), who said he did not recollect, upon being questioned, seeing them, or hearing that they were there; and further remarked, "I cannot recall anything about it."

Second, by Capt. Augustus P. Martin, his chief of artillery, who was also a witness on the original trial for him, who, after testifying with a view to show that he was where he knew everything that was going on at the head of the petitioner's column that day at Dawkins' Branch, nevertheless did not know (Board's Record, p. 1131) of any other information coming in from the front than that of Colonel Marshall's Thirteenth New York Volunteers, and upon being questioned by the petitioner whether he noticed "any body" of Union cavalry of 50 or 70 men in the vicinity of the front that day, or anywhere thereabouts, answered nothing more than a few orderlies. Relative to the battery off to the right and front of the petitioner's column as to whose operations this witness testified quite minutely, he was obliged, on cross-examination, to make the following admissions:

Question. Do you know of any effort being made to take that battery that was towards your front during the day and fired upon you?
Answer. The enemy's battery?
Question. Yes.
Answer. I do not.

From the evidence of some of the witnesses for the petitioner, who were in the Confederate service, as well as from the evidence of other officers of that service, called on behalf of the government, it has been made manifest here that the only cavalry in those operations belonged to the division of Maj. Gen. J. E. B. Stuart, in the command of Major-General Jackson (Board's Record, pp. 174, 524, 526, 694); and that Longstreet had no cavalry whatever with him at that time. Part of the day Col. T. L. Rosser's regiment of Fifth Virginia Cavalry (Stuart's division) was picketed down near the front of the petitioner, and afterwards Brig. Gen. Beverly H. Robertson's brigade of cavalry, belonging to the same command of *Jackson* (Board's Record, p. 173). These cavalry had met the advance of Major-General Longstreet's column between Haymarket, or in its neighborhood, and Gainesville, and had then moved off down to the right in order to be on the extreme right flank of the Confederate force, and was undoubtedly the cavalry reported by Brigadier-General Buford (G. C. M. Record, p. 84).

Such being the case, assuming that two or three cavalry scouts, or cavalrymen, were captured by our First Pennsylvania squadron of Morell's command, the scouts belonged to Jackson's command, had been with him on all his movements down to Bristoe Station and present at the destruction, at Manassas Junction, of the Union supplies, and then gone up by a night march to Centreville, Stone Church, and Groveton, and thence back in the direction of Gainesville. Therefore, on this state of facts, the scouts captured were not Longstreet's men; it is not probable that any of them stated that they were of Major-General Longstreet's command. The latter had no cavalry whatever (Board's Record, p. 74). Therefore, when the petitioner, on this record, has expressed a strong desire to ascertain the whereabouts of those three scouts, had he secured their attendance here they would have been of no possible advantage for the reason that they belonged to Jackson's command and not to Longstreet's. Had he deemed them material on his trial they could possibly then have been easily secured.

That they were mounted cavalrymen was testified to by Brig. Gen. Charles Griffin, petitioner's witness on the trial in 1862 (G. C. M. Record, p. 165).

This petitioner, in his evidence before General McDowell's court of inquiry, swore that he knew from Brigadier-General Gibbon that the order which the latter brought from General Pope—

Was to prevent the junction of the advancing enemy and Jackson's force, then near Groveton; and that the object was to strike the turnpike to Gainesville before the advancing column should arrive.—(Board's Record, p. 1009.)

He testified that General McDowell had seen *that* order, "And when he altered it, as I conceived he had the authority, I presumed he knew more fully than I did the plans of General Pope."

The petitioner's presumption was a *non sequitur*, illustrated by his presumption in attacking the reputations of the court that tried him and all concerned.

It is a difficult matter to follow this petitioner in all his many material contradictions of himself.

In this evidence, we see he states, as I have just quoted (Board's Record, p. 1009), that he conceived General McDowell had authority over him sufficient to alter General Pope's order received by the hand of General Gibbon that morning; yet the latter himself was produced by petitioner as a witness, so far as this point is concerned, to show indirectly that McDowell did not even claim to exercise any command over him until receipt of the "joint order" (Board's Record, p. 245), and in petitioner's closing arguments we find him insisting on the same theory, although he *knew* that while King's division of McDowell's corps was on the Manassas and Gainesville road, and McDowell himself was there awaiting arrival of Ricketts' division to put him in on the same line, the old sixty-second article of war provided for just such a contingency.

General McDowell himself testified on this subject on the original trial that when notified at Manassas Junction by petitioner that General Pope had directed petitioner to take King's division with him, he, McDowell, was under some embarrassment at seeing one of his divisions going off under a junior, and that petitioner "mentioned to the effect that as I [McDowell] was the senior officer, I naturally and necessarily commanded the whole, his force as well as my own, and with that understanding the division followed after his corps on the road he was ordered to take * * ."—(G. C. M. Record, p. 82.)

Therefore, while McDowell *could* exercise command over both corps, if occasion required, he did not interfere as to the march conducted by petitioner, ostensibly up to the battle-field of the night before, until after the head of column had halted at Dawkins' Branch, he meanwhile remaining back on the road where he could communicate with Ricketts' division, then coming up from Bristoe.

Having received the joint order, he rode forward to communicate with petitioner. As it was issued to them *jointly*, it showed that it was the purpose of General Pope that they should act independently of each other, and each in direct subordination to himself; and General Pope testified that such was *his* intention.

"Under these circumstances," as was said by the Judge-Advocate-General in the able review he presented to President Lincoln under the latter's instructions (G. C. M. Record), "it may be well questioned whether under the sixty-second article of war General McDowell could continue the command he had assumed over their joint forces."

Whether or not McDowell was in command of both corps under the joint order, under the operation of the sixty-second article of war, is and was a question of *law* which was directly presented to President Lincoln for his consideration and decided by him, and his decision may be properly considered as final and conclusive.

Accepting, however, for argument, the view that under the "joint order" General McDowell necessarily commanded both corps while acting together, it is to be noted that the order said if any considerable advantages were to be gained by departing from it, it should not be strictly carried out. McDowell, therefore, had the right as joint commander to vary its terms—and his decision fixed the execution in the manner indicated. His decision, however, under a positive order of this character would be valid only as to the *way* of complying, not as to the primary military *end* to be obtained, viz, to unite the wings of the army then separated during a contest with the enemy.

Petitioner himself knew, as his statements and dispatches show, that no pretended order from McDowell to remain where he was, with an undeployed column stretching at least three miles to the rear, fulfilled in the slightest degree the purposes for which the joint order had been given, interpreted as it was by the *three* previous orders this petitioner had received that morning from General Pope.

They were all to push *forward* to fight the enemy.

Petitioner's own dispatches and reports during the day to McDowell and to his own division commander, Morell, "to push over to help Sigel," and that he "failed in getting Morell over," show that he knew McDowell never gave the improbable order he pretends he did, and that such an order, even had it been given, would have had no validity, because of its being in direct contravention of the letter and spirit of Pope's orders *to fight.*

One can but be amazed in considering the various excuses and pleas of this petitioner, that he should attempt to place on McDowell, who was *loyally* and anxiously striving to carry out General Pope's orders, the responsibility for their direct disobedience by himself.

Major-General McDowell's evidence, on cross-examination (Board's Record, p. 791), throws additional light as to the object of his meeting petitioner at the head of the latter's column at Dawkins' Branch:

Question. What was the purpose you went up there for [to the front at Dawkins' Branch]?
Answer. I went up because we came to a halt, and because I was in great anxiety in reference to the firing that was going on to the right. I went up there to see the condition of affairs, to see what was to be done with this force of ours on the left; going up there I received this letter of Buford.
Question. While you were there, if I am rightly informed, you decided, under the latitude allowed you by the joint order of General Pope, that General Porter should put his troops in to the right of where the head of his column then was, and that you would take yours away from the road on which those two commands then lay, up the Sudley Springs road? * * * * * '
Answer. Yes, sir.
Question. Did not you have any idea as to how far it was or how long it would take you?
Answer. I thought I could get my troops into action quicker that way than I could by bringing them up in the rear of General Porter's, because the road was blocked up with his corps. I was excessively anxious to join Reynolds.
Question. Was it not for the purpose of coming in on the left of Reynolds with both of your divisions?
Answer. I should have done so if left to myself.

Here, incidentally, permit me to allude to a point which is not material so far as the petitioner is concerned, but which has been raised according to the method of procedure on his part, as to the why and wherefore of the time General McDowell's corps, viz, King's division, under Hatch, and Ricketts' division, took to get up into the fight. General

McDowell before this Board answered this question (Board's Record, p. 817):

Question. Why did it take your troops so long as it did take them to get around into action that day?
Answer. Those troops had marched day and night without much food, without much rest, for so long a time that they were excessively tired; officers, men, and horses were all very tired. The rate of their advance was not fast; when they went up they were sent forward by me. I first found them halted. Do you mean on the evening of the 29th?
Question. Yes. It must have been about those hours.
Answer. They went up towards the left of Reynolds; they were recalled by order of General Pope back to the road upon which they started; and I think one or two brigades, by direct orders from him, were taken off in several directions. These marches and countermarches consumed considerable time before they were sent up the road in the evening to make the last attack, which last attack was made by the direct orders of General Pope.

*　　　　*　　　　*　　　　*

Question. Did you not go to the right with your two divisions on that day because that was the direction, from the right in front, that the enemy were coming?
Answer. I went up there because there is where I heard a battle going on.

We find from the evidence of Col. *Timothy Sullivan*, of the Twenty-fourth New York Volunteers, King's division, a witness for the petitioner (Board Record, p. 98), that it took a couple of hours, may be two and a half hours, to get up towards the position where they finally went in. Bvt. Brig. Gen. *E. D. Fowler*, of Hatch's brigade, King's division, under Hatch, says that they arrived nearly at the Henry house hill, between it and the Chinn house, about 2 p. m., or between 1 and 3 (Board's Record, p. 548).

WHAT WAS THE CHARACTER OF THE ENEMY IN PETITIONER'S FRONT AT DAWKINS' BRANCH, AND DID HE ATTEMPT TO ASCERTAIN ITS STRENGTH?

His witness (Maj. *G. K. Warren,* Corps of Engineers) says (Board's Record, p. 18) that they were fired at by artillery somewhere about Carrico's, somewhat concealed. Could see mounted men, such as cavalrymen.

*　　　　*　　　　*　　　　*　　　　*

Question. If that battery had not been put in that position, would there have been any difficulty in crossing that open space in order to reach that ridge by Morell's division?
Answer. I regarded that artillery as only an indication. I should not have considered it alone as any obstacle at all. It might have been attached to cavalry and run away at the sight of a demonstration. But as an indication of what might be—it might be a whole line of battle along there.
Question. If you had been placed there with Morell's division in that way, as a military man, what, in your judgment, would have been your duty in the premises?
Answer. Of course I should have had to obey orders.
Question. Supposing you were there as he was, in a semi-independent character, at that moment of time, as far as that battery was concerned, what, in your judgment, would have been your duty in the premises?
Answer. I should have considered the battery of no account at all.
Question. You could have moved forward and taken it if it had not been well supported?
Answer. I suppose I could if *I had chosen to go that much out of my way.* I should not regard a section of artillery as being an object to divert me or attract me. (Pages 37, 38 B. R.)

*　　　　*　　　　*　　　　*　　　　*

Question. You have been asked by General Schofield what you would have done if you had had 30,000 men. Let me ask you whether, with not exceeding 10,000 men, you could have made an attack with any expectation of success?
Answer. From what I *now* know I am satisfied that I could not. The most that could have been done would have been to so far develop the force as to be satisfied whether it could be engaged or not. If you were satisfied that it was too many for you, it would be imprudent to do it.

By the RECORDER:

Question. Do you know whether there was any such effort to develop it or not?
Answer. I do not, to my personal knowledge. (Board's Record, pp. 48, 49.)
*   *   *   *   *   *   *

Question. What was the character of the enemy you saw?
Answer. I saw enough of them to see that there was an enemy there. I didn't know how strong it was and could only have found out by some kind of a reconnaissance.
*   *   *   *   *   *   *

Question. You say that, in order to have gone along to the right of the Manassas and Gainesville road toward the left of General Pope's army, indicated by Reynold's position, that you thought at first a demonstration should have been made off in this direction to the southwest of that road?
Answer. Yes.
Question. Was that done during that day?
Answer. Not that I know of. Will you repeat what I said?
Question. In order to have moved along in a northeasterly direction towards Dawkins' Branch, it would have been first necessary, in your judgment, to have pushed off a column to the left of the Manassas and Gainesville road?
Answer. Yes. What I said was this: that if I had been ordered to make a movement in that direction, I should have considered it necessary to have made a demonstration here and see what would be on my flank. If I could not shake them out of their position, I would not have exposed my flank by moving northeasterly.
Question. Would you know if such a demonstration had been made by Morell's division in your front, they being to the right of the Manassas and Gainesville road and you to the left?
Answer. I don't know what that demonstration should have been. A skirmish-line might have been sufficient.
Question. My question is, would you have known?
Answer. I know that he did make a skirmish-line demonstration, but of the nature of that I am not cognizant.
Question. In which direction did he send out those skirmishers?
Answer. As far as I know they moved to the front.
Question. Not in the direction that you in your judgment say the demonstration should have been made in order to develop the strength of the enemy?
Answer. I cannot say that, exactly. It was in the same direction; of course I don't know whether it would have been as far to the left as I would have made it.
Question. It would have been to the northeast of the Manassas and Gainesville road rather than to the south and west of it?
Answer. It would have been in the direction of this road generally.
Question. Would you not have known if any demonstration had been made to the south and west of that road that day?
Answer. I think I would.
Question. Was any made to your recollection or knowledge?
Answer. No; I think there was not. (Board's Record, pp. 36 and 37.)
*   *   *   *   *   *   *

W. W. Blackford, captain of Confederate engineers, on Maj. Gen. J. E. B. Stuart's staff, called by government, testified as follows (Board's Record, p. 694):

Question. Then you followed the railroad down?
Answer. Then we followed it down in this direction somewhere. [Southeast.]
Question. Did you come to any point of observation?
Answer. We very soon opened communication with the cavalry videttes around *here* (near Hampton Cole's).
Question. Whose cavalry videttes were those?
Answer. Robertson's.
Question. Belonging to Jackson's command?
Answer. No, sir; Stuart's command of cavalry.
Question. Do you know when they had been put out there in observation?
Answer. No, sir; I could not make out what command it was hardly, but it must have been some of Robertson's.
Question. When did you first see the advance of the Federals?
Answer. Not long after we got out there. There were reports that they were advancing, and Stuart sent me out to verify the reports.
Question. State about the point you went to in order to get a view?
Answer. I went to every point I could see. I just rode to wherever I could get a view.
Question. Beyond Vessel's?
Answer. Yes; I went down on this side [south of Vessel's]; then, I think, over this

road [from Vessel's toward Dawkins' Branch]; and then came down by Carrico's. I examined it from every point of view that it was possible to get a view of it from. I had a very powerful pair of glasses that I could observe with. The main point to establish was whether it was infantry or dismounted cavalry.

Question. What did you observe?

Answer. As this was a powerful glass, I could tell by the bayonet-scabbards and the color of the trimmings whether it was cavalry or artillery.

Question. What did you see?

Answer. The head of the column then was just about making its appearance. I think they deployed on both sides of the Manassas and Gainesville road.

Question. What did you do?

Answer. I went back as soon as I ascertained that it was infantry.

Question. Did you come into any close proximity to any of these advancing parties?

Answer. As close as the skirmishers would let me. I drew their fire.

Question. Did you return it?

Answer. No, sir; I only had two or three men with me.

Question. Do you recollect just what took place?

Answer. I went back and reported to General Stuart.

    *   *   *   *   *

Question. Do you know of any movement, during that day, of the corps that was on this Manassas and Gainesville road, beyond Dawkins' Branch?

Answer. No, sir.

Question. Was your position such that it would have fallen under your observation if there had been such a movement?

Answer. I think we would have been sent over there if there had been.

Beverly H. Robertson, then a Confederate brigadier-general in Major-General Stuart's cavalry division of Jackson's command (Board's Record, pp. 173, 174, 524, and 526), says that after Major-General Longstreet's command, or a portion of it at least, arrived on the field and finally deployed, he was placed on the enemy's extreme right, and had his skirmishers in front of Dawkins' Branch (Board's Record, pp. 175 and 181), with his brigade massed half a mile in rear in the woods.

He put his brigade as fully 2,500 men on the 29th August present under arms, this being additional to Fitzhugh Lee and Rosser's regiments of Stuart's division under Jackson.

It is curious to notice how this witness, who went from Jackson that morning to Haymarket, and Longstreet and Charles Marshall and other Confederates who came from beyond Haymarket that day, give large estimates as to the forces under their commands. In the consideration of such estimates and in any other matter where there may be a contradiction as to a fact, as this is a military case, the opinion *at the time* of the *Union* officer will be accepted in this argument in preference to that of the enemy, after stating each. Even petitioner's Confederate witnesses, on whom he has so much relied, do not agree in their estimate of the force under Longstreet.

Thus the latter (exclusive of Anderson's division, which did not arrive during the battle of the 29th) says (Board's Record, p. 72) that his divisions present, viz: Hood's, Kemper's, Wilcox's, and D. R. Jones' had each between 6,100 and 6,300 men; while C. M. Wilcox, one of his division commanders (p. 228), put his own force at between 5,000 and 5,500 men—nearly 5,500.

Therefore, assuming Longstreet's extreme estimate as correct, he had about 24,800 men (no cavalry) on the ground, while assuming Wilcox's estimate as correct, about 21,600 would have been the numbers; a difference in the four divisions of 3,200 men; enough for another division.

However, we are not left in much uncertainty as to the actual number which passed through Gainesville in a body at 8.45 a. m., because Brig. Gen. John Buford, U. S. volunteers, chief of cavalry, accused's witness on the trial—who saw this force pass through Gainesville—swore as to the "extent of their entire force" (G. C. M. Record, p. 188), that it consisted of "seventeen regiments of infantry, one battery of artillery, and about 500 cavalry"; that he "made a particular estimate," and thought the. regiments would average 800 men; also that there were besides the organized force "some stragglers following."

This intelligent witness did not have to trust to a recollection of sixteen years through many vicissitudes of intermediate military service, but made his estimate and report *at the time* to Major-General McDowell. The latter received it as he went towards petitioner's head, of column at Dawkins' Branch and showed it to him. Buford's estimate, it will be perceived, made Longstreet's force about 14,100 men, instead of the extreme computation of 24,800.

Major-General *Morell*, in a dispatch to petitioner (No. 35, Board's Record, p. 303), said in the afternoon, "No infantry in sight"; and his assistant adjutant-general, Earle (Board's Record, p. 419), *did not see the enemy's skirmishers that day.*

Lieut. *James Stevenson*, Thirteenth New York Volunteers (petitioner,s witness), who came down *along the front* from the left of General Pope's army to his regiment on the skirmish line, bringing the regimental mail, says in the trial (G. C. M. Record, p. 201), that he judged the enemy that afternoon, whom he saw, to have been 12,000 or 15,000 strong; a fact, if fact it was, which came directly before the court that tried this petitioner.

This case must be considered, if at all, *in the light he then had,* based upon what he THEN KNEW OR BELIEVED WERE THE FACTS, *in connection with the character of the specific orders he was acting under.*

With every disposition to make his case appear as favorable to himself as possible—he having been on trial for his life—and with nothing to restrain him from estimating that separate force under Longstreet, the senior Confederate division commander, at as large a figure as would serve his purposes, this petitioner deliberately stated before the court that tried him, on the 10th January, 1863 (G. C. M. Record, p. 266), that this separate force was from *ten to fifteen thousand strong.*

This accords with the estimate of his own witness, Brigadier-General Buford, as to the number Major-General Longstreet brought to Jackson's assistance that day (29th August) as an *organized* force, divided into four divisions of three brigades each, and each brigade containing as an average three regiments, each about 375 strong.

This, it is to be understood, is considered a *very* liberal estimate of the number of men Longstreet brought to Jackson's assistance, exclusive of stragglers, that day.

When Longstreet's divisions did *finally* get into position, two of Hood's brigades were north of the Gainesville, Groveton, and Centreville turnpike, with Wilcox's division in support; and facing those south were Stevens's brigade of Reno's division, also Schenck's division of Sigel's corps, about 4,500 strong, and Reynolds's division of thirteen regiments and four battalions, besides petitioner's corps, on the right flank of Longstreet, enough to have overwhelmed this fragment of Lee's rebel army, had he loyally "pushed in."

Brevet Brig.-Gen. *Horace Bouton*, then captain Thirteenth New York Volunteers, who was on the skirmish picket line front of petitioner's corps, testified as follows (Board's Record, p. 332):

Question. What force of the enemy did you perceive there?
Answer. All we could see were occasional skirmishers that we developed.
* * * * *
Question. In the morning when you were deployed and went into the woods, or to the edge of the woods, what was the apparent strength of the enemy's skirmishers?
Answer. They seemed to be fully the strength of ours. It was a regular skirmish-line deployed. We could only see them occasionally; we could not tell the number.

There was no regular line except a line of skirmishers; there was no line of battle that we discovered.

* * * * * * *

Question. I would like you to fix as near as you can the earliest hour in the day when you heard any such movement or sound which indicated such a movement of troops, in the rear of the enemy's skirmish-line.

Answer. As we did not get in there until about noon, according to my impression it must have been somewhere *about the middle of the afternoon or a little after that.* We pressed forward immediately after deploying; and at that time was the first time that we developed the enemy. I suppose not more than half an hour would have elapsed from the time we halted to the time we made the advance and discovered the skirmishers.

This petitioner has heralded the testimony from *Confederate* sources as the "newly discovered testimony" which should show that he was justified in not attacking them under the orders he had for fear of destruction.

In my opening argument, which was purposely full in order to apprise petitioner of the principal points in the government case, I observed that "Confederate" testimony as to the *strength* and *position* of their own force was not "newly discovered" evidence of the kind that would be entitled to consideration in any court of justice having appellate authority, for the reason that subsequently acquired knowledge must be excluded in determining what was *then* known by the petitioner in connection with the orders he had.

The enemy might have had 50,000 men on his front, instead of the 25,000 he now asserts it was, as against the 10,000 or 15,000 he insisted it to have been when on his trial in January, 1863.

The prospect of a "repulse" in an attack, made under lawful orders, would be no excuse for failing to make it.

"Confederate" testimony, therefore, as to the numbers in his front on the 29th August, has nothing to do with the case in considering whether he did attack under his orders or did not attack. If he made *no vigorous efforts to develop and ascertain what force of the enemy was in front of* him, he cannot, even on the assumption that he had no orders to attack, justify, palliate, or excuse his fatal inaction on the 29th August, 1862.

To ascertain what he did do, the testimony of those who were at the front must be considered. His witness, General Morell, thus testified on cross-examination (Board's Record, p. 432):

Question. When did you first see the enemy?
Answer. I did not see them at all. Except that section of artillery, they were all in the woods [around Vessels's]. I believe those who were farther to the left could see something of them; but where I was I could not see them. I relied very much upon Colonel Marshall. He was an educated Army officer, and I had perfect confidence in him.

* * * * * * *

Question. The moment you heard a little skirmish in front you halted and began to deploy?
Answer. I did not hear the fighting. Colonel Marshall sent back word; then we halted immediately and began to deploy on the crest of the ridge.

* * * * * *

Question. Then I understand you did not hear any skirmish-firing at all in your front?
Answer. I heard a few dropping shots, and the report came in immediately from Colonel Marshall; that is what really stopped me.

* * * * * *

Question. Could you see the dust raised by the enemy advancing during the day?
Answer. I could see dust off on the left.
Question. They appeared to be coming in pretty much all the afternoon?
Answer. There was a cloud of dust in the direction of Gainesville.
Question. Did you understand they were coming up all the afternoon?
Answer. From Colonel Marshall's report I did, and I inferred so from the appearance of the country.

Question. As soon as you heard the skirmish-line as you were marching along that road, do I understand you to say that you immediately began to deploy?
Answer. As soon as what?
Question. As soon as you heard the fire of your skirmishers?
Answer. Yes; as soon as we heard that Longstreet's skirmishers and ours had met we began immediately to deploy.
Question. How long afterwards was it before General Porter came up?
Answer. I think he was with me at the time.
Question. You deployed under his orders?
Answer. Under his orders.

It will be perceived that this witness assumes that *Longstreet's* skirmishers were in his front, which, in point of fact, from petitioner's own "Confederate" witnesses, we have seen was not the case. They were skirmishers from Stuart's cavalry division of Jackson's command.

Maj. *George Hyland, jr.*, Thirteenth New York Volunteers, the next in rank in his regiment to Colonel Marshall that day on petitioner's skirmish line, called by him, testified (Board's Record, p. 115) that petitioner came up to the head of column at Dawkins' Branch and requested Colonel Marshall *to find where the enemy were in front;* and he, witness, took the left wing of his regiment and deployed it as skirmishers. He then answered as follows:

Question. Where did you halt; what was the topography of the country?
Answer. The division halted on a hill, and I deployed my skirmishers directly to the front of that hill, and as we passed down at the bottom of the little valley there was a stream passed through it to our right; it was quite a swamp. I had to take the left of the line, as they were advancing a great deal faster than the right. As we came up the opposite side of the valley we fell in with the enemy's skirmishers at the edge of the timber. About the same instant there was a squadron of cavalry upon my right in a corn-field. I sent word back to General Griffin to send some shells into their position. He placed half a dozen shells in there, and dislodged them. We were skirmishing the balance of the afternoon with the enemy's skirmishers; sometimes they would drive us back a few rods, then we would regain our former position.

*　　*　　*　　*　　*　　*　　*

Question. What were the actions of Colonel Marshall, that you know of?
Answer. He came out to see me once or twice. He advanced to my left with one of my men. I didn't go with him; I staid with my command. He went out, and I think he reported to me there were cavalry there, but I didn't see them; I was not in a position where I could see them.
Question. What was the impression made upon your mind; that it was a large or a small force?
Answer. A very large force.

By the PRESIDENT OF THE BOARD:
Question. What arm or troops did those rebel skirmishers belong to?
Answer. I don't know. They were infantry, in the woods.

On the trial of petitioner, Major Hyland was then a witness in his behalf, and on the direct examination (G. C. M. Record, p. 174) answered as follows:

Question by accused. Was there any enemy formed in your front during that time [viz, about 1 p. m. that day until daylight 30th August]?
Answer. There was.
Question by accused. Do you know at what hour they commenced forming, or about what hour?
Answer. *They commenced forming between two and three o'clock,* I think.

This evidence will be found in entire harmony with the government view of this case.

This witness, "*judging from the columns of dust*" that he saw "coming from the same direction," stated as his conclusions to the court-martial that there were probably 10,000 troops in front of petitioner.

Capt. *Henry Gecke*, Thirteenth New York Volunteers, a witness for government (Board's Record, p. 668), was ordered out by Colonel Marshall in command of the left wing of the regiment on the skirmish line, Major Hyland having command of all of the regiment which went on this duty. He has put the time when he went out later than it actually was. His evidence, however, as to what he could hear is confirmed by his colonel, Marshall. Captain Gecke testified as follows (Board's Record, p. 668):

Right before me was a piece of wood and an open corn-field between me and the woods. I remained and deployed my skirmish line outside of the ditch there. At the same time when I came there I saw skirmishers, dismounted cavalry, marching before me in that corn-field. My men fired at them and they fired over to us. Then they went back into the woods and I gave the command to cease firing. Then the adjutant of the regiment came up between four and five o'clock with an order to the commanding officer of the skirmish line. I stepped up, and he said I should find out immediately what was going on in the corner of the woods; so I took a sergeant and a file of men and went up there; and the sergeant went ahead and looked in that direction, and then we came down and reported to the adjutant that the enemy has been marching out of the woods, and that they were moving cannon and ammunition-wagons to form their proper companies, and turning to the left. A little while after this I heard a few shots fired over in that direction.

* * * * * *

Question. When you went out with the skirmishers and deployed your men, what orders did you have?
Answer. I had no special order except to see what was going on. I saw no line formed on the left; no line formed on the right.
Question. When did you first observe the enemy coming down on your front?
Answer. That was about four o'clock.
Question. Up to that time what indications were there of an enemy in your front?
Answer. I should say I saw a few of a skirmish line moving through the corn-field into the other side of the wood.
Question. During that day did you see any artillery firing?
Answer. I heard artillery firing.
Question. In what direction did you hear it?
Answer. The fire of artillery that forenoon I heard on the front of us; in the afternoon on our right.
Question. What was the character of that artillery firing that you heard?
Answer. It commenced at five o'clock in the morning; then it was in the far distance. Then about eleven or twelve o'clock we heard it better; we heard heavier firing. Then between one and two o'clock there was no firing whatever. Then from about three o'clock and afterwards there was heavy artillery firing and musketry firing up to most nine o'clock at night and yelling by the enemy and cheering by the Union men. We heard that off on our right.
Question. Did you at any time during that afternoon undertake to feel the enemy and find out what their strength was?
Answer. No; I only carried out the order I had.
Question. About what time in the day would you say you moved across Dawkins' Branch to go forward with your skirmishers?
Answer. About three o'clock.
Question. Did you know the position of the enemy after you got up on the skirmish line?
Answer. No; I didn't see no other part of the troops except this dismounted cavalry.

* * * * * * *

Question. This yelling and cheering that you heard by the enemy and the Union troops, was that before or after you moved your skirmish line across Dawkins' Branch.
Answer. Afterwards.
Question. How long after?
Answer. That commenced about five o'clock or half past five, and kept on until darkness.
Question. The yelling and cheering that you heard was between five o'clock and sundown?

[The Confederate General R. E. Lee's official report of that action says that the battle continued until nine o'clock at night (Board's Record, p. 520).]

Answer. Up to nine o'clock at night.
Question. Did you make any report of that to anybody?
Answer. No.

Question. Do you mean to say that you did not send any messages to Colonel Marshall at all that day?
Answer. No; except this one, because I was not so far off from them. They could hear all these things going on themselves.
Question. Then you could hear and he could hear?
Answer. He could hear the firing. It took me about ten minutes, more or less, to get there from my position back.

Sergeant *Ferdinand Mohle*, Thirteenth New York Volunteers (Board's Record, p. 676), a government witness, has stated as follows as to his position to the front:

Answer. I think we staid as skirmishers up towards night, and then we were withdrawn on to a hill. It is kind of rolling country here. I think it was hollow along that way and then it raised again.
Question. What did you see while you were on the skirmish line so far as the enemy was concerned?
Answer. Saw a couple of rebel pickets in front of us.
Question. Infantry or cavalry?
Answer. I could not say exactly; I guess it was dismounted cavalry.
Question. What other indications of an enemy did you see during the day; what enemy did you see in front of you?
Answer. I saw no enemy where I stood. I have just said it was a kind of hollow place where we went through and we could not see many of the enemy except a line of pickets; they were not very active. We exchanged a couple of shots, and I recollect a couple of cannon shots flew right over our line and came I guess from our rear—our own men—two or three shots.
Question. Was there any cannonading going on then?
Answer. There was.
Question. Where was that?
Answer. That was to our right.
Question. What was the character of it?
Answer. It was heavier towards evening than the time we went up there. We heard the noise more in the evening—the noise of artillery and cheering—than when we first came up there. But still firing was going on.
Question. When did the enemy come down in force on your front that day where you were?
Answer. What do you mean by the enemy; the line of pickets?
Question. Yes, or heavy force; did you see any heavier force in front of you?
Answer. I could not see any heavy force; I could hear more. I could hear moving; I did not know whether it was artillery or cavalry, but I heard some words, some commands.
Question. How late in the day was that?
Answer. It was in the evening; towards night, I guess.
Question. When you went out there on that line, did you hear those commands and movements?
Answer. I cannot remember; I did not hear any command that time; but there was a couple of shots exchanged between the pickets; and finally, I think, the rebel pickets went back a little, and word was brought to cease firing.
Question. Could you hear any musketry firing in the afternoon where you were and infantry firing?
Answer. Yes; I could hear that.
Question. How long in the afternoon did you hear infantry firing?
Answer. I cannot tell exactly when it commenced, but I could hear cannon firing when we were marching up there.
Question. After you got up there, was there any cannon firing?
Answer. There was cannon firing at intervals; it ceased sometimes, and toward night it went on pretty heavy.
Question. Any musketry firing in the afternoon to your front or right?
Answer. I think there was musketry firing, but we could not hear it so plain as in the evening.
Question. About what time did you hear this cheering which you speak of?
Answer. About sunset.

Captain *Mark I. Bunnell*, then lieutenant Thirteenth New York Volunteers, who was also on the skirmish line of petitioner's column, testified as follows:

Question. What could you see and hear during that day?
Answer. I saw some skirmishers from the opposite side—two or three cavalrymen I saw come out in a corn-field in a front a little to the right; and heard firing.

Question. In which direction?

Answer. Soon after we were in position there was some firing in front, and a little to the right of the front.

Question. Artillery or infantry?

Answer. Artillery and some carbine firing—cavalry. That was the skirmish line, I judge.

Question. Could you see any enemy in your front?

Answer. Only those few cavalrymen that came out there.

Question. Do you know whether the enemy came down in force in your front that day; if so, when?

Answer. The impression was that there was some force there in the latter part of the afternoon. I did not see them; I could not see them.

Question. Was there any contest of any description in any other direction than directly in your front and right?

Answer. Judging from the firing there was at the right.

Question. What was it; infantry, or artillery, or both?

Answer. Both.

Question. How near were you to that contest?

Answer. It would be almost impossible to tell.

Question. You could hear musketry distinctly?

Answer. Yes; very distinctly.

Question. Could you hear anything else indicating a contest or battle?

Answer. Late in the afternoon we could hear the huzzas and howling of the soldiers, apparently as though they were charging, and going backwards and forwards a number of times.

The rest of this witness' evidence has already been cited in another connection; but it will be perceived that the enemy's force in front of petitioner's head of column, of which the witness was well placed to judge, was cavalry skirmishers, and if there was any infantry force there at all it was not until the latter part of the afternoon; meanwhile he and his comrades *were aware that General Pope's army was fighting,* although petitioner, with his headquarters 2¾ miles to the rear from Dawkins' Branch, insists that he, himself, was not.

Assistant Surgeon *William L. Faxon,* Twenty-second Massachusetts Volunteers, Martindale's brigade, Morell's division, called for government, said (Board's Record, p. 890), as to the halt at Dawkins' Branch:

Answer. We halted on a small knoll; part of it overlooked quite a large valley; quite a large part of it was cleared, and on the right I saw the line of the Manassas Gap Railroad.

Question. This point that I have indicated on the map as Dawkins' Branch?

Answer. I should take the branch to be a little farther away. I should take the branch to be about a mile away from the place where we halted; there might have been a dry run at the foot of this knoll, but I think not.

Question. What did you do after you came to a halt there?

Answer. I went down on the railroad; I went around generally in the woods and looked at the situation generally; saw firing was going on along the right of us, over toward Thoroughfare Gap.

Question. Did you see any indications of an enemy immediately in your front?

Answer. I did not see any for a mile or more; I looked along through the field close; General Porter came up and borrowed a glass of me; he asked me what I had seen. I told him I thought there was a battery coming in about a mile from us on the Washington side of the road. Not very far from it, I think, there was a small house, and I saw something that led me to suppose that there were men going in there.

Question. Do you recollect what reply he made?

Answer. I do not know that he made any reply to me.

Question. Did that battery open upon you?

Answer. It opened shortly afterwards; of course I cannot tell you how many minutes, because I did not keep any note of the time. I had no intention of making any memorandum. It opened and fired before the troops were withdrawn, I think, not exceeding three, might have been four, possibly but two shots.

Question. Where did those shots strike?

Answer. One of the shots struck a man in the front rank of the First Michigan Infantry, and passed through his abdomen, and struck the first man in the rear rank in the thigh.

Question. You were there at the time?

Answer. I was at the place and saw the men; they were sitting or lying just a little lower down on the slope of the hill in front of me.

Question. Then what was done?

Answer. Shortly after that we withdrew.

Question. What indications, if any, did you see of an enemy in your front, or to your right and front, or to your right?

Answer. To the right and front.

Mr. CHOATE. I do not know that an assistant surgeon is a military expert.

The RECORDER. I asked him what he saw.

Mr. CHOATE. I have no objection to what he saw.

Answer. (Continued.) Beyond this general clearing to quite a large extent there was a smaller clearing, only a part of which could be seen; there was a small opening in the wood; across that opening there came a small body of men; they halted in the opening where there was evidently a depression, but their heads and shoulders could be plainly seen.

Question. About how many men?

Answer. I should judge not over 20.

Question. What else did you see of an enemy in your front, or to your right and front, or to your right?

Answer. Nothing.

Question. Could you see anything that would indicate the march of troops; if so, what?

Answer. I could see a large cloud of dust on the Warrenton turnpike moving towards Centreville.

Question. After that where did you go?

Answer. I went into camp with troops at night, *after they withdrew.*

Question. Did they remain in this advanced position during the day?

Answer. *They were withdrawn in the afternoon; the sun was declining in the heavens.*

Question. How far were they withdrawn?

Answer. *I should judge inside of a mile.*

Question. More than a half a mile or less?

Answer. That I could not tell you; I could go to the spot, to the place where they came, because we withdrew on the same road, and then came back and went into camp again after dusk.

*   *   *   *   *   *

(Board's Record, p. 898.)   (Redirect).

Question. You say you heard firing off to the right. What firing was that?

Answer. There was firing over, I should judge, somewhere on the northwest side of the Warrenton pike; and on the pike that was lying between us and Thoroughfare Gap there was quite hard fighting; volleys of musketry and artillery firing. There was some musketry firing over beyond that point, and but little artillery firing; you could see the smoke of the rebel guns, and the shells exploding beyond, but not as hard there as over on the right.

[It will be observed as I go along that Captain Monteith, petitioner's then aide-de-camp, also saw those shells bursting in air.]

Q. How long did you hear that during the day?

Answer. More or less all the time there was sound of fighting, and we expected to be in it. I would like to make an explanation in regard to distance, which the gentleman refused to allow me to make. The body of men that came out *here* was fired at by Hazlitt's battery, and the shell was exploded right in the place where these men were; they ran away. I asked the sergeant for what time he cut his shell, and he said for a mile; that is how I locate the distance of those men in front of me.

Question. The sergeant of Hazlitt's battery fired the piece?

Answer. Yes.

Bvt. Lieut. Col. *Jos. P. Cleary*, then of the Thirteenth New York Volunteers, under Colonel Marshall, testified as follows (Board's Record, p. 673):

Question. Do you know of any action in this direction [north]; if so, what was its character?

Answer. To the right of where we lay along toward dark in the evening there was musketry firing. I could hear the cheering of our men and the peculiar yell of the enemy as if they were charging and recharging.

Private *Charles E. Brahm*, Fifth New York Volunteers, Warren's brigade, Sykes' division, a government witness, testified as follows (Board's Record, p. 936):

Question. Did you hear any firing at that time?

Answer. We heard firing mostly all day; artillery. I could see the artillery in the morning at nine o'clock down toward the direction of Groveton. We laid alongside of the road two or three hours, and heard musketry firing all that time—towards night very heavy.

Question. Did you see any enemy in your front?

Answer. I did not. There was some artillery firing in our front—two or four shots that I can recollect. This was the closest firing we had to our line.

Question. Did you hear any musketry firing during the afternoon?

Answer. Yes; a great deal toward the right and rear of us.

Question. Off in what direction?

Answer. Toward the right and rear.

Private *Joseph Robbins*, Eighteenth Massachusetts Volunteers, Martindale's brigade, Morell's division, kept a diary at the time, in which he said (Board's Record, p. 845): "On the 29th marched to Manassas; then orders came to move towards Manassas Gap. *Now we expect to have some fighting.*" He says he "heard considerable firing on their right" until dark, up to the time of bivouacking.

By this witness' diary it is very evident the volunteers under Morell in petitioner's corps knew what they were moving up towards Dawkins' Branch for.

They were not looking back to see how they could get behind "Bull Run that night," but forward to meet the enemy. They knew a battle was going on and that they should be in it.

Col. *E. G. Marshall*, United States Army, retired, a graduate of the United States Military Academy at West Point, called by the accused, and since recalled before this Board, and his prior statements accepted without question by petitioner (p. 190, G. C. M. Record, and p. 75, Board's Record), has testified as follows:

Question. State the position and force of the enemy in the immediate vicinity of General Porter's command as far as you know it.

Answer. Immediately after going there my skirmishers were fired on by a body of dragoons, and shortly afterward there was a section of artillery which opened fire upon General Porter's command. Soon after that, perhaps about two o'clock, the head of a large column came to my front. They deployed their skirmishers and met mine, and about three o'clock drove my skirmishers into the edge of the timber. We were all on the left of the Manassas Railroad, going toward Gainesville. Their force continued to *come down all day;* in fact, until one o'clock at night. It was a very large force, and they were drawn up in line of battle as they came down.

I reported at different intervals to General Morell, my immediate commander, the position of the enemy; but at one time I deemed it so important that I did not dare to trust orderlies or others with messages, and I went myself up to him to confer concerning the enemy. This was about dusk. General Morell told me that he had just received orders from General Porter to attack the enemy—to commence the attack with *four regiments.* He seemed to be very much troubled concerning the order, and asked my advice, my opinion. I told him by all means not to attack; that it was certain destruction for us to do so; that I, for one, did not wish to go into the timber and attack the enemy. Their position was a strong one, and they were certainly in force at that time—twice as large as our force—all of General Porter's corps. He had expressed to me the tenor of General Porter's order. I also deemed that we had executed the same with reference to the other part of the army—General Pope's army—by keeping this large body in force, and better than we would by attacking them, because if we had attacked them, I felt that it was certain destruction, as we would have had to move our line of battle across this ravine into this timber, and then perhaps our line of retreat would have been entirely cut off from General Pope's army.

I may say that this army that came down in our front was a separate and distinct army of the enemy from that *which we saw General Pope's army fighting with.*

About the same time—before I went in to General Morell—I could hear and judge of the result of the fighting between the force of the enemy and General Pope's army.

I could see General Pope's left and the enemy's right during the greater part of the day, about two miles off, perhaps more, diagonally to our front and to the right. The enemy set up their cheering, and appeared to be charging and driving us, so that not a man of my command but what was certain that General Pope's army was being driven from the field.

In the different battles I have seen, I have learned that there is no mistaking the enemy's yell when they are successful. It is different from that of our own men, our men giving three successive cheers, and in concert, but theirs is a cheering without any reference to regularity of form—a continual yelling.

Thus did this witness testify on the original trial. It will be perceived that the point that the petitioner has undertaken to raise here, of a separate and large force in his front during that day, was raised then before the court; nevertheless it is to be observed that the receipt by Morell of petitioner's order to attack with four regiments, at dusk or about dusk, is a fair indication of the number of the enemy the petitioner at *that* time thought were in front of him to permit of two regiments supported by two others making an attack.

Capt. *John S. Hatch*, First Michigan Volunteers, Martindale's brigade, Morell's division, a witness for the government, testifies as follows (Board's Record, p. 600) as to what transpired at the front, near Dawkin's Branch, on the 29th August:

Question. Tell what you saw when you got there at that point.
Answer. When we turned off into the woods we were preparing to go into action, as I supposed. I think the pieces were loaded. Caps were left off the guns, and cartridges examined and cartridge-boxes, and some such things as that. We remained in the woods a little time, and then we moved off to an eminence where we could look off into the depression or ravine; and then the Thirteenth New York was thrown out as skirmishers.
Question. How long had this been after you had arrived at that point before the Thirteenth was thrown in?
Answer. It is my impression that we were loading pieces and preparing, as we supposed, to go into action. I recollect we were talking of it together; that it was about noon. I do not recollect looking at a watch. It was about twelve o'clock, I should say; not far from that any way.
Question. That the Thirteenth were thrown out?
Answer. Yes, sir.
Question. You remained there during the day?
Answer. Remained there all that day.
Question. After the Thirteenth were thrown out what did you see?
Answer. We came out of these woods, I guess, almost entirely, so that we could see the Thirteenth New York maneuver, and see the ravine and woods on beyond. I think our arms were stacked—our brigade. We lay there and saw the Thirteenth New York moving; they kept moving on until they met with some little check on the other side; there were some shots fired; then, some time after that, a solid shot came over. General Porter was there with his staff. I do not know whether there were any other generals there or not. There was a little scattering there and a little commotion all around, until pretty soon another one came over, and there was a piece run out of the woods where the Thirteenth New York had met with some opposition from the infantry; there was another shot fired soon after that, and we supposed the work was commencing. There were three shots, I think, or four shots fired. We supposed that they were firing at General Porter and his staff, because they were mounted and conspicuous.
Question. Then what was done?
Answer. There was nothing done by us during that afternoon. We were lying there at ease until early in the evening, when our brigade, a portion of it—my regiment at least—was thrown out, you might say, as skirmishers. We were thrown out to guard against a surprise that night—thrown out to the right of where the New York Thirteenth went down.
Question. How long did you remain there?
Answer. Two hours; about that.
Question. What indications, if any, did you observe of the presence of the enemy during the day?
Answer. We saw fighting going on on our right and front.
Question. What kind of a contest was it?
Answer. There was heavy artillery firing.
Question. How long did that continue?
Answer. From the time we came out on to that eminence, out of the woods; there was firing all the afternoon, but not continuous; there was at times heavy firing, rapid firing.
Question. From the character of the firing what were the indications?
Answer. It was heavy—artillery fire.
Question. I understand you to say that you could see the action going on?
Answer. I could not see the troops that I recollect. I do not think I could, but the smoke and the bursting of shells could be seen, and we could hear the sound of the artillery, and see the lines of smoke; towards evening we heard musketry firing.

Question. How long was it after the Thirteenth New York went out before you saw that gun run out that you speak of?

Answer. They had time to get down three-quarters of a mile or more—perhaps half an hour.

Question. During the day what enemy did you see in your front besides what you have mentioned at that time?

Answer. Saw a line of dust on the left making towards Jackson, who we understood was opposing our forces.

Question. At the time?

Answer. At the time.

Question. Did you see any enemy directly in your front?

Answer. These woods were there; nothing more than artillery. There were infantry opposed to the Thirteenth New York.

Question. How long did they remain there, artillery and infantry?

Answer. I do not know that; they did not remain all the afternoon.

Question. Had no more artillery firing from them?

Answer. The artillery, three or four shots, was all that bothered us.

Cross-examination by Mr. BULLITT:

Question. What time was it, in the afternoon or toward evening, that you heard that musketry firing?

Answer. The day was well advanced.

Question. Five or six o'clock in the evening.

Answer. I should judge so; before sundown sometime.

Question. What you had heard, prior to that time, was all artillery firing?

Answer. I do not recollect any musketry firing until toward sundown; perhaps the sun an hour or two high.

Question. What time was it that you were sent out on that picket-line?

Answer. The Thirteenth New York was sent out, and I was in the same brigade with them. As I say, we were preparing for action in the woods about twelve o'clock, I should think.

It is plain that a portion of the petitioner's corps was, on the 29th August, 1862, as charged in the first and second specifications of the second charge, "in sight of the field and in full hearing of its artillery."

Even the petitioner, in his opening statement (p. 28), had to admit that as early as when he was at Manassas Junction that day "the sound of artillery in the direction of Groveton" was heard by him.

From these witnesses, both petitioner's and the government's, is obtained concurrent testimony to material facts, which can neither be evaded nor disposed of by "want of recollection" on the part of others who were called, or statements from others still that they "did not hear" or see the contest or hear the cheers of the Union soldiers and yells of the Confederates. As for the petitioner himself, he had taken good care to locate his headquarters sufficiently far to the rear to interpose the heaviest woods between himself and the action and see and hear the least of the battle.

One of the most remarkable pieces of evidence in this remarkable case is found in that of Maj. Gen. Samuel G. Sturgis, United States Volunteers, now colonel Seventh United States Cavalry and brevet major-general United States Army, of a conversation he had with petitioner at the front, which tends to show that at that time (after McDowell had gone) the petitioner did not believe that the enemy was in force in his front. We have also seen by the evidence of Dr. Faxon, which has just been cited, that when the petitioner borrowed his glass, in order to look to the front, he seemingly was not aware of artillery there. The following comprise the extracts from General Sturgis' evidence (Board's Record, p. 711):

Question. State your rank in the Army.

Answer. Colonel Seventh Cavalry, and brevet major-general.

Question. What rank and command did you hold on the 29th of August, 1862?

Answer. I was brigadier-general of volunteers. I had on that day only one brigade of a division, the principal part of which was back of Alexandria. On that day I had only one brigade with me, General Piatt's brigade.

Question. Where did you move from on the morning of the 29th of August, and up to what place?

Answer. I am not exactly certain where I moved from on that morning, because the march of the 28th of August is not clear in my mind; but I think it is in the neighborhood of Bristoe Station.

Question. To whom were you ordered to report?

Answer. General Porter; ordered by General Porter himself to join him; that order I received at *Warrenton Junction*.

The Board will recollect from what I have cited of the petitioner's opening statement, and of his own dispatches, that the petitioner knew that Sturgis was at Warrenton Junction at the time that Sturgis here says he was; he speaks of him as there (p. 89, petitioner's opening statement):

Question. Where did you find General Porter's column?

Answer. I found it on the road leading from Manassas Junction in the direction of Gainesville; I should think a mile and a half, about, beyond Bethlehem Church.

Question. Did you bring up this brigade with you?

Answer. O, yes.

Question. You say you went a mile and a half beyond Bethlehem Church toward Gainesville?

Answer. That is my recollection.

Question. What did you then do?

Answer. I reported to General Porter. I rode in advance of my brigade. I found troops occupying the road, and I got up as near as I could get and then halted my command, and then rode forward to tell General Porter that they were there. He said, "For the present, let them lie there."

Question. What did you do then, individually?

Answer. Well, I simply looked about to see what I could see. I was a stranger to the lay of the land, and the troops, and all that; so, without getting off my horse, I rode about from place to place watching the skirmishers, and among other things I took a glass and looked in the direction of the woods, about a mile beyond which seemed to be the object of attention—beyond the skirmishers; there I saw a glint of light on a gun; and I remarked to General Porter that I thought they were probably putting a battery in position at that place, for I thought I had seen a gun.

Question. State what the conversation was.

Answer. I reported this fact of what I had seen to the general; *he thought I was mistaken about it*, but I was not mistaken, because it opened in a moment—at least a few shots were fired from that place—four, as I recollect.

The Board will please recollect this remark and the evidence of General Sturgis when we consider it in connection with the petitioner's statement as to what he (petitioner) saw when he was riding back from his interview with General McDowell:

Question. What force of the enemy did you see in that direction at that time?

Answer. *I didn't see any of the enemy at all.*

Question. Then what did you do.

Answer. Then when they had fired, as near as I can recollect, about four shots from this piece, General Porter beckoned to me; I rode up to him, and he directed me to take my command to Manassas Junction, and take up a defensive position, inasmuch as the fire seemed to be receding on our right.

Question. What firing do you mean?

Answer. I mean the cannonading that had been going on for some time on our right, probably in the direction of Groveton.

It will be recollected here that when Maj. S. N. Benjamin (then Second United States Artillery) got to Groveton and put his battery in position, that at first there was a lull, he says, of half an hour (Board's Record, p. 614).

Question. How long had you heard that cannonading.

Answer. I don't recollect exactly where I heard it first. My impression has been that I heard it all along the march from Manassas to General Porter's position. I do not recollect distinctly that I did hear it, but I know I heard it all the time after I arrived there until I left.

Question. What time of day was this that you received the order to move back with your command to Manassas Junction?

Answer. I have no way of fixing the time of day. I have carried in my mind the impression that it was more about the middle of the day—about one o'clock.

In that connection the Board will notice in Major Benjamin's evidence that the latter puts it exactly between half past twelve and one o'clock for that lull. This was not long after petitioner had returned from the railroad to the head of his column at Dawkins' Branch, and while General McDowell must have been taking Brigadier General Patrick's brigade up the Sudley road.

Question. What did you do when you received that order?
Answer. I sent word to General Piatt to move back to Manassas Junction, and that I would join him there.
Question. Do you know whether your order was obeyed?
Answer. Yes; it was obeyed.

Cross-examination by Mr. BULLITT:

Question. What next did you do after that?
Answer. I rode back myself as far as *Bethlehem Church.*

So it is apparent that this witness did not go the entire distance with the brigade.

Question. Did you receive any order from General Porter subsequent to that?
Answer. Yes, sir.
Question. What was it?
Answer. To bring forward my brigade again.
Question. What did you do?
Answer. Brought it forward as far as Bethlehem Church.
Question. What then?
Answer. I was ordered to encamp there.
Question. You did encamp there?
Answer. Yes.
Question. How long was it after you got the order to fall back to Manassas before you got the order to march back to Bethlehem Church?
Answer. I cannot say exactly, but as soon as I got the order to come forward again I brought the brigade forward and night overtook us at Bethlehem Church—dusk; then we were *ordered to encamp there*

Thus it will be perceived that a considerable time must have elapsed between the time of the order to go to Manassas Junction and the time when that order was received to go forward again—several hours.

Question. So that the order to fall back to Manassas might have been given late in the afternoon, might it not?
Answer. No, sir; I don't think it could have been beyond two o'clock. I have no way of fixing the hour except by my impression of the day, as it looked; and I recollect the heat of the day.
Question. In going back after receiving this order to fall back to Manassas, did you meet troops coming up to the front?
Answer. Yes; we met some troops. We met some of a division.
Question. Whose was it?
Answer. I think it was Ricketts' division. That is my recollection of my inquiries at the time.
Question. At what point was it?
Answer. Near Bethlehem Church; *we turned off to their right.*

So that he must have got back here, between Bethlehem Church and the Sudley road, at the time he met Ricketts.

Question. Did you halt your command at that point?
Answer. I was not with my own command. It had preceded me. They had gone back. I rode back following them.
Question. Were you not left at Warrenton Junction on the 29th to guard a train until the arrival of General Banks? Do you recollect that?
Answer. On the 29th? No, sir.
Question. On the 27th?
Answer. Yes; on the 27th?
Question. You remained there until you were relieved from that duty?
Answer. My orders from General Porter were to march and join him as soon as General Banks would come up, who was bringing up the rear; but inasmuch as General Banks got possession of the road in advance of me, I brought up the rear myself.
Question. Do you recollect about what time of day it was when you reported to General Porter that you were on the ground with your troops?

S G

Answer. Yes; I think it was about the middle of the day. I cannot fix it definitely

Question. Had General Porter's troops then deployed?

Answer. No, sir; they were not deployed; many of them were occupying the road. I don't know what troops were immediately there with them, except a battery.

Question. Did you see his troops deployed in front?

Answer. No, sir; nothing but skirmishers. I saw the skirmish line.

Question. You did not see Morell's division deployed?

Answer. No, sir.

Question. Were you up at the front?

Answer. Yes; it might have been, but I don't recollect now seeing it. I don't recollect that there were any troops deployed.

Redirect examination:

Question. You have stated that you saw Ricketts' division come up toward Bethlehem Church while you were stationed at Manassas Junction?

Answer. No; as I was reaching *Bethlehem Church* on my way back I met it.

Question. As you were going back to Manassas Junction you met Ricketts' division coming up?

Answer. Yes, sir.

Question. Do you recollect any incidents connected with the arrival of General Ricketts' division which impressed that fact on your memory?

Answer. *Yes; I recollect a fact that it struck me as strange that we should be going back while they were apparently going in the direction of the firing off to their right.*

Question. Off toward the Sudley road?

Answer. On the right as they came up from Manassas Junction, off in the direction of the firing.

Question. By looking at the map would you be able to indicate whether it was the Manassas and Sudley road that you refer to?

Answer. That is on so large a scale that I doubt if I could. Ricketts was taking the right-hand road, the Manassas and Sudley road; my impression is it was right at the church; the junction of the roads was as far as I went back. My brigade had moved back to Manassas Junction.

* * * * * * *

Question. Where did you see a battery on the road that you have mentioned when you went up to the front? I understood you to say you saw some battery on the road.

Answer. There was a battery at the point where I reported to General Porter—in that vicinity.

Question. What were the troops of General Porter's corps doing when you saw them?

Answer. I don't recollect that they were doing anything. They were perfectly quiet, apparently waiting.

Question. Were their arms stacked?

Answer. Everybody seemed to be lying around, just the way you do before a battle, in anticipation of news of some movement.

* * * * * *

Question. Was that General Piatt's regular brigade which you brought up?

Answer. It was known as Piatt's brigade; I was not familiar with it. The fact was that there was a division forming for me, and this brigade had been sent down to Warrenton Junction; I was not so familiar with that brigade; I don't know that I had seen it at that time.

* * * * *

Question. How did you learn that those were Ricketts' troops that you saw?

Answer. I simply inquired at the time what troops they were, and was informed—I do not recollect by whom; simply general notoriety at the time.

Question. Were they then on their march toward the Warrenton pike along that Sudley Springs road?

Answer. All I know about them was that they turned off to their right on a road close to the church.

Question. Did you see General McDowell at that point?

Answer. I did; but not at that time.

* * * * *

Question. Did you see General McDowell in that neighborhood that day?

Answer. I met him at Bethel Church on my way up to the front.

Question. When you were going up to General Porter?

Answer. Yes.

Question. You went up to the front. You remained there how long?

Answer. Probably we remained there an hour and a half, or two hours.

Question. Then you came back, and was it when you returned that you saw these troops of General Ricketts moving in the direction toward Warrenton?

Answer. Yes.

By the PRESIDENT OF THE BOARD:

Question. Was it on your return that you met General McDowell?
Answer. When I was going up.
Question. When you were coming up you met General McDowell at Bethlehem Church?
Answer. Yes, sir.
Question. In what direction was he coming?
Answer. He told me where General Porter was; whether he told me he had been up there I don't know. He had just arrived from some point, and told me where General Porter was.
Question. Where did he go then?
Answer. I left him there.
Question. Did you see anything of King's division?
Answer. I did not.
Question. It was when you came back, then, that you saw Ricketts' division?
Answer. We met a division which, on inquiry, we were told was Ricketts'.

It is apparent from this evidence, in connection with what had happened just before off to the right of Dawkins' Branch and the "Manassas and Gainesville" road, towards the Manassas Gap Railroad, that the portion of Morell's division under Griffin which had moved over to the right had been brought back and had been put back on the road, and that the moment petitioner saw any indications of an enemy, irrespective of the number, he actually began to retreat.

Brig. Gen. *A. S. Piatt*, United States Volunteers, of Sturgis' division, also testified as follows (Board's Record, p. 1045):

Question. From Manassas Junction where did you go?
Answer. I was ordered up the Thoroughfare Gap road, and I marched up, as near as I could judge, between three and four miles. I cannot tell exactly the distance. There I was halted by General Sturgis on the left of the railroad.
Question. Left of what railroad?
Answer. The Manassas Gap Railroad.
Question. That road that you went up, what place did it go to or pass through?
Answer. As near as I know, it went through Manassas Gap.
Question. Were there troops in front of you?
Answer. There were troops in front of me. When I came to a halt, there was a brigade or more than a brigade in front of me; they passed a little in front, in fact out of sight of where I was halted.
Question. Whose troops were they?
Answer. I could not say.
Question. Did you hear any firing?
Answer. Yes; I heard firing from 10 o'clock in the day. There was continued firing from the time I left Manassas Junction, according to my remembrance of it, up to the time I halted, and afterwards.
Question. Where was this firing?
Answer. It was to my right and front, as it were. There was less firing out where I was halted. While I was standing there I had time for observation. It was to my right and front, and also to my right and back; I seemed to be perpendicular to two parallel lines of firing.
Question. That which was more nearly in your front, what was it?
Answer. I supposed it to be a Confederate force. While I was standing there were three shots fired, and, as I judged at the time, they were to my right and front, on the right of the road, as I faced up the road. There were three shots fired there that I could see the smoke rise from the guns from where I stood.
Question. Apparently a Confederate battery?
Answer. Yes; where I stood there was quite a number of trees; then there were patches of road; there was an opening, and then there was a screen of trees or timber, not very tall, that screened the position of this artillery which was fired from there. At the time of seeing this position, it struck me as a very favorable one. I did not know at that time that it was the Confederate artillery.
Question. What did you next do?
Answer. The next I did, I was ordered to march to Manassas Junction from that point by General Sturgis.

*　　*　　*　　*　　*

Question. What was the character of the country between you and the battery?
Answer. It was up hill, slightly an elevation.
Question. Go on as near as you can recollect and describe the country.
Answer. The country was undulating, rolling slightly, not very much, from Manas-

sas Junction up to the point I had reached. There was a little depression in the ground that I had passed; and it continued, as I recollect, to rise gradually up to this point where I saw these three columns of smoke that rose from the artillery that was fired.

Question. Did you see any other Confederate force there?

Answer. I saw no Confederate force. I only saw this battery.

Question. Did you form any estimate at the time as to what force would be sufficient to take that battery?

(Objected to.)

Answer. I could not form that estimate, for I did not see the force before me. The only idea that struck me was the feasibility of attacking it.

Question. In the position in which that battery was placed, what opportunities presented themselves to you from your observation, made at the time, for attack?

Answer. As the ground was interspersed over the road with timber, a little opening, and beyond was a screen of woods, and that could have been approached very easily, and any force by open order passed through, it struck me that the battery might have been assaulted without great difficulty.

Question. After you marched back to Manassas Junction, what were the next orders you received?

Answer. I received orders to march back to Manassas Junction. I marched back towards Manassas Junction, but before I reached Manassas Junction I was overtaken by an order to countermarch and march back again, which I did, back to the original position.

Question. What time was that when you got back to your original position?

Answer. It was along towards the close of the evening.

Question. What did you do then?

Answer. I then was ordered into camp for the night.

Question. How long during the day did you hear this firing that you say you heard off to the right?

Answer. I think it was about from ten o'clock in the day, as near as I can recollect, that there was a continued firing, more or less.

Question. Up to what time?

Answer. I think the firing, if I recollect correctly, was until I got back, or nearly back, to the original position. They had ceased before I got quite back.

Question. What was the firing that you heard?

Answer. My remembrance is that it was artillery firing that I heard.

* * * * * * *

Question. How far did you march backward?

Answer. About two-thirds of the distance from my position there, as I judge, to Manassas Junction, before I was ordered back again.

Question. How long did your march take you?

Answer. When I got back it was in the evening.

* * * * * * *

Question. Do you know that that was a Confederate battery at all?

Answer. I judge it was from the direction of the fire, it being perpendicular to where I stood.

Question. Your line formed a right-angle with the two lines?

[Witness indicates the relative situation.]

Question. Was that the only way you inferred that it was a Confederate battery?

Answer. Yes, sir.

Question. Were there any batteries near you that responded?

Answer. No, sir.

Question. There was no response?

Answer. None that I heard; those were the only three shots while I was there.

* * * * * * *

Question. Were you in the vicinity of any large body of troops when you encamped?

Answer. Griffin's brigade was right over the railroad from me when I encamped that evening.

Question. Where was Sykes' regulars?

Answer. I will state this: it was either Griffin's brigade or Sykes' regulars.

Question. Over the railroad—to your left or right?

Answer. That would be to the right of the railroad. In taking the right I am always facing toward the gap.

General McDowell, as we have seen, stated on the original trial that when he and the petitioner went half a mile to the right to the Manassas Gap Railroad the "sound of battle seemed to be at its height."

In the cross-examination on the direct evidence he had given in 1862— not the cross-examination *then* concluded, but that instituted against objection before this Board—General McDowell said (Board's Record, p. 801):

Question. Then if, after you took King away, there was not only a large army of the rebels, twice as large as you thought, between Gainesville and Groveton, but actual information of its being there was brought in the way I have stated to General Porter, would you not consider that he was then bound to act on his own discretion, without regard to the suggestion or direction you had given on leaving him?

* * * * * *

The WITNESS. My opinion at the time was formed upon the belief that in front of General Porter was a force reported by General Buford. If there had been a different force I do not doubt I should have acted differently, but how differently I do not now know.

The question was then repeated.

Answer. I should say to this extent: I do not think it would have justified him in doing nothing. I think he should have made some movement, some tentative operation, at least.

Question. I do not ask you what he should have done.

Answer. You made a certain supposed state of facts. You have supposed a condition of affairs and asked me what should have been done.

Mr. CHOATE. I have asked the witness whether General Porter was then to act on his own discretion, without regard to the suggestion or direction that General McDowell had given to him.

The WITNESS. No. If that is the way you put it I will say this: I concede that at the time I left General Porter, and for some short time previous to that, he was subject to my orders. If I had given him an order, my separating from him—but that is a question for this Board to determine—but if he were under my command at that time, and I at that time had power to give him a valid order, I think that my separating and going away from him would not have relieved him from the operations of that order, and he should have carried it out without it was either countermanded by some superior authority, or that the execution of it became impossible.

Question. Didn't you think that when you left him he was left to the unrestrained operations of General Pope's joint order?

Answer. No, sir; as modified by me. It is for the Board to decide that question.

Question. Suppose that General Porter ascertained after you left him that the rebel force in front of him was twice what you had supposed it to be and spoken of to him, and twice Porter's own force, do you think then that he should have made an attack?

Answer. I think he should have found out the force.

Question. You say he should have tested and found out the force?

Answer. I think so; that is a question for this Board.

Question. Now, having tested and found out a force quite as large as his own, do you think he should have attacked them?

Answer. He should have made some tentative operations. There are a number of ways of attacking. You attack headlong, or you skirmish, or you shell. But to do nothing whatever certainly would not be complying with the order—to make no effort with the troops.

Question. Now, I ask you, if after making efforts necessary for the purpose he had ascertained there was a force there double his own, after you left him and took King away, do you say that he should have attacked?

Answer. He should have made an attack, yes.

Question. He should have made an attack just as you ordered it?

Answer. My order was, I confess to you, a very vague one. It was made to a person whose zeal and activity and energy I had every knowledge of—I did not pretend to give him any particular instructions or directions that he should skirmish, or shell, or charge, or anything of the sort; I merely indicated the direction in which his troops should be applied. Further than that I did not think and would not think now if I had the thing to go over again to direct.

Question. You did not construe it as an order given by you to an inferior general?

Answer. Certainly I did.

Question. What did you mean, then, by giving orders that were vague and amounted to nothing?

Answer. I did not say that.

Question. Well, gave orders of the kind you have described?

Answer. What orders?

Question. What did you mean by giving orders "vague," and merely an indication?

Answer. I meant just what I said: that General Porter commanded a corps. I did not tell him that he should deploy so many troops, or that he should put in so many skirmishers, or so many batteries, and do this, that, or the other. Those are questions of detail which as an army corps commander he was to carry out. All I did was to give line to his operations.

Question. You meant that with the indication you gave him he should act on his own discretion?

Answer. Yes; but he should act.

*   *   *   *   *

Question. Would it not make a difference, in your opinion, as to the probable result of an attack by General Porter, whether the rebel force in front of him was confined to the troops mentioned in Buford's dispatch, or was an army twice as great?

Answer. Yes, sir.

The RECORDER. I submit before that is answered that this is a line of questioning that is foreign to my direct examination.

The PRESIDENT OF THE BOARD. I understand that this cross-examination is upon his original testimony.

The RECORDER. I submit to the Board that he has no right to that.

The PRESIDENT OF THE BOARD. It is already decided.

Question. On page 95 you said:

"Question. Had the accused made a vigorous attack with his force on the right flank of the enemy at any time before the battle closed, would or would not, in your opinion, the decisive result in favor of the Union army, of which you have spoken, have followed?

"Answer. I think it would."

That was in reference to what you had said about five or six o'clock, namely:

"Question. What would probably have been the effect upon the fortunes of that battle if between five and six o'clock in the afternoon General Porter, with his whole force, had thrown himself upon the right wing of the enemy, as directed in this order of 4.30 p. m. of the 29th of August, which has been read to you?

*   *   *   *   *

"Answer. I think it would have been decisive in our favor."

Would it not have made a difference, in your opinion, on those questions, if General Porter's attack was to be made, not upon the force mentioned in Buford's dispatch, but upon the whole of Longstreet's army of twice that number?

Answer. You will understand that that attack there, at least as it was propounded to me for an opinion, was to be an attack in conjunction with the attack made along the Warrenton pike, or with the forces that were confronting what was known as Jackson's force. If you read a little farther on that same question, and give the whole of what I said there, and give all the bases I then gave of the opinion that was asked of me—it was that, even if there were a superior force opposed to General Porter, he should have attacked that superior force; that he would have withdrawn the enemy from and relieved the front of another part of the line.

Question. Would it make no difference, in your opinion, whether he had 12,000 or 25,000 troops in front of him?

Answer. Of course.

Question. It would just make the difference between decisive in our favor and not being decisive?

Answer. I will not say that.

Question. What difference would it have made?

Answer. I cannot tell you.

Question. No man can tell, can he?

Answer. No, sir. Let me say this: If the main contest was equally balanced, and under those circumstances an attack by 10,000 men had been vigorously made, it certainly would have turned the scale in our favor.

*   *   *   *   *

Question. * * * Did you intend that he should get into a general engagement with the enemy while you were removed from the scene back on the Sudley road so as to be out of all possibility of rendering him immediate assistance?

Answer. When I left General Porter I left him a corps commander, for him to operate in the direction indicated. How quickly he was to get in an engagement, whether an hour or an hour and a half, and how he would do it, whether in one way or another, I did not indicate, nor did I take it into my mind; it was simply that he was to operate on the left, and necessarily when he got over there the nature of his operations would be determined by the condition of things that he would find. What those conditions would be, I could not at that time tell. As to saying that I did not want him to do any fighting until I got around to a certain place, I made no such calculations.

Question. I ask you what you expected or intended?

Answer. I say what I expected or intended.

Question. You did not expect that he should become engaged with the enemy until you should get around on the left of Reynolds?

Answer. Yes, I did.

It will be observed, in reference to these questions so skillfully put by the very able counsel who cross-examined General McDowell here on his "original" testimony, that he has been asking him as to what he expected or supposed the petitioner was to do. But that I submit was not and is not the light in which it is to be taken. We are to take the words and acts of General McDowell, what he said to the petitioner, and what the petitioner did under those orders that were given him, as indicating what was expected, or supposed, or understood. What he might have had in his mind might have been very different from the language that he used. I merely invite attention to this line of questioning on the part of the petitioner; it, in my judgment, has no bearing upon the case. However, upon examining the language that General McDowell swore on the trial he did use, and the acts of the petitioner immediately afterwards in simulating to do precisely what General McDowell had told him to do, we find that the orders of General McDowell at that time correspond exactly with what he says, namely, that the petitioner was *to attack*.

We have now concluded as to what petitioner did on the 29th August in the way of developing the enemy's strength except as to his dispatches. If the petitioner knew then all he claims to know now as to this force, it is certain that he did not communicate his knowledge to General McDowell; and his dispatches to and from his officers, to which he refers as being some of the sources of his information, do not warrant the claim he has made that he *then* knew of this assumedly large force being on General Jackson's right, or whose it was.

From his skirmish or picket line was certainly the quarter from whence such information in this case had to be obtained, yet those who were out there gave no evidence of it.

See Morell's dispatch No. 30, where he says:

GENERAL: Colonel Marshall reports that two batteries have come down in the woods on our right, towards the railroad, and two regiments of infantry on the road. If this is so it will be hot here in the *morning*.

See Colonel Marshall's report to General Morell (No. 34), where he says, late in the day:

GENERAL MORELL: The enemy must be in a much larger force than I can see. From the commands of the officers I should judge a *brigade*. They are endeavoring to come in on our left, and have been advancing. Have also heard the noise on the left as the movement of artillery. Their advance is quite close.

In these there is nothing to indicate the knowledge it is claimed was then possessed of this large force of Longstreet; two batteries and two regiments in one instance, and at least a brigade in another.

And petitioner did not give evidence of such knowledge when, late in the afternoon, he gave his order to push up "two regiments supporting two others to attack" (see dispatch No. 37), at, as he says, about 6 p. m.

Petitioner claims that by his course he held in check a force of the enemy at least double his own, and thus saved Pope from total defeat. But in the reports of their operations on the 29th, Generals Stuart and Longstreet both concur in stating that, after they had taken preliminary measures to resist petitioner's advance, he, after firing a few shots, retired—one said to Manassas—and thereafter they were not materially influenced by him.

They were however in error as to petitioner's having gone to Manassas; he had only been successful in "putting everything out of their sight"; and, it will be seen, so far as his force was concerned, out of their minds as well. Part of his troops did go back to near there.

I have already said that in my judgment Longstreet's testimony as to having about 25,000 men more or less on the ground or near it, most of the 29th, was not an important element in this case.

The question is solely what petitioner knew was in front of him. *His own exhibits are conclusive against him.*

In dispatch No. 30, Major-General Morell stated two batteries and two regiments to have come down on their right, and then hazards the remark, based on this report, "If this be so, it will be hot here in the morning," showing conclusively that at *that* time Longstreet was not thought to be in force in his front.

It was sufficient, however, for the accused, and immediately the gallant Fifth Corps was put out of sight, and part ordered to fall back to Manassas Junction, several miles distant.

In this connection it seems pertinent to ask why No. 33 was sent, viz:

GENERAL MORELL: Hold on if you can to your present place. What is passing?

This does not betray much confidence in his *defensive* position, nor that he himself was in a place where he could know what was going on nor his corps ready to resist assault.

If there was danger of being crushed, why instead of writing did he not go at once to the front?

It seems certain that he made no sustained, or vigorous, or even fitful effort to ascertain during that day the strength of the force opposed, as he claims, to him, or to establish communication between his corps and the left of General Pope's army.

To say that because he then or now believes the force on his front to have been very much greater than his own, and to offer such statement as an excuse for failing to go to the aid of General Pope's army or failing to attack is in derogation of the traditions and history of the American army, some of whose most glorious victories have been won against superiority of numbers, or apparently insurmountable obstacles. Major-General Jackson at New Orleans, Taylor at Buena Vista, Scott at Lundy's Lane and in his battles from Vera Cruz to the city of Mexico, and Grant in the Wilderness campaign are pertinent illustrations of the point raised.

Mr. Pendergrast in his "Law relating to Officers in the Army" (revised edition, 1854, p. 53), says:

The duty of military obedience to the commands of superior officers is most fully recognized by courts of law; and it has been held that disobedience never admits of *justification;* that nothing but the physical impossibility of obeying an order can excuse the non-performance of it; and that when such impossibility is proved, the charge of disobedience falls to the ground. The learning on this subject is to be found in the great case of Sutton *vs.* Johnstone (1st Term Reports, p. 548), which was an action by Captain Sutton, of His Majesty's ship Isis, against Commodore Johnstone, for arresting and imprisoning him on charges of misconduct and disobedience to orders in the action with the French squadron under M. Suffrein, in Porto Praya Bay, in the year 1782; and there the two chief justices, Lord Mansfield and Lord Loughborough, laid down the law in the following terms:

A subordinate officer must not judge of the danger, propriety, expediency, or consequence of the order he receives; he must obey; nothing can excuse him but a physical impossibility.

A forlorn hope is devoted; many gallant officers have been devoted.

Fleets have been saved and victories obtained by ordering particular ships upon desperate services, with almost a certainty of death or capture.

Mr. Pendergrast in his citation makes the reservation always understood that the order given is not manifestly and clearly illegal.

The General in Chief of the American Army (Sherman), in referring to this principle of obedience to orders in action (24th February, 1870), re-enunciated the rule laid down by the two eminent lord chief justices, for he said "that the stronger the force of the enemy present at the time the officer received the orders, the greater the necessity for him and his troops to pitch in, even if roughly handled, to relieve, *pro tanto*, the other forces engaged."

WAS THERE A BATTLE ON THE 29TH?

One of the most astonishing things in the petitioner's case is the effort he has made to prove no battle on the 29th August, and to do this he has brought several officers to testify they did not hear any.

It is necessary for petitioner to establish this, because, as the Count de Paris said, in a letter dated 8th October, 1876:

Under his first instructions, his duty would have been to attack the large and well-posted forces of the enemy which he unexpectedly met near the railroad only in two cases:

1. If he had received from a superior the positive orders to do so.
2. If he had been aware that a great battle was raging near enough for him to take a direct or indirect part in it.

In this case it will be perceived the Count assumes a large force in presence of petitioner.

Was there a battle *raging* that day? Let the official reports, Union and Confederate, which form part of the evidence now on file in the War Department, attest the fact.

The theory of the petitioner on this head is the theory of civilians without military experience—one like his 27th August theory, that the night was too dark, &c., for him to even undertake to begin earnestly to obey a peremptory order.

This petitioner was as much convicted by the evidence he himself brought on his original trial as by that of government.

Take, for example, the 4.30 p. m. order, to move at once into action. Where was he when he got it?

He was 2⅔ miles from his front, at the forks of the Sudley Church and Manassas and Gainesville roads,

Brigadier-General *Sykes* was with him. and, on the original trial, testified to the receipt of a written order from General Pope and then answered on cross-examination as follows (G. C. M. Record, p. 178):

Question. Did General Porter make known to you the character of that order?
Answer. He did not.
Question. Did he read it in your presence?
Answer. Not that I know of.

* * * * * *

Question. How long did you remain with General Porter on that occasion after the receipt of that order?
Answer. I continued with him from that time all night.

One thing may be considered as quite certain, and that is, if the petitioner had at any time, from the moment of receipt of that imperative order, any intention *loyally* to obey it, he would have acquainted his division commander and personal friend.

It is almost an insult to the memory of the Union dead who fell on that field that day, while obeying orders, to discuss the question as to whether there was a battle.

No effort has been made here by me to ascertain the actual losses. General Pope, in his official report (introduced by petitioner), estimated them, from the reports he received, at six or eight thousand killed and wounded.

Maj. Gen. *Hooker*, says that his division alone, of Heintzelman's corps lost between 1,000 and 1,200 men (Board's Record, p. 947), and Maj. Gen. *Franz Sigel* swears that his own corps lost about 1,400 or 1,500 men. If to these losses are added those equally severe in Kearney's division of Heintzelman's corps, and Maj. Gen. Reno's division of Burnside's corps, together with the heavy losses experienced by King's division, under Hatch, of McDowell's corps—without considering the losses in Reynold's division of McDowell's command, one of whose brigades, under Brig. Gen. G. G. Meade, very late in the day (Board's Record, p. 500) got seriously into action while supporting King's attack, it will be seen that General Pope's rough estimate was very near, if not below, the actual loss.

The battle, like most of the battles of the war of the rebellion, consisted in a series of detached assaults, instead of a united movement, until late in the day.

Whether, in a military sense, this was the best under the circumstances, or whether different strategical or tactical movements would have resulted in greater advantage to the national arms, is a question wholly foreign to this case, which is as to what petitioner did or failed to do under his orders.

In the afternoon—after the 4.30 order had been sent him—the commanding general endeavored to make a combined attack. Why it was not completely successful will be found explained in petitioner's inaction.

Capt. *A. M. Randol*, First United States Artillery, Fifth Corps, a witness for petitioner, says (Board's Record, p. 94) he heard artillery firing occasionally during the day, sometimes quite heavy, evidently batteries engaging one another.

Heard no infantry firing until evening, and then "a very severe infantry fire, which attracted the attention of everybody as being very severe, and evidently considerable fighting going on over towards Groveton."

At that time, according to his evidence, he was back where the petitioner was, near the forks of the Sudley Springs and the Manassas and Gainesville road.

Lieut. *S. M. Weld*, petitioner's then aide-de-camp, admits (p. 268) that when General McDowell and the petitioner moved over to the railroad he could see "shells bursting high in the air." Severe artillery fire at times.

Col. *George D. Ruggles*, assistant adjutant-general, U. S. A., then chief of staff to Major-General Pope, was called by petitioner on the original trial, and said (G. C. M. Record, p. 159):

Question by Court. Was or not the musketry fire, on the 29th August, which you have spoken of in your testimony, indicative of a severe engagement between large bodies of men?

Answer. The musketry fire was; but I desire to say that I did not hear the musketry firing myself until I came on the ground. The musketry firing which I heard after I came on the ground indicated an engagement between large bodies of men.

Commissary Sergeant *John Bond*, First Maryland Cavalry Volunteers, Sigel's Corps (Board's Record, p. 882), government witness, saw three distinct charges in the afternoon about one or two o'clock.

Capt. *LeGrand Benedict*, assistant adjutant-general, Carr's brigade, Hooker's division, Heintzelman's corps (Board's Record, p. 934), government witness, read from the official report of Col. Joseph B. Carr, commanding, as follows:

　　　　　Headquarters Third Brigade, Hooker's Division,
　　　　　　　　Camp near Fort Lyon, Virginia,
　　　　　　　　　　　　September 6, 1862.

*　　*　　*　　*　　*　　*　　*　　*

At two (2) o'clock Friday morning, August 29, I received orders to march at three a. m. and support General Kearney who was in pursuit of the enemy. A march of ten miles brought us to the Bull Run battle-field. About eleven (11) a. m. was ordered in position to support a battery in front of the woods, where the enemy with General

Sigel's troops was engaged. Remaining about one hour in that position, was ordered to send into the woods and relieve two regiments of General Sigel's corps. I went in the 6th and 7th New Jersey Volunteers. Afterwards received orders to take the balance of the brigade in the woods, which I did at about two (2) p. m. Here I at once engaged the enemy, and fought him for a space of two hours, holding my position *until our ammunition was all expended.* About four (4) o'clock we were relieved by General Reno and Colonel Taylor, but did not reach the skirt of the woods before a retreat was made and the woods occupied by the enemy. When I arrived out of the woods I was ordered to march about half a mile to the rear and bivouac for the night.

The witness assisted in preparing the report, and knew of its accuracy.

Col. *M. B. Lakeman,* commanding Third Maine Volunteers, Second Brigade, First Division, Heintzelman's corps, said (p. 934) there was "very severe fighting on our front the whole time."

His regiment went into action three times; once at 11 a. m., again at 12 m., and again at three p. m. There was continuous fighting all the time, from 11 up to dark, in his own brigade. (Board's Record, p. 935.)

B. F. Butterfield, Sixty-third Pennsylvania Volunteers, Robinson's brigade, Kearney's division, Heintzelman's corps, said they arrived on the field about noon (Board's Record, p. 939). "Before we went into action there was an incessant firing on our left, and had been ever since we arrived on the field—heavy infantry firing." This corresponds with what Captain Monteith, General McDowell, Dr. Faxon, and Captain Hatch have said, who could see the bursting of the shells.

Maj. Gen. *Franz Sigel* (Board's Record, p. 940) says the greater part of his corps was in action the whole day until evening.

Bvt. Brig. Gen. *Thomas F. McCoy,* colonel One hundred and seventh Pennsylvania Volunteers, Duryea's brigade, Ricketts' division, McDowell's corps, says (Board's Record, p. 642) they left Gainesville at daylight, and heard heavy cannonading when they left Manassas Junction.

Question. In going up from Manassas Junction toward Sudley Church, on that road, what indications, if any, were there of an action on Friday the 29th?
Answer. Heavy cannonading. We heard, as I remarked before, heavy cannonading when we left Manassas Junction, which continued until we arrived within view of part of the movements and actions; we could then see the infantry on the left of Pope's line.
Question. What could you see going on?
Answer. When we came in view on a prominent piece of ground where the road passed, we saw the left of Pope's line advancing partly on a charge into a wood or to a wood; there was cheering from their troops and ours.
Question. You mean Ricketts' division?
Answer. Yes. There was a good deal of excitement about that time among the soldiers.
Question. What musketry firing was there, if any?
Answer. There was musketry firing at that time. That was about the closing of the day.
Question. About where was your regiment at that time, would you say, upon the road?
Answer. I don't know whether I could show it upon the map or not. It was a prominent piece of ground upon the Sudley road that gives a good view of the battleground—a pretty good view of it. When we came there we first saw the infantry.

That I assume to be the Henry house hill, where we find from other evidence that General McDowell's corps was encamped that night.

Question. As to this cannonading that you heard from early in the morning, what was the character of it, heavy or intermittent?
Answer. Sometimes it was heavy.
Question. Did you see any troops, other than of your own division, when you were at Manassas Junction?
Answer. Yes, sir.
Question. Whose troops were they?
Answer. I understood them to be General Porter's corps.

Question. At that time?
Answer. Yes.
Question. When you first arrived at Manassas Junction, was the cannonading then in progress, or had it ceased?
Answer. I don't recollect now about that.

Maj. Gen. *Samuel P. Heintzelman*, U. S. A. (retired), then United States Volunteers, kept a diary, in which he noted the time of events. He says (Board's Record, p. 610):

Question. Will you read to the Board from the diary those events which you noted at the time, August 29, 1862?
Answer. "Centreville, Friday, August 29, 1862: Kearney did not get off until after daylight" that night; the night before the 29th General Kearney was advanced as far as Centreville. I think General Pope was quite near on the opposite side of the river from Centreville. In the night an order came for Kearney to advance at 1 a. m. and attack the enemy. Hooker at 3 a. m. was to support him. The report was General McDowell had intercepted the enemy, and the next morning I started at daylight as I was directed. When I got to where Kearney was, his division had not started, and he was killed not long afterward, before I made my report.
Question. Now, will you be good enough to read what you made notes of on the 29th of August, as to the events of that day?
The witness read as follows:
"Kearney did not get off till after daylight. We are all detained by him. There is a heavy cloud of dust on the road to Leesburg, upon which the rebels are retreating or rather advancing. It is now a quarter past 7 a. m.; arrived at the bridge at 9 a. m. Firing commenced some two hours ago and has just ceased. Report that we are driving the enemy. At 10 a. m. reached the field, a mile from the stone bridge. Firing going on, and I called upon General Sigel. General Kearney was at the right. Part of General Hooker's division I sent to support some of Sigel's troops. General Hooker got up about 11 a. m.; General Reno nearly an hour later. Soon after General Pope arrived—about quarter to two. I rode to the old Bull Run battle-field, where my troops were. The enemy we drove back in the direction of Sudley's Church, and they are now making another stand. We are hoping for McDowell and Porter. *I fear we will be out of ammunition.* We have sent for it. At 3½ p. m. our troops driven back. At forty-five minutes past three McDowell's troops reported arrived. Firing closed at fifteen minutes past four. At half past four General Reynolds's troops arrived. Five p. m. our troops engaged on the enemy's right. Twenty minutes past five p. m., musketry firing commenced on our center. General Kearney has held his position. Forty-five minutes past five General McDowell on the field at headquarters. Heavy firing on our center. Kearney reports he is driving the enemy back. GENERAL PORTER REPORTS THE REBELS DRIVING HIM BACK, AND HE RETIRING ON MANASSAS. Twenty minutes past six very heavy musketry and artillery. McDowell's troops just entering the battlefield. Kearney on the right with General Stevens's troops, and our artillery drove the enemy out of the woods they temporarily occupied. The firing continued until after night, but left us in possession of the battlefield."

Bvt. Maj. Gen. *William Birney*, U. S. Vols., testified as follows (Board's Record, p. 681):

Question. What was the character of the action from twelve o'clock noon until the sun set?
Answer. My recollection is that, with occasional lulls in the firing, there was some heavy firing. The artillery was sounding all the time, and there was repeated and very heavy musketry firing. It was not an action as heavy as the one of the day following, but if I had not witnessed the one of the day following I should have thought the one of the day before very heavy.

* * * * *

Question. What I want to get at is whether there was any continuous musketry firing beginning at the time you first approached that battlefield up to the night, indicating a general engagement along the whole line?
Answer. I should say that in the morning the firing was that of a series of assaults and skirmishes—at least more of that character; occasional pretty heavy musketry; and in the afternoon it had more the sound of a continuous battle, although even then there were intermissions, as in a battle.
Question. I understand you that you were on General Kearney's extreme right?
Answer. Yes, sir.

* * * * *

Question. At other times than these you speak of, towards the middle and towards the close of the afternoon, about how large a force of infantry was at any one time engaged, as indicated by the sound and smoke which you heard and saw?

Answer. Do you mean on both sides?

Question. On our side.

Answer. I should not think there were over 8,000 or 10,000 at a time.

Question. You speak of a period somewhat near the middle of the afternoon when there was a somewhat general engagement, as I understand you?

Answer. My impression is that towards the close of the afternoon the fighting became more persistent—along about four o'clock.

Question. This persistent and more extended attack, as indicated to you by the sound and the smoke, was then towards the close of the afternoon?

Answer. Yes, sir.

Question. About what hour would you say?

Answer. I should think from four on there was a good deal more firing.

Question. How long did it continue?

Answer. The heaviest firing, of course, did not continue a great while at its heaviest point.

Question. I mean this *general* engagement in the latter part of the day.

Answer. My impression is that it was after four o'clock.

Bvt. Brig. Gen. *Charles Barnes*, then captain Ninth Pennsylvania Reserves, Reynolds' division, McDowell's command, testified as follows (Board's Record, p. 661): "There was a heavy contest going on on our right all day, or nearly all day." Heavy infantry firing at 3.

Bvt. Maj. Gen. *Abner Doubleday*, U. S. A., commanding brigade, King's division, McDowell's corps (Board's Record, p. 688), speaks of of the heavy fighting between five and six p. m., of his division.

Capt. George Shorkley, Fifteenth United States Infantry, then adjutant Fifty-first Pennsylvania Volunteers, Ferreros' brigade, Reno's division (Board's Record, p. 689), answered as follows:

Question by RECORDER. In the afternoon, say from twelve o'clock up to sunset, what was the character of the action?

Answer. Decidedly heavy fighting in the evening. * * * In the middle of the afternoon we were fighting and we were then moving up to a new position.

Bvt. Brig. Gen. *Rufus R. Dawes*, Sixth Wisconsin Volunteers, Gibbon's brigade, King's division, McDowell's corps, testified as follows (Board's Record, p. 834):

·Question. Where were you on the morning of August 29, 1862?

Answer. We retreated from King's engagement and arrived near Manassas Junction. about daybreak on the morning of the 29th.

Question. Did you see any other troops there during that morning aside from your own division; if so, what?

Answer. During the morning I saw the corps of General Porter.

Question. Which direction were they taking?

Answer. They were moving along parallel with the Manasses Gap Railroad in the direction of the battle.

Question. Which direction do you mean by that?

Answer. That is about the position we occupied [between the forks of the Manassas and Gainesville road and Manassas Junction] when we were in bivouac alongside the Manassas Gap Railroad. The corps of General Porter passed by, going up in that direction. [Up the Manassas and Gainesville road.]

Question. At what time did they pass you?

Answer. About nine o'clock.

Question. While you were there, what indications were there, if any, of a battle that day?

Answer. *At that time there was artillery, and during the day at different times there was musketry. It is my recollection that there was musketry firing about the time that General Fitz-John Porter's troops passed up, for the reason that our men talked with those troops in regard to the battle that they expected to take part in—that appeared to be in progress at that time.*

Question. How long did you hear during that day artillery and musketry firing?

Answer. My recollection is at intervals all day.

Brig. and Bvt. Maj. Gen. *Jos. B. Carr*, United States Volunteers, commanding Third Brigade, Hooker's division, Heintzelman's corps, says (Board's Record, p. 836) his brigade marched from Blackburn's Ford and was at the Matthews house about 11 a. m., supporting some batteries. There was, up to 12, firing in front and scattering infantry fire; that

Generals Sigel and Schurz reported to him that their ammunition was all expended, and he sent in his brigade to their relief and became immediately engaged and expended all their ammunition and had to send for more.

About 2 p. m. a general attack took place.

Question. Then that contest, within your own knowledge, or battle, extended from what time to what time during that day?

Answer. I should judge from the appearance of the woods that I had entered about twelve o'clock with my command, that they had been engaged all the morning—from the appearance of the woods and the wounded and dead; there were a great many wounded and dead.

Question. Federal?

Answer. Yes, sir.

Question. Have you been in other actions?

Answer. Yes; several of them.

Question. How would you characterize that battle as to severity, and the proportion of loss of those engaged?

Answer. Along our front I should say that it was as hotly a contested battle as I had been in, with one or two exceptions. I would except Gettysburg and Chancellorsville. Our loss was not as heavy there as in those other battles, although it was very severe.

Question. On the 29th?

Answer. Yes, sir.

Bvt. Brig. Gen. *James M. Deems*, then major First Maryland Cavalry, on General Sigel's staff, has described (Board's Record, p. 839) a charge of the enemy on General Schurz's division, about 11 or 12 o'clock.

Brig. and Bvt. Maj. Gen. *G. W. Mindil*, then assistant adjutant-general to Kearney's division, Heintzelman's corps, says (Board's Record, p. 845), that before his division reached the field, which was about 9 or 9½ a. m., the indications of a battle were wounded men coming to the rear, "and a considerable number of Confederate prisoners."

At noon, when he reached the extreme right of the army in view of the battle-field, there was some infantry fighting going on by the troops of General Carl Schurz's division, and considerable cannonading.

Question by RECORDER. Do you understand that the battle continued pretty much all day?

Answer. There were no intermissions. * * *

First Lieut. *Wm. Conway*, Twenty-second United States Infantry, then Seventy-fourth New York Volunteers, Taylor's brigade, Hooker's division, says (Board's Record, p. 847) his brigade made a charge about 4 p. m.

The action was very severe; men were knocked down with stones.

When we come to look at the evidence of some Confederates of Jackson's command, we will find that they were considerably out of ammunition at that time.

Brig. Gen. *Gilman Marston*, United States Volunteers, then colonel Second New Hampshire Volunteers, Grover's brigade (Board's Record, p. 859). He was in Brig. Gen. Cuvier Grover's heroic bayonet charge and lost 123 out of 300 men. He says that from twelve o'clock up to between three and four there was a little musketry fire on each side of their position at Peach Grove (Dogan House,) and some artillery firing to the left.

(Board's Record, p. 860.) There was pretty heavy artillery firing a little to the left at dark.

That artillery firing was evidently the firing of Cooper's battery, Meade's brigade, Reynolds' division, in order to be at the left of the position of Brigadier-General Marston.

Capt. *James Haddow*, Thirty-sixth Ohio Volunteers, said as follows (Board's Record, p. 875):

* * * On the morning of the 29th we were at Manassas Junction.
Question (by RECORDER.) Did you hear any firing that morning? If so, where and in what direction?
Answer. We did not leave there very early; we were waiting for orders; the major under whom we were conveying these supplies would go off to get orders; we must have remained there until near nine o'clock. In going from the station out toward a large building which the troops who were there said was McDowell's headquarters or had been, there was considerable cannonading, partially to our rear and off to the left. I recollect distinctly, as we went out toward that building [Weir house], there were quite a number of people at the building looking toward the direction of the battle; we ourselves could see the smoke; there was considerable cannonading some time between daylight and eight or nine o'clock.

Asst. Adjt. Gen. *Hazard Stevens*, United States Volunteers, Stevens' brigade, Reno's division, Burnside's corps (Board's Record, p. 524), refers to four assaults known by him to have been made by the national troops on the enemy's lines, viz, one by his brigade, one by Hooker's division, one by Kearney's division, and one by Nichols' brigade of Reno's division.

Bvt. Maj. Gen. *George H. Gordon* United States Volunteers, Third Brigade, First Division, Banks' Corps, introduced by petitioner (January 3, 1879), says, substantially, that the sounds of the battle of the 29th were heard in Major-General Banks' corps, and alludes to their anxiety as to the result.

Lieut. *Stephen M. Weld*, formerly petitioner's aide-de-camp, who was called on his behalf, testified to going with petitioner and General McDowell from Dawkins' Branch to the Manassas Gap Railroad (Board's Record, p. 268), and says that while there he could both hear and see the firing—

Severe at times; then it would slacken off and be slight, and then start off again.
* * * In a northerly direction we could see the shells bursting high in the air, which would indicate it somewhere about Groveton.

Despite *this* witness' testimony, the petitioner has severely criticised General McDowell for saying there was a battle raging.

We see, however, by Lieutenant Weld, who was there, the petitioner's own witness, that there *was* a battle raging to the right.

Brig. Gen. *I. H. Duvall*, United States Volunteers, then major First West Virginia Volunteers, says (Board's Record, p. 861) he went into action with Milroy's brigade at 8 a. m., or earlier, and in referring to the battle said, "It was a severe one at the start." He witnessed one assault about 2 or 3 p. m. Some fighting, more or less, all day.

Maj. Gen. *Gershom Mott*, United States Volunteers, then colonel Sixth New Jersey Volunteers, Third Brigade, Kearney's division, Heintzelman's corps says (p. 868) he arrived on the field at noon and heard artillery firing to the left.

Bvt. Brig. Gen. *H. E. Tremaine*, United States Volunteers, then acting assistant adjutant-general Taylor's brigade, Hooker's division, same corps, says he arrived on the field a little before noon (Board's Record, p. 869).

The troops on the left, which I at that time understood to be General Sigel's, were pretty actively engaged. The troops off to the right, under Kearney, as I then understood, were more or less engaged.

Maj. *Oliver C. Bosbyshell*, then captain, Forty-eighth Pennsylvania Volunteers, first brigade, second division (Reno's) of the Ninth Corps (Burnside's) (Board's Record, p. 872), says his regiment went into action at three and lost one-fifth of the men.

Capt. *John C. Brown*, Twentieth Indiana Volunteers, Robinson's brigade, Kearney's division, Heintzelman's corps, says (p. 873) "There was heavy infantry firing on our left and we expected it to strike us." His regiment lost about a hundred.

Maj. Gen. *John C. Robinson*, U. S. A. (retired), then brigadier-general commanding brigade in Kearney's division, says his brigade lost 578 men (Board's Record, p. 834).

The record shows other witnesses to the fact that there was a battle on the 29th August, but these citations seem sufficient to show that there was fighting all day, artillery and infantry, and on Sigel's front particularly from noon to 3½ p. m.

Maj. *Samuel N. Benjamin*, assistant adjutant-general, U. S. A., then first lieutenant commanding Battery E, Second United States Artillery, says he got into action as near as he can recollect about 1 p. m. at Groveton, and for two hours was actively engaged with eighteen guns of the enemy ranging from 1,000 to 1,500 yards from him (Board's Record, p. 613), and that they soon brought in eight more against him.

In discussing a military question it is quite needless to say that the heavy fire of artillery is generally but a prelude to the infantry assault at the moment when the opposing forces are broken or the opposing fire silenced.

It may be that the infantry will remain hours in expectation of such opportunity while the cannonading continues. Therefore it is the duty of co-operating forces to be ready and to move into action, in order to create such a diversion as will enable the main attack to be successful.

CONFEDERATE ACCOUNTS OF BATTLE.

When we look at the Confederate accounts of the battle of the 29th August, 1862, we find them in perfect accord with those of the Union commanders on the question whether there was a battle that day or not.

In his official report to the Confederate Government of this day's battle, the late General *Robert E. Lee* said (Board's Record, p. 520), "*the battle raged with great fury*"; that, in one part of the field, there were "*several hours of severe fighting*"; that the "contest was close and obstinate"; that "the enemy was repeatedly repulsed, but again pressed on the attack with fresh troops"; that "the battle continued until 9 p. m."; that it was "the darkness of the night" which "put a stop to the engagement," and that his "loss was severe."

All through the report he uses the expressions "battle was raging," "warmly engaged," and "severe contest," showing how this superior military critic viewed the battle of the 29th (Board's Record, p. 519).

Maj. Gen. *A. P. Hill*, in his report to Maj. Gen. T. J. Jackson, dated 25th February, 1863, speaks of the repulse of "six distinct and separate assaults, a portion of the time the men being without a cartridge," and says that "soon his reserves were all in."

A critical examination of all the Confederate reports will not prove uninstructive in this connection.

In examining the testimony of "Confederate" witnesses before this Board, we find further corroboration.

Henry Kyd Douglass, formerly major and assistant adjutant-general to the Confederate General T. J. Jackson, called by government, testified as follows (Board's Record, p. 704):

Question. The force that advanced against A. P. Hill's division—what was its character as to strength and numbers?
Answer. Well, being on the other side, it would be difficult for me to determine. Whether it was attacked by divisions or brigades, I really do not know; but there

were a number of attacks made, not less, I should suppose, than half a dozen, at different times.

Question. How were those attacks carried on?

Answer. Those attacks were vigorous dashes; brief, but *very determined, and very gallant.*

Question. How close did the opposing lines get?

Answer. Very close. Our line was driven back once or twice; then they moved forward again.

Question. What was the character of losses of that day's battle—heavy or light?

Answer. I think the loss in A. P. Hill's division was heavy enough to be called serious; I should not say it was very heavy or very disastrous.

Question. I understand you to say that the battle lasted from between two and three o'clock up to what time?

Answer. Dark. There was some little skirmishing or firing after dark, but you cannot call it an attack.

Question. About what time did the final attack begin upon your lines?

Answer. Do you mean the last assault?

Question. Yes. There were a series of attacks, one after the other?

Answer. Yes; at different intervals. The first attack was something after two; the last may have been about sundown.

Question. Were the attacks made by heavy bodies of troops or by a light body, comparatively?

Answer. The attacks covered Hill's division front; with what commands they were made on the other side, I would have hesitation in saying; they were vigorous.

* * * * * *

Question. At the close of the day's action, on the 29th August, do you recollect what was the state of the supply of ammunition in your division?

Answer. General A. P. Hill was in a very bad way. His ammunition was in some brigades almost entirely exhausted.

James Longstreet, late lieutenant-general in the Confederate army, so called, says (Board's Record, p. 62):

At the time we approached, General Jackson was engaged making a very severe fight * * * a severe artillery combat going on * * * Infantry fight lasted from about 5 o'clock until dark. * * * Knew of no terrific battle raging that day with continuous fury from daylight until after dark that day.

He previously said:

I did not note the time by my watch of any occurrence of that field.

He thus disputes the accuracy of Robert E. Lee's report, but in his own official report dated near Winchester, Va., 10th October, 1862, (Board's Record, p. 521), he said, after describing his march to join Jackson after passing through Thoroughfare Gap on the 29th:

The noise of battle was heard before we reached Gainesville. The march was quickened to the extent of our capacity. The excitement of battle seemed to give new life and strength to our *jaded* men. * * *

His recollection would seem to be very much less vivid and exact than in 1862, for he testified before this Board in reference to that march as follows:

Question by RECORDER. Were your troops in a *jaded* condition at that time?

Answer. I should hardly think they were.

This witness from his position during the rebellion as an officer of high rank in the rebel army was brought prominently into this case as one whose testimony would apparently have to be considered as conclusive even if it did conflict with that of respectable Union officers.

Two instances have been given of the uncertainty of his recollection, viz:

1. His statements here as to the size of Cadmus M. Wilcox's division, contradicted by the latter.

2d. His statements here as to the condition his men were in when they passed through Gainesville, contradicted by his own official report as well as by Col. Thomas L. Rosser (Fifth Virginia Cavalry, Stuart's division), who testifies (Board's Record, p. 1153) that Longstreet's command came from the direction of Thoroughfare Gap "in a very forced and disordered march * * moving rapidly and straggling badly."

3. A third instance is found in the numbers he says Brig. Gen. Beverly H. Robertson, of Stuart's cavalry division, Jackson's command, had there in his brigade. Longstreet (Board's Record, p. 73) puts them at 3,000, but Robertson himself says he had 2,500 (Board's Record, p. 173).

A fourth instance is found in Longstreet's statement (Board's Record, p. 72) that he has no recollection of seeing any cavalry that day.

John S. Mosby, formerly colonel of Major-General J. E. B. Stuart's staff, testified as follows (Board's Record, p. 887):

Question. When did that battle begin on the 29th—what time of day?
Answer. Pretty early on the morning of the 29th there was heavy fighting.
Question. How long did that continue?
Answer. My recollection is that there was heavy fighting during most of the day. Early in the morning I suppose I was about the rear of the center of Jackson's line, and I suppose about eight, or nine, or ten o'clock there came a report that our left flank had been turned, over in the direction of Sudley; I went over there with the First Virginia Cavalry, according to my recollection, for the purpose of checking that, and we were there the whole of the day.
Question. What of the action could you see and hear? Describe all that you recall of that action.
Answer. We could not see the fighting. I was with this cavalry, and I suppose we were half a mile, or part of the time within a mile of it. In the morning this regiment that I got with I suppose was not half a mile in the rear of Jackson's line; but when the report came that the Federal cavalry was over on Jackson's left, and there was danger of their capturing his wagons and ambulances that were in the rear of Sudley Church, this cavalry was sent over there to protect Jackson's left, and I went with it.

*   *   *   *   *   *   *

Question. Do you know what the losses of Jackson were in that action?
Answer. No, sir.
Question. From twelve o'clock noon up to three o'clock in the afternoon, do you recollect the character of the fighting as far as you could judge from the sound?
Answer. My general recollection of it is that most of the day there was heavy fighting. I cannot particularize.
Question. Musketry and artillery?
Answer. Musketry and artillery.

Charles Marshall, formerly aid-de-camp to the Confederate General R. E. Lee, having been called for petitioner (Board's Record, p. 1000), in asserting that he was at the Gibbon wood on or about 12 o'clock, and noticing Confederate dead and wounded on the Warrenton pike, said, "There was a good deal of artillery and musketry firing on that road" before he got up there.

The petitioner has been forced to the assertion that there was no battle on the 29th August, 1862 (Opening Statement, pp. 42 and 57), in order to excuse his inaction in consequence of the Count de Paris's rule, cited by me.

Unfortunately for the petitioner, he has advanced too many and contradictory defenses, which can only be explained on the ground that his case as here presented and on his trial is largely an afterthought.

When he was at the Weir House at Manassas Station that morning, conversing with Major-General McDowell (Board's Record, p. 875), the smoke of battle could be seen, and persons there were watching its progress and listening to the cannonading.

The unqualified statement of petitioner that there was no battle on the 29th is positively disproven by two of his own dispatches of that day, found in his own opening statement before this Board, viz:

First. (No. 28, to General Morell.) To push over and aid Sigel. * * * See if you cannot help Sigel. If you find him retiring, move back toward Manassas.

Second. (No. 29.) The enemy appear to have driven our forces back, the fire of the enemy having advanced and ours retired. I have determined to withdraw to Manassas.

He says he (petitioner) went to the head of the column, and found he had been misinformed, and no action was therefore taken by him to carry out the determination expressed so positively in that dispatch.

These dispatches are fatal to petitioner's theory, even if Col. E. G. Marshall's evidence alone was not.

We have seen that he undertook, *even earlier in the day*, to carry out the same determination to retire, based *on the same belief as to our repulse.*

If he was misinformed at that second time, as he alleges in his opening statement, *when did he again ascertain we were being beaten on the right? for he sent another recently-discovered dispatch*, addressed to General McDowell OR *King*, in which he said:

How goes the *battle?* It seems to go to our rear.

Does this indicate no knowledge on his part of a battle?

Again, in another newly-discovered dispatch, this time to General McDowell, he said:

The firing on my right has so far retired that, as I cannot advance and have failed to get over to you, except by the route taken by King, I *shall* withdraw to Manassas.

Did he withdraw as he, in this dispatch, positively announced he would? We shall find that he commenced the movement. In the previous dispatch he said he had determined to withdraw to Manassas. He afterwards concluded not to. In this dispatch to McDowell, dated 6 p. m., he said he did withdraw Morell, who held the advance.

As to whether there was a battle on the 29th, he is precluded from denying it by his own dispatches, officially made at the time, and having failed in proving the alternative expressed by the Count de Paris, was properly convicted of "*shamefully failing to go to the aid of Major-General Pope's troops, and did shamefully retreat and fall back with his army and leave to the disasters of a presumed defeat the said army, and did fail, by any attempt to attack the enemy, to aid in averting the misfortunes of a disaster that would have endangered the safety of the national Capital.*"

It was not necessary he should go back to Manassas Junction, though a considerable portion of his troops did move back by his direct orders.

He put his troops where they were not available, and he did it knowing a battle was—to use the language of General Lee—"raging" at the time.

No argument, however skillful, can influence these facts. General Pope or any of his subordinate corps-commanders may have made movements which to others may not seem to have been as effective as if some other movement had been made. His plan of battle may be criticised, his mode of attack commented upon by unfriendly critics, but none of this has any relation to the petitioner. The duty of the latter was plain and obligatory. He did not do it, and judgment came, the judgment of his peers.

In vain did he on that fatal 29th August go to the point in his column most remote from the sound of the enemy's cannon, and calmly wait the issue between the contending forces with a safe line of retreat open to himself.

Did he hope for a favorable opportunity to come at the last moment to protect a retreat? Such things history shows have happened before.

LONGSTREET'S DEFENSIVE POSITION 29TH AUGUST.

The next point to be considered is the position of the co-operating Confederate forces which arrived on the 29th August to the support of Jackson's hard-pressed troops.

118

By glancing at the map it will be seen that "Gainesville" was the key to the Confederate position on that day. It was of vital importance to General R. E. Lee—

First. To prevent a flank movement from any portion of the Army of the Potomac, via Warrenton Junction.

Second. To maintain communication with Thoroughfare Gap, through which advancing re-enforcements, including Anderson's division of Long-street's command, were expected.

General Lee did not and could not properly know what peculiar influences were operating to retard the arrival of additional assistance from the Army of the Potomac. Therefore we find from the official Confederate reports that at 8 a. m., the 29th August, while Lee was still at Thoroughfare Gap, he dispatched Major Hairston, commissary of subsistence on Major-General Stuart's staff, to Warrenton, Va., to ascertain whether any of our Army was there.

The turnpike from Centreville, it will be noticed, passed by the stone house and through Groveton and Gainesville to Warrenton; consequently any Union force from the Rappahannock, via Warrenton, would have struck in his rear and interposed, if in sufficient force, between his command near Gainesville and Thoroughfare Gap.

It was not until 8 p. m., the 29th August, that Lee became apprised that there was no danger from that quarter.

The following is the report (Board's Record, p. 540):

REPORT OF MAJOR S. H. HAIRSTON, DIVISION QUARTERMASTER, STUART'S CAVALRY DIVISION.

GAINESVILLE, *August* 29, 1862—8 p. m.

To Colonel CHILTON, *A. A. G.:*

In obedience to General Lee's order I started this morning at eight o'clock with one hundred and fifty cavalry to go to Warrenton, "to find out if any of the enemy's forces were still in the vicinity of that place." I went from Thoroughfare to the right on a by-road, which took me into the Winchester road two miles below Warrenton, and came up to the rear of the town. I inquired of the citizens and persons I met on the way, but could not hear that any of their forces were in the vicinity of that place. They informed me that the last left yesterday in the direction of Gainesville and Warrenton Junction. We picked up on the way forty-six prisoners, thirty muskets and rifles, one deserter from the Stuart horse artillery, and one sutler, with his wagon and driver. I also paroled two lieutenants in Warrenton, who were too sick to travel. What shall I do with the prisoners?

SAMUEL H. HAIRSTON,
Major Commanding, by order of General Lee.

NOTE.—This was made of men from every regiment in your command, with one entire company, headed by the captain, that General Lee had handled at Thoroughfare and turned over to me when he ordered me to go on the expedition.   S. H. H.

On the 29th August, therefore, the Confederate General in Chief may be said to have been fighting what General Pope termed a "defensive" battle, because he had not all his forces available, viz: the large divisions of Maj. Gen. D. H. Hill, consisting of five brigades with artillery; Maj. Gen. L. McLaws' of four brigades, and Maj. Gen. R. H. Anderson's "very full division" of Maj. Gen. Longstreet's special command (Board's Record, p. 61.)

Already had Heintzelman's Corps, and Reno's division of Burnside's corps, Reynolds' division of Pennsylvania Reserves, and petitioner's corps, all of the Army of the Potomac, joined General Pope from the Peninsula.

Sumner's Corps (second) and Franklin's corps (sixth) and the remainder of the Army of the Potomac had been afforded reasonable time to evacuate Harrison's Landing on James River and come into position, and the latter was at Alexandria.

At that time there were no regular *corps* organizations in the Confederate army (Board's Record, p. 950), and the senior division commanders commanded the right and left wings and center of the army.

The fact that Lee left all his reserve artillery under Col. Stephen D. Lee at Thoroughfare Gap on the 29th, shows that he was not prepared for an offensive movement against unknown forces (Board's Record, p. 120).

Part of the forces which came up to Gainesville on the 29th appear, according to Longstreet's testimony, if his recollection is reliable, to have arrived at Thoroughfare Gap nearly half a day before attempting to shove through.

He testified as follows (Board's Record, p. 70) on cross-examination:

Question. Was not the delay at Thoroughfare Gap for half a day due partially at least to the uncertainty as to General Pope's movements?
Answer. I think it must have been.
Question. Would you not have been likely to know, being one of the two superior commanders?
Answer. I would be likely to know if General Lee expressed an opinion as to the occasion of the delay, more likely than anybody else. I think if he had known that Jackson was pressed and wanted re-enforcements he would not have allowed us to halt on the west side of the gap. I think it is probably because he did not know anything about it that we were detained there. If he had expected that gap would have been occupied by Pope's troops, we would have moved immediately through. I think we had some mounted stragglers who had been ont to the front and reported to us that there was nothing up there in that direction, and we were a little surprised when we found our troops driven back into the gap on the afternoon of the 28th.
Question. Then you are not prepared to say whether or not your delay there was due partially to the fact that General Lee was not aware exactly of the movements of General Pope?
Answer. All those things, you know, have their relations one to another.

(Also Board's Record, p. 157, Charles Marshall's evidence.)

Longstreet further testified (Board's Record, p. 68), on cross-examination, that when he heard, on the 26th August, of Major-General Jackson having been detached to make the movement around to the rear of General Pope's army he expressed considerable surprise to Lee, and intimated his opinion that Jackson was in a very hazardous position and liable to be cut off.

That Lee was apprehensive for Jackson's safety is evident from the fact of his sending a dispatch to the latter.

William W. Blackford, then captain of engineers in the Confederate service, called by government, testified as follows (Board's Record, p. 693):

Question. Can you fix, with any degree of certainty, about what time in the morning that was?
Answer. No, sir; not exactly. The only thing I recollect about it is that it was early in the day. We had been looking for Longstreet's coming with a great deal of anxiety, and I recollect the feeling of relief that I had when Stuart told me that he was going to open communication with him; and the impression made upon my mind at the time was that it was sufficiently early in the day for him to be there by any time within which the enemy would probably make an attack.

* * * * *

Question. Can you swear at all as to the hour at which you met General Lee before reaching Gainesville?
Answer. No, sir; I could not swear to the exact hour, except that it was quite early in the day.
Question. What fixes it in your mind that it was quite early in the day?
Answer. The fact that we had been rather nervous about Longstreet's joining us; and as soon as I heard that we were going out to open communication to meet General Lee, I recollect the feeling of relief that I had in knowing that that junction would be made so soon in the day.

* * * * *

Question. You say that the morning of the 29th you were nervous about Longstreet's joining you, and that you experienced a feeling of relief when you found that you were going to join him. What do you have reference to?

Answer. Jackson had been occupying an isolated position there, and we were anxious for Longstreet to rejoin us. We knew that the enemy were concentrating, and we were anxious for our concentration to take place too.

* * * * * * * *

Question. Was it the time you left the turnpike in company with General Stuart to go down to make this reconnaissance that I am to understand a division of Longstreet's troops had already passed the point where you were?

Answer. I suppose a division had passed. I know while standing there the men were very anxious to know what news there was from Jackson, and we were standing on the turnpike telling them as they passed. Then they would cheer. That was the first intelligence they had of Jackson's safety.

Alexander D. Payne, then first lieutenant Fourth Virginia Cavalry, commanding Lee's body-guard, called by petitioner, on cross-examination said (Board's Record, p. 381):

I have reason to know that General Lee was very uneasy about General Jackson all the day before.

Capt. *Robert McEldowney,* Twenty-seventh Virginia Confederate Infantry, says (Board's Record, p. 951) that, on the 29th, Jackson's command was in "a rather exhausted condition," and Col. Henry Kyd Douglas, assistant adjutant-general that day with Jackson, says the latter that morning was "rather trying to avoid" an engagement (Board's Record, p. 707).

As Major-General Sigel, by General Pope's orders, attacked Jackson at daylight of the 29th, and as the night before Ricketts' and King's divisions were so interposed as to prevent Jackson's withdrawal, Lee was forced to come up sufficiently near to prevent Jackson being crushed; *but not knowing what forces he had to contend with he remained in such a position as to cover Gainesville and protect his line of communication with Thoroughfare Gap.*

This is the explanation why his co-operating divisions under Wilcox, Kemper, Jones, and Hood, comprising part of Longstreet's command, were not shoved into action.

They were strong enough to hold open the line of retreat for Jackson, and towards evening, at sunset, Hood's division and Evans' brigade, supported by Wilcox's, was ordered to attack one of McDowell's divisions (King's), under Hatch, down the Warrenton pike, but was anticipated by the latter (Board's Record, p. 529).

For Longstreet to say that General Lee was very anxious for him to bring on a battle on the 29th, is to say that which is very unlikely to have been the actual case (Board's Record, p. 64).

1st. Because Lee did not know how many or where all the Union forces then were.

2d. Because petitioner's corps was on his right flank.

3d. Because Banks' corps, over ten thousand strong, was also on his right flank at Bristoe on a *direct* road into Gainesville in his rear, and not more than five miles from it.

That he may have desired Longstreet to make some tentative movement to develop the strength of the opposing Union forces is not improbable.

Even on the next day (30th August) after his reserve artillery and Anderson's division had joined him and he felt assured that there was no army of the Potomac corps coming up from the Rappahannock, through Warrenton on to his rear, he did not attack, but awaited the attack which General Pope made in the afternoon.

With this insight into the plans of the Confederate general, his operations on the 29th can be readily understood, and we can see why Wilcox's, Kemper's, and Jones' divisions never fired a shot on the 29th (Board's Record, p. 232), while Jackson's command on the other hand expended quite all their ammunition (Board's Record, p. 707).

Longstreet makes a *very* significant admission in his evidence. He says that with Lee's permission he made a personal reconnaissance and got as far forward along by Young's Branch as he dared venture, and thought there was a force along above the Warrenton and Gainesville pike—artillery, and infantry too—"a considerable force," and that it would be a *little hazardous* to make a front attack, that is making a parallel battery, throwing his troops forward so as to breast the storm. So he reported to General Lee that he had some doubt of their being able to carry the position (Board's Record, p. 63).

While he and Lee were still discussing this, he says General Stuart sent—

A report of the advance of a force against his right.

As soon as that came, General Lee ordered him (Longstreet) to cross to that point to re-enforce it, which he did with three brigades under Wilcox.

Now Longstreet, in his official report, dated 10th October, 1862, puts this circumstance at a *late hour* in the day. This is what his report says (Board's Record, p. 521):

Three brigades, under General Wilcox, were thrown forward to the support of the left, and three others, under General Kemper, to the support of the right of these commands. General D. R. Jones' division was placed upon the Manassas Gap Railroad to the right and in echelon with regard to the three last brigades. Colonel Walton placed his batteries in a commanding position between my line and that of General Jackson, and engaged the enemy for several hours in a severe and successful artillery duel. At a late hour in the day Major-General Stuart reported the approach of the enemy in heavy columns against my extreme right. I withdrew General Wilcox, with his three brigades, from the left, and placed his command in position to support Jones in case of an attack against my right. After some few shots the enemy withdrew his forces, moving them around towards his front, and about four o'clock in the afternoon began to press forward against General Jackson's position. Wilcox's brigades were moved back to their former position, and Hood's two brigades, supported by Evans, were quickly pressed forward to the attack.

The expression at a "late hour" is somewhat indefinite—though it is quite unlikely he could have intended it to apply to as early an hour in the afternoon even as 2 o'clock, at which he now puts it (p. 72)—yet he says before this Board that this advance reported by Stuart was what he *afterwards learned* to be McDowell's and petitioner's forces on the Manassas and Gainesville dirt road (Board's Record, p. 63).

Unfortunately the information which he received *afterward* does not correspond with the facts, as neither petitioner nor General McDowell made any advance whatever on that road after noon.

We are left in no doubt as to the time when Stuart made a report of the advance of Union forces on Longstreet's right, because Cadmus M. Wilcox, one of Longstreet's division commanders (Board's Record, p. 530), who had been stationed with his division a considerable time in reserve on the north of the Warrenton turnpike, in his official report, dated 11th October, 1862, said as follows relative to his own three brigades:

At half past four or five p. m. the three brigades were moved across to the right of the turnpike, a mile or more, to the Manassas Gap Railroad. While here musketry was heard to our left, on the turnpike. This firing continued, with more or less vivacity, until sundown. Now the command was ordered back to the turnpike and forward on this to the support of General Hood, who had become engaged with the enemy, and had driven him back some distance, inflicting severe loss upon him, being checked in his successes by the darkness of the night.

Before this Board, Wilcox, who was one of petitioner's witnesses, also testified as to this movement of his division as follows:

Question. Next after that what order did you get?
Answer. In *the afternoon, about half past four or five*, I was moved over to the right of the pike. * * * (Board's Record, p. 230). I remained there until near sundown. Meantime there had been some musketry heard on the pike, &c.

He thus corroborates his official report in this interesting particular and fixes the hour.

Longstreet, on cross-examination (Board's Record, p. 68), said he was informed of the position of petitioner's troops about 2 o'clock p. m.

If, as soon as his divisions were all deployed, Lee wanted him, according to his statement, to bring on a general engagement, and if he took a little time to make a reconnaissance of the ground and reported at once to Lee on the field, and while discussing the matter received Stuart's report at what he himself terms a "late hour in the day," it is plain—

First. That his troops were not all up from Gainesville so as to be deployed into line before 3 p. m.—possibly nearer 4 p. m.—despite the earlier hour given by him; because, according to Col. *E. G. Marshall*, Thirteenth New York Volunteers (now colonel, U. S. A., retired), petitioner's witness, who commanded the latter's skirmish-line, the enemy's *"force continued to come down all day, in fact until one o'clock at night"* (G. C. M. Record, p. 190); and Major *George Hyland, jr.*, same regiment, another of petitioner's witnesses on the latter's trial, who had been on the skirmish-line, swore as follows:

Question by accused. Do you know at what hour they [the enemy] commenced forming, or about what hour?
Answer. They *commenced* forming between *two* and *three* o'clock, I think (G. C. M. Record, p. 174).

Thus two of the best-informed officers under petitioner confirmed this particular evidence of Longstreet.

Brigadier-General Charles Griffin, United States Volunteers, another of petitioner's witnesses on his trial, said (G. C. M. Record, p. 163):

That heavy bodies of troops were passing from Thoroughfare Gap down towards our front all day long—that is, that they passed. Some of them may have been three miles, some of them may have been five miles, and some of them may not have been over 2,000 yards from us.

Therefore, all of Longstreet's assumed 25,000 men could not have been up in position by 1 or 2 or 3 p. m.

Second. It is also plain that when Longstreet made his reconnaissance about 4 p. m. he gave no heed or attention to the position where petitioner's corps was lying inactive, quite out of sight, but devoted his attention to the Union forces near the Warrenton, Gainesville, Groveton and Centreville turnpike.

This, we shall see, harmonizes exactly with the evidence of distinguished Union officers who have testified in this case.

Third. It is also plain that it was the presence of Union troops wholly north of petitioner's position which made Longstreet reluctant to attack, and induced him to tell Lee it would be a "little hazardous."

This fact, with the report between 4 and 4½ p. m. of the advance from Bristoe toward Gainesville, toward Lee's rear, of the brigade of observation sent out by Major-General N. P. Banks, United States Volunteers, caused the Confederate commander to maintain his condition of inaction until apprehension from that quarter had disappeared, and at sunset he shoved in down the pike Hood's division and Evans' brigade, with Wilcox's division as support, into an action with King's division, near the

Gibbon wood, which lasted, according to General Lee's and other official reports, until NINE P. M. (Board's Record, pp. 521, 537). Longstreet also puts it until 9 p. m. in his report.

As, after noon, it is certain that petitioner's corps were kept by him in a state of complete inactivity, stretched in column along a road concealed by woods for at least three miles to the rear, it is quite clear that Lee and Longstreet gave him no attention.

If, as Longstreet says, a reconnaissance to his front, near the Warrenton pike, made him believe a front attack, even with his assumed 25,000 men, would be "hazardous," the inquiry naturally suggests itself, What would have been the consequences to his command had the petitioner pushed *forward* on his (Longstreet's) right flank, supported as he would have been by the gallant Reynolds, with his division attached to McDowell's corps, and by Schenck's division of Sigel's corps and Stevens' brigade of Reno, all of which were south of the Warrenton turnpike, and supported by King's division of McDowell's corps?

All our movements of the left wing south of the Warrenton turnpike were absolutely paralyzed that day and rendered of no avail in consequence of petitioner's lamentable failure.

His pretense that his skillful arrangements to put his own forces out of sight and in a "*defensive*" position, so as to *hold* the enemy in his front, while at the same time, on the right flank of General Pope's Army, assault after assault was being made on the Confederate lines, is a pretense such as was, possibly, never before ventured upon in a judicial investigation by any defendant having military training.

Indeed, his own witness, *Charles Marshall*, aide-de camp to Lee, says (Board's Record, p. 171), on his (petitioner's) assumption of facts that Lee withdrew Wilcox's division of Longstreet's command from the right late in the afternoon and sent him up on to the pike to support Hood, *because he believed "there would be no further movement against his right."*

Brig. Gen. *John Buford*, U. S. Volunteers, petitioner's original witness, did, as appears of record, observe the advance of Longstreet and Lee through Gainesville on the 29th August, and estimated their numbers liberally at 14,000.

Cadmus M. Wilcox, division commander under Longstreet, (petitioner's witness), testifies that the brigades and divisions were all together (Board's Record, p. 230).

Longstreet, and *Charles U. Williams*, then aide-de-camp to D. R. Jones, another division commander (both petitioner's witnesses), confirm this (Board's Record, pp. 60, 221).

Buford's estimate and report, made from personal and careful observation at the time, is much more reliable than the recollection of these Confederates, which, as we have seen, varied among themselves to the extent of several thousands.

Buford testified in 1862 that the cavalry with that marching column was about 500 (G. C. M. Record, p. 188); and also so reported to Major-General McDowell on the morning of the 29th August; yet Beverly H. Robertson and Longstreet each, as we have seen, *put it now*, from recollection merely, as respectively 2,500 and 3,000.

These discrepancies are glaring.

At the close of the evidence before this Board (3d January) petitioner reproduced the witness Leachman, and inquired, not however in sur-rebuttal of anything developed during the recess, as to the character of the country behind Pageland Lane, which he declared to be a "morass." He also previously said (Board's Record, p. 141), men could only have gone down the Manassas Gap Railroad to J. W. Jeffers' in single file, as the culverts were open; and yet, we know, General McDowell galloped rapidly down.

His reliability is further exemplified when cross-questioned as to "Monroe's" or Stuart's Hill, which overlooks his house (Board's Record, p. 142):

Question. Is there any commanding elevation south from the Warrenton pike from which you can see Centreville?

Answer. No, sir; not in the topography of the country at that time, nor is there now.

As to the ground west of Pageland Lane, Longstreet himself indicates that he came into position back of it, and threw out one battery northwest of Pageland Lane (Board's Record, p. 68). The Board has got to take what may, for explanation, be termed "judicial" notice of the character of the country, and I insist that the country back of Pageland Lane is high ground.

James Mitchell, formerly a captain, First Virginia Volunteers, Kemper's division, called by petitioner (Board's Record, p. 385), says that to the best of his recollection they must have advanced to *near* Pageland Lane, and then filed on to the right and passed down an old and unfrequented road for some distance, and then diverged into the fields through the woods. Further on he said as follows (Board's Record, p. 386):

I saw no Federal troops at all that day.

This is the only witness who has been produced in this case from Kemper's division of Longstreet's command, and his statement shows conclusively how far back that division must have been placed, so far as the battle was concerned.

The *position* of the portion of Longstreet's command which arrived near the field on this 29th of August, is only indirectly of importance.

Assuming it to have been as far east as the easterly edge of the "Gibbon wood," where petitioner seeks to put it, such position would only have put the petitioner in a better position to attack the enemy's flank and possible rear, than the position actually taken by Longstreet as indicated by me.

Some few of the Confederates brought before this Board by petitioner give evidence directly contradictory to that formerly and now given by Union officers, as indicative of the enemy's position. And this evidence of the Union officers is supported by that of citizens and Confederates.

It must be remembered that the enemy occupied substantially the same ground for two days, having been moved back or forward in some instances half a mile or more.

On the other hand, the Union officers were up on that line only *one day*. Consequently there is no possibility of confusion when they indicate that they were located in a particular position.

As to the Confederates, there is strong probability that what was said, for example, by Charles Marshall, of Lee's staff (Board's Record, pp. 158, 995), as to Longstreet's position, really referred to the 30th instead of the 29th August.

A good illustration of this is found in the Rev. Franklin Stringfellow's testimony (Board's Record, p. 1034). He was on duty with Maj. Gen. J. E. B. Stuart, mentioned several incidents which occurred, and gives his recollection of seeing regiments in position back of Pageland Lane, yet when he came to describe positions subsequent to the first seen by him, he became confused; and confounded the two days' battles so completely as to ask to have his testimony not considered.

There is great discrepancy between petitioner's witnesses Longstreet and Chas. Marshall as to the former's station.

Longstreet (Board's Record, p. 68) put his line on the easterly slope of the Douglas Browner house hill (where it would have been exposed to the fire of the Union batteries), and carried it down on a line with Meadowville Lane. (See his map.)

Chas. Marshall, equally positive, puts Longstreet far in advance of Longstreet himself and to the east edge of the "Gibbon" wood (Board's Record, pp. 157, 240, and 1000) by 11 a. m.

However (Board's Record, p. 996), in another part of his testimony, he says that some time on the 29th or 30th, *he does not recollect which,* he was sent on a certain duty.

Alexander D. Payne, formerly first lieutenant Fourth Virginia Confederate Cavalry, commanding Lee's guards, having been called for petitioner, says (Board's Record, p. 382), that Hood's division formed in the Gibbon wood, very soon after Lee got there, between 10 and 11 a. m., nearer 10.

Jubal A. Early, then brigadier-general Confederate service, a government witness, says (Board's Record, p. 850) that Hood came up about 11 a. m. He further testifies as follows:

I moved my own brigade across Pageland road and waited there some time until these two regiments [Thirteenth and Thirty-first Virginia Infantry] could be withdrawn; their place had to be supplied by some other troops on the flank.
I suppose it was in the afternoon sometime, before those regiments got there. I lay there waiting for *some time* and then moved off to the left in the rear of our line.

It will be noticed that these two regiments of Early's had been early in the day pushed down to guard Jackson's right flank.

Henry Kyd Douglas, assistant adjutant-general to Maj. Gen. T. J. Jackson on the 29th August, a government witness, testified as follows (Board's Record, p. 705):

Question. Do you recollect seeing General Longstreet coming into position?
Answer. I do not. I don't recollect seeing General Longstreet until about the time Hood's command became involved, late in the evening. I think I had gone to General Jackson, and was sent to Longstreet to see what that was.
Question. That was along the line of attack?
Answer. That was rather on Longstreet's left. There was a gap between Jackson's right and the position taken by Longstreet. That gap was a *series of hills,* as far as I can recollect, occupied by artillery controlled by Colonel Kirchner, Jackson's chief of staff. I have not been there since the war. I do not attempt to be accurate about topographical features.

William W. Blackford, then captain of engineers, on Stuart's staff, subsequently lieutenant-colonel of engineers, a government witness (Board's Record, p. 701), when asked whether, according to his recollection, the Confederate lines included Cundiffe's and the ravine near "Meadowville Lane," answered as follows:

Answer. Longstreet's first line was back of that; I think his first line was in *these* woods. [West of Pageland Lane.]

This witness had, just before testifying, been on the ground (Board's Record, p. 696), and knew the country.

Lewis B. Carrico, who resides on the battle-ground, called by government, testified as follows (Board's Record, p. 982):

Question. Where do you reside?
Answer. Prince William County, Virginia.
Question. Where did you reside on the 29th of August, 1862?
Answer. Where I now reside, very near the Manassas Gap Railroad.
Question. Were you there on that day?
Answer. I was.
Question. Up to what hour in the day did you remain there?
Answer. I was there until very late Friday evening.
Question. During that day did you see any Confederate forces? If so, where?

Answer. I saw some cavalry scouts during that day, and in the evening there was a battery firing some 75 or 80 yards back of my house, just west of my house, and an officer came there and told me I was in danger, and to take my family and go back of the line.

Question. Where did you go then?

Answer. I went up the road about a mile, to a farm owned now by Major Nutt.

Question. Towards Gainesville?

Answer. Between there and Gainesville.

Question. Did you meet any Confederate force on that trip? If so, about where?

Answer. I saw them a little beyond Hampton Cole's, a very small number. They were sitting down on the side of the railroad, and their battery, that was planted at the back of my house—that opened upon the Federal troops directly after I passed it; and when I got up there against them, they got up and took shelter on the embankment of the railroad.

Question. Did you at that time see any troops to the south of the railroad?

Answer. None at all except a little picket force that was a little to the south of the railroad, just above there; a small picket force.

Question. Did any Confederate force pass to the east of your house during the day? If so, in what direction did they go?

Answer. I saw none pass to the eastward. I saw some shelling from the back of what is called the Britt farm, and a disabled Federal wagon at the mouth of a lane called Compton's lane.

Question. About what time in the day was that?

Answer. I could hardly say; twelve or one o'clock.

* * * * * *

Question. What do you mean by the expression "evening"?

Answer. I mean something like three or four o'clock; somewhere thereabouts.

Question. How do you fix the time?

Answer. I fix the time by having to leave home, and having to go the small distance I did go.

* * * * * *

Question. What room did you stay in?

Answer. I was all over the house; very often up-stairs, looking out of the window.

Question. Which way?

Answer. Towards Dawkins' Branch.

* * * * * *

Question. What time was the cannon posted there?

Answer. Possibly four o'clock.

Question. You are positive about that?

Answer. I am not positive; but according to the best of my judgment it was probably as late as four.

Question. Was it earlier or later than four?

Answer. It was not earlier, I do not think; not earlier than three I am very sure.

* * * * * *

Question. Were there any soldiers of any description about your house, except the battery?

Answer. On Friday there was a Federal force in Mr. Lewis' field, to the east of my house.

Question. Where was Lewis' field?

Answer. Within 300 or 400 yards to the east of my house.

Question. Were there any about your house?

Answer. Yes; there were some of the Federal forces; two men that I had had some acquaintance with, who were in my house when this wagon was disabled at the end of Compton's lane.

* * * * * *

Question. About where is the place where you carried your family?

Answer. Immediately at the Manassas Railroad, one mile past Hampton Cole's.

Question. You say you did not meet any considerable body of the Confederate force on your way there?

Answer. Yes; I do say it; and I saw no considerable body there as I stated to you and General Porter, if he was with you, until I got home next morning, about sun-up. They came there to my house and destroyed a great deal.

William T. Monroe, residing on "Stuart's Hill," called by government, testified as follows (Board's Record, p. 986):

Question. Do you recollect anything of the occurrences of the 29th of August, 1862?

Answer. I recollect about eleven o'clock General Longstreet's troops first came in there, or about twelve; I reckon that battery was posted on that hill—it may have been a little earlier, but not later than twelve o'clock.

Question. Do you know in what direction that battery was fired?

Answer. It fired in the direction of Groveton.

Question. Did it continue to fire in that direction?

Answer. It fired in that direction some hour, or maybe more.

Question. Do you know where it went to from that point?

Answer. It went down by, just into the depot which is now upon the railroad, and from there to the hill at the Britt house.

Question. Did you see it there in position?

Answer. At the Britt house? Yes.

Question. In which direction did it fire from there?

Answer. At first it fired in the direction of the Lewis house. [Witness indicates Leachman's.] Whether it fired in that direction all the time, I don't know.

Question. You did not see it fire in any other direction?

Answer. No, sir; the Federal troops at the time were around the Leachman house, and this battery graped them, fired grape and canister.

Question. Do you know where the Confederate lines were, or forces, on that day, aside from that particular battery that finally got down to the Britt house?

Answer. There was infantry just in here, running from the Warrenton and Gainesville pike [back of Pageland lane]. There was an army-road running through there, and then they were posted on this road. [Witness marks the map.]

Question. Do you know how far down they were posted?

Answer. I don't know. [Witness closes his marking at the road just northwest of Charles Randall's.] The skirmish line was drawn down as far as Vessel's.

Question. When did you first see the Confederate lines advance beyond Pageland lane during that day—the infantry?

Answer. I don't know when this part of the line advanced at all. [Down near the railroad.] It moved down under the hill, out of sight of the house. I did not see them.

Question. Off in what direction?

Answer. Off in this way, I suppose. [In the direction of Hampton Cole's.]

Question. Down along the railroad, do you say?

Answer. They moved in that direction, down along the railroad.

Question. About what time of day was that?

Answer. I would not say positively. I think it was about the middle of the afternoon, say three or four o'clock.

Question. You were describing some portion of the line that you did see.

Answer. This portion of the line marched through by the house—that was about three o'clock. [The line just north of the house.]

Question. That portion of the line between your house and the turnpike, you mean?

Answer. Yes, sir.

Question. Marched to the front about four o'clock?

Answer. I think it was General Hunton's brigade. General Hunton was along with the brigade, and I thought he was commanding.

Question. Do you know of the advance of any of the other Confederate forces that day, during the day?

Answer. I do not.

*　　　*　　　*　　　*　　　*　　　*

Cross-examination:

Question. How do you fix the time of the arrival of the Confederate force by your house in the morning?

Answer. The first came in about ten o'clock.

Question. Where did they come?

Answer. Marched around in here then. [On the army road.] But by eleven o'clock that line was formed, and the troops were lying there in the line of battle.

Question. How do you fix those times?

Answer. Well, I had a time-piece.

Question. Did you look at the clock?

Answer. I do not say that it was exactly that time.

Question. It was in reference to the clock that you fixed it at about that time?

Answer. Yes.

Question. How far down had they formed—down the railroad—by ten or eleven o'clock?

Answer. They had formed down as far as the railroad by eleven o'clock.

Question. How long did they remain there?

Answer. I know that they were there about one. When they left I don't know. They had gone about four o'clock.

Question. Did you hear any cannonading anywhere within a mile to the south or southeast of your place before their arrival?

Answer. I did not.

Question. Did you hear any firing of guns off towards Carrico's house at or about the time of their arrival?

Answer. I didn't hear until after they arrived.

Question. How long after?

Answer. Some hour; maybe hour and a half.

Question. Did you hear any about three or four o'clock in the afternoon at Carrico's house?

Answer. Yes; I heard that. But the first guns I heard at all were—well, I heard this battery.

Question. I do not refer to the battery near your house.

Answer. The first fire I heard after that was one o'clock.

Question. Where was that?

Answer. That was off here in the direction of Dawkins' Branch.

Question. Can you see Dawkins' Branch from your house?

Answer. No, sir; we cannot see the branch, but we can see the hills on both sides.

Question. Can you see the hill near Dawkins' Branch?

Answer. Yes, sir.

* * * * * *

Question. Do you know of any firing by Carrico's house about twelve o'clock?

Answer. I know there was none at twelve or one o'clock, either.

Question. Do you know that all that arrived there remained there until one o'clock?

Answer. I know they staid there on this part of the line until one o'clock.

Question. The whole force that was there?

Answer. I understood the skirmish line.

Question. Could you see from your house to Hampton Cole's?

Answer. Very plainly.

Question. Could you see any lines of troops that would be formed along what is called Meadowville lane?

Answer. I did not see any troops at all formed along Meadowville lane, but about some time between three and four o'clock there were some Confederate troops formed right along here in the woods [south of Hampton Cole's], I think one regiment.

Question. Did you see the effect of the fire from the hill near your house in the direction of Groveton?

Answer. I saw that there was infantry in this field [east of Gibbons' battle-ground], lying along in there [south of the pike]. When this battery commenced firing, they got back into the woods.

Question. You mean along the branch running up from Lewis' lane No. 1 towards the letter "V" in "Gainesville"—the line was just alongside of the strip of woods between the branch and that?

Answer. Right along in the edge of the woods. [Witness marks the point on the Douglass Pope map as "Monroe."] That was about 12 o'clock.

Question. They retired then?

Answer. Yes; they got back into the woods.

Question. How long did you remain where you could see the direction of that firing?

Answer. Just as long as that battery was on the hill. That was some hour and a half.

* * * * * *

Question. How do you fix the time of the advance of a Confederate force from behind your house at three or four o'clock?

Answer. I don't know when they moved, but about 4 they were gone. They were there as late as one o'clock, and at four o'clock they were gone.

* * * *

Question. If troops had been lying along here parallel with and east of Pageland lane west of Meadowville lane, in the direction of Douglass Hill, would you have been able to see them?

Answer. I would if they had been in here. [East of Pageland lane, west of Meadowville lane, and parallel to Pageland lane, about midway between.]

* * * *

By the PRESIDENT of the Board:

Question. The troops you saw coming up marched along what road?

Answer. I did not see them march at all. When I first saw them they were standing in line, back of Pageland lane.

Question. That was about what time?

Answer. Between ten and eleven o'clock.

Question. The first you saw was the skirmish line?

Answer. The first troops I saw was the skirmish line.

From the evidence of *Lewis B. Carrico* it appears:

1st. That during the day some of the Union soldiers came to his house.

2d. That the first Confederates who came near his house did so in the afternoon between 3 and 4 o'clock, although he saw some scouts possibly earlier.

3d. That a Confederate battery was not posted back of his house until about 4 p. m.; and

4th. That the first Confederate troops he saw were a little beyond Hampton Cole's when he went back at that time towards Gainesville.

5th. That he saw some shelling from back of the "Britt" farm.

6th. That there were some Union troops in the Lewis fields.

From the evidence of *William T. Monroe* it appears:

1st. That Longstreet's troops came into position back of Pageland lane between 11 and 12 m.

2d. That Longstreet's troops formed down the railroad about 10 or 11 a. m., and were there about 1 p. m.

3d. That a battery was placed on the hill and forced first towards Groveton, for an hour, maybe more, and then moved down first near the depot on the railroad, and then to the Britt house from whence it fired for a time in the direction of the Lewis-Leachman house.

4th. That some of Longstreet's forces moved, he supposes, in the direction of Hampton Cole's, somewhere between 3 and 4 p. m.

5th. That about 4 p. m. Hampton's brigade moved forward.

6th. Some time between 3 and 4 p. m. there were some Confederate troops along in the roads south of Hampton Cole's, he thinks one regiment.

7th. He noticed effect of firing on Union forces between Gibbon battle-ground and strip of woods east.

The battery continued firing an hour and a half.

Bushrod W. Frobel, then major commanding artillery of Hood's Confederate division, Longstreet's command, a government witness, says that he was ordered to go to the right or south of the Warrenton turnpike, somewhere between 10 o'clock and noon or about 11 o'clock.

He then testifies as follows (Board's Record, p. 709):

Answer. I was ordered by General Byrne to General J. E. B. Stuart, and Captain Johnson, of General Lee's staff, was sent with me to show me where I could find him.

Question. Where did you find J. E. B. Stuart?

Answer. I found him near the Manassas Railroad. I stated in that report that it was near the Orange Railroad; it was a mistake, owing to not having a map to refer to. It was near the Manassas Railroad.

Question. What then transpired?

Answer. He said the enemy were advancing up the road and for me to go into position and fire.

Question. What road did you understand the enemy were advancing on?

Answer. I don't recollect. My impression is now some one told us they were advancing on what was called the Ocoquan.

Question. From what direction?

Answer. The direction of Manassas Junction.

Question. What did you then do after you came into position?

Answer. I fired about fifteen or twenty rounds.

Question. Where was General Lee at this time?

Answer. He came over there just about the close of the firing.

Question. Did he have anything to say in reference to the firing?

Answer. I think he told us not to waste any ammunition; that we would have a use for it before the day was over.

Question. When you fired those shots in what direction did you fire them?

Answer. As near as I can recollect it was in the direction of the railroad; pretty nearly in the direction in which the railroad passed.

Question. What did the Federal troops that were advancing do when you fired?

Answer. I think they commenced to retire and moved, as near as I can recollect, toward our left and their right.

Question. What was it that prevented your seeing the direction of that attack?

Answer. Woods.

Question. The woods near which they were?

Answer. Yes.

Question. Were they deployed when you saw them or were they advancing?

Answer. We could see them, very indistinctly indeed, to the rear of the woods; it seemed as if they were advancing. After they got into the woods, we could not see at all.

Question. How long did you remain in that position?

Answer. I don't recollect; probably an hour.

Question. Was there any return to this artillery fire of yours?

Answer. No, sir.

Between Major Frobel and Mr. Munroe there is a contradiction as to the point to which Frobel fired. However, he says his impression is that some one at the time told him our forces were advancing on the Ocoquan road, which is designated on the map as the "Manassas and Gainesville" dirt road.

The time at which he places himself on Munroe's or Stuart's Hill corresponds to the time of arrival of the head of petitioner's column on the ridge back of Dawkins' Branch.

We must not forget that it appears in evidence (see Mr. Wheeler's latest testimony, corroborated by Leachman's, if the latter's evidence is reliable in anything) that the Manassas Gap Railroad at Dawkins' Branch could be seen from Munroe's or Stuart's Hill, and also several hundred yards towards the Manassas and Gainesville dirt road, and the ridge back of the branch along which Griffin's brigade, after McDowell left, moved up to and across the railroad into the little pine bushes which, without exploration *of any kind on the part of anybody*, were found sufficient pretended obstacle to prevent the infantry complying with General McDowell's orders given before he left, to go into action where the dust indicated the arrival of reinforcements to Jackson.

Col. *Thomas L. Rosser*, Fifth Virginia Cavalry, Stuart's division, a government witness, testified, from Saint Paul, Minn., as follows:

7th interrogatory. Where were you at daylight on the morning of the twenty-ninth of August, eighteen hundred and sixty-two?

Answer. I was on Jackson's extreme right, with pickets under my command, on the Alexandria and Warrenton turnpike, and other roads leading in from the direction of the Orange and Alexandria Railroad.

8th interrogatory. Do you know where Sudley Church is? If so, where were you in reference to that point?

Answer. I do; and I was further up the stream, and to the west of the church.

9th interrogatory. Did you join General Stuart that morning? If so, state at what time, and narrate what happened.

Answer. At daylight I moved out, crossing the Alexandria and Warrenton turnpike, and occupied a road leading off to Manassas Junction, a mile or two beyond the turnpike. At this point, about ten o'clock, I was joined by Stuart and his staff. Longstreet's command was coming in in a very forced and disordered march from the direction of Thoroughfare Gap, moving rapidly and straggling badly. My position was taken up with reference to their protection from a gun of the enemy who were in my front. When Stuart joined me, he notified me that the enemy was moving upon our right flank, and ordered me to move my command up and down the dusty road, and to drag brush, and thus create a heavy dust as though troops were in motion. I kept this up at least four or five hours.

10th interrogatory. Did you see Capt. John Pelham, or Major Patrick, or both, that morning? If so, where, under what circumstances, and what did they do to your knowledge?

Answer. I do not remember Patrick. Pelham came to where I was, late in the day, with some artillery, and was moved out to the right, where he engaged the enemy. There was firing—at this time a cavalry command, with Stuart, moved out and relieved me from my position. I then took position on the extreme right of Longstreet's line, which was then forming.

*   *   *   *   *   *

15th interrogatory. Were you south of the Warrenton, Gainesville and Centreville pike after this? If so, where did you go, what did you do, and by whose orders?

Answer. I was all the time south of it. I assumed it in the first place without orders, and remained there afterwards by General Stuart's orders.

16th interrogatory. Do you know of any artillery firing south of the pike in the direction of Manassas Junction or Bristoe Station, on the twenty-ninth of August, eighteen hundred and sixty-two? If so, where was it from, what was it directed to, what was its character and result?

Answer. The horse artillery, as I have stated, under Pelham, directed by Stuart, moved out and engaged the Federal forces. It was east of Hay Market and south of the turnpike. It was directed to a marching column or advancing column. It was so reported to me by my scouts. They also reported that the column had halted.

17th interrogatory. If you were south of the Gainesville pike did you see any Federal forces advancing from the direction of Manassas Junction or Bristoe? If so, do you know whether any measures or expedients were taken by General Stuart or yourself, or directed to be taken to retard, impede, or prevent such advance, or to divert such forces? If so, please state what they were.

Answer. Stuart reported the advance of a Federal force, and that led to the dragging of brush as previously related.

* * * * *

1st cross-interrogatory. Please mark upon the map (hereunto attached) with a red letter A the various places where you know of your own knowledge your pickets were placed about daylight on the right of Jackson's forces, Aug. 29th, 1862.

Answer to 1st cross-interrogatory. My pickets were posted along the line indicated by the letter A marked on the map, as requested, on the date given. [From Pageland lane on the pike to letter A in word Warrenton, then northeast to first brook.]

2d cross-interrogatory. If you cannot do so, designate the roads which you know of your own knowledge were guarded by your pickets at that time.

Answer to 2d cross-interrogatory. My reply to the first question answers that.

3d cross-interrogatory. Mark with a red letter B the road leading off to Manassas Junction which you say you occupied at daylight a mile or two beyond the turnpike.

Answer to 3d cross-interrogatory. My position was at the point which I have marked on the map with the letter B 1, and my pickets were extended out on the roads indicated by the other letters B, which I have marked, as requested. [B is on Meadowville lane, 1,400 feet north of Hampton Cole's; B, B, B are at the junction of Meadowville lane with old Warrenton and Alexandria road, on that road 2,200 feet east of junction, and 1,800 feet southeast of junction on railroad.]

4th cross interrogatory. Mark with red letter C the point where General Stuart joined you with his staff about ten o'clock of 29th Aug., 1862.

Answer to 4th cross-interrogatory. It was at the forks of the roads which I have marked on the map with the letter C. [Junction of Meadowville lane and old Warrenton and Alexandria road.]

5th cross-interrogatory. Mark with red letter D where the forces of General Longstreet were when you first saw them on that day.

Answer to 5th cross-interrogatory. I have marked the points with the letters D, as near as I can on this map. [2,800 feet west of Pageland lane on the pike, then south half-way to railroad.]

6th cross-interrogatory. Mark with the letter E the position of the "few of the enemy who were in my (your) front," against whom you were posted to protect Longstreet's advancing forces, as I understand you to state.

Answer to 6th cross-interrogatory. They run in front of my pickets at the points I have marked on the map with the letters E. [On the railroad 2,200 feet west of Dawkins' Branch, then into the woods to the southeast to the Manassas and Gainesville dirt road.]

7th cross-interrogatory. Mark with red line and letters F F at each end of the line the distance and road along which your command dragged brush.

Answer to 7th cross-interrogatory. I have marked the map as requested. [From junction of Meadowville lane and old Warrenton road on the lane north 2,800 feet.]

8th cross-interrogatory. Did you, yourself, see this dragging of brush?

Answer to 8th cross-interrogatory. I did.

9th cross-interrogatory. How many men were present for duty in your regiment on said 29th August?

Answer to 9th cross-interrogatory. It was somewhere between three hundred and four hundred.

10th cross-interrogatory. How many were dragging brush?

Answer to 10th cross-interrogatory. There was a large detail—several companies— in the neighborhood of a hundred.

11th cross-interrogatory. With a view to getting their opinions as to hour and place of dragging brush on 29th of August, 1862, please state if you remember the names and addresses of any officers or men now living who were eye-witnesses of such dragging.

Answer to 11th cross-interrogatory. The regiment was subsequently so badly cut up that I do not now remember the name of a single living officer who was present, unless it may be Hon. B. B. Douglas, now a member of Congress from Virginia.

12th cross-interrogatory. What time in the day did you begin dragging brush, and when did you end it? State particularly how you fix the time.

Answer to 12th cross-interrogatory. We began it, as near as I can remember, about ten o'clock in the morning. It must have been in the neighborhood of one,o'clock when we quit. I state the time from my recollection.

13th cross-interrogatory. Draw a red line from the point where you said you met General Stuart when he directed you to drag brush to a place marked New Market, another from the same first-named point to Manassas Station; a third line to a point where Milford road runs off at foot of map, and a fourth to Langley's Mills, and then state the position with reference to either of these lines of the Union forces to delude whom you dragged brush as Stuart reported them advancing.

Answer to 13th cross-interrogatory. I have marked the lines on the map as requested. The forces I desired to delude were reported to be in the direction of Manassas, between the points I have previously marked on the map with the letters E and Manassas.

14th cross-interrogatory. Along what road did you understand the Union forces were moving upon our (your) right flank, because of which you were ordered to drag brush? Please mark the road with red letters G G and the position of the Union forces with red bars

Answer to 14th cross-interrogatory. I only understood the Union forces were moving as stated. I did not see them, and cannot locate their position.

15th cross-interrogatory. In whose command was Major Pelham; in that of Longstreet or of Jackson?

Answer to 15th cross-interrogatory. Major Pelham was chief of artillery with Stuart, under Jackson.

16th cross-interrogatory. Where were you when Pelham came to you? Mark with red letter H.

Answer to 16th cross-interrogatory. I was near the point I have marked with the letter H; about at the point marked C [near junction of Meadowville lane and old Warrenton and Alexandria road].

17th cross-interrogatory. To what point and in which direction did Pelham "move out to the right" where he engaged the enemy? Mark point with red letter I and direction with red arrow and letter K, →.

Answer to 17th cross-interrogatory. I have marked the direction in which he went. I do not know to what point he went. [A little east of south, towards Union skirmishers.]

18th cross-interrogatory. How many guns had he with him?

Answer to 18th cross-interrogatory. It is my impression he had only two.

19th cross-interrogatory. In which direction did he fire? Mark with red arrow and letter L.

Answer to 19th cross-interrogatory. I did not see him fire. I heard artillery in the direction he took.

20th cross-interrogatory. Where were the enemy at whom he fired? Mark with red letter M.

Answer to 20th cross-interrogatory. That I could not tell.

21st cross-interrogatory. What cavalry command relieved you then, and from where did they move out? Mark point with red letter N.

Answer to 21st cross-interrogatory. It is my impression that I was relieved by General Bev. Robinson. They came in from the direction of Gainesville. I at once left upon being relieved.

22d cross-interrogatory. Where was your position on extreme right of Longstreet, which was then forming, as you say? Mark this position with red bars and letter O.

Answer to 22d cross-interrogatory. I have marked the map as requested. The point near Brewer's Spring. [One thousand three hundred feet east of junction Meadowville lane and old Warrenton and Alexandria road.]

23d cross-interrogatory. Do you know of your own observation that Jackson's infantry was engaged all the morning?

Answer to 23d cross-interrogatory. I know there was more or less firing all morning. I did not consider it a regular engagement. There was no battle.

24th cross-interrogatory. Have you had your memory refreshed lately? If so, state when, where, and by whom, or what.

Answer to 24th cross-interrogatory. I have not. I have not even read the proceedings of the present trial.

25th cross-interrogatory. Have you ever been over the ground you speak of since 1862? If so, state when, and if you have examined the topography particularly.

Answer to 25th cross-interrogatory. I have not been on the field since that day. I had previously examined the topography of the country particularly, and made a map of the first battle of Manassas.

B. S. White, then major and assistant inspector-general of the *regular* Confederate army, serving on Maj. Gen. J. E. B. Stuart's staff, called by the government, testified as follows (Board's Record, p. 1052):

Question. Where were you on the morning of Friday, August 29, 1862?
Answer. Near Sudley Church.
Question. Do you know anything that transpired in your immediate vicinity on that morning? If so, what was it? [Map shown and explained to witness.]
Answer. On that morning we were looking south; there were some troops appeared on our left, Federal troops, and there was some little confusion in our ambulance train just north of Sudley Springs.
Question. What then transpired?
Answer. There were some artillery and troops put in position to open on the enemy in *that* direction (witness indicates that the artillery was west of Sudley Church), firing east across Bull Run.
Question. Do you know whose battery that was that was put in position?
Answer. Pelham's battery; he commanded the Stuart horse-artillery.
Question. What then transpired?
Answer. Major Patrick was ordered to charge, and did charge the enemy in that direction, and lost his life there.

* * * * *

Question. That morning after Major Patrick had those orders to charge, what did you do?
Answer. The enemy were driven away.
Question. Then what was the next event that transpired?
Answer. We moved off across the country to find out what had become of Longstreet's corps; we moved off in this way, towards Thoroughfare Gap.
Question. Did you find General Longstreet's column or corps advancing?
Answer. We did, between Hay Market and Gainesville.
Question. What did General Stuart then do?
Answer. General Stuart then threw his command on Longstreet's right and moved down with his right flank in the direction of Bristoe to Manassas Junction.
Question. What did you then observe?
Answer. We took the road leading directly down the Manassas Gap Railroad; there is a road running parallel with it.
Question. How far down did you go?
Answer. General Stuart threw his command on the right of Longstreet, and passed down the Manassas Gap Railroad to about that point [west of Hampton Cole's; point marked "W"].
Question. Then what did you do?
Answer. We discovered a column in our front—discovered a force in our front coming from the direction of Manassas Junction to Bristoe.
Question. What sort of a point was that where you discovered this column coming, so far as observation is concerned?
Answer. It was a good point for observation; a high position, elevated ground. We could see Thoroughfare Gap and Gainesville and all the surrounding country.
Mr. MALTBY. Do you refer to the point where he was?
The RECORDER. Yes; where they saw this column approaching.
Question. How near the point on the railroad was it that this commanding ridge is?
Answer. Not very far from the railroad; I suppose a half or three-quarters of a mile—something like that.
Question. Could you indicate about where you think it was?
Answer. I think it was about *there.* [Marked thus: + .]
Question. You saw the column of troops advancing?
Answer. Yes.
Question. Did you at that time judge about how much of a column it was?
Answer. I did not see it all, but it seemed to be a very large body of troops.
Question. What did General Stuart then do?
Answer. He put a battery in position on that hill.
Question. Did you receive any instructions at that time?
Answer. I did.
Question. What were they?
Answer. My instructions were to put a battery in position there and open on the column advancing in this direction. His instructions to me were to go to General Jackson and report the fact of this column moving in that direction.
Question. Did you go and do it?

Answer. I did: I went across *here*. [Parallel with Pageland lane.] General Jackson's corps was here—that is, his command was along the Independent Manassas Gap Railroad, and the batteries were posted right on a range of hills in the rear of that. I found General Jackson on a range of hills just in the rear of his battery.

Question. Having reported, what did you then do?.

Answer. I then started to return to General Stuart.

Question. Where did you go?

Answer. I tried to take a little short cut going back to him. I made a little detour; I passed where there had been a skirmish the evening before.

Question. Did you find any dead and wounded there?

Answer. I did.

Question. North of the pike or south of the pike?

Answer. On the north side.

Question Did you find General Stuart at once?

Answer. It was some time before I found him; a half or three-quarters of an hour.

Question. Did you halt on the way going back?

Answer I passed a little time with General Jackson after I reported to him, because the batteries were engaged; his batteries were on Stony Ridge. (Witness indicates a point back of the words "Stony Ridge.") His line of battle was along the Independent line of the Manassas Gap Railroad; there was a battery that came out about the point of that woods (just northwest of the Matthews house and west of the Sudley pike); just about that point there was a battery from the Union side that came out there and took position, and I staid there some time watching the artillery duel between the guns stationed *here* and that battery. Then going back to General Stuart I took a little short cut and passed over some ground where there had been a fight the evening before, and there was some dead on the field. In going back I met a cousin of mine, who commanded a battalion connected with Ewell's corps, which was engaged in this fight; he was reconnoitering; I went along with him, and saw what was in my front; I suppose it was half or three-quarters of an hour, or maybe an hour, before I got back to General Stuart.

Question. When you got back to General Stuart, where was he?

Answer. Where I left him, on that hill.

Question. At that time where was General Longstreet's command?

Answer. They had come down and were forming *here*. (Witness indicates a point back, westerly of Pageland lane.)

Question. About what time of day was it that this affair occurred at Sudley Springs; before you and General Stuart started to cross the country towards Thoroughfare Gap?

Answer. Early in the morning.

Question. At what would you fix the time?

Answer. I suppose eight or nine o'clock in the morning.

Question. Did you remain at this point with General Stuart after you got back on this hill?

Answer. I did.

Question. What became of this column of troops that you saw advancing?

Answer. I don't know what became of them; they disappeared from our front.

Question. Do you know of any other position being taken up by General Longstreet's command during the day in advance of the position that you have indicated? If so, when and where? You indicated a position back of Pageland lane.

Answer. I do not.

Question. How long were you down in the neighborhood of this hill which you have marked with a cross during that day; up to what time?

Answer. We were down there the greater part of the day; we were on the extreme right all the time afterward. The cavalry remained on the extreme right until the morning of the 30th.

Question. Do you know of any other measures taken to retard the advance of this column of troops from the direction of Manassas Junction or Bristoe that day by General Stuart, other than the planting of the battery in that position?

Answer. I do not. Before that battery was put in position Robertson's brigade of cavalry and Rosser were engaging the enemy in our front. When the battery was put in position and opened on the enemy it checked them, and they retired. Then General Stuart told me to go to General Jackson and report the fact that this column was advancing in this direction.

Question. During that day what sort of an action was going on, on the 29th, to your knowledge?

Answer. There was very heavy fighting going on up here in Jackson's front.

Mr. MALTBY. Did you see it?

Answer. I heard the musketry firing and I heard artillery.

Question. This engagement which you speak of between Robertson's cavalry and the enemy—what was it?

Answer. It was a skirmish simply.

* * * * *

Question. What time do you think you met General Longstreet between Haymarket and Gainesville?

Answer. It was about eleven o'clock.

Question. Was General Longstreet at the head of his column?

Answer. He was near the head of the column.

Question. Were there many troops in front of his command?

Answer. Not many.

Question. Were they advancing?

Answer. They were.

Question. Rapidly?

Answer. They were marching at an ordinary pace.

Question. State the style of march; how many front?

Answer. They were marching in column.

Question. How many front?

Answer. Marching in column of regiments, perhaps four abreast.

Question. Were they in close order?

Answer. Yes, sir.

Question. Would you swear it was eleven o'clock?

Answer. It was about eleven o'clock.

Question. You are confident that none of Longstreet's forces had passed through Gainesville before eleven o'clock?

Answer. I don't think they had.

* * * * *

Question. Those hours are stated purely from memory?

Answer. From memory simply.

Question. How did General Stuart throw his cavalry to the right of Longstreet's column?

Answer. By passing through Longstreet's line of march.

Question. Were they passed through in column.

Answer. No, sir.

Question. How?

Answer. By single file.

Question. What became of the cavalry then?

Answer. They took the road leading parallel with the Manassas Gap Railroad, and moved down in the direction of Manassas Junction.

Question. Did you remain with the cavalry or did you go with General Stuart?

Answer. I was with General Stuart.

Question. Did General Stuart have any conversation with General Longstreet or General Lee?

Answer. He did.

Question. About where was that?

Answer. At the point where we met Longstreet's column.

Question. Was that while you were on the march, or was it while you were personally stationary?

Answer. We were stationary at the time, of course, when we met Longstreet's column; they were together when this conversation took place. General Lee passed his command on the road, and Longstreet then moved down with Stuart, and they then and there moved down in the direction of Manassas Junction.

Question. How long a conversation did General Stuart have with General Lee or General Longstreet?

Answer. Ten or fifteen minutes.

Question. Did you converse at all with the men.

Answer. No, sir.

Question. Any of the command?

Answer. No, sir.

Question. How long was it before you arrived at the point marked "W" by you on this map?

Answer. It could not have been over three-quarters of an hour or an hour.

Question. Then about what time would that make it when you arrived at the point marked "W"?

Answer. Between 11 and 12 o'clock.

Question. Nearer which?

Answer. Nearer 12 than 11.

Question. Where were Rosser's cavalry at that time, if you know personally?

Answer. I judge they were right in *here*. (Witness indicates a point about south-west of Hampton Cole's.)

Question. Were they all there, do you know?
Answer. Yes; they were there.
Question. All?
Answer. All.

*   *   *   *   *   *

Question. You say that the distance from the railroad, or from the point "W" to where those two cannon or that battery were posted by General Stuart, was from half to three-quarters of a mile; this map being on a scale of three inches to a mile, you have marked it within half an inch, which would be far less than either of those distances; how do you come to put it there—that cross-mark?
Answer. That is about the distance they were; about three-quarters of a mile from this ridge.
Question. That not being three-quarters of a mile, where would you put their position?
Answer. *There* is about where the battery was. (The witness measures the map and marks the point indicated thus: +².)
Question. How did the forces of the enemy coming from the direction of Manassas or Bristoe appear; how were they formed; in column, or line of battle, or how?
Answer. They were in column.
Question. How far off?
Answer. They were about *here.* (Witness indicates a point on a line with "SS" in the word "Manassas" on the Manassas Gap Railroad.)
Question. On the railroad?
Answer. Coming up this road running parallel to the railroad.
Question. From the position where you were, did you see any house in the direction of those troops?
Answer. Of course we could see the whole surrounding country.
Question. Did you see any house in the direction of those troops between you and those troops, or nearly between you and those troops?
Answer. There were several houses; yes.
Question. Were those troops near any house that you could see?
Answer. They were near the Carraco house.
Question. Very near?
Answer. Perhaps a little beyond.
Question. Did not you see any troops in the direction of the place marked "Lewis-Leachman house" on that day?
Answer. Yes; there were troops there, too.
Question. How were they disposed.
Answer. I could not say.
Question. Are you certain that no shots were fired from that direction at the men about in the neighborhood of the Lewis-Leachman house? [The position indicated being +²].
Answer. No, I am not certain; though I believe that there were.
Question. Are you not certain that most of the shots were fired in that direction?
Answer. I am unable to answer that, for this reason: at the time that battery was put in there [+²], firing in this direction upon the Manassas Gap Railroad, General Stuart requested that I should go here and report the fact to General Jackson, which I did; I went off *there*, and was gone at least three-quarters of an hour or an hour. [Witness indicates a direction towards the Independent line of the Manassas Gap Railroad.] The firing commenced in the direction of the Manassas Gap Railroad.
Question. How many shots?
Answer. I do not know.
Question. Much firing?
Answer. Yes; a good deal.
Question. Fifty shots.
Answer. I could not say whether there were one or fifty, because when the firing commenced, as I tell you, and that battery came in position, firing in this direction— I know there were troops off here [towards the Lewis-Leachman house]—some shots may have been directed there in that direction [the Leachman house], and I went away to report to General Jackson.

*   *   *   *   *   *

Question. Are you positive that there were two shots?
Answer. Yes; I am positive that there were two shots.
Question. Three?
Answer. Yes, there were three.

*   *   *   *   *   *

Question. Was there not firing due south from +², in the direction of Langley's Mill?
Answer. That I cannot answer. The object of putting that battery in that position

was, we saw troops coming from this direction, and it was put there for the purpose of firing in that direction [Manassas Gap road.]

Question. Have you been informed during the last month of the position of the column of troops commanded by General Porter, with reference to this map, on the morning of the 29th?

Answer. I have not; I do not know whether this was General Porter's column, or whose column it was.

*   *   *   *   *   *   *

Question. How did they appear to you; to be on top of a hill, or in a depression, or in woods, or by woods, or in an open field?

Answer. The position we occupied was a commanding one, of course. They were in a depressed situation from the position we occupied. We were on this hill and they were here. [Witness indicates.]

Question. In column, marching along the Manassas Gap Railroad?

Answer. Yes.

Question. Did you see the Manassas Gap Railroad right in their vicinity?

Answer. The road they were marching on was parallel to the Manassas Gap Railroad.

Question. When you came back to that position did you see any Federal troops anywhere?

Answer. Yes. There were Federal troops off here. [Indicating the lines of the regiments.]

Question. When you came back did you see Longstreet's command?

Answer. I saw Longstreet's command on my way back from General Stuart; they came and formed in here. [Pageland lane.]

Question. Did you remain in that position all day?

Answer. We were there most all day. Do you mean me individually?

Question. Yes.

Answer. No. I was backward and forward several times during the day. I went with messages from Stuart to Lee and Longstreet and to Jackson.

Question. Then, during that whole day, you were in the vicinity of Longstreet's troops and knew of their position?

*   *   *   *

Question. You say you were on a hill that commanded views of the country in front of you?

Answer. We had a battery off here [W. 5]; that is, there was a park of artillery in position and Longstreet's command was about that way [south].

Question. Were there any artillery in front of the position called "W. 5"?

Answer. Right there we had 19 or 20 pieces of artillery.

Question. Where "W. 5" is?

Answer. Yes; between Jackson's line and Longstreet's line.

Question. Are you as positive about the position of the guns marked "W. 5" as you are about the position of Hood "W. 3"?

Answer. Right here was where Hood was [witness indicates]; beyond the piece of woods there was a little branch running down; over on a hill was a battery of the Union troops.

By the RECORDER:

Question. Do you know what these red lines stand for?

Answer. No, sir; I do not.

Question. These red lines are contour lines marking the heights, and these numbers, 200 and 210, and so forth, mark the elevations.

Answer. Hood was here [W. 3]; then there was a small branch.

Question. Do you know the marks which indicate branches?

Answer. No, sir.

Mr. MALTBY. They are the black marks.

Answer. Well, that is the branch [Young's Branch]. My recollection is there was a battery or several batteries of the Federal forces right there.

Question. At Britt's?

Answer. Wait a moment; it may be that piece of woods [between Britt's and Cunliffe's]. There is where they were—in there [about south of the word "Meadowville," under Cunliffe's]. There was a hill—I don't know how you mark it here—there was a hill, a very nice position for artillery, where there were several batteries that were firing off here [at W. 5] in that direction; with Longstreet's command right in here [W. 3].

Question. Did Longstreet's line curve from the position of the artillery [W. 5.]?

Answer. I cannot answer that question. I had no connection with Longstreet's command; it was only observations in passing with messages from Stuart to Lee or Jackson.

Question. Where was Lee's position, headquarters, where he could be heard from, in reference to Longstreet's line, in front or behind it?

Answer. It was behind it.

Question. Can you locate on the map where General Lee's headquarters were? Describe as near as possible what his headquarters were. Were they a house?

Answer. No; the times I reported to him he was in the field; he would move sometimes to one position, sometimes to another.

Question. How far behind Longstreet's front line was General Lee?

Answer. I found General Lee at one time just on a hill, just behind General Hood, when I went with a message to him, just behind General Hood's command; he was there with a glass looking off in the direction where this battery was. [Southeasterly towards Britt's.]

Question. Do you know Col. Charles Marshall, of General Lee's staff?

Answer. I do.

Question. Did you see him during the day?

Answer. I did; several times.

. Question. Was he in a stationary position, dismounted, or riding about?

Answer. Riding about. Whenever I saw him he was mounted. I saw him several times during the day, at different parts of the field.

* * * * * *

Question. If his actual headquarters were about in the position marked P, would the position of Hood be in the position you have assigned it or in advance of the letter P, that being on the edge of a hill, as you see by the map, Cunliffe's being in a depression—where would you put the line of General Hood?

Answer. General Hood's line was just here. [Witness indicates.]

Question. Suppose Lee's headquarters were where the letter P is, where would the line of General Hood be on this map?

Answer. I never said that General Lee's headquarters were there [at the point marked P.]

* * * * * *

Question. What time do you put it that you came back from General Jackson after being sent over by General Stuart?

Answer. Half past two or three o'clock.

Question. Do you know of any action that occurred along the Warrenton pike: infantry?

Answer. I heard firing.

Question. What time was that?

Answer. In the evening.

Question. About what time?

Answer. General Jackson's command was engaged all the time.

Question. Was Hood's command engaged at all?

Answer. That evening they were.

Question. What time that evening?

Answer. I suppose about three o'clock in the evening they were engaged; two and a half to three o'clock.

Question. Were they engaged vigorously?

Answer. Quite a severe fight.

Question. Describe the action, so far as you observed it.

Answer. I was not present. I didn't see it. I heard the firing; it lasted, I suppose, half to three-quarters of an hour.

Question. Was it very vigorous?

Answer. It was a very sharp fight.

Question. Was that the only occasion in which Hood's command was engaged that day, to your knowledge?

Answer. To my knowledge that is the only one until next morning.

Question. You say it was three o'clock?

Answer. Between two and three o'clock. It may have been after three. It was after he had got in position.

Question. How long after he got in position?

Answer. He got in position, I suppose, about twelve or one o'clock. This engagement took place about two and a half, or maybe three, or three and a half.

Question. Was it as late as five?

Answer. I can't recollect. I don't think it was.

Question. What is your recollection about the time that that engagement took place upon the Warrenton turnpike by Hood's troops?

Answer. I was away on the right. Of course there was fighting on the line. I don't know what troops were engaged, but I know that Hood's troops had a fight there that evening. I don't know whether it was three, or three and a half; it may have been five o'clock. I know they had a sharp fight there, and I heard it.

* * * * * *

Question. Do you fix that time with more or less precision; and, if so, why, than the time you arrived at the point marked $+$?

Answer. Hood's command had not formed at the time we left here; he formed afterwards.

* * * * * *

Question. Does your memory serve you equally well as to all the hours stated by you?

Answer. The hours that I spoke of at the time I was connected with our command, of course, are more clear in my mind.

Question. Than the time when you heard the sound of vigorous battle near you?

Answer. The cavalry were around on the right. Hood was right in there [W³]; and three and a half or three o'clock, to the best of my recollection, is the time I heard this sharp fighting in Hood's front. From the position he occupied I supposed it was his front, because we were just to his right.

* * * * *

Question. If it were proven that no Union troops were upon the Manassas Gap Railroad in the position you have marked, and that the position which they actually did occupy—the corps referred to in that neighborhood—was invisible from the position that you occupied——

Answer. I never said it was a corps; I said it was a column of troops.

Question. The corps referred in that neighborhood, would you or would you not say that those troops were in the neighborhood of Leachman's?

Answer. I saw troops in both directions.

Question. Might they not have been on the Alexandria and Washington road, about the junction of Lewis' lane No. 1 with that road?

Answer. No, sir; there were troops off there; we could not see them from the position we occupied. There were troops over here both in the direction of the Lewis-Leachman house and off in the direction of the Manassas Gap Railroad.

Question. How much of the column did you see there on the Manassas Gap Railroad?

Answer. I saw a good many troops there. I don't know how many they were.

Question. A regiment?

Answer. I suppose there were more; two.

Question. Two regiments?

Answer. Yes; perhaps more than two regiments.

Question. How much of the line did you see?

Answer. I saw the column; they were moving in column.

* * * * *

Question. How many regiments should you judge you saw?

Answer. I don't know how many regiments. When the head of that column appeared there, this battery was put in position and opened on them. I went by direction of Stuart to Jackson to report to him.

* * * * *

By the RECORDER:

Question. Assuming Hood's division to be in the place you have indicated by W³, and suppose there had been a battery placed on this rise of ground marked C, would that have fulfilled what you understood was the position of a battery firing off in the direction of "W⁵"?

Answer. Yes. Just beyond a small branch there was a hill, a very fine position for artillery, and it was firing off in the direction of "W⁵." The highest ground of that hill is where that battery was placed, or rather a park of artillery; 19 or 20 of our guns were in that position.

Question. Suppose that the column of troops that you saw on that morning, or on the noon of Friday, August 29, had been coming up the dirt road from Manassas Junction to Gainesville and was in the neighborhood of Dawkins' Run, would that have been the position of the column that you saw according to the map?

(Objected to as leading.)

Answer. The troops that we saw approaching came more from the direction of Bristoe than from Manassas.

Question. Therefore what road indicated on this map best fulfills the direction from which you saw those troops coming?

(Objected to as leading.)

Answer. They were approaching more in the direction from Bristoe than from Manassas.

Question. Therefore what road best of the roads you see on this map shows the direction from which you saw those troops coming [map explained to the witness]? Now where were the Federal troops?

Answer. I remarked a while ago that the column that was advancing advanced more from the direction of Bristoe than Manassas.

Question. Here is Bristoe and there is Manassas. Now where do you put it, what direction? Make a line indicating the direction.

Answer. They must have come in here or in here.

Question. Then you are not positive that you saw them on the Manassas Gap Railroad?

Answer. I never said I saw the Manassas Gap Railroad. I said I saw them on the road running parallel with the Manassas Gap Railroad. They were not marching on the railroad. They were marching on a road that I supposed, from the position I occupied, was a line parallel with the Manassas Gap Railroad; they may have been on this road [from Gainesville to Stuart's Hill] and took position there [at + ²]. From that position we saw the column coming up, but they were not on the railroad.

* * * * * *

Question. Did you see the railroad in conjunction with seeing them, or at the same time in connection with seeing them?

Answer. I could not say. I was not looking for railroads. I was looking for troops. I don't recollect now whether I saw the railroad or not, because my attention was directed to more important matters.

Question. Would you swear that those troops, Bristoe being *here* and Manassas *there*—that those troops were not on this road to Milford?

Answer. No; they were not in that direction at all. They were off here [witness indicates in the direction of the Manassas and Gainesville dirt road].

Question. Had you been to Bristoe that day?

Answer. No, sir; we had been there the day before.

Question. How do you know where Bristoe was?

Answer. Because I have been there a thousand times since.

Question. Could you see it from that position?

Answer. I don't know that you could see the station, but I knew the general direction, and had been all over that country time and again.

Question. Did you see any of the shot fired fall near that column?

Answer. Yes, sir.

Question. What did the column do?

Answer. The column seemed to retire.

Question. Did you see them retire?

Answer. Yes; I saw them give back.

Question. How did they retire?

Answer. You know how troops retire. They gave back into a piece of woods; and just at that time I went off with a message, as I stated before—went off with a message to General Jackson from General Stuart.

Question. Did anybody mention a piece of woods to you in connection with those troops within the last month?

Answer. Not if my memory serves me.

Question. Were you reminded of a piece of woods by any marks on the map?

Answer. No, sir; because my memory serves me clearly that it was just in a piece of woods when the head of the column showed itself, and they retired back into the woods, and we fired our artillery into this piece of woods.

Question. Did you see a smaller column march from this main column in advance and deploy?

Answer. I don't recollect. When we took position there was a column advancing more in the direction of Bristoe than from Manassas.

Question. Looking at the map where you made a mark somewhat south and east of Carraco's on the Manassas Gap Railroad, if that country was all open at that time, would that position fulfill the position you have just indicated as where those troops were that you saw that fell immediately back into the woods upon being fired upon?

Answer. My recollection is that the scale of this map is about the distance they showed themselves in our front. I suppose that would indicate about three-quarters of a mile, or something in that neighborhood—half or three-quarters of a mile. That is about the distance that they were in our front when we discovered them and opened upon them. At the same time we saw troops off in this direction [the Lewis-Leachman house]; just about here there was a narrow range of wooded hills.

By Mr. MALTBY:

Question. You say that the artillery were stationed on the right of Jackson at the highest point on the ridge. Now, did Longstreet's line bend back from the line of Jackson, or did they make an angle more nearly approaching right angles?

Answer. I had nothing to do with Longstreet's position.

Question. But you saw it?

Answer. I passed in his rear several times.

Question. Take a pencil and mark Longstreet's line.

Answer. There was an angle formed between Jackson and Longstreet's line; Jackson's line ran along here. [Witness indicates.]

Question. Draw it in pencil. There is the Independent line of the Manassas Gap Railroad. [Indicated to the witness.]

Answer. Jackson's artillery was posted on this stony ridge.
Question. Draw a line where the nineteen or twenty guns were posted.
Answer. I had no connection with Longstreet's command or Jackson's. I passed in the rear of both lines several times with messages. I did not inspect their lines. I just speak from general recollection of their lines.
Question. Then you do not recollect precisely where any one line was?
Answer. I do; yes. I have indicated there is Jackson's line; his artillery was posted on this range of hills; General Longstreet formed here. [Witness indicates the different positions.] Their lines did not join; there was an angle there, an opening, and there is where the battery of artillery was.
Question. Draw Jackson's line and the cannon of Longstreet.
Answer. I have indicated it. [Witness indicates the line of the Independent line of the Manassas Gap Railroad.] His line did not go down that far [indicating Sudley Church]; it went to about there.
Question. Where do you run Jackson's line?
Answer. Jackson's line ran about in this direction. [Marked with a pencil.] That is about the direction of Jackson's line.
The line indicated by the witness by means of a pencil is followed in ink by the Recorder.
Question. Where were these eighteen or twenty guns of Jackson's?
Answer. That did not have reference to Jackson's command; Jackson's artillery was posted on this range of hills back of his line of battle. This park of artillery is where W⁵ is and W⁶.
Question. You still say that Hood occupied that position, and that his right was where + and + + are?
Answer. There is where Hood was; right there.

By Mr. MALTBY:
Question. Did you see General Longstreet's troops or General Hood's troops while they were forming in line of battle on the 29th, and after they were formed?
Answer. I saw Hood's command after they had taken position.
Question. But not while they were forming?
Answer. Not while they were forming.

By the RECORDER:
Question. Did you see them before they were formed? If so, at what time?
Answer. When we parted with them on the pike between Haymarket and Gainesville, we took the right and moved down to this position where we saw the column advancing. When that battery took position there and opened in that direction I went with a message immediately to General Jackson, and passed over the ground where I saw Hood's command. Afterwards, when I went on a message from Stuart to Lee, I found him on that hill in the rear of Hood's line and delivered my message to General Lee, looking to the south of the Warrenton pike on that hill.
Question. He was not in that position when you went to General Jackson with that message?
Answer. No, sir; he had not taken position there then.

Rev. *John Landstreet*, called by the Recorder, and examined in the city of Baltimore October 22, 1878 (present, the Recorder and Mr. Maltby, of counsel for the petitioner), being duly sworn, testified as follows:

Question. State your residence and occupation.
Answer. Minister of the gospel in the Southern Methodist Church; I reside at Reisterstown, Baltimore County, Maryland.
Question. What position did you hold in the Confederate Army of Northern Virginia on the 29th of August, 1862?
Answer. I was chaplain of the First Virginia Cavalry during the entire war. Before I was commissioned I was with General Stuart. I received my commission while with him. I had a little more liberty than some of the others had, in view of my position, preaching to the different commands, and would often absent myself with less formality than some of the rest would. I was with him in all his important engagements, or, if I was not with him, he would generally send for me if he knew where I was.
Question. Where were you on the morning of August 29, 1862?
Answer. I was between Sudley Springs and Aldie, about midway in the mountain.
Question. Did you join General Stuart that day?
Answer. I joined him for the first time for eight months, after our Catlett's Station raid. I think I reached Sudley between eight and nine o'clock in the morning.
Question. Was General Stuart there?
Answer. Yes, sir.
Question. Do you recollect any circumstance transpiring after you arrived there?

Answer. No, sir. Just before we arrived there was a little confusion or kind of stampede among the baggage-train. I don't know that I noticed any of our cavalry there unless it was those connected with the commissary and quartermaster's department. But there was a little skirmish there about that time which attracted my attention.

Question. Did you see Captain Pelham any time that day?

Answer. Yes; I saw him. I was very intimate with him. But where I saw him I cannot tell. I have a journal in which I noted everything. I kept it at the request of General Stuart and partly for my own gratification, but especially at his request.

Question. Do you know at what time you left Sudley?

Answer. No, sir; I recollect that the next place where I was was called Cole's. It was an elevated position, rather in the angle between Gainesville and Bristoe; Bristoe being much farther off. [Witness looks at the map.] It was Hampton Cole's.

Question. At what time in the day were you at Hampton Cole's?

Answer. I did not have a watch, but I think it was somewhere towards ten o'clock in the day.

Question. What did you do or see there which has impressed itself upon your attention?

Answer. There was considerable dust in this direction [witness indicates], indicating a body of troops; there was considerable down in this direction somewhere. At any rate, General Stuart ordered some of the Fifth Cavalry to go and cut brush and drag it along the road.

Question. [By Mr. MALTBY.] Did you hear the order?

Answer. Yes; to drag the brush along the Gainesville road, so as to serve as a feint and to convey the impression that there was a force coming down the Gainesville road. It was given, I distinctly recollect, to a member of the Fifth Virginia Cavalry.

Question. Who was the colonel of that regiment?

Answer. T. L. Rosser. We frequently after that conversed about it.

Question. What was done after that, while you were in the neighborhood of Hampton Cole's?

Answer. There was some firing from this position [+2], in the direction of this approaching force; and from my recollection of it the force was a considerable distance down. If 3 inches indicate a mile here, and if it was a life and death case, I would say that it was inside of a mile that they were off.

Question. You should say it was a distance of about a mile?

Answer. I should say it was inside of a mile. It was not beyond a mile, certainly. [Witness indicates from Hampton Cole's.] There were several shots fired from this point in the direction down there.

Question. In what direction?

Answer. That depends entirely upon where the man was standing at the time, and what he was looking at. I did not charge my mind much with this Manassas Gap Railroad, though I knew it very well. But I would not say whether it was here or there [whether right or left]. It was pretty much in line with this railroad. [Manassas Gap Railroad.]

Question. What became of this column of troops upon those shots being fired?

Answer. I did not see them.

Question. They disappeared from your sight?

Answer. Yes, sir.

Question. Did they remain in the position they were in when they were fired upon?

Answer. No, sir. When my attention was directed to them they were where I could see the column, or a considerable portion of it; and they were marching in good order, close column.

Question. Do you recollect how many shots were fired at them?

Answer. I do not; but I am positive I didn't hear half a dozen; I know I did not.

Question. How long did you remain in that position in the neighborhood of Hampton Cole's that day?

Answer. I was sent off after that to hunt up the First Virginia Cavalry, not very far from there at that time; and I paid very little attention, indeed, from that time. When Longstreet came and formed there, General Jackson being in position, I came out from the command, and I was not in any of the fight at all except in the cavalry movements—skirmishing.

Question. Where did General Longstreet form his command?

Answer. It seems to me I struck a portion of Hood's command on General Longstreet's left, before I got anywhere in the direction of Longstreet's right. They seemed to come in a good ways in the direction of General Longstreet's left, if they were not immediately on his flank.

Question. About where would you put them; north of the pike, across the pike, or south of the pike?

Answer. Which?

Question. Hood's division of that command?

Answer. From my recollection, there was a portion of Longstreet's command that crossed the Manassas Gap Railroad [the witness marks a point with a pen]; crossed it, I am sure, some distance, but how far I don't know. I do not think it was far. It extended, I think, up in this way. Hood's was in front of it; part of it in the body of the woods. My impression is that Hood came in a little in advance of Longstreet's left. I am certain I came to Hood before I came to Longstreet's force in position [marked "Longstreet" and "Hood"].

Question. What time of day was that that they were all in position?

Answer. It is my recollection that it was somewhere between two and three o'clock.

Question. Do you know whether or not either Hood or the remainder of Longstreet's that was in advance to the east of Pageland lane at any time that day?

Answer. I do not.

Question. Was your position such that you could see the location of Hood and Longstreet during the afternoon?

Answer. O, yes; I could go where I pleased.

Question. How long did this action of that day continue?

Answer. The firing to my recollection continued up to about dark. It was near dusk. At times it was heavier than at others; and at times severer than I ever heard it in any engagement.

Question. What were your opportunities during that day of knowing the fact, provided General Hood had advanced east of Pageland lane? [Points of compass upon the map explained to the witness.]

Answer. My answer is, that if I had a desire to know it, I could have known it very easily; but I didn't think about it at all. It was not in my mind. I was well acquainted with Hood and his command, and that made the impression upon me in coming to this point. I came from the direction where Jackson's command was, and passed this heavy battery at the time, though I think there were a few more guns there than I have heard stated to-day.

Question. How late in the day do you recollect seeing General Hood's division.

Answer. Between three and four o'clock.

Question. Where was it then?

Answer. Where I have indicated on the map.

Question. Relative to the command that you heard given by General Stuart to the member of the Fifth Virginia Cavalry to drag brush, what do you know about whether that order was obeyed or not?

Answer. After hearing this order given, and being very much interested in the approach of this column below there, I kept a lookout, and it was not long—I am sure not more than 40 or 50 minutes—before the column of dust on the Gainesville road appeared.

Question. You saw the column of dust arising?

Answer. I saw a cloud of dust.

Question. Arising from this dragging of brush?

Answer. Yes.

*   *   *   *   *

Question. Who arrived first at Hampton Cole's, you or General Stuart?

Answer. He did; he was there when I got there.

*   *   *   *

Question. Will you describe the position on that map about where you saw the column of dust arising after General Stuart gave the order?

Answer. I think it was midway between this point and that.

Question. About midway between Hampton Cole's and Gainesville, along on the line of the Manassas Gap Railroad?

Answer. Yes. It may have been farther. There is some wood-land beyond that.

Question. Were you on this commanding ridge where the guns were stationed, of which you have spoken?

Answer. Yes; right there at Hampton Cole's.

Question. Are you certain it was at Hampton Cole's, and not at Carraco's?

Question. Did you arrive at Hampton Cole's before this battery was stationed upon this ridge?

Answer. Yes; the battery was put in position after I got there. This column from this direction made its appearance after I got there.

Question. What battery was placed there?

Answer. I don't know.

Question. Were they guns belonging to Stuart's command?

Answer. I think they were; I am not certain of that.

*   *   *   *   *

Question. From your station at Hampton Cole's, in which direction was Longstreet's command when you first saw it, without reference to the map?

Answer. I am sorry you brought me a map with anything on it now, because my impression is that Longstreet's line commenced on the other side of the Gainesville road and crossed it, but did not cross it far, and came up and passed the Warrenton turnpike; and that Hood's command was extended beyond his left.

Question. Didn't you understand Hood's command to have been a part of Longstreet's command?

Answer. I mean Hood's division.

Question. In which direction, as you stood at Hampton Cole's facing the enemy, was Longstreet's command from you, with reference to your own person—to the left, right, front, or rear?

Answer. Looking down in the direction from which the enemy were coming, a portion of it was in my rear and a portion of it was not.

Question. At the time you arrived there at Hampton Cole's?

Answer. No, sir. They did not get in this position at the time I arrived at Hampton Cole's. I arrived at Hampton Cole's about ten or eleven in the morning.

Question. Where were the guns stationed in reference to Hampton Cole's?

Answer. The guns were pointed down a little to the left of the railroad.

Question. How near were you to the guns?

Answer. Right up by them.

Question. How much of that column did you see?

Answer. I could not say how many regiments there were. The column indicated that it was the head of a considerable body of men.

Question. What was that indication?

Answer. They were marching in close column.

Question. Would not a regiment march in close column?

Answer. Might not in as close column as that, and in good order. My judgment in the matter was that it was the advance of a large army.

Question. Did you see a quarter of a mile of that column?

Answer. No, sir.

Question. An eighth of a mile?

Answer. That is somewhere near it.

Question. Was it marching upon a plain?

Answer. I cannot tell you that. It did not appear to me as if they were coming up a hill, nor as if they were coming down a hill.

Question. As if they were marching upon a plain?

Answer. It looked pretty much as if they were on a level.

Question. Can you state whether any bushes were to their right or left, or trees?

Answer. No, I could not. My impression is that the country was pretty well open left and right of where I first saw them.

Question. Did you see them in flank at all?

Answer. No, sir.

Question. I don't know whether it is a military expression or not.

Answer. Do you mean did I see the rear of the enemy?

Question. No, sir. I mean the side of the column as it advanced?

Answer. No, sir; it was the shortest space of time before the firing commenced here at Hampton Cole's before I saw them no more.

*　　　*　　　*　　　*　　　*

Question. Was this column to your right or left?

Answer. From the position I was in, it was almost directly in my front. I think if I had advanced in a straight line, I would have come up face to face with them. I was a little to the right of Hampton Cole's and looking right straight down.

*　　　*　　　*　　　*　　　*

Question. Did you see troops in the neighborhood of the Leachman house?

Answer. I knew there were troops there, but how I knew it I am not now prepared to say.

Question. How did they disappear? Did they march out of sight in the rear, or did they retire in the bushes?

Answer. If you will let me use an illustration: It was a very common thing for a column of cavalry to advance, and one shot into a column of cavalry would make them disappear in the woods, and that was the end of it. I never saw a column that got out of sight quicker than this column did.

Question. How do you fix it as being eleven o'clock in the day?

Answer. During the war, when I did not carry my watch, I was accustomed to average the time—how long it took to go to this place, and how long it took to go to that place, and I often came very close to it.

Question. Did you average the time in this instance?

Answer. I speak now simply from my recollection of what my impression was at the time, when the time was that these things occurred. I have no doubt in the world that my impression was taken exactly from my diary as I wrote it; the times of the day were specified in that, where I stated the times of the day.

*　　　*　　　*　　　*　　　*

Question. You say you arrived at Cole's about ten o'clock?

Answer. I should say between ten and eleven. I think it was nearer eleven than half past ten.

Question. You cannot swear positively whether it was half past ten or eleven?

Answer. No, sir; only that it was in the forenoon; before twelve o'clock.

Question. From your position at Hampton Cole's, after the formation of Longstreet's line, could you see them?

Answer. Could I see who?

Question. Could you see Longstreet's line?

Answer. I was not there when Longstreet's line was formed. I visited the line after it was formed.

Question. How long did you remain at Hampton Cole's?

Answer. I suppose I staid there until—well, it was just after the brush expedition; shortly after that; and I went in the direction of Gainesville from there. I don't know but what I went right across to Gainesville; I think I did.

Question. How did you go?

Answer. I struck out on this Gainesville road that I had traveled hundreds of times towards Gainesville; pretty much along the line of the railroad.

Question. How long did you say that it was that you were at Hampton Cole's?

Answer. I said I was there until after twelve o'clock.

Question. Were you there about an hour in all?

Answer. I was there more than an hour; I was there fully an hour and a half.

Question. You passed along the Manassas Gap Railroad?

Answer. I passed along the Gainesville turnpike.

Question. What did you see on your route in the shape of troops?

Answer. I met some of, I think, Longstreet's forces on the Warrenton pike.

Question. Did you see any of Longstreet's troops?

Answer. I have no recollection of seeing them.

Question. Were there any troops marching on that turnpike?

Answer. There may have been. I did not pay any attention to it.

Question. How long did you stay away in the direction of Gainesville?

Answer. I staid away until about three or half past three o'clock, I think.

Question. Then what did you do?

Answer. Then I returned to the First Regiment of Virginia Cavalry.

Question. Where was that?

Answer. If my recollection serves, it was between Hampton Cole's and Sudley.

Question. Was that the detachment that had been sent off to drag brush there that day?

Answer. No, sir. That was the Fifth Virginia Cavalry, commanded by Colonel Rosser.

Question. When did you first see the place where Longstreet's line was formed after you went off towards Gainesville?

Answer. I saw it for the first time a little after three o'clock.

Question. Was it then formed?

Answer. Yes; it was then formed in good order.

Question. All along the whole line?

Answer. Well, I did not ride along the whole line.

Question. Where were you?

Answer. I could not tell you how it was along the whole line. I rode in along *here* and I passed on out *here*. I passed around on Longstreet's left, and I found Hood's division in front of Longstreet, and rather extending beyond his left. [Witness indicates near Pageland lane.]

Question. Then what did you strike?

Answer. I didn't know what the name of the road was. I made for Sudley neighborhood, and there I met a portion of the First Virginia.

Question. On Hood's left or Longstreet's left, did you find artillery?

Answer. Yes, sir.

Question. Did Hood's line extend quite up to the artillery?

Answer. No, sir; it did not. *There was a gap.*

Question. How much of a gap?

Answer. I don't recollect how much it was, but it was a considerable gap.

Question. Half a mile?

Answer. I don't know whether it was that much, but it was a considerable gap, a considerable elevation.

Question. Do you know where that artillery was in reference to the Browner or Douglass house?

Answer. No, sir; I know nothing about houses there.

Question. Were the batteries in advance of Hood's line?

Answer. Well, rather.

Question. Much?

Answer. No, sir; they were rather a little in advance of his left.

Question. Was the distance between Hood's left and the right of the artillery as great as the gap?

Answer. According to my recollection, the battery was pretty nearly in the center of the gap.

Question. Did the line of the battery run in the same direction that Hood's line ran, or did Hood's line form an angle with the battery?

Answer. It was at an angle.

Question. Was the right of the battery much in advance of Hood's left?

Answer. No, sir; it was not much in advance, but still it was in advance.

Question. Was it a half-mile in advance?

Answer. O, no.

Question. Was it a quarter of a mile?

Answer. No, sir; I don't think it was that.

Question. Or an eighth?

Answer. I don't think it was that. It was a very short distance in advance. I would not say positively that it was in advance at all.

Question. If the actual position of the artillery on Jackson's right and on Hood's left was in the general line A A, where would the left of Hood have joined him, and where was the left of Hood in reference to that?

Answer. Pretty much where the right of Jackson was in reference to it; they sustained pretty much about the same relation.

Question. Where was the right of Jackson?

Answer. Pretty much to the left, in the rear of that battery, from my recollection, and about nearly the same distance that Hood's left was to the left.

Question. How far?

Answer. About intermediate.

Question. Did you see Jackson's right come in there?

Answer. No; I did not see it.

Question. Mark where it did come.

Answer. I cannot tell.

Question. You saw Jackson's right?

Answer. Yes; but my recollection is that that distance is pretty much about equal, the battery being in advance of both, between Hood's left and Jackson's right.

Question. Where was Jackson's right?

Answer. Jackson's right at that rate would be somewhere about here (witness indicates).

Question. Where would Hood's left be?

Answer. Somewhere about here (witness indicates).

Question. Is there the same distance between them?

Answer. To my mind they look about the same.

Question. This is a third of a mile from Hood's left to that position?

Answer. There is no third of a mile about it.

Question. You have not got the full distance?

Answer. It was just the difference between tweedledum and tweedledee. It was a very fine position for artillery, which guarded both the left of Hood and the right of Jackson.

Question. You say that Jackson was back of the left of that line of artillery as far as Hood was back of the right of the artillery?

Answer. That is my recollection of it.

    *   *   *   *   *

Question. You saw no troops marching?

Answer. No; I didn't say that. I say I didn't know what troops they were. I saw occasionally troops on the road.

Question. Many?

Answer. At times I saw quite a number.

Question. How large a force did you see on the turnpike?

Answer. I don't know.

    *   *   *   *   *   *   *

Question. Did you see one thousand?

Answer. I may have seen that; maybe more.

Question. Two thousand?

Answer. I cannot tell you.

Question. Did you see three thousand?

Answer. I cannot answer the question, because I did not charge my mind with it.

Question. Was it your impression or opinion that they were the advance or the rear of Longstreet's command?

Answer. It was my opinion that it was the rear, if I knew anything about it.

    *   *   *   *   *   *   *

Question. Allow me to refresh your recollection. These guns were under the command of Major Froebel?

Answer. I don't know; I have never asked the question.

Question. How long did you watch this cloud of dust back between Hampton Cole's and Gainesville, which occurred immediately after the sending of that order to drag brush?

Answer. It didn't occur until thirty minutes afterwards; I suppose I watched it four or five minutes.

Question. How long was that dust there?

Answer. I don't know; the dust extended down a considerable distance. I am satisfied that whenever I looked in that direction the dust was there.

Question. For how long a period?

Answer. I am not willing to answer the question, inasmuch as I cannot answer it with positiveness.

* * * * * *

Question. Did you see it at various times during the period of one hour?

Answer. I say I saw it at various times during the period of twenty-five or thirty minutes; I know that in that space of time I was somewhat interested in it; but no further.

* * * * * * *

Question. Did you follow the line of the railroad at all in going back there?

Answer. I went part on the railroad after I left Hampton Cole's.

Question. How far did you follow this railroad?

Answer. I don't recollect anything more than that I went part of the way on a railroad.

Question. Did you turn to the right or left after striking the railroad?

Answer. I don't recollect that; I recollect nothing at all about it, in regard to the items, as to my taking such a road as that.

* * * * * *

Question. Would not any considerable body of men in line of battle have made an impression upon you?

Answer. No, sir; would not have made a bit of impression, unless there was something in the case to particularly strike me.

Question. Then they might have been there or not?

Answer. Might have been there or not. I could not testify as to whether they were or not.

* * * * * *

Question. About what time of day did you first see Longstreet's troops in position after that?

Answer. I saw them in position, I think, somewhere about three o'clock, or a little after three, or a little before three.

* * * * *

Question. This position that you have given General Jackson here as his right, was that based on the supposition that was given you by the counsel on the other side, or from your recollection?

Answer. I base nothing upon any supposition from anybody. I have had no conversation with anybody about these things.

Question. You misunderstood my question. Did you notice a mark that you put there?

Answer. I told you a while ago I was sorry that map was marked, because I wanted to do my own marking. I was trying to locate that thing all the time, and what bothered me was that somebody else had been marking.

Mr. MALTBY. There was only one mark there. That is the Henry Kyd Douglas map.

The WITNESS. Intermediate between Hood's left and what I recollect on Jackson's right there was a space. It was an elevated position, and this large battery not only guarded Hood's left, but Jackson's right, if necessary. That is the impression I wanted to make.

It will be perceived that Major White, the Rev. John Landstreet, Mr Carrico, and Mr. Munroe all speak positively of Union troops at and in the vicinity of the "Lewis-Leachman" house during the morning and into the afternoon, which is confirmed, as we shall see, by the evidence of Brevet Major-General Sickles, Brevet Brigadier-General Barnes, and other Union officers of the Pennsylvania Reserves.

Therefore when Longstreet says he was at the Lewis-Leachman house between 11 and 12 on that day (Board's Record, p. 73) we must charitably conclude that he has confounded the twenty-ninth with the thirtieth day's operations.

He undoubtedly was there on the 30th, but the Union troops were then nowhere in the vicinity. One thing is particularly noticeable in this case, and that is that witnesses' recollection as to the time of occurrence of events in which they were not immediately and directly concerned, or which they saw, varies so much that it must be taken with very great allowance.

The sequence of events, or a diary made at the time, will give a better indication of the facts, and in this connection I regret that the diaries which some of the government witnesses had were not spread upon the record.

All these witnesses, White, Landstreet, and Munroe, put the formation of the divisions under Longstreet *behind* "Pageland lane."

Hood's division appears to have been somewhat in advance of the rest of the line, with the Texas brigade on the south of the pike.

Henry Kyd Douglas, Jackson's assistant adjutant-general, has indicated Jackson's right, which was turned off northwesterly beyond the beginning of the word "Independent." (See map.)

That ridge there, "Stony Ridge," was 270 feet high, and along it in rear of Jackson's line was placed the artillery which played over his own lines 50 feet below and behind the "Independent Manassas Gap" embankment into the Union lines formed parallel to his own.

It was on the continuation of this 270 feet high ridge, which formed a perfect glacis down to the northerly fringe of the "Gibbon wood," that Colonel Walton's eighteen or twenty guns were placed, just where the Rev. Mr. Landstreet and Major White placed them, and not on the low ground southeast of the "Browner-Douglas" house, where petitioner, for purposes of his own, would put them in order to get Longstreet's line forward of its actual position.

The map before us, prepared under Major Warren's direction by Capt. J. A. Judson, who is in the government service under him, omits many very material points on this end of the line, as, for example, Stuart's Hill, and the continuation of the ridge which runs northwest from the westerly end of the "Gibbon wood" and joins the ridge on which Longstreet's artillery was placed and the high ground west of Pageland lane.

POSITION OF UNION FORCES SOUTH OF THE WARRENTON PIKE.

The position of the troops south of the pike is important in determining what were the petitioner's opportunities which were lost by his fatal inaction on the 29th.

In the first place the battle was directed against Jackson, who awaited attack in a position of great strength behind the Independent Manassas Gap Railroad cut and filling; the right of his line following the direction of the railroad approached the turnpike at a small angle.

The position of General Pope's line accommodated itself to Jackson's, and thus Heintzelman's corps, part of Reno's division of Burnside's corps, and part of Sigel's corps, were north of the pike, and the remainder of Sigel's and Reynolds' division south of the pike, not in the position petitioner places them, due south, along Lewis Lane No. 1, but conforming to Jackson's line.

Thus, after Schenck's division of Sigel's corps and Reynolds' division of McDowell's command had moved forward in line of battle south of the pike, driving Early's skirmishers from the Thirteenth and Thirty-first Virginia of Jackson's command before them, they swung around by a right half-wheel, with the right of Schenck's division pivoted on Groveton, and brought up the left (which was under Reynolds) to and across the Warrenton Pike, near Meadowville lane, *in order to attack Jackson's right.*

Maj. Gen. R. C. Schenck, as we shall see, and also Maj. Gen. Franz Sigel, express great doubts as to Longstreet having been in their front in any force during these movements.

Emor B. Cope, then sergeant Company A, First Pennsylvania Reserves, Reynolds' division, called by petitioner (Board's Record, p. 918), in rebuttal, puts Reynolds' division just east of Compton's lane, where it remained most of the day, and near dusk General Reynolds was at a point south of Young's Branch and about 400 feet east of Lewis' lane. The witness positively stated that there was very little skirmishing— "very feeble indeed."

The late Col. *Owen Jones,* formerly First Pennsylvania Cavalry, who succeeded this witness, also in petitioner's behalf, and heard his evidence (Board's Record, p. 926), swore that Reynolds "advanced with one or two brigades of reserves and had quite a severe skirmish"; and Reynolds, in his official report, mentions the very brigade of the witness Cope as one of those engaged. The latter put his regiment in camp east of the Chinn house hill on the night of the 28th (Board's Record, p. 921), in a place where, according to his story, they were shelled, but the contour map shows conclusively that the location was such as to screen them from the enemy.

Col. *Owen Jones,* First Pennsylvania Cavalry (Board's Record, p. 929), says he first thought that about 2 p. m. he was on Reynolds' left near Compton's lane, but on cross-examination admitted that up in the direction towards Cundiffe's and Meadowville he "passed very near the head of that ravine, and moved out into an open field, and forward, and then discovered that there was a large force in the woods, which Reynolds went over to attack." He fixes the time at about 2 p. m., and says he kept within 500 feet of Reynolds' left, but would not attempt to designate the woods on the map, but says that at one time during the day (Board's Record, p. 928) he came across a hospital, that had been, of King's division the night before. This, of course, must have been the hospital in the Gibbon wood, as there was no other. It is also plain that as Col. Owen Jones, petitioner's witness, thus corroborates the numerous government witnesses as to Reynolds' division being near Meadowville lane at 2 p. m.

Longstreet could not have been east of Reynolds, and behind him in the Gibbon wood by 10.30 or 11 a. m. The position Col. Owen Jones admitted Reynolds was in at 2 p. m. shows that petitioner could have moved his own corps up without hindrance to the point General McDowell had indicated before he left him (petitioner) two hours before.

Maj. Gen. *Franz Sigel,* United States Volunteers, a corps commander, called on behalf of government, testified as follows (Board's Record, p. 941):

Question by RECORDER. Do you know how far Schenck's division advanced that day?

Answer. I know from his report that it advanced as far as the battlefield of Gibbon and Doubleday of the evening before, the night of the 28th, and from this I suppose that he was there; but I know by my own eyes that he marched from the Bald Headed hill, where I posted him first, and where the artillery was posted; that he advanced through the woods, and tried to get in and get across the road, across the Warrenton road, and attack the enemy's right wing; and he was prevented from getting across the road by the enemy's position on the ridge, which enfiladed his advance on the right.

Question. Then as to the afternoon?

Answer. In the afternoon one of my divisions on the right was relieved by the troops of General Hooker, and, I think, General Reno; but General Schenck and General Milroy remained in line of battle.

By the PRESIDENT OF THE BOARD:

Question. You spoke of General Schenck's division having advanced on the left of the Warrenton pike with the design of striking Jackson's right; at what hour of the day did he reach his most advanced position?

Answer. I think it was between twelve and one, or about one o'clock; it may have been a little later; but that was the time, about.

Question. Then he was induced to retire by some firing that you speak of, and he crossed the Warrenton pike toward the north for the purpose of striking Jackson's right, because the fire was received from what direction?

Answer. From the right of Jackson on a ridge, there were artillery there; and when he advanced he presented his left flank to this fire; but then he was under the necessity of assisting Milroy, who was on the right; and this space between Schenck's right and Milroy's left was almost uncovered; so I know very well that I ordered General Schenck to draw more to the right to connect with Milroy, and then he sent one of his brigades to the right to connect with Milroy.

Question. Was Schenck wholly to the left of the Warrenton pike?

Answer. He was, at the commencement of the advance; but then during the movement in advance he sent one of his brigades—he had two brigades—he sent one of his brigades to the right, across the pike, to assist Milroy; that was only temporary. Then afterward, when the troops of General Stevens came and I put him in there, I ordered him to the left, and he took line with Schenck on the left of the road.

* * * * * * *

Question. Where was General Reynolds' division during your advance; did you know of it then?

Answer. I knew that it was somewhere near to our line.

Question. On which flank?

Answer. On my left.

Question. You knew Reynolds was somewhere near your left?

Answer. Somewhere near my left; I don't know exactly where he was, because I was so much engaged with my own troops that I could not get away to look for him. I found out that during the day he maneuvered on the left; advanced on our left, and was with General Schenck in communication; and it was reported to me so when he came there.

* * * * * *

Answer. Some of them—only the division of General Schurz was relieved; this was at two o'clock: Schenck remained here all day.

Question. After he fell back from this position (Gibbon's)?

Answer. Yes, and so did Milroy.

By Mr. BULLITT:

Question. It was McLean's brigade that was south of the pike, was it?

Answer. Yes; he was under General Schenck; he commanded the left brigade; this brigade was on the left, Stahel's was on the right, therefore he was this side of the road (south).

By the RECORDER:

Question. You say that General Schenck maneuvered through Gibbon's battle-ground, and got there, I think you said, about one o'clock. Now, do you know how long he remained on that battle-ground before falling back, according to the report that was made to you? There was a battery in action, was there not, there?

Answer. My impression is this, that he remained there and around there about an hour, I think, from one to two o'clock; at least I would not say that he was always in one place, but he maneuvered around there (Gibbon's battle-ground).

By the PRESIDENT OF THE BOARD:

Question. That you get from the report of General Schenck?

Answer. Not only from the report, but from the reports sent me. I identify the place from his report, and reports were sent by his officers and by my own that he was about a mile in advance.

Question. The reports received on the battle-field at that time?

Answer. Yes; and I see from his report that this is the place.

Maj. *S. N. Benjamin*, U. S. A. (then first lieutenant, Second Artillery, Stevens brigade, Reno's division, Burnside's corps), thinks he himself went into position with his battery about 12½ p. m. (Board's Record, p. 614). He says it was very still for half an hour and then got engaged himself. Benjamin put his battery with his right near the Warrenton turnpike and his left south of it on the ridge about two hundred yards from Groveton. The Board will recollect that General Sigel, after hav-

ing given his evidence and been cross-examined (p. 944), said, after
the brief recess, that he desired to correct his testimony, to the effect
that General Schenck retired from his advance position between twelve
and one, instead of between one and two, because Brig. Gen. Isaac I.
Stevens, of Reno's division, came up and went into position in Sigel's
line between eleven and twelve. He added, however, that he was not
absolutely positive in regard to the time in this case; this, although
Colonel Chesebrough's official report to himself of Schenck's division on
that day, with specific hours noted, had been put before him.

The invaluable diary of Major-General Heintzleman, however, who
noted the hours, said Hooker got up about eleven; General Reno about
an hour later. At this time of day, Heintzleman fixes his own headquarters on the field near Stone Bridge. His headquarters
must have been on Buck Hill north of and near to Warrenton pike, because he says, after mentioning Reno's arrival, that soon after General
Pope arrived, about a quarter to two.

For Reno to march from stone house, on the Warrenton pike (which
was a little nearer Sigel than Heintzleman's headquarters), to the position of Sigel's corps at Groveton was a trifle over a mile and a quarter;
Sigel's own headquarters were on the "Chinn house hill."

From this it is apparent that Stevens did not get up with Sigel's corps
to go into position until within a quarter to one, or one o'clock.

This is confirmed by the evidence of Maj., then Capt., Oliver C. Bosbyshell, Forty-eighth Pennsylvania Volunteers, first brigade, Reno's division, Burnside's corps, who says the division arrived on the field at 1 p. m.
(Board's Record, p. 872).

Sigel says Schenck was a mile in advance of his corps' position, near
Groveton, maneuvering around Gibbons' battle-ground (p. 944).
Chesebrough, the assistant adjutant-general, puts this at between 1
and 2 p. m., and Sigel, before having his attention called to the matter,
gave about the same time as his own impression in response to a question of the President of the Board (p. 942). He also was disposed to
admit (p. 944) an hour's time as having elapsed between the arrival of
Stevens and the retirement of Schenck from his most advanced station
during the day. Thus, by the aid of General Heintzleman's diary, we
find that General Sigel's impressions as he first gave them in evidence
correspond with the specific statements of Colonel Chesebrough, who,
as assistant adjutant-general, appears to have noted the time. It is to
be regretted that his absence abroad has prevented his own corroborative evidence being obtained.

Brigadier-General *Stahel's* brigade, which was the right brigade of
Schenck's division, had to be taken still farther to the right to aid Milroy,
and Stevens' brigade supplied its place, but it soon returned (Board's
Record, p. 507).

When General Sigel says that he took line with Schenck on the left
of the road (p. 943), it must not be supposed that this line was formed
perpendicular to the Warrenton pike; on the contrary, they were nearly
parallel to it, making but a slight angle at Groveton, because Milroy's
independent brigade and Schurz's division of Sigel's corps were north
of the pike, and fighting Jackson, who was behind the Independent
Manassas Gap Railroad, running also nearly parallel with the pike. In
other words, the line that General Pope's army was taking in attacking,
was conformed to the "Independent Line of the Manassas Gap Railroad."
Thus having a line of battle parallel to Jackson's, the left of Schenck's
division was up near Gibbon's battle-ground of necessity, and Reynolds
on *his* left.

Therefore, when Reynolds undertook to attack Jackson's right naturally he was up near Cundiff's, at Meadowville lane.

That this was deemed by Sigel both possible and probable is evinced by his own report of the 16th September, 1862 (Board's Record, p. 504); said he:

Scarcely were these troops in position when the contest began with renewed vigor and vehemence, the enemy attacking furiously along our whole line from the extreme right to the extreme left. The infantry brigade of General Steinwehr, commanded by Colonel Koltes, was then sent forward to the assistance of Generals Schenck and Schurz, and one regiment was detailed for the protection of a battery posted in reserve near our center. The troops of Brigadier Reynolds had meanwhile (12 o'clock) taken position on our left. *In order to defend our right, I sent a letter to General Kearney, saying that Longstreet was not able to bring his troops in line of battle that day, and requesting him (Kearney) to change his front to the left and to advance, if possible, against the enemy's left flank.*

Therefore, if General Sigel did not think Longstreet was able (when he wrote his letter to Kearney after twelve) to bring his troops in line of battle that day, it is plain he had not then any ground for withdrawing Schenck from the position near Gibbon's battle-ground, which Schenck, as we shall see and have seen, maintained nearly all that day.

On this subject the report of Brigadier-General R. C. Schenck (by Col. William H. Chesebrough, A. D. C. and A. A. A. G., Schenck's division, Sigel's corps), says (Board's Record, p. 514):

WASHINGTON, D. C., *September 17, 1862.*

* * * * * * * *

On Thursday, 29th ultimo, we left Buckland's Mills, passing through Gainesville, and proceeded on the Manassas Junction pike to within some four miles of that place, and then turned eastwardly, marching toward "Bull Run." The scouts in advance reported a force of the enemy, consisting of infantry and cavalry, in front. We were hurried forward and formed line of battle with our right toward Centreville. Some few shells were thrown into a clump of woods in front, where the enemy were last seen, but without eliciting any response. Some two hours elapsed, when heavy firing was heard on our left, which we concluded was from McDowell's corps and the enemy, who had worked around from our front in that direction. We were immediately put in motion and marched on the Warrenton road, and took position for the night on a hill east of the "stone house," our right resting on the pike. On Friday morning early the engagement was commenced by General Milroy on our right, in which we soon after took part, and a rapid artillery fire ensued from both sides. For some time heavy columns of the enemy could be seen filing out of a wood in front, and gradually falling back. They were within range of our guns, which were turned on them, and must have done some execution. An hour after we received the order to move one brigade by the flank to the left and advance, which was done. We here obtained a good position for artillery, and stationed De Beck's 1st Ohio Battery, which did excellent service, dismounting one of the enemy's guns, blowing up a caisson, and silencing the battery. Unfortunately, however, they were poorly supplied with ammunition, and soon compelled to withdraw. Our two brigades were now put in motion. General Stahel, commanding first brigade, marching around the right of the hill to a hollow in front, was ordered to draw up in line of battle and halt. Colonel McLean advanced around the left of the hill under cover of the woods, pressing gradually forward until he struck the turnpike at a *white house,* about one-half mile in advance of the stone house. General Milroy's brigade arrived about the same time. We here halted and sent back for General Stahel, who took the pike and soon joined us. We then formed our line of battle in the woods to the left of the pike, our right resting on the road, and then pushed on slowly. Milroy, in the meanwhile, had deployed to the right of the road, and soon became engaged with the enemy. Our division was advanced until we reached the edge of the woods and halted. In front of us was an open space (which also extended to the right of the road and to our right), beyond which was another wood. We remained here nearly an hour, the firing in the meanwhile becoming heavy on the right. The enemy had a battery very advantageously placed on a high ridge behind the woods in front of Milroy, on the right of the road. It was admirably served and entirely concealed. Our position becoming known, their fire was directed towards us. The general determined, therefore, to advance, and so pushed on across the open space in front, and took position in the woods beyond. We here discovered that we were on the battle-ground of the night before, and found the hospital of Gibbon's brigade, who had engaged the enemy. The battery of the enemy still continued. We had no artillery. De Beck's and Schirmer's ammunition having given out, and Buell's battery, which had reported, after a hot contest with the enemy (who had every advantage in position and range), was compelled to retire. It was now determined to flank the battery and capture it, and for this purpose General Schenck ordered one of his aids to reconnoiter the position. Before he returned, however, we were requested by General Milroy to assist him, as he was very heavily pressed. .General Stahel was immediately ordered to proceed with his brigade to Milroy's support. It was about this time, one or two o'clock, that a line of skirmishers were observed approaching us from the rear; they proved to be of General Reynolds. We communicated with General Reynolds at once, who took his position on our left, and at General Schenck's suggestion he sent a battery to our right in the woods for the purpose of flanking the enemy. They secured a position and were engaged with him about an hour, but with what result we were not informed. General Reynolds now sent us word that he had discovered the enemy bearing down upon his left in heavy columns, and that he intended to fall back to the first woods behind the cleared space, and had already put his troops in motion. We therefore accommodated ourselves to his movement. It was about this time that your order came to press towards the right. We returned answer that the enemy were in force in front of us, and that we could not do so without leaving the left much exposed. General Schenck again asked for some artillery. General Stahel's brigade that had been sent to General Milroy's assistance, having accomplished its object under a severe fire, had returned, and soon after General Stevens reported with two regiments of infantry and a battery of four twenty-pound Parrott guns. With these re-enforcements we determined to advance again and reoccupy the woods in front of the cleared space, and communicated this intention to General Reynolds. He, however, had fallen back on our left some distance to the rear; he was therefore requested to make his connection with our left. The Parrotts in the meanwhile were placed in position, and under the admirable management of Lieutenant Benjamin did splendidly. Two mountain howitzers also reported, and were placed on our right in the edge of the woods near the road, and commenced shelling the woods in front of the open space, which were now occupied by the enemy, our skirmishers having previously fallen back. The artillery fire now became very severe, and General Schenck was convinced that it was very essential that he should have another battery, and so sent me to you to get one. I arrived to find one, Captain Romer's, just starting. You also directed me to order General Schenck to fall gradually back, as he was too far forward. This he had perceived, and, anticipating, fell slowly back, placing his division behind the slope of the hill in front of the one we had occupied in the morning. Captain Romer's battery in the meanwhile had taken position in front of the white house on the right of the pike, a little in advance of the hill on which we were. Lieutenant Benjamin's battery had suffered severely, so much so that he reported only one section fit for duty, the other having lost all its cannoniers. They were placed in position and fired one or two rounds at the woods in front of the position we had just left, more to get the range than anything else. We were now ordered to descend the hill, cross the road, and take up our position behind the house, in front of which was Captain Romer's battery. This we did, deploying the brigades in line of battle, the second brigade in front and the first brigade in the rear. We remained so during the night.

The above report is respectfully submitted, with the remark that it is made without any communication with General Schenck, he being severely wounded, and prevented by his surgeon's orders from attending to any business whatever. And although fully assured that the main points are correct, there may have been some orders or movements of minor importance, which, in my position as aide, carrying orders, might not have come within my notice.

As General Schenck, who had been wounded the day before, was unable to make the report, Colonel Chesebrough made it; though it appears in the evidence of General Schenck that he was with him at the time and in constant communication with him.

Colonel Chesebrough wrote a letter to General McDowell in reply to Brigadier-General Reynolds' letter on the subject (Board's Record, p. 501) which is as follows:

LETTER OF COLONEL CHESEBROUGH TO MAJOR-GENERAL M'DOWELL.

WASHINGTON, D. C., *October 20, 1862.*

GENERAL: In reply to General Reynolds' letter of the 9th instant, I have the honor to make the following remarks:

I can discover but little difference between the statements of General Reynolds and my report.

He states firstly. "That his division manœuvred on our left from early in the morning until we had gained the position alluded to on the pike, near Gibbon's battle-ground of the evening previous." This I do not attempt to deny. I merely give in my report the time when we first became acquainted with his (General Reynolds') position.

He then says that "it was here that General Schenck asked me for a battery," which agrees entirely with my report, with the exception that I did not enter so much into the details. He then remarks that, "in returning from this position to bring up the other battery and Seymour's brigade, I passed through Schenck's troops drawn up on the *right* of the woods before alluded to, in which Gibbon had been engaged." But in bringing up the battery and Seymour's brigade, he noticed that "Schenck's troops had disappeared from this position, and were nowhere in sight." In the first place General Reynolds is incorrect in his impression of our position.

Our troops were always on the left of the pike throughout the day, except when the brigade under General Stahel was sent to Milroy's assistance.

Our position before Stahel moved was in the woods which had been occupied as a hospital by Gibbon's brigade, to the left of the pike, General Stahel's right resting on the road and Colonel McLean's brigade on his left, the woods in which Gibbon had had his principal fighting being across the pike and to our right.

At the time that General Reynolds returned from placing the battery and Meade's brigade it is probable that he passed through General Stahel's brigade, which was in motion and had gained the right of the pike on its way to join Milroy, and that afterward, when General Reynolds was bringing up Ransom's battery and Seymour's brigade, they were gone, which accounts for his impression that "he was left alone." He soon discovered his error, however, as he states in his letter, "in doing which McLean's brigade was discovered."

Colonel McLean still held his position, and was immediately moved so that his right would rest on the pike, and General Reynolds made his movement to correspond.

It was about this time that our position was changed, but not because we had ascertained that we were disconnected with the rest of Sigel's troops.

We *had been* and *were* well aware of our position.

It is true we had advanced further than was intended, being constantly urged by General Sigel to advance, and pressed toward the right, he evidently not understanding our true position. We fell back, however, on account of the information received from General Reynolds that the enemy were bearing down on his left. General Reynolds did not communicate directly with General Schenck, as it would appear from my report, but the information was received through Colonel McLean, who told General Schenck that General Reynolds had informed him "that the enemy were bearing down, &c., and that he (Reynolds) intended to fall back, and has actually commenced the movement." Colonel McLean wished to know if he should act accordingly. General Schenck directed him to accommodate himself to General Reynolds' movement.

We retired slowly across the open space to and within the woods and halted. General Stahel rejoined us here, and General Stevens as reported with two regiments of infantry and a battery. General Stevens' force was thrown to the right of the pike, General Stahel on the left of the pike, and Colonel McLean on the left of Stahel. I here state in my report that General Schenck, on receiving these re-enforcements, determined to advance again, and communicated his intention to General Reynolds. I carried this message myself, and after some difficulty found General Reynolds, and requested him to halt and form on the left of McLean. He had fallen back, however, some distance to the rear of McLean's line of battle, so much so that the enemy's skirmishers had actually flanked us, and in returning to the division I had a narrow escape from being captured. I also asked General Reynolds to ride forward to meet General Schenck, who had directed me to say that he would be at the extreme left of our line for that purpose. General Reynolds neither gave me any positive answer as to whether he would meet General Schenck or any information as to what he intended to do. I do not know if he complied with the request to make his connection on our left, as, on my return to General Schenck, I was immediately sent to General Sigel to represent our position; and when returning again with the order to General Schenck to retire slowly, I met the command executing the movement.

My report was intended merely as a sketch of our movements for General Sigel's information, and I endeavored throughout to be as concise as possible, and confine myself solely to the operations and movements of our division. I now submit the above statement, trusting that the explanations will be satisfactory to General Reynolds.

Hon. *Robert C. Schenck*, late envoy extraordinary and minister plenipotentiary to Great Britian, brigadier-general of volunteers, commanding the first division of Sigel's corps, wounded and promoted major-general on the 30th August 1862, being duly sworn, testified as follows: (Board's Record, p. 1082):

Question. Where was that division early on the morning of that day, August 29?
Answer. We were upon the hills below Bull Run, up in the neighborhood of Young's Creek.

Question. North or south of the Warrenton turnpike?

Answer. South of the Warrenton turnpike.

Question. In reference to the Manassas and Sudley road, running up there to the stone house and Sudley Springs—east of it or west of it?

Answer. That must have been west of it.

Question. Where did you go to from that point where you camped the night before?

Answer. Along the left side, the southerly side of the turnpike.

Question. What formation was your division in?

Answer. I had Stahel's brigade upon the right and McLean's brigade to the left, moving along south of and parallel with the turnpike.

Question. Were they in column or in line of battle?

Answer. They were for the most part of the time in line of battle?

Question. About what time did you make that forward movement westerly?

Answer. We set out very early in the morning, I cannot recollect the hour, and continued moving, with rests and delays, until we reached the farthest point that we attained to, which, as I recollect, was a wood, in which some of Gibbon's troops had been engaged the night before. After that, I withdrew toward the position that I had occupied in the morning, though not quite as far as to that position; by those two movements I occupied the day.

Question. In moving up to this position, did you have in the morning of the 29th August any enemy in front of you?

Answer. None, that we felt; throwing forward skirmishers and supposing the enemy was present somewhere. Pretty early in the day a force of the enemy was developed upon this ridge, where there were a number of batteries placed to our right; that would be to the north of the turnpike road.

Question. Do you recollect passing that lane, Lewis lane No. 1?

Answer. I have a very indistinct impression of it. I have a remembrance floating in my mind having crossed some road which was not the turnpike, but I don't recall it distinctly.

Question. At what time of the day did you reach your farthest point in advance.

Answer. I think it must have been somewhere about the middle of the day; perhaps a little earlier than the middle of the day.

Question. Did you see General Reynolds' division during that day?

Answer. No; but I understood he was off on my left.

Question. Did you see General Reynolds himself during the morning or afternoon?

Answer. No; I think not. I don't recollect.

Question. How far did you get beyond the Gibbon's wood in which the wounded of the night before were?

Answer. I don't know that we got beyond the Gibbon woods. My remembrance is that the farthest point we reached was somewhere about the west edge of the Gibbon wood—that is, the wood in which Gibbon's troops were engaged the night before. We found there his wounded and the evidence of the battle that had taken place.

Question. Was anything done with these wounded that you found there?

Answer. I ordered all the men in that and the piece of woods this side of that where there were, I think, a few scattered, to be sent to the rear and taken care of. I don't know that that is the Gibbon wood; I mean the wood farthest in advance that I reached was the wood in which the engagement took place. My impression is we did not at any period go farther in that direction than to, perhaps, the west edge of that wood.

Question. Look at the map; which piece of timber is it that you consider to be the Gibbon wood?

Answer. This I suppose to be the wood. [In which the word "Warrenton" ends; marked S on the Landstreet map.] That I suppose is intended for the wood in which Gibbon's engagement took place.

Question. How long did your division remain in that woods?

Answer. We must have been in that wood altogether two or three hours.

Question. Did you see any battery of the enemy while you were in that position? If so, where was it?

Answer. There was a battery off to our right somewhere, which I recollect all the more distinctly because it seemed to me to be detached from the general line of the enemy, and I conceived the purpose of attempting to capture it, and sent one of my staff over to reconnoiter with a view to see how it might be approached. But about that time Milroy, who was engaged with the enemy off to my right, communicated with me, or General Sigel for him—I think the message came from Milroy himself—begging assistance, and I detached Stahel's brigade to support Milroy northeast of the pike, and then gave up the idea of attempting to capture that battery.

Question. That battery was in the neighborhood of where?

Answer. It was on a hill on my right, to the right of the wood where Gibbon's fight had taken place. It was upon elevated ground, and seemed to be the spur of a hill. I thought we might by a sudden and decisive movement upon it capture it.

Question. While you were up in this position, McLean's brigade, I understand, was on the left. What was the position of Reynolds' division of Pennsylvania reserves as reported to you at that time in reference to your own position?

Answer. I did not see them, but they were reported to me as being upon our left, and I may add that it was reported to me that they had stationed a battery somewhere in advance of Gibbon's wood, I think Cooper's battery.

Question. In which direction was that battery operating?

Answer. Did not see the battery.

Question. At what time did you quit with your division this Gibbon wood?

Answer. I should think, to the best of my recollection, somewhere between one and three o'clock. I don't think I can be more positive than that. My recollection is that it was some time after noon.

Question. To what point did you go then with your division?

Answer. In consequence of reports made to me in reference to the movements of General Reynolds, I thought it best for me to fall back, and I came into a strip of woods which I supposed to be these [south of the syllable "ville" in "Gainesville"]. I formed in line of battle near the west edge of that woods. There we lay most of the afternoon.

Question. Up to what time?

Answer. I can scarcely tell you. I should think at least until the middle of the afternoon, perhaps later. I recollect withdrawing from that point from wood to wood as we had advanced. We found it quite late in the afternoon, or quite sunset, by the time I reached my original position. The whole distance, I should think, was about two miles from the point where we started in the morning to the farthest point to which we advanced.

Question. While you were in the Gibbon wood, what enemy, if any, did you see in your immediate front?

Answer. I cannot say that I saw any enemy in our immediate front. There were skirmishes in that direction, and as my skirmishers were thrown forward we would have an occasional shot, but there seemed to me at that time to be no enemy in front—in my immediate front. The first intimation that I had that the enemy in considerable force were upon our left was through Colonel McLean, the commander of my second brigade, who told me that a messenger, or staff officer, or orderly, or some one from Reynolds, apparently with authority, had come to him, as he was in command of a brigade, and communicated the fact that the enemy were upon our left, and I think that was coupled with the information that Reynolds intended to fall back. I tried to communicate with Reynolds again, but did not succeed, but I thought that there was no occasion for immediately falling back; but not finding any response from General Reynolds, I concluded to withdraw slowly to at least a short distance and then come across an open space into the next wood [into a little strip marked S 2], where I rested the troops in line.

Question. While you were holding position in that little strip of woods, do you know whether or not the enemy obtained the possession of the Gibbon wood?

Answer. I am satisfied that they were not there in any force; they had their skirmishers thrown forward as I had men toward the Gibbon wood, and there were occasional shots fired with or without good cause for them, but there was no movement in force, nor was there indicated to me any presence of an enemy in force.

Question. Can you fix with any degree of relative certainty the time in the afternoon when you quit the little fringe of woods marked "S 2"; whether it was two or three or four or five or six o'clock?

Answer. The days in August are pretty long. I should say it was at least the middle of the afternoon, or probably later. I reached my conclusion from measuring it by the movement forward and the gradual withdrawal of the troops. I should think it was after the middle of the afternoon.

Question. Do you mean to say three or four o'clock?

Answer. I should think later, perhaps; from one to seven. I should think it was as late as four o'clock; of that I cannot be positive at all. Such is the impression when I attempt now to recall the circumstances and the movements.

Question. Have you seen the official report of the action of your division that day, made by your assistant adjutant-general, Colonel Chesebrough?

Answer. Yes.

Question. Was that report made under your direction or with your knowledge?

Answer. It was brought to my attention after it was made, when I was able to see and read it, and of course I read it with a great deal of interest, but my recollection is that I was neither able to dictate to him nor did I give him any points in regard to his report unless it was to suggest that favorable mention should be made of certain officers.

Question. Did you see that report before it was finally filed?

Answer. I doubt if I did. I think it must have been before I saw it.

Question. During the day did you know of any battle in progress at any time; if so, what was its character and where was it?

Answer. The fight was principally on our right. There was apparently a range of batteries to our right, which in the earlier part of the day directed their fire against a battery of Benjamin's that was drawn up upon the spur of a hill. There was fighting which I did not see, but which was reported to me as going on, and of which I could hear by the continual reports of musketry, that I supposed to have been Milroy's forces. But on our side of the turnpike there was no serious engagement of any kind during that day.

Question. Do you know when any of the rest of General Lee's command of the army of North Virginia came to the assistance of Jackson's forces? If so, when?

Answer. I do not; I can only give you the impression we had at the time of when they effected anything like a junction.

Question. What was it?

Mr. MALTBY. I object to impressions.

Answer. I think there was no junction of their forces until in the night or very early next morning. That I do not know, however. That was our conclusion, situated as we were.

Question. This firing that you heard to your right—what was its character—artillery, infantry, or both?

Answer. Principally artillery.

Question. How long did it continue during the day?

Answer. That I cannot tell you; but during a part of the time there was evidently a sharp engagement with small-arms.

Question. Towards dusk, do you know of any firing? If so, what was its character?

Answer. I don't recollect.

Question. What were the losses of your division that day?

Answer. I cannot tell you without refreshing my recollection.

Cross-examination by Mr. MALTBY:

Question. Where did you start from on the morning of the 29th?

Answer. On these hills, as I recollect, south of the turnpike, and not far from the position where the fight took place on the 30th.

Question. Under whose immediate command were you?

Answer. General Sigel's.

Question. At what time did you leave that position? Was it near the Chinn house, or where was it?

Answer. It must have been somewhere in the neighborhood of the Chinn house. I recollect the Chinn house more in connection with the fight of the next day. It was upon those hills.

Question. What time did you leave that position?

Answer. Quite early in the morning. I cannot indicate the hour.

Question. At daybreak?

Answer. I think I ordered the men to take their breakfasts, but it must have been an early breakfast; it must have been at least by sunrise or earlier. We began the movement, perhaps, at daybreak.

Question. Where did you first take possession in line of battle?

Answer. That I cannot distinctly recollect, but it was some time before we reached the wood where Gibbon was engaged, and I think the greater portion of the distance we were thrown into line, and Stahel with his first brigade marching on the right and McLean on the left in line.

Question. Those were the only two brigades composing your division?

Answer. Those were the only two brigades that I had there at that time.

Question. How far did Stahel advance with you?

Answer. Up to near the wood in which Gibbon was engaged, I think.

Question. Did he retire before you retired from that position?

Answer. He was sent over to sustain Milroy.

Question. Then you were left with McLean's command alone?

Answer I think Stahel did not join us until after the backward movement.

Question. Did Stahel move up on the right of the turnpike in advancing?

Answer. I think a portion of the time his command was upon the right of the turnpike, but I am not sure that his right did not rest on the turnpike, making the whole of my line to the left of the turnpike. I recollect riding in the turnpike myself.

Question. Did you march rapidly from your position where you breakfasted to where you formed line of battle; previous to your forming line of battle, did you advance rapidly?

Answer. No. My recollection is that all the way through the day we moved but slowly from one patch of woods to another across the intervening distance, feeling our way; we would generally rest in a piece of wood and sent forward skirmishers, and then move forward across the open space.

Question. How many men had you in your command?

Answer. I cannot recollect; they were average brigades.
Question. Do you recollect a battery under Benjamin?
Answer. Yes, sir.
Question. Where was that stationed?
Answer. On a point which I could indicate if I were on the ground.
Question. Have you been on the ground since the battle?
Answer. No; not that part of the ground. Immediately after the war I went down to Manassas and went across in a wagon, out of curiosity, to see the ridge upon which I had been wounded, but I did not go over the field.
Question. How far to the front did Benjamin's battery get, as you recollect?
Answer. It was placed to our right. I should think somewhere upon a spur about here.

When General Schenck thus places Benjamin's battery on the right of the division, he does not mean that his line of battle was perpendicular to the pike at Groveton and at right angles to the rest of General Pope's line on *his* right, but that his own line was nearly parallel with the pike, in continuation of General Pope's line, conforming to the Independent Manassas Gap Railroad, and that his left was up in the Gibbon wood.

Question. Across the pike from you?
Answer. Across the pike.
Question. How far to your rear was he, or to your front, when you reached that farthest point, according to your recollection?
Answer. It was some distance to the right, and some considerable distance. I cannot say how much; possibly a quarter or a half a mile to the rear, the farthest point that we reached; half a mile, I should think, at least; probably more.
Question. At what time did you reach the position in which he was placed?
Answer. I was in the advance of that position before he was placed there; it was to meet the fire from those batteries as we advanced that I had Benjamin's battery placed upon an eminence here; and I discovered very soon afterwards that he had drawn upon himself the concentrated fire of a number of batteries upon the *stony ridge* where the enemy were, beyond.
Question. Where were you when Benjamin's battery was placed in the position of which we are speaking?
Answer. I think I may have been, as I said, from a quarter to a half mile farther west than the point where he was placed on the south side of the turnpike.
Question. With reference to your advanced point, where were you at the time Benjamin was placed where his batteries were?
Answer. That I cannot tell.
Question. Have you any recollection as to whether you were then in Gibbon's woods?
Answer. I do not recollect. My impression rather is that I was not at that time in Gibbon's wood.
Question. How long after Benjamin being placed in that position do you think that you reached Gibbon's wood?
Answer. I cannot tell you.
Question. How long after that opening fire began with such severity upon Benjamin?
Answer. After he was placed there?
Question. Yes.
Answer. I think he had occupied the position for some little time. Perhaps half an hour or more. He was firing an occasional shot before the enemy seemed to discover his range and position and concentrated their fire upon him.
Question. In what direction from your own command were those guns at that time? Were they immediately upon your right or far to your front and right?
Answer. You mean Benjamin's?
Question. No, sir; I mean the rebel battery?
Answer. No. If this map is to be relied upon as showing where the ridge is, if the line had been continued they would have made an acute angle with the point towards which I was moving.
Question. How far would it have been, according to your recollection, from your front to the point where their line, if prolonged, would have struck the turnpike road?
Answer. Their line, if prolonged, I should have thought would strike the road some hundreds of yards, perhaps a quarter of a mile, beyond the Gibbon woods; that is, if their line had been protracted.
Question. How long did you remain in the position where you were when Benjamin's battery opened?

Answer. I cannot tell you; I don't recollect.

Question. You were there in line of battle perhaps half a mile in his front, or perhaps a quarter?

Answer. From a quarter to half a mile in front.

Question. Did you lie a long time in that position before advancing?

Answer. We moved slowly, resting in each of these successive pieces of wood, and then marched more rapidly across the open spaces between, after having felt the wood in advance of us, until by these successive delays and marches, occupying the forenoon, we reached finally what we call the Gibbon woods.

* * * * *

Question. If Lieutenant Benjamin has sworn that that was his place, and if you place his battery there as opening, how far in advance of that position would you judge you were?

Answer. Wherever his battery was we were to his left in advance, and I should say from a quarter to a half a mile.

Question. Do you think you were in this strip of woods, marked S², at the time his battery opened?

Answer. That, as I understand the map, is a strip of woods back to which we fell when we left Gibbon's woods, where I formed a line fronting towards the open space and towards the Gibbon woods.

* * * * *

Question. How do you fix it as between one and three o'clock the time when you left Gibbon's woods?

Answer. Because we consumed about half a day or more in advancing to that point. We rested there for some time, and we consumed pretty much all the rest of the day in regaining our original position to which we withdrew. I make it out, therefore, that we must have reached there about midway of that time. I will add that after I was able to examine the report made by my aide, I found that he had stated the time in his report, and was satisfied that he had stated it correctly; and I think, though I have not his report now to refer to, that he makes it somewhere between one and two o'clock.

Question. Have you ever read the report of General Reynolds?

Answer. I dare say I have, but not for a long time.

Question. Did General Reynolds retire from his advance at the time that you retired?

Answer. General Reynolds, as I have stated, was reported to be commanding the troops which were on my left when we were up in the Gibbon's woods. I had no intention of retiring from that position then, at least, nor did I know that it would become necessary for me to do so. We had then advanced about two miles on the south side of the road from the point from which we started in the morning [Warrenton turnpike]. I sent a staff-officer to communicate with General Reynolds. He returned and reported to me that there were indications of the presence of the enemy off in the front of Reynolds' skirmishing parties or pickets, and that he had mistaken his way, as he thought, and came very near being captured. I heard subsequently, or about that time, from Colonel McLean, then commanding my second brigade, that he had received a message from General Reynolds, which had been delivered to him instead of being conveyed to me, stating that Reynolds found the enemy were on his left, and to my left, of course, therefore, in sufficient force to make him think it advisable to withdraw. I had no proof of any such indications, and I wanted Reynolds to hold on, and sent accordingly to get into communication with him, so as to preserve our line, but my message, I think, never reached him, or at least he had left his position, as was reported to me, and I did not have communication with him.

Question. Is your recollection as to the time when you retired from your advanced position so strong that if General Reynolds swore (December 30, 1862) that he retired between twelve and one o'clock, or it may have been after one, that you would still say that it was between one and three, or nearer three, that you retired from Gibbon's woods?

Answer. I should not base my recollection upon anything that you informed me as to Reynolds' recollection. My remembrance is, as I now recall the circumstance, that it was not earlier than one—nor, perhaps, later than three. It was after I had had indication from Reynolds, derived in the circuitous way I tell you, of his purpose to withdraw, and while I was in the Gibbon's wood; and a messenger was sent to communicate with Reynolds, and we found he was gone; so that he must have retired before I did. I should say I certainly did not retire before one, and as certainly not after three; but I do not think it is possible for me, from my present recollection of the circumstances, to fix it more definitely than that.

Question. What was your final position that evening?

Answer. We fell back to this hill which looks down into a ravine occupied by Young's Creek.

Question. You moved back to Young's Creek, on the ridge just behind that?

Answer. Yes; I slept in a little grove. It could scarcely be called a grove. It was a clump of woods. It was made disagreeable by some cattle that had taken shelter there during the day. They were driven out that I might find shelter. It was nearly dark, and I went soon to sleep.

Question. At what time did you reach that position?

Answer. It must have been, I should think, not earlier than sunset. It was near to the end of the day.

Question. Was there no fighting going on on the pike in your vicinity at that time?

Answer. I have an indistinct recollection that shots were fired along in the evening. I cannot recall the circumstances.

Question. Did you know of King's division?

Answer. I had no immediate personal knowledge of them.

Question. Did you not know that they had a very severe fight in the neighborhood of Groveton that evening?

Answer. Evening of the 29th?

Question. Yes.

Answer. I think I must have known of it.

Question. In reference to that fight what was your position when it took place?

Answer. I was back on this hill, looking down into the ravine; I should say, at least as early as sunset.

Question. Was your whole line back there?

Answer. Yes, sir; I had withdrawn my force.

* * * * * * *

Question. Did you have a watch?

Answer. I am in the habit of carrying a watch. I don't recollect to have been without one for a great many years.

Question. Did you fix times at all by reference to your watch on that day?

Answer. I dare say I did at the time, but I have no recollection now when or where I took out my watch to consult it as to time. This is sixteen years ago, you must recollect; but certain prominent facts or incidents would be, as it were, burned upon my mind without a recollection of the connecting details.

Question. Do you say that you were in the woods, the Gibbon woods, when General Reynolds retired?

Answer. Yes; I should say I was.

Question. Then this statement of your aide-de-camp, Colonel Cheseborough, is incorrect?

Answer. What is the statement?

Question. "With these re-enforcements we determined to advance again and re-occupy the woods in front of the cleared space, and communicated this intention to General Reynolds."

Answer. What re-enforcements?

Question. From Stahel's brigade.

Answer. Stahel retired.

Question. Yes. "He, however, had fallen back on our left some distance to the rear. He was, therefore, requested to make his connection with our left."

Answer. My impression was that I got this report as coming from General Reynolds in relation to his movement when I was in the Gibbon woods. . When I come to consider the matter a little further my remembrance is, as I think I said before, that it was not until we fell back to the strip of woods behind the Gibbon woods [S. 2] that Stahel rejoined me, and therefore the probability is that I may have been there, and prevented from making an advance again upon the Gibbon woods by hearing that Reynolds was not going to remain on my left.

Question. You have stated that the enemy did not occupy Gibbon's woods during the time that you were in this strip of woods marked "S 2."

Answer. No; I am very sure they were not.

Question. Could you see through those woods?

Answer. No.

Question. Then how do you know?

Answer. Because I had skirmishers forward, observing Gibbon's woods, while I lay in this strip here.

Question. What time did you lie in that strip?

Answer. From the time we fell back from Gibbon's woods, between one and three o'clock, and we lay for several hours in the strip of woods.

Question. Do you know how far your skirmishers advanced into that wood?

Answer. No.

Question. Do you know where the line of the enemy's skirmishers was?

Answer. The enemy had skirmishers, I think, in the same wood.

Question. Were they advanced far into the wood?

Answer. I do not know. I was not on the skirmish line, but there was no serious encounter between skirmishers anywhere; still we knew of the presence of the enemy by an occasional shot fired—or supposed presence.

Question. In reference to the time that you retired, do you think that it was rather two o'clock, as between one and three, or was it before or after that period?

Answer. I should say nearer two than one. I think when I say from one to three that about the average of that, two, would be perhaps the time. I will add here, because it is a part of my answer, that I may be distinctly understood, I am perfectly certain that the enemy did not occupy in force that which you call the Gibbon wood while I was yet in this strip of woods with my line of battle there. [Marked "S 2."] While I was remaining in that wood marked "S 2" the enemy did not in force at any time occupy those woods.

Question. But you did not see them yourself?

Answer. No, sir. It would be very easy to distinguish what you call Gibbon wood "S 1" from the other woods by the presence of indications of a battle having taken place there the night before; the wounded that we found there and the dead from that battle; and also somewhere in the turnpike, near there, I stopped to look at a caisson that was blown up.

Question. The way you have of fixing this in your mind is only in reference to the time occupied in advancing from your position in the morning by slow stages up to that point, and retiring by slow stages to a point where you camped at night, somewhat in advance of where you marched from in the morning?

Answer. No. If I were called upon now for the first time after a lapse of sixteen years, perhaps I should have no other standard by which to determine it than a vague recollection of that kind of measuring—marching and falling back; but after the battle, within a short time, within a few weeks, as I was well enough to become acquainted with what was said and known about the battle, there began in my mind a distinctive impression that it was not later than 1 o'clock, that my aide, who had made a report, was not wrong in his report; and by that help I have ever since carried in my mind a remembrance of the time.

Question. When did you recover from your wound?

Answer. I was carried to Washington, and I was out of the hotel in about seven weeks.

Question. Had you seen the report prior to your coming out?

Answer. Yes. Colonel Cheseborough remained with me during all or most of the time while I was lying wounded, in attendance upon me, with two or three of my staff; and during that time, as soon as I was well enough to know what he had reported, and what had been done, my attention was called to it, and he related to me the sort of controversy into which he had been drawn by reason of this statement of General Reynolds.

* * * * * * *

By the RECORDER:

Question. You say that you are satisfied that the enemy had substantially no considerable force in the Gibbon wood after you had fallen back to the fringe of woods S²?

Answer. Not while I remained in the next woods east [S²].

Question. How do you know that?

Answer. The space between is not so great but that you could fire across from one wood to the other. If we had had artillery, or they artillery, we could soon, either of us, have riddled the other out from the wood. That is one reason why I suppose they were not there in force. Another reason is that my skirmishers were out in advance and entered that wood, and occasional shots were fired over to the left of the wood, indicating that the enemy also had skirmishers in that neighborhood, but nothing more. My conclusion from that condition of things was that the enemy could not possibly be there in any very great force or any force at all. You could not very well be in one strip of woods, with another strip of woods opposite to you, neither of them large, without knowing whether there was an enemy in the other wood. An army has a good many eyes and feelers.

Question. Assuming that Lieutenant Benjamin was in a position just south of Groveton, right on the pike, firing off in a northwesterly direction toward the word "stony," where would that bring him so far as your troops are concerned?

Answer. I was to his left and in the advance; wherever I was to his left and advance. My impression would lead me now to think that he was just on the north side of the turnpike; he could not have been very far from the turnpike; he was upon a sort of spur or hill. I have not been on the ground.

* * * * *

Question. Could not a force of the enemy have a line of pickets in the edge of this Gibbon's woods without your knowing it—in the westerly edge?

Answer. Hardly; until after we left this strip of woods.

Question. Were there skirmishers thrown out in your front?

Answer. I hardly think they could have been there at any time until we left in the middle of the afternoon; I think we should have known it. As I see by your map, and as I have always understood, there are other portions of the wood farther west still, and about these I can give no information. There may be a discrepancy between my recollection and the recollection of others in regard to the piece of woods, but I speak quite confidently that Gibbon's woods up to the time of my leaving that strip of woods to the east were not occupied by the enemy.

Question. Did you carry from Gibbon's wood the Union dead and wounded?

Answer. Yes; it was left to others to execute the order. I gave the order that they should be taken from there. While we were in the wood I recollect them gathering the soldiers who had suffered in the engagement the night before.

By the RECORDER:

Question. Do you mean wounded or dead, or both?

Answer. I think both. I was particularly concerned for the wounded.

Question. Do you recollect firing by the enemy or any battle on your left?

Answer. I do not recollect.

Maj. T. C. H. Smith, paymaster, United States Army, then lieutenant-colonel First Ohio Volunteer Cavalry, testified as follows (Board's Record, page 367):

Question. What was the situation of affairs, as you understand it to have been, on the afternoon of August 29th?

Answer. The situation of affairs on August 29 was that early in the afternoon the head of Longstreet's column got on to the turnpike and fired a few shots that we heard, not knowing where they were from. I have since learned that they were from Longstreet.

Question. I ask you what you saw?

Answer. What I saw was this: that our left was up on the turnpike beyond Groveton and that it commanded the ground beyond Groveton, the very ground that Longstreet testifies his troops were on up to as late at least as one o'clock that day. I cannot indicate the exact position that our troops were in. I knew that they were up and beyond Groveton. * * * * I was out once or twice during the day to the Dogan house.

Question. Whose troops were those which you saw on the left?

Answer. Reynolds' and Schenck's; they were out there maneuvering for a position for attack.

Brig. Gen. N. C. McLean, United States Volunteers, commanding Second Brigade, Schenck's division, Sigel's corps, testified as follows (Board's Record, page 937):

Question. What time did you go into action?

Answer. We were ordered quite early in the day, as I supposed at the time, on the extreme left of our troops; we advanced toward the position of the enemy in line of battle with a very heavy line of skirmishers; the skirmishers were engaged more or less as we advanced, sometimes severely, sometimes very lightly, but the opposition to us was not so heavy as to prevent our advance. We advanced slowly and regularly; that was the condition of affairs. We halted at times to examine the position, and then went on again until the afternoon. Quite late in the afternoon we were ordered back into camp. During the day, exactly at what portion of the day I cannot now state, General Meade came to me and said he was ordered to take position on our left; he was in General Reynolds' division; General Meade was commanding the brigade.

Question. George G. Meade?

Answer. Yes, afterward commander of the Army of the Potomac; I halted and he came up with his troops; we then went on, and he took position on our left. Some time afterward—the intervals of time I cannot give you at all, regulated more by events than time then—General Meade came back with his brigade, saying to me that he had placed a battery, and he had been shelled out of his position by the rebel batteries, and had got into a hornet's nest of batteries; he was then coming back, and advised me to do the same.

Now General Meade had placed that battery upon the left and west of that "Gibbon wood," on this *same ridge on which some of the enemy's guns were placed;* and according to the official report of Brig. Gen. Jno. F. Reynolds, he appears to have been in action there—Cooper's battery and Brig. Gen. George G. Meade's brigade—for about an hour or an hour and a half. (Board's Record, p. 501.)

I reported to General Schenck, my division commander, the facts, and in a short time we were ordered back a little distance, and remained there until night-fall; we were, on the approach of night, ordered back into camp, some little distance farther back toward the position from which we had started in the morning. The position that we got into camp that night was a hill upon which our reserve batteries were placed. I cannot indicate it to you upon the map, because the map does not indicate to me what the ground was at all.

Question. Did you know Maj. George B. Fox, of Cincinnati?
Answer. He was in my own regiment, the Seventy-fifth Ohio.
Question. On that day?
Answer. Yes; he was there in that regiment, in that brigade. I had four regiments and an Ohio brigade. I was from Ohio.
Question. Major Fox has been here and testified.
Answer. He was a very competent and good officer.

* * * * * * *

Question. How far do you suppose you advanced forward?
Answer. I cannot give you an estimate; we were in line of battle the whole time from the time we moved early in the morning. We moved along for some time before we found any reply to our skirmishers; then it was continuous dropping fire; sometimes it was very severe, and sometimes not severe. We kept advancing very slowly; occasionally we would halt and skirmish along to find out where we were and what the enemy were doing, and then advance again. That was kept up all the day until in the afternoon when General Meade came back; we did not advance any more after that; we halted then and waited until it was time for us to retire—to go into camp where we were ordered to go; we then went back.

Bvt. Brig. Gen. *W. P. Richardson*, in answer to telegraphic interrogatories sent him, has testified as follows:

MARIETTA, OHIO, *Oct.* 15, 1878.

A. BIRD GARDNER, *Recorder*,
   Governor's Island, N. Y.:

I was colonel and in command of the 25th O. V. I., 2d brigade, Schenck's division, Sigel's corps.

Came on the field the evening of the 28th. Halted on a hill on the south of the road (which I supposed to be the Warrenton pike), at a point east of, and in full view, looking westward, of the ground occupied by King's division during the engagement of that division and Jackson's force on that evening, all of which we saw. Laid there in position until daylight on the 29th.

Moved forward in line of battle, south of the road, early in the morning, slowly; passed over the ground fought on by King's division on the previous evening; saw a few of the dead and wounded. Passed this point about 1 p. m.

Proceeded until we came near the road at the foot of a high hill, on which was a rebel battery.

Supposed we were about to attempt to take it, as we were formed in close column by division. There was at this time a force belonging to our Army on our left and seemed to be crossing the road in front of us on our left.

Soon an artillery fire was opened on our left and rear, and we were withdrawn slowly over the ground we had traversed in the morning, to a narrow strip of timber, where we halted. This was perhaps 2 or half past 2 p. m.

The artillery fire on our left and front increased, and we were withdrawn further across the fields to a heavy piece of timber, where we halted and remained until evening, when we were still further withdrawn and placed (as I believe) on the north side of the road in reserve in the rear of our corps. Here we remained during the night and the greater part of the 30th.

The furtherest point westward from where we started on the morning of the 29th reached by us on that day, was at the foot of the hill just described. Our own brigade was where I have stated; the 1st had crossed the road on our right.

I have not been on the ground since the battle, never was on it before, therefore will not say I know where the Lewis house was.

W. P. RICHARDSON.

Although this witness was not furnished with any map, the movements of his brigade, as narrated by him, can readily and with precision be followed on the map used in this proceeding.

Maj. *George B. Fox*, then captain Seventy-fifth Ohio Volunteers, Mc-

Lean's brigade, Schenck's division, Sigel's corps, called for government, testified as follows (Board's Record, p. 732):

Question. Where were you on the early morning of August 29, 1862?

Answer. We camped about, I should say, 200 or 300 yards from the Chinn house, as indicated on the map, the night previous—night of the 28th.

Question. And on the morning of the 29th did you move forward from that position; if so, at what time and in what direction?

Answer. I should say about eight o'clock, perhaps nine, we commenced to advance through the woods.

Question. Will you please describe on the tracing all the events of the day within your knowledge?

Answer. I was there yesterday. About *this* point on *this* ridge [northeast of the Chinn house] we advanced down through these woods in line of battle—heavy woods—until we came to this ravine at Young's Branch. We adjusted our lines and went up through these woods, and came out on *this* open field [west of Lewis' lane No. 1], where we again adjusted our lines, expecting to find the enemy in *this* clump of woods. [Little fringe of woods south of the word Gainesville.] As soon as we reached this point we saw a charge made. It was over across *that* field and across *this* field; it was off to our right. It seemed to me as though it was a little further in the rear than *this*. I think it was north of the Dogan house. It was about *there* [peach grove] that charge was made northwest and was repulsed. We could see the enemy drive them back down the hill. After they were driven back we concluded to make an advance into these woods. [South of the word Gainesville.] I was in advance. The skirmish line halted in these woods; these are a narrow woods here. From that point we advanced by flank movement, with the right in front parallel with the road. [Gainesville and Centreville pike.] I think when we got into these woods, at this point, we deployed in line; the left came up and we deployed. We were lying along right in front, the left back along the pike; and I think when the right reached here—I am almost sure—it deployed in line of battle. [In the thick woods between the words Warrenton and Gainesville.] After going out of these woods some distance we discovered a great many dead and wounded, which we assisted in carrying off the field.

Question. Whose command did they belong to?

Answer. I do not know; but we heard firing there the evening before, and I suppose that the troops were killed and wounded at that time.

Question. Wounded troops?

Answer. Yes; said to be King's division, but I am not certain about that.

Question. Where did you go?

Answer. We remained there some little time. I advanced out so that I could see through *these* woods. [Trees to the west.] While out in there the Confederates opened their battery from about *this* position, I should judge, at an angle across the road, striking in the rear. [Battery to the west of the Douglass house.] Not many shots were fired; I do not think to exceed a dozen. That was as far as we advanced; and in looking down in this direction [southwest] there were some troops which did not belong to our brigade. I do not know what troops they were.

Question. Union troops?

Answer. Yes, sir.

Question. In what direction?

Answer. To our left; down *this* way.

Question. Diagonally to the left from the pike?

Answer. To the left, forward.

Question. Can you indicate the direction on the map?

Answer. I should say down in this direction [toward Cunliffe's].

Question. Then what did you do?

Answer. We fell back from this point; I think perhaps these troops moved back first, because I could not hear any firing that would indicate that they were driven back; there was no infantry firing at all. They moved back from some cause, I don't know what.

Question. At that point could you see any enemy?

Answer. No, sir; I could see no enemy; I saw none at all on that day on our immediate front.

Question. Then you fell back from these woods?

Answer. Fell back from those woods and remained there some little time—on the edge of the woods. Of course we were a little in advance as skirmishers. We had orders to be on the lookout and watch the column and rear, and move back if they moved back. I know we moved back following them until we got to these woods [little fringe of woods south of the word "Gainesville"]. Then we moved back again on Lewis' lane No. 1, where we remained probably three hours, and rested there.

Question. Did you see or know of any action going on that day; if so, what? State what you saw and what you heard that indicated such.

Answer. In our immediate front there was no fighting.

Question. You mean south of the pike?

Answer. Yes, to the left of the pike, toward Page Land lane; there was no firing from this direction [Page Land lane] that I know of; but there was some firing from that direction [from the pike northwest]. In the morning, when we advanced to this point [west of Lewis' lane No. 1], we saw a charge made by our line; the line had been moved out from these woods, and were in some position here behind a knoll [south of the school-house], up toward this position, held by the enemy [Independent line of the Manassas Gap Railway]. A terrible volley was fired at them and our troops fell back.

Question. What time of day was that?

Answer. That was the first charge; I suppose half-past nine or ten o'clock in the morning. We started from the Chinn house about eight, and it took us about an hour and a half or two hours to get to this house [Lewis' lane No. 1].

Question. What other evidence of an action did you witness?

Answer. After we fell back we saw two other charges later in the day over the same ground, exactly the same ground where we saw the fight in the morning; could see the men moving out away up in this direction later in the day [northwest of the school-house]. That firing and fighting continued throughout the day at intervals.

Question. What was the character of the contest that you witnessed?

Answer. It was a very hotly-contested contest; so much so that we felt we ought to have gone over there, and wanted to go over to their assistance when they drove our troops back. It was the intention of our general to move over there and help them if he could, but I think he had orders to hold them on the left; still, I don't know anything about it.

Question. How long during the day did the battle continue?

Answer. Throughout the day; not continually, but at intervals.

Question. Those intervals which you speak of, were they in the nature of assaults?

Answer. They were assaults on our part, none on the part of the enemy, except when our folks were repulsed they would drive them back from that hill.

Question. From the Independent Manassas Gap Railroad line?

Answer. Yes; it was from a hill up there.

Question. To how late an hour did that battle continue?

Answer. My recollection is that there was firing even after dark. I know that up to dusk in the evening, and I think after dark, there was firing over to the right.

* * * * * *

Question. In going to the point where you encamped that night did you march along a road?

Answer. No, sir, across fields; that is, personally with my company.

Question. Was there any road in your immediate vicinity?

Answer. I think there was none that I saw; we had difficulty in advancing and moving along; the enemy were in our immediate front; there was a few cavalry.

Question. Did you cross any stream?

Answer. I know we crossed several small ravines—no stream of any consequence.

* * * * * *

Question. About what time did you reach that?

Answer. I should say about twelve or half past twelve; we did not remain there long. [In the fringe.]

Question. That was the farthest point to which you advanced?

Answer. Yes, sir.

Question. How long did you remain there?

Answer. Not very long; I think probably an hour, or not that.

Question. That would bring you to about what time?

Answer. Between twelve and one; then we fell back again to this fringe of woods gradually, not pressed back, but moved back very carefully.

Question. About what time?

Answer. Immediately.

Question. One o'clock?

Answer. About one o'clock.

Question. How long did you remain there in falling back?

Answer. We did not remain in this fringe of woods very long; just went and loitered through, and fell back to this position [back to Lewis' lane No. 1], where we remained for probably three or four hours.

Question. Up to what time?

Answer. I should say four or five o'clock.

Question. Then you fell back to what point?

Answer. Then we fell back on our camping ground; the men had nothing to eat all day long. I recollect a little controversy that occurred on the battle-field when the brigade was brought back. General Sigel rode up to General Schenck to know why he was moving back; he told him that the men had had nothing to eat all day long, and he thought it best to get back where they could make some coffee.

Question. What time did you get back?

Answer. About dusk; it was so you could not see a mile and a half away. I recollect in looking out in front we heard some firing on our right; when we got up on this knoll the firing became indistinct; we could not see it, but we could hear it.

* * * * * * *

Question. Do you know whether there were any troops to your left at all?

Answer. I do not. Do you mean in the morning?

Question. Yes.

Answer. I don't know in the morning.

Question. Were there any troops there in the afternoon?

Answer. Yes; to our left, when we were in this advanced position, we saw troops in *this* direction.

Question. Please indicate where you saw them.

Answer. Down on our left, to these woods.

Question. How far?

Answer. Well, I would occasionally through the trees see—well, I don't suppose over 100 yards, if that far. It was wooded there.

Question. Can you, on that map, point out about where you saw those troops?

Answer. Right down in *these* woods, from "G. B. F." to "C. B." [Tracing so lettered.]

Question. State about the hour at which you say you saw those troops?

Answer. I should say it was between one and two o'clock.

Question. Did I understand you to say that there was no musketry firing south of the pike that morning?

Answer. I never heard a musketry shot fired all the day along to the left of the pike.

Question. Neither skirmish line nor anything else?

Answer. No, sir.

Question. Did you hear any artillery firing south of the pike that morning?

Answer. When we fell back the firing that I supposed to have been here might have been along the line, probably a little south of here, but my opinion was all day long that the most firing was north of the pike.

Question. And towards your front?

Answer. Yes, sir; one reason why I am pretty positive of it is that when we were in this wood [the Gibbon wood] I looked back over this field, and the angle of the shooting was right my way. I noticed from the firing of the shots that it would come close by.

Question. A northwesterly direction?

Answer. Yes, sir.

Question. What hour was it when you first saw that movement of Federal troops up against that Independent line of railway?

Answer. In the morning, when we first saw it.

Question. About what time?

Answer. I guess about eight or nine o'clock.

Question. How long did that last?

Answer. The charge, I suppose, occupied a space of fifteen or twenty minutes.

Question. Then did the troops fall back?

Answer. They did.

Question. When was the next one?

Answer. I think we saw four charges during the day. Whether we saw another one that morning before we came back I do not know, but my impression is that I saw a second charge before we advanced.

Question. You think you saw a second one before you made your advance from Lewis' lane No. 1?

Answer. Yes, sir.

Question. How long did it last?

Answer. About the same in character.

Question. Fifteen or twenty minutes?

Answer. Yes.

Question. When was the next one?

Answer. After we fell back in the afternoon, then for two or three hours we could hear them firing, and saw two or three charges in the afternoon.

Question. About what time was it in the afternoon?

Answer. Some time between three and five o'clock.

Question. Not earlier than three?

Answer. That is my recollection. Of course I took no notice of the time by a watch.

Question. In other words, you saw two charges in the morning, and then you saw several in the afternoon?

Answer. I saw one or two in the morning; I know I saw one. The impression is very distinct, for we expected, of course, to go over and assist them, and that was the first notice that we had when we were out in front; so that the probabilities were that if they drove them any farther back we would come in and assist them; that is, I expected to.

* * * * * * *

Question. What is your estimate of the whole distance you advanced over that day?

Answer. Probably a mile and a quarter to a mile and a half.

Question. From the point where you camped the night before to the extreme advance?

Answer. Yes, sir.

Thus it will be perceived that General Schenck is corroborated by General McLean, by the report of Colonel Chesebrough, by the evidence of General Richardson, and by that of Major Fox, who was also in Brigadier-General McLean's brigade and commanded the skirmishers as they advanced. Major Fox was on the ground before he came to testify here and identified the position; so that while Charles Marshall, the former aid of Lee, was there to identify, we have a Union officer also to identify the points to which he advanced on the 29th August, and to which he did not get the next day.

Attention is next invited to the evidence of an important witness on the original trial, now deceased, viz, Brig. Gen. *John F. Reynolds,* who was called by the accused, in 1862, and testified as follows (G. C. M. Record, p. 169):

* * * * * * *

Question. Please to state the position of your command on the 29th, in the afternoon, and the distance between your left and General Porter's command.

Answer. On the 29th I was on the left of General Sigel's command, engaged with the enemy, who was then wholly on the right of the Warrenton pike as we faced it. General Sigel moving up obliquely across the pike; I was on his extreme left. I had no knowledge of General Porter's position at that time, but I suppose that the nearest he must have been at any time was within two and a half or three miles, probably three miles, across this broken country.

By the JUDGE-ADVOCATE:

* * * * * *

Question. Do you, or not, know where the enemy's right flank was on the afternoon of the 29th, say towards sunset?

Answer. *I was on the extreme left of our troops, facing the enemy, and their right, towards sunset, had been extended across the pike, with fresh troops coming down the Warrenton turnpike. But up to twelve or one o'clock it was not across the pike, and I had myself made an attack on their right with my division, but was obliged to change front to meet the enemy coming down the Warrenton pike.* I was forming my troops parallel to the pike, to attack the enemy's right, which was on the other side of the pike, but was obliged to change from front to rear on the right, to face the troops coming down the turnpike. *That was, I suppose, as late as one o'clock,* and they continued to come in there until they formed and extended across the turnpike.

Question. Will you now answer the question as to the probable effect upon the battle of an attack made about that hour on the right flank of the enemy by General Porter's command?

Answer. Supposing General Porter's command to have been on the road from Gainesville to Manassas Junction?

Question. Yes, sir.

Answer. A vigorous attack made there ought to have resulted favorably to our success; ought to have contributed greatly towards it, certainly.

* * * *

Question. Did you see any of the enemy's forces, on the 29th, on the south of the pike leading from Gainesville to Groveton, and do you not know that the right of the enemy's line rested on the north of that road?

Answer. Their line changed during the day. It was on the right up to twelve o'clock, or about that time. In the afternoon it was extended across the pike; I cannot state how far; the country was very wooded there, and I could not see how far across it was. *I thought at the time they were extending it that afternoon until dark.*

Question. You have stated that the country between your left and General Porter's position was a broken country. Will you look at the map which is on the table and designate at what point, in making that statement, you assumed the command of General Porter to have occupied at that time?

Answer. (Going to the map.) [Map used on trial in 1862.] This map is very inaccurate, and, as a military map, is not worth much, particularly this portion of it (indicating the portion referred to). My left was somewhere about here (indicating the place by the letter R), and I take it to be about two miles and a half in a straight line across to where General Porter was, as I understood it (pointing to place marked M. S.). If there had been no troops in his front I suppose he could have made the attack.

By the COURT:

*   *   *   *   *   *   *

Question. On the 29th of August did or did not the enemy's right outflank your left at any time?

Answer. I think it did toward evening. It was late, not dark, toward the dusk of the evening.

So Reynolds, even, did not believe that Longstreet was in force down in front of the petitioner's column during the day.

Question. Will you look at the map and point out the positions your division occupied on the 29th?

Answer. The division was maneuvering almost all the morning, and indeed the whole day in action on that day up to twelve o'clock, with what was supposed to be Jackson's forces, which were in there the day before. (The witness indicated upon the map several positions as occupied by his division during the day.)

Question. Did the enemy outflank you at sunset on the 29th?

Answer. My division, with a brigade of Sigel's corps, lost its connection for a time with the remainder of General Sigel's corps, but at sunset we had closed in to the right, so that the enemy, I think, did outflank us at sunset; that is, I think his flank extended beyond ours, although distant from us, not near enough to be engaged.

Question. Did the enemy that forced you to change front take position between your command and that of the accused on the 29th?

Answer. I think his position was partially between myself and the position occupied by the accused as far as I can judge. I wish the court to remember, in all this testimony, that I had no knowledge at the time where General Porter was. *I knew that troops were over toward Manassas, and was expecting to have them brought up on my left.* I was informed that such would be the case; but they were not brought up there.

Question. Did you think that the force of the enemy, of which you have spoken, was large?

Answer. I thought it a pretty heavy force. I thought it amounted to about a division. It extended, apparently, as far as my division did.

Question. Did not the enemy, in attacking the left and rear of General Pope, on Saturday, the 30th of August, pass with artillery and infantry over much of the country that General Porter would have had to pass over on the 29th to attack the right of the Confederates?

Answer. I think not; I think he had gotten in, as it were, between that broken country and our position on that day, occupying a ridge which crossed the turnpike there, and having the broken country behind him. Because I maneuvered the day before, 29th, all over up to that broken country, and got partially on that ridge with one brigade.

*   *   *   *   *   *

Question. Do you know where the enemy commenced the movement of which you have spoken, to draw around General Pope's left flank?

Answer. I supposed it commenced about the time I changed front, on the afternoon of the 29th, between twelve and one o'clock; it may have been after one o'clock. I suppose that to have been the commencement of that movement; their re-enforcements were constantly coming up, and their line was extended accordingly; they commenced throwing troops out on Jackson's right as they came up, and extended their right out along the ridge.

If anything else was needed confirmatory of the gallant Reynolds, it will be found in his official reports, made at the time of these occurrences. They absolutely contradict the two Confederate witnesses, Marshall and Paine, introduced here by petitioner, and are as follows (Board's Record, p. 500).

REPORT OF BRIGADIER-GENERAL JOHN F. REYNOLDS, COMMANDING DIVISION OF PENN-
SYLVANIA RESERVES, ATTACHED TO M'DOWELL'S CORPS.

HEADQUARTERS REYNOLDS' DIVISION,
Camp Near Munson's Hill, Va., September 5, 1862.

General McDowell joined the command at daylight, and directed my co-operation
with General Sigel.

The right of the enemy's position could be discerned upon the heights above Groveton, on the right of the pike. The division advanced over the ground to the heights
above Groveton, crossed the pike, and Cooper's battery came gallantly into action on
the same ridge on which the enemy's right was, supported by Meade's brigade. While
pressing forward our extreme left across the pike, re-enforcements were sent for by General Sigel for the right of his line under General Milroy, now hardly pressed by the
enemy, and a brigade was taken from Schenck's command on my right. The whole
fire of the enemy was now concentrated on the extreme right of my division, and,
unsupported there, the battery was obliged to retire with considerable loss, in both
men and horses, and the division fell back to connect with Schenck.

Later in the day General Pope, arriving on the right from Centreville, renewed the
attack on the enemy and drove him some distance. My division was directed to
threaten the enemy's right and rear, which it proceeded to do under a heavy fire of
artillery from the ridge to the left of the pike. Generals Seymour and Jackson led
their brigades in advance; but notwithstanding all the steadiness and courage shown
by the men, they were compelled to fall back before the heavy fire of artillery and
musketry which met them both on the front and left flank, and the division resumed
its original position. King's division engaged the enemy along the pike on our right,
and the action was continued with it until dark by Meade's brigade.

List of brigades, regiments, and batteries in Reynolds' division as per his report of killed,
wounded, and missing.

FIRST BRIGADE (Meade).

First Rifles, Colonel McNiel.
Third Infantry, Colonel Sickles.
Fourth Infantry, Colonel Magillon.

Seventh Infantry, Lieutenant-Colonel
Henderson.
Eighth Infantry, Captain Lemon.

SECOND BRIGADE (Seymour).

First Infantry, Colonel Roberts.
Second Infantry, Colonel McCandless,

Fifth Infantry, Major Fentmyer.
Sixth Infantry, Colonel Sinclair.

THIRD BRIGADE (Jackson).

Ninth Infantry, Colonel Anderson.
Tenth Infantry, Colonel Kirk.

Eleventh Infantry, Lieutenant-Colonel
Jackson.
Twelfth Infantry, Colonel Hardin.

ARTILLERY.

Battery C, Fifth Artillery, Captain Ransom.
Battery A, First Pennsylvania Artillery.

Battery B, First Pennsylvania Artillery.
Battery G, First Pennsylvania Artillery.

SUPPLEMENTAL REPORT OF BRIGADIER-GENERAL JOHN F. REYNOLDS.

HEADQUARTERS FIRST ARMY CORPS,
October 9, 1862.

GENERAL: I observe in the report by General Schenck's acting assistant adjutant-
general, published in the Philadelphia Inquirer of to-day, of the operations of that
general's division when General Sigel advanced to attack the enemy on the morning of
the 29th of *August last* (you will yourself observe the error in the dates), several misstate-
ments, unintentional no doubt, when referring to the movements of my division. My
division maneuvered on his left from early in the morning until he gained the position
alluded to on the pike near Gibbon's battle-ground of the evening previous. It was
here that General Schenck asked me for a battery. *Cooper's battery, with Meade's*
brigade as a support, was immediately placed in position on the ridge to the right of the pike
and on the left of the woods where Gibbon's brigade had been in action by General Meade and

myself. In returning from this position, to bring up the other battery and Seymour's brigade, I passed through Schenck's troops, drawn up on the *right* of the woods before alluded to, in which Gibbon had been engaged. But, in bringing up Ransom's battery and Seymour's brigade along the pike, I noticed that Schenck's troops had disappeared from this position and were nowhere in sight. I understood that Schenck had detached a brigade to the right to the support of Milroy, and that I was therefore left alone as far as I knew. I immediately arrested Seymour's movement, and directed the division to occupy the position across the pike from which it had moved, in doing which McLean's brigade was discovered occupying a piece of woods just on the left of the pike, and as soon as could be this movement was arrested and made to correspond with his position. It was subsequently ascertained that he was disconnected from the rest of Sigel's troops, and the position was again changed to make them correct.

I sent no word to General Schenck of the kind indicated in this paper of the movement of the enemy at the time this change of position was made, nor at any time. There was a report came later in the evening that the enemy were moving over the pike, but I am not aware that I communicated it to General Schenck, as at that time I had no connection with him.

I am, &c.,

JOHN F. REYNOLDS,
Brigadier-General Volunteers, Commanding.

Major-General McDowell, *Washington, D. C.*

I make this correction to you, and without any desire to enter into a controversy in the paper on official matters.

J. F. R.

Thus we have fixed with a certainty which approaches the absolute that the Union forces were in and beyond that "Gibbon wood" as late as one o'clock, and held those positions as late, certainly, as three o'clock in the afternoon. No wonder, therefore, that Longstreet thought "it would be a little hazardous to make a front attack," and expressed to General Lee a doubt of being able to carry the position held by Generals Schenck, Stevens, and Reynolds, south of the pike, and, as Charles Marshall says, "for reasons satisfactory to himself [Longstreet], rather advised against it" (Board's Record, pp. 63 and 169.)

But there is still further evidence as to Reynold's position.

Bvt. Maj. Gen. *H. G. Sickles,* United States Volunteers, called by government, testified as follows (Board's Record, p. 1096):

By the RECORDER:

Question. What position did you hold in the military service of the United States on the 29th of August, 1862?

Answer. I was colonel of the Third Regiment Pennsylvania Reserves, second brigade. I do not recollect what our division was. We returned from the Peninsula and rejoined our old corps.

Question. With what rank did you leave the service?

Answer. Brevet major-general.

Question. Whose corps?

Answer. General McDowell's.

Question. Who commanded your division?

Answer. General John F. Reynolds.

Question. Who commanded your brigade?

Answer. General George G. Meade.

Question. Do you know where your regiment was encamped on the morning of Friday, August 29, 1832, if it was encamped at all, or bivouacked?

Answer. I took it that, in looking over the map shown me here, it was near the Lewis house, on the battle-field.

Question. What did your brigade do that morning of August 29, 1862?

Answer. We broke camp about daylight, I think, and moved out to the front on the left of Sigel, I think.

Question. How long did you remain with the brigade?

Answer. It was probably eight o'clock, or nine, in the morning; eight, perhaps.

Question. When you left it?

Answer. Yes.

Question. You did not then remain with it the remainder of the day?

Answer. No, sir; I did not.

* * * * * * *

Cross-examination by Mr. BULLITT:

Question. You say it was in the neighborhood of the Lewis house where your camp was; will you indicate on the map where it was?

Answer. I don't know that it was really the Lewis house; I judge from the location. I think that here is about the position (the Lewis-Leachman house) where we were massed that evening; but I am not very sure; I have such an indistinct knowledge of the ground, and was with the command so little, that it would be hardly fair to depend upon my testimony.

Question. You really do not recollect where it was?

Answer. No; I have not a distinct recollection; but I think that is the neighborhood, judging from that stream there. (Witness indicates the Lewis-Leachman house.) I saw a map upstairs which locates a stream of water which I am pretty sure I have a recollection of.

Question. May it not have been this stream (Chinn's Branch), or this (Young's Branch)?

Answer. I think it was not so far to the rear as that.

Question. Do you feel any certainty about it?

Answer. Of course I am not certain; but yet I am inclined to think it was here (Lewis-Leachman house).

*   *   *   *   *   *   *.

By the RECORDER:

Question. Is there anything else in the neighborhood of that location that fixes it in your recollection?

Answer. On the previous evening, the 28th, I think, I recollect there was a battle took place, or a fight, between Gibbon's troops and the enemy near our front, and General Meade's brigade was ordered front. We advanced some distance, and formed on a hill where we could overlook the fighting. It was then about sunset. I think we remained there until dark, when the firing ceased; then we returned again to where the first and third brigades were in camp.

Maj. *William H. Hope*, Ninth Pennsylvania Reserves, Third Brigade, Reynolds' division, called by government, testified as follows (Board's Record, p. 931):

Question. Where was your regiment camped on the morning of the 29th of August, Friday?

Answer. We arrived on the morning of the 29th, about one o'clock, on the Bull Run battle-field.

Question. And encamped near or at what place?

Answer. Near Groveton, I think.

Question. Did you move out from that place after daylight?

Answer. We did.

Question. At about what time?

Answer. About daylight. We were ordered to the rear of General Sigel's troops to support him.

Question. Describe all your movements that day.

Answer. We were marching and countermarching nearly all day, until about between four and five o'clock in the afternoon; our brigade was ordered in to the extreme left to try to take a battery; we went down through a corn-field, and came to this dry ravine, and General Reynolds was there; he says, "General Jackson, you are too damned slow." The regiment, the right wing, passed around to the right, and the left wing passed to the left. I commanded the third company from the right, Company D; we got between the rebel battery and on a line with a battery and sharpshooters; Colonel Hardin, commanding the Twelfth Regiment, and the lieutenant-colonel of my regiment were talking together; the sharpshooters opened on us. I was standing probably ten feet from Colonel Hardin when a ball cut the cord of his hat; it was a little too hot, and we could not return the fire. The sharpshooters were under cover; the battery had been supported by this time, and we could do nothing with it, and all about-faced and got away from there.

Question. That was about what time?

Answer. Half past five o'clock; probably a little later.

Question. Do you know where the Lewis house is?

Answer. I do.

Question. Were you at any time in the day in the vicinity of that house?

Answer. We passed that house, I think, where we went to try to capture a battery, rather in front and to the left of the Lewis house.

Question. Off in the neighborhood of Britt's?

Answer. I don't know that I can locate it. I think probably the battery was nearly a mile from the Lewis house.

Question. Can you indicate about where that battery was?
Answer. I cannot locate that battery on that map.
Question. It was a little to the left and front?
Answer. Yes, sir.
Question. How far forward did you get on that day, in reference to the position of the Lewis house?
Answer. About a mile from the Lewis house.
Question. Forward?
Answer. Yes.
Question. In which direction, west, northwest, or southwest?
Answer. Northwest.

* * * * * * *

Question. What time in the day did you first see the enemy?
Answer. About daylight.
Question. Where did you see them then?
Answer. To the left of Groveton.
Question. When you say to the left of Groveton, do you mean the north or south of it?
(The witness indicates on the tracing northwest of Groveton.)
Question. Did you see any fighting that day in that direction?
Answer. I know we were not particularly engaged; we were under fire, and some of them gave us a little railroad iron that day. We went in to take a battery, and when we came back they gave us some grapeshot in a corn-field.
Question. Did you hear any cannonading that day?
Answer. Yes, sir.
Question. Which direction?
Answer. Groveton.
Question. Did you hear any infantry firing?
Answer. Yes, sir.
Question. How long?
Answer. More or less all day. In the morning there was quite a sharp cannonading.
Question. Do you recollect the Lewis house, whether it was a one-story or two-story house?
Answer. A two-story house.
Question. Do you recollect distinctly being there that day?
Answer. Yes, sir.

By the PRESIDENT OF THE BOARD:

Question. What was the formation of this division during this day?
Answer. I do not know, only my own brigade.
Question. What was your formation?
Answer. The 9th, 10th, and 12th; we were on the extreme left.
Question. How were you formed—in line or in column?
Answer. I could not say as to the first and second brigades, how they were formed. Our brigade was formed in column of battalions.
Question. You did not see the formation of the other brigades?
Answer. No, sir.

Bvt. Brig. Gen. *Charles Barnes*, United States Volunteers, then captain Ninth Pennsylvania Reserves, Third Brigade, Reynolds' division, called by government, testified as follows (Board's Record, p. 660):

Question. Where were you at daylight on the morning of August 29?
Answer. We were to the left of the Lewis house.
Question. From there where did you go?
Answer. From there we moved to the front, or between that and Groveton and the Lewis house, in a ravine to the left of the Lewis house.
Question. The Lewis house that is now called Leachman's?
Answer. The Lewis house was a two-story white frame house, one of the best in that section of country.
Question. At what time did you arrive at that point?
Answer. To the best of my recollection we arrived in the position that we lay, to the left of that house, about three o'clock in the morning.
Question. What were your movements from that position during the day?
Answer. We were on the extreme flank of General Pope's army, and we kept moving backwards and forwards from different points on the extreme left; my regiment was on the skirmish line a good part of the day, that is, we were kept flanking.
Question. Was there any contest going on that day; if so, what was the nature of it?
Answer. There was a heavy contest going on on our right all day, or nearly all day;

there was heavy cannonading in the fore part of the day, and there was heavy artillery fire in the after part of the day on as late as dark.

Question. At how early a period in the day did that heavy infantry firing begin ?

Answer. To the best of my recollection there was some infantry firing in the fore part of the day, but the heavy infantry firing was, I should think, about three o'clock.

Question. How long did it continue ?

Answer. It continued heavy at intervals until dark.

Question. Do you know of any infantry firing between, say, about twelve o'clock noon and three o'clock ?

Answer. I cannot say that I do. There was some cannonading.

Question. Can you indicate on the map the farthest point to the front that you got that day ?

Answer. I believe I can.

Question. Is this house called the Leachman-Lewis house the one that you refer to ? [Douglas Pope map shown to the witness.]

Answer. We were ordered late at night to charge up in this ravine, with two brigades. [In the direction of J. W. Cunliffe's.]

Question. Will you mark it on the map ?

Answer. As near as I can tell from this map I should think that was the ravine. [Marked C. B.] Just south of the word Cundiff.

Question. With reference to the point farthest in advance that you reached that day, do you know where the right of your brigade was located ?

Answer. The right of our brigade was over near to Groveton, towards Groveton. Our brigade kept flanking backwards and forwards down in this direction and off in that direction, feeling for the enemy, as we were directed.

Question. From about twelve o'clock in the day where was your company ?

Answer. About twelve o'clock we were resting in a piece of woods up near, I should think, in here somewhere. [In a piece of woods northwest of Britt's, marked No. 2 C. B.]

Question. And the farthest point you reached was where ?

Answer. Where it is marked "C. B.," southeast of Cundiffe's. The enemy were firing off in this direction somewhere. . [From Pageland lane towards Gainesville.]

Question. Indicate the direction in which the firing was.

Answer. I should think it was off in this direction somewhere. [Near to the railroad.] We were ordered to move up into a run, just a dry ravine. We moved up by the flank, three regiments. General Seymour was with us. As we got up near, I think, this piece of woods, we were ordered to halt. [Just west of the words "Meadowville lane."] General Reynolds came riding up to the rear of the column—we were moving by the left flank—and ordered Seymour to halt, that he was too late, and for us to move right back ; he gave the order himself to about-face and march back. We marched back, and moved, I should think, down this ravine towards the Lewis house. [Following the line of the branch.]

Question. At the time that he ordered you to move back, did he state anything more ?

Answer. He stated nothing more. He stated to General Seymour that he was too late ; that the enemy were showing themselves off in this direction. [Beyond Pageland lane.] We could see their skirmish line coming in off in this direction ; that would be to the right of where we were moving up.

Question. Put down with your pencil and mark it C. B. 3 where you noticed the enemy's skirmishers coming in.

(The witness does as directed.)

Question. What time of day was that ?

Answer. At the time we made this movement up here it was as late as four o'clock. I recollect the time, because the sun was sinking in the west quite perceptibly.

Question. I understand you to say that you were on the left of General Reynolds' division ?

Answer. On the left of General Reynolds' division, and my regiment did the flanking, or, rather, the skirmishing.

Question. When you say did flanking, what have you reference to ?

Answer. In moving the brigade backwards and forwards to feel the enemy. Men were put to moving out in flank as feelers.

Question. Were you in that body ?

Answer. Yes, sir.

Question. The right of the division rested over in the direction of the Warrenton pike ?

Answer. In the direction of Groveton and the Warrenton pike.

Question. During that time where was the enemy, so far as you were concerned, from noon up to dusk ?

Answer. The body seemed to be on the right, where the heavy firing was, north of the Warrenton pike, about Groveton.

Question. Could you see the enemy during the day from twelve o'clock ?

Answer. Not where we were, we couldn't see them. We were kept kind of down in the ravine a little.

* * \~ * * * *

Cross-examination by Mr. BULLITT:

Question. Will you locate on the map your position at three o'clock in the night or on the morning of the 29th?

Answer. I don't know that I can.

Question. As nearly as you can, about where were you at three o'clock?

Answer. That was the time when we got where we bivouacked.

Question. Indicate that as well as possible. [Douglas Pope map shown to witness.]

Answer. I don't know that I can indicate where we bivouacked that night.

Question. You can somewhere in the neighborhood?

Answer. It must have been off here. It is in this direction from the Lewis house.

Question. Give your recollection of about the locality; you arrived there about three o'clock?

Answer. Yes, sir.

Question. Now the point you arrived at where you bivouacked that morning and night?

Answer. It is pretty hard for me to state, but it was near the Lewis house.

Question. Which Lewis house?

(The witness indicates Leachman's.)

Question. It was near the Lewis house, which is west of Lewis lane No. 1. Now what time did you leave that point?

Answer. It was after daylight.

Question. How far did you march?

Answer. We marched a short distance in the first place, then we marched again, and we kept marching and remarching.

Question. Please show the point to which you marched when you first left there after daylight.

Answer. We marched direct, I should think, from the Lewis house up toward Groveton. We marched from where we were bivouacked to the direction of Groveton.

Question. Was it a northerly direction?

Answer. It was a northerly direction, if that map is correct.

Question. How near did you go to Groveton?

Answer. We went in sight of it. In the first place, you could see a long distance there at some of those points.

Question. You know where the Warrenton and Centreville pike is?

Answer. I do.

Question. Were you immediately south of that? Were you marched directly north toward that road, at right angles with it?

Answer. I don't know that we were marched at right angles, but in that direction toward Groveton.

Question. How near did you go to Groveton?

Answer. I suppose we were three-quarters of a mile.

Question. Groveton was in which direction from you?

Answer. Groveton was in a northerly direction. It was a little to our right.

* * * * * * *

Question. Which way did you march and which way did you countermarch? Give your movements as nearly as you can.

Answer. In marching up this ravine we marched off in this direction (toward Cunliffe's) In moving back, we moved back right down the ravine.

Question. In countermarching, did you at any time go east of the point at which you had bivouacked the night before?

Answer. I think not, to the best of my recollection.

Question. Then, during the whole day, according to your present recollection, you were west of what is marked on this map as Lewis lane No. 1?

Answer. Yes; that is the best of my recollection. At night we fell back and took position in here somewhere [north of Compton's barn].

* * * * * *

Question. Did you see no enemy along about in the vicinity of what you have marked here as "C. B."?

Answer. There was an enemy up in here. [Towards Pageland lane.] We saw a few mounted skirmishers.

Question. You saw no heavy bodies of troops?

Answer. Had no heavy bodies of troops at that time until they commenced firing upon us from this position.

Question. Do you recollect having seen Owen Jones, of Pennsylvania, with his cavalry, there?

Answer. I don't recollect seeing any Pennsylvania cavalry there. There were cavalry moving backwards and forwards.

•   •   •   •   •

Question. Now I ask you whether or not General Reynolds did not that day move into the woods in front of you with more than one brigade, and whether he was not driven out within fifteen minutes or half an hour afterwards?
Answer. He was not driven out. He ordered the troops out; they were not driven out.

Question. That was a wood?
Answer. That was up a dry ravine in an open field; there was a little woods to our left.

Question. Will you indicate where that woods was?
Answer. If this map is correct, I would suppose that is it; it is a small piece of wood. [West of the words "Meadowville lane."]

Question. You took a route along here, I suppose—you marched along that road? [Manassas and Sudley road.]
Answer. On the 28th we were moving along this road. [From Gainesville east along the Warrenton and Centreville pike.] One of our brigades was fired into, and the eighth regiment had several men killed.

Question. Then which way did you go?
Answer. Soon afterwards—after that the enemy left our front and we made a detour off towards Manassas.

Question. That is, you moved off towards the Manassas and Gainesville road on the Manassas Gap Railroad?
Answer. We moved off towards the Manassas Gap Railroad. I don't recollect that we crossed it; yet I am not positive but what we did cross it. Then we moved along to Manassas or near Manassas.

Question. What time did you leave there?
Answer. I cannot tell.

Question. About what time?
Answer. We came in here and halted.

Question. Came in where and halted?
Answer. Some point either on this side of the railroad or on that, I cannot tell which. We halted for an hour or two and then we moved off, and it was after dark when we passed Manassas; we marched on from Manassas; we seemed to just turn right up towards the Warrenton pike.

Question. Came up in this direction? [Along the Manassas and Sudley road.]
Answer. I suppose that is the road; from there we went up to this point that I indicated, where we bivouacked.

Question. How did you get to that point from the Manassas and Sudley road?
Answer. Across the country.

Question. Look at it there; did you march right across here?
Answer. I cannot tell; it was after night.

Question. You do not know how you got there?
Answer. I don't know how we got there, but I know we were at Manassas, and I know we marched that night during the night.

Question. Did you see the attack which was made late in the afternoon or evening by King's division?
Answer. I did not.

Question. Where were you at half past five to six o'clock?
Answer. At half past five or six, at the time that this charge was made up in here—I put this at a later date than some of my comrades—but at the time when we made this charge, or just before it, this heavy musketry firing was going on.

Question. Then about what time?
Answer. While we were falling back there was heavy musketry firing.

Question. About what time would you say it was that you were there at "C. B."?
Answer. I should say that it was not earlier in the day than five o'clock.

Question. That is, the movement by which you were at "C. B." was not later than five o'clock on that day?
Answer. I should say that it was not later than five o'clock in the afternoon.

Question. Not earlier than that?
Answer. Not earlier than that.

Question. How long did you remain in that point?
Answer. Not ten minutes.

Question. Before you fell back to what point?
Answer. We flanked right around this ravine, I should think, and we halted there for a little while.

Question. That is the ravine right under "Lewis lane, No. 2"?
Answer. Yes.

Question. What I want to know is where you were at the time General Hatch's division and King's division, General Hatch in command, charged up the Warrenton pike?

Answer. The time the troops charged up there I cannot tell who commanded the troops. We were in here.

*　　　　*　　　　*　　　　*　　　　*

Question. Was there any heavy fighting along on the Warrenton pike just north of you?

Answer. There was to our right very heavy firing in the vicinity of Groveton?

This evidence, it is noticeable, corroborates Geneal Reynólds' official report, before cited, of the 5th September, 1862, that *after* General Pope arrived on the field he proceeded, under the latter's orders, to threaten the enemy's right and rear "to the left of the pike," viz: to the north of it, and had a sharp contest.

It is a curious tact that Maj. G. B. Fox, of Schenck's division, and Brevet Brigadier-General Barnes, of the Pennsylvania Reserves, Reynolds' division, each put the lines that they marked on the map in exactly the same relative position, Reynolds having been on Schenck's left, near Meadowville lane, and one being a continuation of the other.

The opportunity here presented to an enterprising and vigorous officer was lost by this petitioner, for instead of pushing into action so as to communicate with the left of General Pope's army, he retired without any effort to carry out the specific orders for his march, *under which he was to halt only when he should have established communication with the forces on his right* (Pennsylvania Reserves), *which, as he knew, were ordered also to march toward Gainesville.*

As, however, from the sounds of battle, it was evident that they had met the enemy, communication could not, of course, be had by continuing in the direction of Gainesville on one side of the triangle, Gainesville forming the apex, but by pushing across to the other side on a more northerly road, parallel to the base of the assumed triangle.

While the petitioner was still at his furthest point of advance, with a portion of his troops, near Dawkins' Branch, General Reynolds was crossing the Warrenton turnpike and attacking Jackson's right.

There were two brigade fronts between Reynolds' division and Groveton, viz, Stahel's and McLean's, of Sigel's corps, and this shows how far his force must have extended on the general line of the turnpike toward Gainesville.

In his official report, General Reynolds says, as we have seen, that "Cooper's battery, with Meade's brigade as a support, was immediately placed in position on the right of the pike and on the left [viz, west] of the woods where Gibbon's brigade had been in action" (*p.* 72 *official printed report*).

In his evidence on the general court-martial, General Reynolds said "*he supposes this to have been as late as one o'clock.*"

In Brig. Gen. R. C. Schenck's official report (p. 140, *ibid.*), it is stated that it was about one or two o'clock when General Reynolds' division was seen coming up on the left of McLean's brigade of Schenck's division.

It was the "left rear" of the force of General Reynolds (thus offered at an angle with our main line) that the Confederate reports speak of as attained by their artillery from the high ground west of Pageland lane in their advance from Gainesville.

From this we may consider what would have been the effect had petitioner moved up to establish communication with our left (Reynolds'), since the ground between them was necessarily entirely unoccupied by the enemy, and since the enemy's check to Reynolds' attack of Jackson's right would have been counterchecked by petitioner's advance.

All these troops south of the Warrenton turnpike were rendered of comparatively little use, by reason of the petitioner's fatal inaction.

As, according to General Schenck's report, Cooper's battery, after going into position (west of Gibbon's battle-ground) between one and two o'clock, was in action "about an hour" (p. 140, *ibid.*), it follows that the enemy could not have attacked and flanked Reynolds with artillery, even so as to have compelled his falling back, until about three o'clock.

When, therefore, it is sought by petitioner's counsel to place the Confederate line of Hood's division in the neighborhood of Gibbon's battle-ground and field-hospital at 10 a. m., we can only believe it by saying that what John F. Reynolds swore to, and Schenck (by his aide-de-camp) officially reported in September and October, 1862, was false, or else you must come to the conclusion that the Confederate sources of information were mistaken.

The field-hospital of our dead and wounded men of Gibbon's brigade has been too well fixed in evidence and too indelibly impressed on the minds of those who passed over the ground on the 29th August, 1862, and who have been witnesses, not to leave its impress. Nearly three hours is a great discrepancy, but as Reynolds' and Schenck's reports and the former's evidence were made and given when the subject was fresh in their recollection, such sources of information are entitled to great respect.

If the Confederates were anywhere near the position it is sought to place them, Reynolds would have been destroyed.

Leaving out of view the question of success or non-success of an attack on the enemy's right, and whether Jackson or Longstreet was there, it will not be questioned that an attack should be made as ordered, because even if it fails it may so employ troops of the enemy as to insure elsewhere against their line such success as to lead to victory.

The battle we are considering affords a striking illustration of this.

When Hood's advance (of Longstreet's command) had, towards the middle of the afternoon, rendered the stay of the two brigades in Jackson's right front in observation of Reynolds no longer a necessity, they were withdrawn and became a reserve greatly needed for Jackson's nearly-exhausted lines.

When General Kearney, at about six o'clock, rolled up the enemy's left upon his center, and Steven's, joining with Kearney, endeavored to sweep their line still further and make the success decisive, it was Jubal Early's Confederate brigade, with the Eighth Louisiana of Hay's brigade, coming to the aid of A. P. Hill's exhausted troops, who had already, says Hill in his report, suffered "six distinct and separate assaults," that checked our advance and drove Stevens back.

Kearney's report says his own division "changed front to the left to sweep with a rush the first line of the enemy. This was most successful. The enemy rolled up on his own right. It presaged a victory for us all. Still our force was too light. The enemy brought up rapidly heavy reserves, so that our further progress was impeded. General Stevens came up gallantly in action to support us, but did not have the numbers."

These were the *last* reserves Jackson had upon the field. The other regiments of Hay's Confederate brigade had been put in some time previously on a similar necessity.

Second Lieutenant *John S. Hollingshead*, Ninth Pennsylvania Reserves, third brigade, Reynolds' division, called by government, testified as follows (Board's Record, p. 932):

Question. Where were you on the morning of that day—29th of August?
Answer. I could not scarcely tell; we were marching during the night, and we lay in an open field until daylight, then we commenced moving.
Question. Do you know where the Lewis house is?
Answer. No, sir; I could not say by name. All I know is that after we had been

marching and countermarching during the day, and after going through a strip of woods into a ravine to charge a battery, we all fell back and got to a white house, and staid there part of the night; I don't know the name of the house. I have never been on the ground since that time.

Question. Was there any branch near that house—any stream?

Answer. The ravine that we went into was dry at that time; just past where our company halted, in sight of that battery, there was a swamp, then a clump of trees on the other side; part of our brigade got into the woods across the swamp; our company and two or three others were just on the edge of the knoll that the battery was placed on. General Seymour sat there on his horse, on the edge of the knoll, within ten feet of where I was standing, and while there General Reynolds rode up and says, "You are too late, too late, about face," and we all went out together as quick as we could get.

Question. You had been moving up this ravine?

Answer. When we moved up that ravine and crossed the corn-field, a battery was playing on us with grape and canister, and we got back there as fast as we could, and got behind a knoll in front. The battery played on us as we went across the corn-field, and when we got upon the knoll, we changed direction; then when we got past where that swamp is the battery changed direction again, and was firing at our men in the woods across the swamp. While we staid there in that position General Reynolds came up, and the words he said were to General Seymour.

Question. How far in advance of this house do you think you went up that ravine?

Answer. About a mile, to the best of my recollection.

Question. Do you know what direction that ravine took which you went up from this house?

Answer. The strip of woods that we went through—we had been marching and countermarching along the roads during the day, and then we went to the right through a strip of woods and through a cornfield at about right angles.

By reference to the map at the time, between 1 and 2 o'clock p. m., when General Reynolds, as he originally testified, was swinging his division by a right half wheel across the "Warrenton" pike, near Meadowville lane, and west of the Gibbon wood, in order to attack Jackson's right, it will be perceived what an opportunity was presented to petitioner, had he been at the head of his column, to move up in the exact direction indicated by his early verbal and written orders from General Pope and personal direction from General McDowell.

The position of Reynolds' division at that time shows quite convincingly that the enemy could not have been in either position or force south of the pike, near enough to have offered any obstruction to a movement by petitioner to connect with the left wing of the "Army of Virginia."

Now with reference indirectly to the position that Maj. S. N. Benjamin, then Second United States Artillery, fired at. The impression sought to be conveyed is, that he fired off in the direction of the "Browner-Douglass house" towards a battery placed down on the easterly slope of the hill, on that natural glacis. There is also a natural glacis from this highest point noted as "Stony ridge,". where Jackson had his artillery in position behind his line down towards the Warrenton pike. If we look at the position taken up by Major Benjamin and examine the contour lines and the respective heights, we find, for example, that, his position being on the southerly edge of the pike at the easterly corner of Groveton, the next height westerly at its highest northerly point is 20 feet above the point at which his battery was located as just mentioned; that ridge which crosses the pike west of Groveton, and which is 20 feet higher than the one on which Benjamin's battery was placed, has still another west of it and east of the "Gibbon" road, which also crosses the pike to a point still more northerly, and is also 20 feet higher, while the northerly edge of the "Gibbon" wood north of the pike is still more northerly on an elevation 200 feet high.

From this topographical description it is plain that he could not possibly have fired westerly down the pike, or towards the "Browner-

Douglass" house, even had he so wished, on account of intermediate hills and "Gibbon" wood, but that his line of fire was northwesterly, in the direction of the word "Stony," which best fulfills his conditions as to distance (Board's Record, p. 613), besides which, we have seen by the evidence heretofore cited of Maj. B. S. White, inspector-general in the regular Confederate army, Jackson's artillery was behind his line on that very "Stony ridge."

This direction of Benjamin's artillery contest corresponds exactly with the government theory of the true situation; for had he been firing westerly down the pike (had the topography permitted), General Reynolds would never have been able to cross it west of the "Gibbon" wood at the time he swore in 1862 that he did, or march Seymour's brigade down it to join his division, which was at precisely the same time Benjamin swears he carried on his remarkably gallant artillery contest.

From the position which Reynolds reached westerly beyond the Gibbon wood between 1 and 2 p. m. of the 29th, and from the fact that the Confederate Capt. James Mitchell, First Virginia Volunteers (called by petitioner), the only witness from Kemper's division of Longstreet (which division has been put in line by petitioner south of the pike next to Hood's), swears he "saw no Federal troops at all that day" (Board's Record, p. 386), it is plain that the re-enforcing enemy under Lee, comprising part of Longstreet's command, that day occupied a *defensive* position only near enough to help Jackson if necessary.

I have now given the evidence of these Union witnesses as to the position they occupied up to a very late hour in the afternoon. If General Reynolds, as his official reports show and as he swears on the original trial of this petitioner, got up in this position on the pike beyond the Gibbon wood at a later hour than one o'clock on the 29th of August, 1862, remaing there a considerable time, and if that is corroborated, as we find it is, by the official report of Colonel Cheesebrough, Schenck's adjutant-general, and by Major-General Schenck himself, and by Major Fox, and by Brevet Brigadier-General Barnes, Major Hope, Lieutenant Hollingshead, and General McLean, besides the citizens Monroe and Carrico, Major White, and Rev. Mr. Landstreet, it is quite plan that Charles Marshall and Alex. D. Payne, the two rebel officers who were brought here by petitioner as witnesses, were mistaken as to that day's position of Longstreet, which they fixed as on the easterly edge of the Gibbon wood by 9.30 or 10 a. m.

4.30 P. M. ORDER.

We now come to the consideration of the 4.30 p. m. order, so called, which is found in the third specification of the first charge, and is the basis of the first specification, second charge, and is as follows:

That the accused, being in front of the enemy during the battle of Manassas on Friday the 29th August, 1862, did receive the following lawful order:

" HEADQUARTERS IN THE FIELD,
"*August* 29—4.30 p. m.

" Major-General PORTER: Your line of march brings you in on the enemy's right flank. I desire you to push forward into action at once on the enemy's flank, and if possible on his rear, keeping your right in communication with General Reynolds. The enemy is massed in the woods in front of us, but can be shelled out as soon as you engage their flank. Keep heavy reserves and use your batteries, keeping well closed to your right all the time. In case you are obliged to fall back, do so to your right and rear, so as to keep you in close communication with the right wing.
"JOHN POPE,
" *Major-General Commanding.*"

The petitioner denies that he received this order at 5, or even 5.30 p. m., or until on or about sunset, when he was at his headquarters at the junction of the Gainesville and Sudley Ford roads, east of Bethlehem Church (petitioner's opening statement, p. 40,) and on the original trial brought several witnesses to this point. He has produced no new evidence upon the subject. He has, however, brought witnesses (Leachman and Payne) to *guess* a road by which the order could have been carried.

As somewhat illustrative of this subject, it will be curious to note the evidence of the petitioner's then aid-de-camp, Lieut. S. M. Weld, as given in the original trial (G. C. M. Record, p. 129).

It seems that he was sent by the petitioner with a message to be delivered either to General McDowell or *General King*, both verbal and written, and that he started about four o'clock in the afternoon of the 29th from the junction of the road that leads from Gainesville to Manassas Junction and the road that leads to Sudley Springs. The purport of this message was that General Morell would now be strongly engaged; that there was a large force in front of us; that large clouds of dust were seen there, &c.

He says that on the road he saw General Hatch, who told him that General King was sick and *not there*, and that he, General Hatch, commanded his division; a fact, by the way, which, as we have seen, the petitioner himself knew beyond peradventure as early as ten o'clock in the morning. He says that General Hatch gave him a message to the petitioner to the effect that we had driven the enemy into the woods, which he sent to the petitioner by an orderly. This was after "quite a heavy fire of musketry broke out to our right and front." He then went in the direction indicated in order to deliver the message to General McDowell, and found him just leaving General Pope. He delivered the dispatch, and General McDowell said he was not the man, and pointed to General Pope. He says that General Pope told him to tell the petitioner "that we are having a hard fight"; that he overheard General Pope tell General McDowell to send one of his divisions to the right, to which General McDowell made some objection. He, Weld, then left General Pope, went down the road, and waited about five minutes; wrote the substance of the message, and sent it by an orderly to the petitioner. He met the orderly on his way back, who told him he could not find the petitioner, and he delivered it himself. He says he got back about sundown, and that he did not see Capt. Douglas Pope until then. He says he occupied at least an hour and a half returning, having come back by a *different* road from that on which he went. He did not go to where he had left the petitioner, because he understood from the petitioner that the latter would be up at the front, and therefore he went to the front, having come out into the Manassas and Gainesville road near Bethlehem Church.

Of course, he did not find the petitioner at the front, because, as we have seen, during the course of the evidence for that day, that was not the place that the petitioner frequented. However, Lieutenant Weld went on up to the front, and then came back. He says he found the petitioner where he left him, right in the forks of the two roads—the Sudley Springs and the Manassas and Gainesville roads.

This message which he delivered to General Pope, with all the delay of going to find King's division, conversing with General Hatch, afterwards receiving a different message from him from the one mentioned colloquially, writing it out and then going to find General McDowell on Buck Hill with General Pope, took him, according to his own evidence, about an hour.

Therefore, at that time the distance from General Pope's headquarters on Buck Hill to where the petitioner was located was not, according to his own witness and aid, more than an hour; and it must be recollected that the message which he gave his aid to carry to General McDowell was not one of urgency, requiring anything specially or immediately to be done on the part of General McDowell; it was in the nature of a report to General McDowell, and shows that he conceived himself to be operating still under the orders and instructions which General McDowell had given him upon leaving him near the Manassas Gap Railroad.

If it took the petitioner's aid but an hour to go to General McDowell at Buck Hill (General Pope's headquarters), even including all these delays *en route* of which I have spoken, it certainly could not have taken a longer time for an officer starting half an hour later from Buck Hill with an urgent message to go to the petitioner.

In considering this subject as to the delivery of this order, we must consider the character of the message which Captain Pope was to take to the petitioner.

There was a battle progressing at the time, heavy infantry and artillery firing, assaults being made upon the enemy's lines; and all this was spread out and under the notice of the commanding general and his staff. Captain Pope himself had shortly before, according to his own statement, been in a position where he witnessed directly some of the serious portions of the contest. The order which Captain Pope received was of an urgent character. It was for the petitioner to move at once to attack the *enemy's* right flank and, if possible, his rear. No description of order which could be given on the battle-field would indicate the necessity of greater speed and haste in its delivery than this. Is it to be assumed therefore, for a moment, that Captain Pope, after receiving such a message, should trot or walk as if on an excursion of mere pleasure to view the scenery? There is every reason to suppose, aside from the evidence of the witnesses on the subject, that Captain Pope rode with that message with all the haste and speed that was possible.

We have seen from the evidence and reports of both Sigel and Reynolds on the left of General Pope's line of operations, that they had been informed and were looking for the arrival of the petitioner upon their left to take part in the action; and the Hon. *E. D. Fowler*, who then commanded the Fourteenth Brooklyn Regiment in Hatch's brigade, King's division, has said (Board's Record, p. 548) that his brigade got into position to support Reynolds west of the Sudley Springs road after having left the Manassas and Gainesville road, about 2 p. m., and that he was "very anxious, and expected, even before we halted, to hear, on what was our front and left, the guns of Porter's division."

General McDowell testified on the original trial (G. C. M. Record, p. 85, and Board's Record, p. 818) that he met Captain Pope when carrying this order near the Manassas and Sudley road, and that his troops were on the Sudley road. Some of them, however, had been put in, as he himself says, and as other testimony has corroborated, west of the Sudley road between New Market and the stone house, to co-operate with General Reynolds.

At the time, therefore, that General McDowell met Captain Pope, it is quite apparent that the latter could not have strayed from the road in the direction that the petitioner would put him in order to show that he lost his way.

It is to be noticed in looking at the map prepared by Major Warren that the road which the government witnesses unite in saying they took on the afternoon of the 29th of August is not fully delineated. For a part of the distance along Chinn's Branch, between two roads running northeasterly from the Chinn house, to the point where they cross the branch, is delineated a path which, so far as the map is concerned, stops at the most southerly of those two roads without any apparent reason.

The witness *Leachman*, and others, have testified to the presence in that country, in camp the previous year, of a Confederate army, and that the country was full of army roads.

The time of the dispatch of the order is fixed by its date, namely, 4.30 p. m. Three witnesses have testified as to the road that was taken, and their evidence as to a part of the road is substantiated by that of Major-General McDowell.

When we come to look into the testimony of Mr. *W. B. Wheeler*, a citizen, who lives on the line of the road which Captain Pope and the orderly, Mr. Duffee, testified as to taking, we find that there was formerly, at the time which we are considering, an army road in that very direction testified to by those witnesses.

As a slight corroborative circumstance it is to be noted that when these two witnesses, Captain Pope and Orderly Duffee, at my request, visited the battle-ground before coming in the presence of the Board to testify, after leaving Buck Hill, General Pope's former headquarters, they moved down the line of the Manassas and Sudley road towards Manassas Junction the entire distance in a light wagon, without personally examining the road that ran up by Chinn's Branch around the spring, and so on to Wheeler's and out by Smith's on to the Manassas and Sudley road. Nevertheless, they distinctly delineated upon the map the general direction that they were confident they had taken on the afternoon of the 29th in delivering that order, a direction which, as we shall see, has since been corroborated by Mr. Wheeler, in placing a road on the general line which they thought they had taken, and which they indicated from memory dating back sixteen years. The testimony of William B. Wheeler on that subject is as follows:

Question. Please look at this map. [Douglass Pope map shown witness.] Tell me what ways there were at that time, on the 29th of August, 1862, of going by roads from Buck Hill down to Bethlehem Church.

Answer. There was an opportunity of going any way that a person thought proper to go. There were no obstructions to any party not in a vehicle of going any way they thought proper to go. On some part of the route they would encounter woodland, and would evade it. The country was all open. There was no fencing there except my own outside fencing. If they went on the west side of what is known with us as the Manassas and Sudley road, or, in other words, the road leading from Manassas to Sudley, there was no fencing whatever except my own outside fence.

Question. Will you please point out and describe any road there was, if there was one, leading down west of the Manassas and Sudley road, and the nearest to it in the direction of Bethlehem Church?

Answer. There was no road at all that was known as a road except the one from Groveton, which crossed the old Warrenton and Alexandria road [Lewis lane No. 1]. But the whole country was a road where any and every person thought of traveling. There was particularly from Mr. F. M. Lewis's, as laid down here, through B. F. Lewis's, and through Mr. Steers's to my own place (the Wheeler place) into the Chinn farm—there was a road that was mostly traveled by soldiers in passing from Manassas to what was then known as the Bull Run battle-field. During the spring of 1862 there was a great many that walked from Manassas up there, and while they were encamped at Manassas, an every-day occurrence.

* * * * *

Question. Was there any road leading down in the neighborhood of Chinn's Branch? If so, will you give its general direction on the map?

Answer. *There was a spring on the west side of that branch;* that is *cleared land; on the west side of that branch there was a road,* or cattle-path; the whole country was open, and everybody's cattle, whose cattle wished to go over that, passed down on the west side of the branch until they made a path or road to the lower point of those woods, not including that small woodland that runs down there [just east of the branch]. *There was formerly a road, when Mr. Hoe owned that Chinn farm, that was on the outside of that woodland, down to that point, and cattle and stock of all kinds passed on this west side because there are bluffs on the east side.*

Question. How would they get out from this Chinn's Branch, from this lower point of that piece of woodland to Bethlehem Church?

Answer. *They could come through by my house*, or they could leave at the Spring. It is in a small oak grove laid down on that map (on the branch). Mr. Chinn used as an inlet and outlet from his dwelling a road crossing that branch road.

Question. Was there any way of getting out from that point to the Manassas and Sudley road, except by going due east on the Chinn road?

Answer. Yes; as I just remarked, they could go where they pleased. The country was entirely open. As far as I know, most of the cavalry that was stationed at Manassas and vicinity passed through my place, sometimes out down here at New Market, and sometimes through Mr. Steers's, and into the road. They went any way they thought proper, that their inclination leaned.

Question. Was there any road at that time between your house and the Sudley road running from that point up here, that you have alluded to?

Answer. No, sir; there was no road. Persons riding about over the battle-field for the first time frequently rode through my field.

Question. Was there any old ruined house in that vicinity?

Answer. There was a tenant house on the Chinn farm, in a northeasterly direction from the residence, standing near a large cherry-tree in a northeasterly direction, but rather nearer the spring branch.

Question. About where would you say that ruined tenement was?

Answer. If I knew the scale of this map, I could locate it. [The scale of the map stated to the witness.] I should say that that tenant house was within a hundred yards northeast of the Chinn house—somewhat nearer—40 or 50, I suppose, nearer to the spring branch. It was totally destroyed, except the heavy frame.

Question. How far from the branch then was it?

Answer. I should think 80 to 100 yards, probably not quite a hundred yards, from the branch. It was northeasterly, in the direction of the stone house, and pretty much in the same direction as the branch.

The petitioner's witness, *John T. Leachman*, another resident of that region, who was called in order to *guess* at a route which Captain Pope took in delivering the order, nevertheless made some curious admissions corroborative of the evidence of the government witnesses.

In taking a route which he pretended Captain Pope might possibly have taken, a very difficult piece of road much to the west of where Captain Pope came out, and near Gaskins'; and yet, as will be perceived by a reference to the evidence that he gave, from which extracts will be made, he admits, although he is an elderly man, to have ridden at the rate of about six miles an hour, including this rough piece of country over which Captain Pope never went, and which he included in his estimate of the general rapidity with which he travelled; and he was making this estimate at the time specially for his own use as a witness in this case. This witness, without knowing anything about the exact direction that Captain Pope took, and although making him start from the Matthews house, a point much farther north than Buck Hill from whence he (Pope) actually started, and although assuming that after he crossed the Warrenton and Centreville pike he (Pope) took a route via the Chinn house, much to the west of the road he actually took, so as to have brought him down via Compton's lane to the old Warrenton, Alexandria, and Washington road, thence out to New Market and so on down the Manassas and Sudley road and around up the Manassas and Gainesville road to Bethlehem Church, five-eighths of a mile farther than the headquarters of the petitioner, nevertheless, the witness Leachman was satisfied that Captain Pope did come out on the old Warrenton and Alexandria road. In this he was correct. We take up his evidence at that point and find that he testified as follows:

He evidently struck this road somewhere.
Question. Which road?
Answer. The old Alexandria road.
Question. Why do you say that he evidently struck that?

Answer. Because he says he came out around a farm-house.

Question. That is on the Sudley Springs road?

Answer. Sudley Springs road.

Question. Where is that house?

Answer. That is at Smith's; he could not have come out around any other house to have done it. That house at that time presented a dilapidated appearance. It had a basement to it, but the wall was very much cut to pieces. It has since been repaired. The chimneys were very much to pieces.

Question. That is the house you suppose he means to designate when he says, "In coming up to this farm-house we struck the road, and went right straight out to where we found General Porter"?

Answer. Yes, that is the point where he struck the Sudley Springs road.

Question. Is that the only house that answers to that description, or that did answer to it at that time?

Answer. That is the only house, and I will give you my reasons for supposing that he came out on that road.

*   *   *   *   *   *   *

Question. From there to Bethlehem Church, of course, it is a perfectly open road, no trouble in finding the way?

Answer. None at all; it is a broad open road.

Question. Taking the route which you supposed him to have traveled, what is the character of the road or roads, or what was it at that time for horses?

Answer. From this point up here until he struck the valley of Young's Branch, I suppose the traveling was very good. There he struck rising ground, running up towards the Chinn house, but not enough to obstruct a horseman but very little, if he came out at Gaskins' until he struck that road.

*   *   *   *   *   *   *

Question. Taking the road as a whole, was it a road over which a man on horseback ordinarily could make a rapid ride, or would it be a moderate ride?

Answer. We rode at the rate of about six miles an hour, and I think it was about as fast as any prudent man would ride over such a road. I was well acquainted with the road and knew in what direction to guide my horse, where to make time and where not to make time.

*   *   *   *   *   *   *

Opposite Wheeler's house the road is comparatively smooth, and you could travel very rapidly over it with a very good degree of safety.

Question. In passing from the junction of the old Alexandria road with the Sudley Springs road down to opposite F. M. Lewis', how rapidly could a man ride with safety and expediency?

Answer. I don't mean to be understood that there are not spots, say of 100 yards, on that road that a man could ride at a brisk gait; but, as a general thing, I wouldn't like to ride over five miles an hour on that road.

Question. Supposing you had a safe horse; with that sort of a horse you say that five miles an hour would be the most rapid gait at which you would be willing to ride?

Answer. Yes, it certainly is. There are young men with less prudence than I now possess who might go faster.

*   *   *   *   *   *

Question. I believe at that time it was very dry?

Answer. My recollection is that it was very dry and dusty.

*   *   *   *   *   *

Question. Please say, from the experience you have had, and the knowledge of that road, how long, in your judgment, would it take a rider upon a good horse, riding as rapidly as a man ought to do who is going upon a somewhat urgent mission—how long would it take them, travelling with prudence and proper regard for the safety of his horse and himself, and only so much as that—how long, in your judgment, would it take him to ride over that road?

Answer. Assuming that the rider took the route that I have indicated here?

Question. I mean from the Matthew house to Bethlehem Church.

Answer. Yes. I don't think it could be done under an hour and a half. I wouldn't like to do it in less time.

*   *   *   *   *   *

. Question. Will you please indicate on that map any house lying between the Warrenton pike and the Bethlehem Church, east of the line at Compton's lane—any wells at any of those houses?

Answer. I will. Coming down this road [the Manassas and Sudley road] in the direction of Manassas, Wheeler's is the first well; Gaskins has a well. We pass on to Smith's, and he has a well between his house and the road. We pass on down to F. M. Lewis', and he has a well. These are all that there is anywhere in that whole country between the Manassas and Sudley road and the Manassas and Gainesville road, except at my house.

Question. I understood you to say that all the fences were down?

Answer. The fences were all down pretty much all through that section of country at that time, and had been since 1861.

Question. Were there any neighborhood roads running along within half a mile or a mile to the eastward of the Sudley Springs road and down in a southerly direction?

Answer. I don't think I can answer that question, for even the fields were roads then. People went where they pleased. If they could cut off a corner by going across a field they would do it, and if many of them went along it would make something of a road, I suppose.

* * * * * *

Question. I understand you to say the country was all open?

Answer. Yes.

Question. Neighborhood roads there?

Answer. Yes; I presume neighborhood roads there.

Question. And that many of them were paths made by people going across that you don't recollect now?

Answer. I cannot speak of the number of roads there at all; as I stated before, the country was all open and people traveled where they pleased.

* * * * * *

It will be seen that, upon his own assumption of the road which Captain Pope took (which assumption was not correct, and which included much difficult ground), he estimated an hour and a half as the time for the delivery of the order, which would have brought it up to about six o'clock. According to petitioner in one of his closing arguments here, 6.30 p. m. was *some time before dark.*

In the delivery of an urgent order, which required speed, it is hardly to be expected that the officer delivering it would bring his horse down below its greatest ability to get over the ground rapidly unless some serious obstacle intervened.

The evidence of the three witnesses, Captain Pope and the two orderlies, Duffee and Dyer, shows that they found the petitioner's headquarters exactly at the point where the petitioner himself located it, namely, at the forks of the two roads. The general route, which has been indicated with much particularity by the three witnesses, was from the southerly side of Buck Hill below the line of the trees, across the Manassas and Sudley road and Young's Branch at the ford there, then down on the easterly side of Chinn's Branch to the place marked as a ford on the map, then down on the westerly side of that branch, on the road indicated partially by the map and wholly by Mr. Wheeler, to the spring east of the Chinn house, thence directly down between Mr. Wheeler's house and barn to the old Warrenton, Alexandria and Washington road, thence easterly by a road across lots between Smith's house and his well, which then existed, and the location of which is still plainly to be seen; so on down the Manassas and Sudley road until near its junction with the Manassas and Gainesville road, nearly; obliquing to the right in the woods there delineated they found the petitioner's headquarters at the very point he himself placed them. That road measures a little short of five miles.

In the evidence as given by these three witnesses there are found some slight discrepancies; as, for example, the witness Dyer, who, while at petitioner's headquarters, noticed Bethlehem Church, and has an idea that there was a spire upon it, though, singularly enough, *all* the witnesses who were on the Manassas and Gainesville dirt-road appear to have recollected Bethlehem Church.

The last two witnesses produced by the petitioner here at the close of the case were called for the purpose of showing that the walls had fallen, and that it was an undistinguishable mass of ruins before this August campaign of 1862. This hardly seems to be borne out, for the reason that so many witnesses have testified to the position of the church, and to the fact of its being impressed upon their recollection by passing by it. As it was but a small structure, if the walls had fallen in and it had become a mere mass of bricks and rubbish, no one would have known but that it was merely the ruins of a dwelling. While, on the other hand, a number of witnesses distinctly recollect the fact of a church being there, or the ruins of one. It is reasonable to suppose that Messrs. *Wheeler* and *Leachman*, in placing the falling of the entire structure as in the spring of 1862, were mistaken. Possibly the roof fell in; possibly even two of the walls; but the remaining brick walls, if standing, would have indicated the presence of a church, not a dwelling.

There were also some discrepancies in recollection as to the road they took back beyond New Market. That is explained by Mr. Dyer, that they cut across from Smith's until they struck the road they had come down on around the Chinn Branch Spring. Captain Pope said that he went to the Henry House hill on his way back to General Pope's head-quarters, and saw General McDowell. His recollection is different from that of Mr. Dyer. However, it may be that Captain Pope himself went to that hill, as he says, and left the orderlies to return to headquarters. If their evidence agreed after the lapse of sixteen years in all these minor particulars, there would, according to the text-books on evidence, be a greater cause for suspicion than if they diverged.

The general route which they took has been positively identified by all three, corroborated by General McDowell, and shown by Wheeler, the petitioner's witness, not only to have been possible but probable; with the additional verification that without such a road being delineated on this map, and without Captain Pope and Mr. Duffee going down that road themselves before coming here they, nevertheless, put a road ex-actly where the subsequent witness, Wheeler, says that there was such a road. It is also in evidence by them that they did not go up on the old Warrenton and Alexandria road into the vicinity of his house.

These corroborative circumstances become of great value in deter-mining the fact as to the route actually taken by Captain Pope and the orderlies, particularly after the severe and unusual cross-examination to which they were subjected by such skillful counsel as represent the petitioner here. The corroborative evidence of General McDowell is peculiarly valuable, given as it was upon the original trial, when his recollection was fresh, as well as before this Board, for the reason that it gives a motive for the change of direction taken by Captain Pope in order to deliver that order.

General Pope, or Colonel Ruggles, his chief of staff, had an idea that the petitioner was to be found much farther up on the Manassas and Gainesville road than the point at which he chose to locate himself. Therefore, as Mr. Dyer has said, Colonel Ruggles indicated the general line of Bristoe Station as the direction which Captain Pope should pur-sue in order to strike the Manassas and Gainesville road in the vicinity of the petitioner's force. That direction would have carried Captain Pope directly through Five Forks.

When the individual named Collins induced Mr. Duffee to go from his home up to Columbus in order to get some sort of testimony out of him—for what purpose I do not know—Mr. Duffee thought at the time, in looking at that map, that the road which he had taken was in the direc-tion through Five Forks, until he went down to the ground. (Board's Record, p. 623.) The fact that he rode up this road by Chinn's Branch in a southwesterly direction shows that his line of travel had been indicated by the proper authority, even if the evidence of the witnesses did not state it.

General McDowell was of course apprised of the road on which petitioner was acting (G. C. M. Record, p. 32), and appears to have indicated to Captain Pope the most convenient route by which to reach him (G. C. M. Record, p. 208), as appears by the evidence in the original trial. This is the explanation why Captain Pope did not keep right on down in the direction the petitioner would have him go. General McDowell even offered to send a guide with Captain Pope, but the orderly, Mr. Duffee, was familiar with those roads, and said that it was not necessary; and Captain Pope (G. C. M. Record, p. 62) relied upon his knowledge of the country. Therefore, at the first point where the road obliqued to the left in the direction that they were going, they came out down by Wheeler's and so on to the Sudley road.

In determining the value to be given to the evidence of witnesses it often is desirable to consider the character of the persons who give the evidence.

In the first place, as to Captain Pope, the evidence shows him to have been an officer in the Regular Army for some years, and to be at present occupying a responsible position under the United States circuit judge for the eighth circuit. The orderlies who accompanied Captain Pope on that day belonged to a detachment of the First Ohio Cavalry, which was doing that duty under Lieut. Col. T. C. H. Smith, their commanding officer, at Major General Pope's headquarters. These men had been neither bounty-jumpers, conscripts, nor mendicants, but farmers and farmers' sons, who had entered the service from patriotic motives, and who evidently were of the most reliable character, or they would not have been selected for the special duty as messengers and orderlies at headquarters. We find, incidentally, in the record that all these men owned the horses that they rode; and it is reasonable to suppose, therefore, that they were much better mounted than the ordinary cavalrymen. It is to be noticed that both Mr. Duffee and the newly-discovered witness Mr. Dyer, place the time of the delivery of that order at less, in their judgment, than an hour.

Mr. Dyer, it appears, is a farmer; he had no watch, and has never been in the habit of carrying a watch, but has been always accustomed to note the lapse of time by the position of the sun. With a practical experience of this description, and without knowing the time at which the order was dated, he placed it, in his judgment, as not later than half-past four, and said that it took about three-quarters of an hour to deliver that order, and that he judged of the time by having noted the position of the sun at the time they started, and the position of the sun at the time the order was delivered. The effort on the part of the petitioner, through his counsel, to make this witness state the degree of rapidity with which they traveled on the different parts of the road when en route to deliver the order was an effort to induce the witness to say that which it would be quite impossible for any one to say, unless he made particular note and memorandum at the time of the localities between which he traveled and the rate of speed at which he traveled between certain points. Possibly as accurate a mode of computing the time taken in the delivery of that order as could be given was that testified to by Mr. Dyer, whose recollection of the length of the journey is fortified by actual measurement, and shows quite conclusively that he is an accurate observer both of time and distance.

To every person who is in the habit of judging time as he was, every object which casts a shadow is a sun-dial to note the progress of the day.

Solomon Thomas, a government witness (Board's Record, p. 841), says that an officer came riding from the Manassas Junction way, having a dispatch, which he gave to the petitioner; that at the time his brigade was moving to the rear; that they were ordered to face about and move again up to the Manassas and Gainesville road; and that the time of the delivery of this dispatch, *judging from the position of the sun*, was somewhere from five to half past five o'clock. The recollection of this witness is that the petitioner was mounted, and that he dismounted and sat down by the roadside. The fact of the delivery of the dispatch, which he says was delivered at that time, is the prominent point in the recollection of the witness, because it is connected with the order which he received to face about and move back towards the front.

On the original trial it was sought to be shown that the hour of the arrival of Captain Pope was near sunset. The chief of staff of the petitioner, however, Lieut. Col. *Frederick T. Locke*, on the original trial (G. C. M. Record, p. 139) said as follows:

Question. How much time elapsed between the departure of General McDowell and the arrival of the order of General Pope to attack the enemy; and what were the accused and his command doing during that time?

Answer. I cannot say exactly as to the lapse of time; but during that time General Morell's troops were in position, and our artillery were engaging some artillery of the enemy, and there was some musketry firing also.

Question. State approximately the length of time that you think elapsed between the departure of General McDowell and the receipt of that order.

Answer. I should think three hours.

* * * * *

General *Patrick*, one of petitioner's witnesses (Board's Record, p. 189), said that General McDowell got back from the front of petitioner's column at about half past twelve to one o'clock, and ordered him to halt, and countermarched him, and then immediately led his brigade through a wood road directly across the country, until it eventually came into the Sudley Springs road. The evidence, however, of petitioner's chief of staff as to the *time* of the receipt of the 4.30 order, although vague, certainly shows that it was received, according to *his* recollection, during the *afternoon*, when the sun was high, and not at or about sunset.

Despite the witnesses produced by the accused on his behalf on the trial, the court convicted of the charges based upon this 4.30 order.

It is to be noticed that that order from General Pope did not state that he was to attack *Jackson's* flank; but merely the *enemy's* right flank, which, according to some statements, particularly his own, was in front of him; though, according to Col. E. G. Marshall, Thirteenth New York Volunteers, on skirmish line—not more than a brigade. Jackson's name was not mentioned. General Pope afterwards expressed his opinion on the subject in his evidence, and also said that it was his belief at the time that the road on which petitioner's command was in column would have conducted "him either to the right flank of the enemy or past the right flank of the enemy, towards his rear." (G. C. M. Record, pp. 33, 34.) *But at the time the order was delivered to petitioner there was nothing to show that General Pope did not understand what the petitioner pretends to say he himself knew was the case.*

The battle on the right of the petitioner continued until some time after dark, as testified to by the witnesses, particularly of King's division, McDowell's corps. *Generals Lee and Longstreet, in their official reports, have stated that it continued until 9 p. m.* This is no doubt true. If King's division, under Hatch, of McDowell's corps (Board's Record, p. 548), could attack as late as 9 p. m., and be in action up to that time, just as it had been in action the night before to a late hour, certainly the petitioner's corps could equally have made some tentative movement. If the petitioner was even so well prepared for *defense* as he assumes he was, and the enemy was in force directly in his front, as he also assumes they were, why should it have taken him an hour or more to get ready to move into action if he really had any intention or desire to assist his companions in arms on the right, where, as the witnesses all say, very heavy musketry firing was at that time heard? (Board's Record, pp. 100, 103, 107, 189, 235, 505, 520, 521, 549.)

The order to the petitioner to move into action *at once* was part of the plan of General Pope under which Kearney attacked and rolled up Jackson's left, and a general movement was made against the enemy's front on the Independent line of the Manassas Gap Railroad, and down the pike by King's division of McDowell's corps and south of the pike by Brigadier-General Meade's brigade of Reynolds' division, against which Longstreet opposed Hood's division with Evans' brigade and Wilcox's division as a support.

All day long, on the 29th, the petitioner, according to his theory, is either ready or getting ready; but never doing anything. Had he been so disposed, the character of the country on the left of the Manassas and Gainesville road by which his corps moved up towards Dawkins' Branch was so open that he could have massed his entire command just behind the ridge which overlooked the branch.

In the delivery of this 4.30 order, the concurrent testimony of Capt. Douglas Pope and the two orderlies is that no time was lost in starting or delay experienced in moving along beyond the incidental ones of the momentary meeting with General McDowell and occasional rough places on the Manassas and Sudley Springs road below New Market.

Captain Pope swore (Board's Record, p. 566) that the entire distance from Stone house to where he met petitioner could have been galloped over, except perhaps 300 yards.

However, it is hardly necessary to discuss this point, as all three witnesses say that in their judgment they were not an hour—not more than three-quarters of an hour—in riding down. Of course if Lieutenant Weld could go from petitioner to General Pope in an hour with all the intermediate delays he experienced, then Captain Pope could go from General Pope to petitioner in less time with an urgent message.

A point has been raised by petitioner that Captain Pope should have seen King's or Ricketts' division while *en route*. It must, however, be remembered—

1st, as to King's division: Heintzelman's diary reports it as arrived on the main field at 3.45 p. m. (Board's Record, p. 611). It had, we know, been previously supporting Reynolds' movements until General Pope decided to put it in another position. Patrick's brigade, which formed the rear of King's division, under Hatch, when it moved up the Sudley Springs road, first halted at Conrad's above where Capt. Douglas Pope struck the road, and afterwards (as well as Doubledays brigade. Board's Record, p. 688) moved west into the shoulder of woods northwest of Conrad's, and afterwards west of the line of road by Chinn's Branch down which Captain Pope came (Board's Record, p. 189), so that of course Captain Pope did not, to his recollection, see any of King's division. Captain Pope also said (Board's Record, p. 572) that while he did not meet any organized body of troops from the time he struck the Sudley Springs road until he met the petitioner, yet that he thought there were Union troops and wagons all along on his left on the Sudley Springs road as he came down Chinn's Branch.

2d. Relative to Ricketts' division being on the road, it must be remembered that after Captain Pope left petitioner, after an interview of fifteen minutes, he went along up the road, stopped at the well near Smith's, and was brought back for a further interview with petitioner. Also that on his second journey up it was late in the day, and after Ricketts had got up to Henry house hill, some of that division having, as we know from Brevet Brigadier-General McCoy's testimony (Board's Record, p. 641), taken the direct army road from Manassas Junction which on the map used here is called a new road. The advantage of having such a road, as shown by the movements during the war, undoubtedly caused it to be regularly made a county road when peace came. There was also a road parallel to the Sudley road which left it westerly at F. M. Lewis' house, ran north through B. F. Lewis' and Steers to Wheeler's; what the latter calls an army road. (Board's Record, p. 981.)

WHAT PETITIONER DID ON RECEIPT OF 4.30 ORDER?

We are now brought to the consideration of what petitioner did when he received the 4.30 order.

That order imperatively required him to *push forward at once* into action on the enemy's right flank.

He had received it at 5.15 p. m., or, with further allowance, 5.30 p. m.

He says here, in the closing argument of his counsel (Mr. Maltby), that 6.30 p. m., an hour later, was some time before dark.

Did he do anything to carry out his urgent orders? Did he move *at once* forward? For if he was, as he says, apprehensive of attack and ready for defense, he must also have been ready for assault.

The answer is, he made at the utmost only the feeblest momentary efforts—the merest pretense, and then put his troops into bivouac, after marching some to the rear.

His own witness, Brigadier-General Sykes, division commander, convicts him of the charge.

It is a melancholy story, but must be repeated.

On the original trial Sykes swore, on cross-examination, after saying that he was with the petitioner when an officer brought him the order from General Pope, as follows (G. C. M .Record, pp. 177, 178):

Question by JUDGE-ADVOCATE. Did.General Porter make known to you the character of that order?
Answer. *He did not.*
Question. Did he read it in your presence?
Answer. Not that I know of.

* * * * * * *

Question. How long did you remain with General Porter on that occasion, after the receipt of this order?
Answer. I continued with him from that time all night.

* * * * *

Question. *You had then, as I understand you to say, no knowledge that a positive order had been given by General Pope on that afternoon for General Porter to attack the enemy on their right flank?*
Answer. *I had no such knowledge.*

The evidence of General Sykes leads *directly* to the conclusion that the petitioner had no intention or desire to attack or he would have told his division commander then and there.

Look at it in any light, there was no effort then, or at any time afterwards on that day, to put Sykes' division into position to support or participate in an assault.

On this point, the evidence of Capt. Douglas Pope is corroborative (G. C. M. Record, p. 57):

Question. What statements, if any, did General Porter make to you in regard to the movements which the order contemplated he should make?
Answer. In a conversation which I had with General Porter, after his reading the

order, he explained to me on the map, where the enemy had come down in force to attack him, and had established a battery. I understood him to say that the enemy had opened upon him; but what he had done I do not now remember.

Question. How long did you remain with General Porter?

Answer. About fifteen minutes, I suppose.

Question. While you were there, or at any time before you left, did you observe any orders given or any indication of preparation for a movement in the direction of the battle-field?

Answer. I did not.

Question. In what condition were the troops there at that time?

Answer. I saw only a portion of them; the portion that I saw I believe belonged to General Sykes' division. They were on the road between the forks of the road and Manassas, what small portion of the troops I saw that belonged to General Porter's corps. It was my impression they were halted there; I saw the arms of some of them stacked.

Question. They had their arms stacked?

Answer. Yes, sir.

Question. Was not the sound of the artillery of the battle then pending distinctly audible at that point?

Answer. It was.

*　　　*　　　*　　　*　　　*　　　*　　　*

Question. Did you, or not, have another interview with General Porter after that time?

Answer. I did not. After receiving a written reply to the order I had delivered to General Porter, I started on my way back, and I suppose I had got a mile or a mile and a half from where General Porter was, when I was overtaken by an orderly, who said General Porter wished to see me. I got part way back when I met an officer, I supposed an aide-de-camp, of General Porter, who said that General Porter wished to see me. I went back and this aide-de-camp told me I better wait a few minutes. I did not see General Porter then.

Question. Had you, or not, seen this officer whom you supposed to be an aide-de-camp, during your first interview with General Porter?

Answer. I had, and had had a conversation with him.

Question. In the presence of General Porter?

Answer. While General Porter was writing the reply to the order I had delivered to him.

Question. What seemed to be his rank?

Answer. He was a first lieutenant, I think.

Question. Did he, or not, perform any act or make any remark in the presence of General Porter which induced you to believe that he was an aide-de-camp? If so, state what that remark and what that act was.

Answer. I do not remember his making any remark to General Porter, or General Porter saying anything to him. My impression is that he told me that he was an aide-de-camp. I firmly believed at the time that he was General Porter's aide-de-camp. I did not see any act indicating that, excepting that he was associated with General Porter; he was very close to General Porter at the time I had the conversation with him; within hearing of General Porter if he had listened to it.

Question. Do you, or not, suppose that his statement to you, that he was an aide-de-camp of General Porter, could have been heard by General Porter if he had been listening to your conversation?

Answer. It could.

Question. Do I or not understand you, then, to say that that conversation occurred in fact in the presence of General Porter?

Answer. In the presence of General Porter; yes, sir.

Question. Were you, or not, charged by that officer with a message to General Pope that a scout had come in, reporting that the enemy were retreating through Thoroughfare Gap?

Answer. I was.

Question. Did you regard that message as given to you seriously or jestingly?

Answer. Seriously.

Question. How long a time had elapsed from the time of your interview with General Porter until your return to General Porter's encampment?

Answer. About three-quarters of an hour, I suppose; between that and an hour.

Question. On your return to his encampment, did you or not observe any preparation on the part of his officers or of the troops for an advance upon the enemy?

Answer. I did not.

And on cross-examination as follows:

*　　　*　　　*　　　*　　　*　　　*

Question. When you were brought back by the orderly and the aide de camp, as you supposed him to be, you did not find General Porter. Do you know where he then was?

Answer. I did not.

Question. Did anything occur to induce you to believe that General Porter had gone to the front?

Answer. There did not. I supposed he had just walked off a short distance, and would be back in a few minutes.

Question. From the time when you arrived to deliver the order to General Porter, up to the time of your second departure from General Porter's location to go towards General Pope, about what period of time elapsed?

Answer. I should suppose about an hour. It may have been a little more than an hour. I should think at least an hour.

Question. How long did you stay at General Porter's headquarters or location, after you were brought back by the orderly and the aide-de-camp?

Answer. A very few minutes.

Question. Would you say five or ten minutes?

Answer. About ten minutes.

Question. Did we understand you correctly to say that it was about fifteen minutes after you delivered the order to General Porter before you first started on your return?

Answer. It was about fifteen minutes.

Question. The remainder of the hour, then, which you spent near General Porter's ocation, was passed in your going about a mile and a half and returning about a mile and a half, and some ten minutes' further delay in General Porter's camp?

Answer. Yes, sir.

Question. Will you state, if you please, at what point General Pope was when you received from him the order of which you have spoken?

Answer. I cannot state exactly where it was. It was on the battle-field, the extreme right of it.

Intent may be gathered from acts as well as words.

This petitioner, with his headquarters 2⅝ miles from the head of his column, never went to the front on receipt of the order, but permitted General Pope's army to attack without rendering the slightest assistance.

While all along the center and right, according to Heintzelman's diary, a direct attack was being made, and while Kearney was rolling the enemy up on Jackson's left, and King's division of McDowell's corps was gallantly pushing in down the turnpike against Hood and Evans and Wilcox in support of Longstreet's command, this petitioner was calmly reposing at his headquarters, while the good, true-hearted men of the Fifth Corps, at the head of his column, held by his commands to a state of inaction, heard, with impatience that they could not do their share, the cheers of our brave soldiers. When the rebel yells indicative of Confederate successes rose on the evening air, grief and indignation filled the breasts of even the private soldiery at the head of that inactive column. They knew they had not done their part, and when, on the next afternoon, they were moved into action up by the school-house against an enemy, re-enforced by the Confederate R. H. General Anderson's large division (Board's Record, p. 61,) and S. D. Lee's artillery, although their own numbers were reduced at least 2,360 by the absence of Brigadier-General Piatt and of Brigadier-General Griffin at Centreville, they stood up courageously against the rebel artillery which mowed their ranks, and the battery of Chapman which unopposed enfiladed them fearfully, until human nature could stand no more.

Sullenly retiring, they felt they had vindicated the honor of their corps from the stain put upon it by this petitioner's conduct of the day before.

I have not inquired into the action of the 30th, nor brought Chapman or others to show how they were permitted to do their dreadful work unchecked, because what petitioner did on the 30th was ruled out on the trial in 1862.

We know incidentally that, with the exception of a section, this petitioner never brought his artillery into action on the 30th during that assault. We also know that Griffin's brigade went to Centreville and never came up during all the action of the 30th, while Piatt's brigade, of Sturgis' division, which followed Griffin, did move up and lost heavily. (G. C. M. Rec., pp. 107, 149.)

The responsibility for the absence of Griffin appears not to have depended on the petitioner. The division commander, Morell, was with it there, and the gallant Butterfield led the remainder of Morell's division.

Returning to the consideration of the 29th, we see that General Lee had formed a good estimate as to what this petitioner might do, and was in nowise apprehensive, for he brought back Wilcox's division to the support of Hood from the point south of the pike, to which he had sent it late in the day, when he received information of approach of Major-General Banks' brigade of observation from Bristoe.

The enemy had no available reserves beyond those in line. Jackson's men were exhausted, their ammunition nearly spent, and the chances for victory for the Union were good. All the prospects of success were blasted by the petitioner's conduct.

He has said in the closing arguments, through his counsel, substantially, that if guilty he ought to have been shot. He had, however, his former and subsequent services under Major-General McClellan to plead for him. The members of the court were largely his personal friends, and to these circumstances may possibly be ascribed its leniency.

The history of the American Army gives but one other comparative illustration, and that is in the case of Maj. Gen. Charles Lee, the second in command, who was charged with having at the battle of Monmouth, in June, 1778, made a shameful and disorderly retreat without engaging the enemy. He pleaded that he did not believe General Washington desired him to attack and that he did make certain efforts. The court found him guilty and sentenced him to suspension for one year. After its expiration Congress dismissed him, believing, doubtless, the punishment was too mild. History has since shown with great directness, that he was not loyal to Washington or to the latter's plans of campaign.

The petitioner, through his counsel, now says there was no *general* battle or continuous battle on the 29th. This is a recession from the first effort to prove that there was nothing but an "artillery" duel.

The reason there was no *general* battle, or continuous line of battle to confront the enemy, was because this petitioner during the day did not go into position or make any vigorous or sustained movement to connect with the Union Army on his right. Had he done so, the country would possibly have been spared the disaster of the following day—the invasion of Maryland and battles of Sharpsburg and Antietam.

When he received the 4.30 order he knew that his force was needed by his commanding general. He made no attempt to actually engage the enemy or aid the troops who were already fighting greatly superior numbers, and were relying on the flank attack to secure a decisive victory and to capture the enemy's army. This the court of nine general officers which tried petitioner believed undoubtedly would have been the result, or they would not have convicted him on that particular specification.

Petitioner had placed before them the evidence of officers on his skirmish line and at the front as to what he and they believed and knew. Unfortunately the want of judicial authority in this Board absolutely prevents any effort to ascertain whether any weight was given to any witnesses' opinion on matters in which the court themselves were experts.

He himself estimated Longstreet at from 10,000 to 15,000 strong; and the court, as military experts, came to its conclusion, which the law permitted. As their decision was based on their judgment of the probable results on a given state of facts, it was final and conclusive.

The petitioner here, however, adds 10,000 to Longstreet, and asks this Board to put its judgment as military experts against the nine.

If such were permissible as a rule of practice, we should never have a final determination in any case involving special professional knowledge and opinions.

PETITIONER'S MOVEMENTS TO THE REAR.

The petitioner has strenuously insisted before this Board that he did not "retreat" during the 29th and that there was nothing in the nature of a retreat in any of his movements.

This point is vital to his assumed case, because he was convicted of shamefully falling back and retreating from the advance of the enemy without any attempt to give them *battle*.

In the crime of larceny it is sufficient to prove that the article stolen was taken from its place by a person with felonious *intent* to appropriate it to his own use, knowing it to be the property of another, even if possession is retained but momentarily. The *gist* of the *offense* is the *intent*, and the one in question is analogous.

It was not necessary for the petitioner to fall·back to Manassas Junction, or four, three, or two miles, in order to complete the offense of which he was convicted. It was sufficient to show that he did move back and conceal his troops so that the enemy considered them no longer an object of special attention.

If he retired even a hundred yards with intent not to give battle when other parts of the army were engaged, and he *knew or had any reason to suppose assistance was needed*, he failed in his duty under the military laws of his country.

The petitioner cannot say with propriety that he did not know help was needed, because his own dispatch to Morell to push over and help Sigel—"See if you cannot help Sigel"—(No. 28), conclusively answers it. In his closing argument on his trial he also spoke of General Pope's "hard-pressed left." (G. C. M. Record, p. 278.)

Now, what did he do looking towards falling back when he should have been *pushing forward?*

First. We have his orders to Col. E. G. Marshall, Thirteenth New York Volunteers, when he went forward with his regiment as skirmishers, *before* McDowell came up, "not to bring on an engagement," although there was a contest then going on on the right, which Marshall soon after saw from rear of his skirmish line." (Board's Record, p. 678.)

Second. His order to Brigadier-General Sturgis, immediately after the first shots from the battery off on the right front, for him to go back with Piatt's brigade to Manassas Junction and take up a defensive position. We know the brigade marched nearly if not quite back to the Junction, and did not get again up near its most advanced position until about dusk. (Board's Record, p. 712.)

Third. His orders to Morell (No. 30) to "move the infantry and everything behind the crest and conceal the guns. We must hold the place and make it hot for them. Come the same game over them they do over us, and get your men out of sight."

Now, this hide-and-seek game which this petitioner thus early began in that day (Board's Record, p. 422,) was in consequence of Morell's first dispatch to him, in which he said (No. 30) that Colonel Marshall reported two batteries to have come down in the woods on their right *towards the railroad* and two regiments of infantry on the road. Morell therefore concluded with the intimation that "*if this be so*, it will be hot here in the morning."

From this it may be inferred—

First. That Morell doubted the accuracy of the information; and

Second. That, if true, there would *probably be enough of the enemy come down during the remainder of the day and night to make it "hot" for petitioner's corps by the next morning;* and

Petitioner, miles to the rear, does not accept Marshall's and Morell's report and conclusions, although for other purposes he asserts the utmost confidence in them.

The pretense, however, of two regiments and two batteries near his front as an obstacle is sufficient for his purposes.

Morell then reported (dispatch No. 31) that he could move everything out of sight except Hazlitt's battery, which was on the right of the road, with Griffin's brigade on its right supporting it, principally in the pine bushes. Also that "*the other batteries and brigades are retired out of sight.*"

Morell then asked of his commander at the rear, "Is this what you mean by everything?" To which petitioner replied:

I think you can move Hazlitt's, or the most of it, and post him in the bushes, with the others, so as to deceive. I would get everything, if possible, in ambuscade. *All goes well with the other troops.*

Sergt. *John Bond*, First Maryland Cavalry, a government witness, testified as follows (Board's Record, p. 882):

Question. What did you then do?
Answer. I then retired to Manassas Junction.
Question. Where did you come to a stop?
Answer. I first met a lot of troops and I met a group of officers; one of them said "Where from, sergeant?" I said, "The battle-field"; he says, "What news?" I says, "Good"; he says, "Do I understand you to say we are holding our own?" I says, "Yes, we have driven the enemy"; he says, "Do I understand you we are holding our own?" I says, "Yes"; he repeated that question three times. He says, "You can go." I went off a short distance from where I was talking with the general, and I asked them who that general was; they told me it was General Porter.
Question. Did you return to the battle-field then?
Answer. No, sir.
Question. After that time what indications were there of any battle going on?
Answer. I could hear firing off and on.
Question. How long after that did you hear firing?
Answer. I could not exactly say.
Question. With relation to sunset or dark?
Answer. I could not exactly say; it was more or less the whole afternoon.

The next dispatch (No. 28) from petitioner was the one to Morell to push over and aid Sigel, of the result of which we know. (Board's Record, p. 423.)

If the petitioner at *the time of that dispatch had known or believed* the enemy in his front in the force he now pretends, he would never—being, as he claims he was at that time, an independent corps commander—have given any such order to Morell, unless in obedience to what McDowell directed before he left him on the railroad.

Still later in the day he sends this interesting and suspicious dispatch to Morell:

Hold on, if you can, to your present place. What is passing?

This he now explains as countermanding the order to push over to aid Sigel.

14 G

This was followed by dispatch No. 32 to Morell, as follows:

Tell me what is passing quickly. If the enemy is coming, hold to him, and I will come up. Post your men to repulse him.

F. J. PORTER,
Major-General.

Morell now began to understand matters a little better, and sent this dispatch in reply (No. 35):

Col. Marshall reports a movement in front of his left. I think we had better retire. *No infantry in sight, and I am continuing the movement.* Stay where you are, to aid me if necessary.

MORELL.

Although there was no infantry of the enemy in sight, the senior division commander now thought they "had better retire," but seems apprehensive his commander will fall back in advance of him.

The petitioner now concluded to give an order with a view to finding out a little about the force of two regiments reported on his front; so he assured Morell in a dispatch (No. 36) that he had all within reach of him, and then said:

I wish you to give the enemy a good shelling, without wasting ammunition, and push at the same time a party over to see what is going on. *We cannot retire while McDowell holds his own.*

This shelling does not seem to have taken place, though if the enemy had been present in the force he pretends they were, he would never, on his assumption as to his own inferiority of force, have given such an order to shell the enemy.

Late in the day Colonel Marshall sent Morell another report, as follows (No. 34):

General MORELL:

The enemy must be in much larger force than I can see; from the commands of the officers, *I should judge a brigade.* They are endeavoring to come in on our left, and have been advancing. Have also heard the noise on left as the movement of artillery. Their advance is quite close.

E. G. MARSHALL,
Col. 13th N. Y.

When Marshall reported two regiments of infantry on his front on the road, petitioner immediately moved back all his own forces.

Now that Marshall reported a brigade about 6 p. m., the petitioner gave orders for an attack, and he declares he did it of his own volition, and not in consequence of receipt of the 4.30 p. m. order.

Assuming it was done of his own volition, we can possibly form some idea of the amount of force under Longstreet he *then believed* was in his front.

AUGUST 29th.

General MORELL:

I wish you to push up *two* regiments, supported by *two* others, preceded by skirmishers, the regiments at intervals of two hundred yards, and attack the *section* of artillery opposed to you.

The *battle* works well on our right, and the enemy are said to be retiring up the pike.

Give the enemy a good shelling as our troops advance.

F. J. PORTER,
Maj. Gen'l Command'g.

Thus did the petitioner wait until late in the day before issuing any orders to move forward, or engage even, until induced to do so by information of success on the right of our line.

If he really believed Longstreet was in his front with five, ten, fifteen, twenty, or twenty-five thousand men, it requires no argument to show that those "two regiments supported by two others," ordered by him to attack, would have been destroyed in a few moments.

The character of the order shows he knew well what sort of operations he should have undertaken, if necessary, early in the day.

In his opening statement (p. 38) he says as follows, viz: *"That about 6 o'clock favorable reports from the right wing, stating that the enemy was retiring up the pike, induced me to direct General Morrell to attack."* By the very order just quoted, to attack with two regiments, &c.

Nevertheless, assuming his own carefully-prepared opening statement to be correct as to what he did at that time, he sent the following dispatch to Major-General McDowell, which constitutes one of those lately found by the latter, viz:

Gen'l McDowell: Failed in getting Morell over to you. After wandering about the woods for a time I withdrew him, and while doing so artillery opened on us. My scouts could not get through. Each one found the enemy between us, and I believe some have been captured. Infantry are also in front. I am trying to get a battery, but have not succeeded as yet. From the masses of dust on our left, and from reports of scouts, think the enemy are moving largely in that way. Please communicate the way this messenger came. I have no cavalry or messengers now. Please let me know your designs; whether you retire or not. I cannot get water and am out of provision. Have lost a few men from infantry firing.

F. J. PORTER,
Maj. Gen. Vols.

Aug. 29—6 p. m.

In this dispatch it is to be noticed he says, "Infantry are also in front"; and yet a previous dispatch of Morell to petitioner said, "No infantry in sight" (No. 35).

These statements and dispatches speak for themselves; they are absolutely and unqualifiedly unreconcilable, and no language which can be used will add to the force of the contrast.

At *sunset* petitioner says he arrested his order to Morell to attack with two regiments by dispatch No. 38, and ordered him to put his men in position to remain during the night, remarking, also, that McDowell says all goes well and we are getting the best of the fight, and concluded the dispatch as follows:

Keep me informed. Troops are passing up to Gainesville, *pushing* the enemy. * * *

He admits that at time of writing this last dispatch just quoted he had received General Pope's 4.30 order to attack at once, and yet, although he knew our troops on the right were in action and moving into action, he put his own corps into bivouac.

Was it that he did not propose to lend a helping hand to General John Pope to win a decisive victory? We shall see when the subject of *"animus"* is considered.

Whether the petitioner did fall back and withdraw from the contest into which duty should have led him or not, the dispatches just quoted afford strong indications that he put his troops far enough out of the way to render them of no avail whatever to General Pope's army.

A reference to some of the evidence will further elucidate this.

Col. *Benjamin F. Smith*, One hundred and twenty-sixth Ohio Volunteers, called for government, testified in 1862 as follows (G. C. M. Record, p. 112):

By the JUDGE-ADVOCATE:

Question. Will you state your position in the military service of the United States?
Answer. I am a captain of the Sixth Regular Infantry, and colonel of the One hundred and twenty-sixth Regiment of Ohio Volunteers.
Question. Will you state to the court whether you were serving with any part of the Army of Virginia, commanded by Major-General Pope, on the days of the 27th, 28th, 29th, and 30th of August last; and if so, in what brigade and division?

Answer. I was serving in Colonel Chapan's brigade, of General Sykes' division.

Question. In what direction did that brigade march on Friday, the 29th of August last?

Answer. We had marched from Fredericksburg, by way of Warrenton Junction, and arrived at Manassas Junction, I think, on the 29th of August, the day before the battle of Bull Run. We arrived exactly at the place where the railroad had been destroyed; the wreck of the train was there, and there we halted. Later in the day, in the morning, we retraced our steps to the branch railroad running, I think, towards Gainesville or Manassas Gap, and followed the direction of that road some few miles. We then halted on some rising ground, where we could see the country beyond, over the woods, the tops of the trees. It was a wooded country. While we were halted there a battery of the rebels opened upon us, but fired some three or four shells only, I think; there may have been a half a dozen. Our brigade then marched into a field, and the regiments were placed in order of battle. I recollect that General Morell's division was in our advance, on the lower ground. Some of our pieces replied to this rebel battery. I received permission from the commanding officer of my regiment to go to a more elevated piece of ground, a few rods distant, and while there I saw our batteries reply.

A short time afterwards (probably half an hour) we received orders to retrace our steps, and march back in the direction we had come. We then marched back to near Manassas Junction, and camped in the woods alongside this branch railroad I have mentioned. That night I was placed on duty as the field officer of the pickets of Sykes' division. About daybreak the pickets were called in, and we marched towards the battle-field of Bull Run, and were engaged in that battle.

Question. What was the effect of the reply of your guns to this attack of the rebel battery?

Answer. It seemed to silence that battery, and it withdrew. At least that was the impression I had at the time.

Question. What amount of infantry force, if any, did there seem to be supporting this rebel battery?

Answer. I did not see them.

Question. Before you received orders to fall back and retrace your steps along this road, had or had not this rebel battery been completely silenced?

Answer. I think it had been.

Question. Were there or not, at that time, clouds of dust in view, showing an advance of the enemy?

Answer. Clouds of dust were distinctly visible further over beyond the trees. Whether there were troops advancing, or whether they were moving in another direction, I could not tell. I could see distinctly the clouds of dust as if there was a large body of troops moving.

Question. Did you or not see the accused, General Porter, at the head of the column on that day?

Answer. No, sir; I do not recollect of seeing General Porter at all that day.

Question. Did you or not see General McDowell that day?

Answer. I saw General McDowell before we arrived at the hill or rising ground I have spoken of.

Question. Do you or not know whether General McDowell had left the command before this engagement with the rebel battery took place?

Answer. I do not recollect about that.

Question. Will you state at what hour on that evening you arrived at your encampment near Manassas Junction?

Answer. It was some time in the afternoon, I think; I do not recollect distinctly.

Question. Was it nightfall?

Answer. No, sir; it was before night. I went on duty to post my pickets just at dark.

Question. Was there or not any such display of the enemy's forces as to make it necessary, in your judgment, to retreat before them?

Answer. I had no means of knowing. When we moved back from that position I supposed it was for some proper cause, but I did not understand at all what the cause was. I did not receive any impression that we were retreating from the enemy. I supposed that we were making a reconnaissance to feel the enemy in that direction, and, having found him, that we had moved back for some other purpose; and, not knowing about the orders to the general, I remained under that impression. The examination by the Judge-Advocate here closed.

Examination by the accused:

Question. Do you recollect the road over which you marched the following morning, the 30th of August, going up to the battlefield?

Answer. Yes, sir.

Question. Was your camp near the junction of that road and the railroad?

Answer. Yes, sir.

Question. Was that road near to Manassas Junction?
Answer. I thought it was about a mile or two from the junction.
Question. It was not at the junction?
Answer. No, sir.
Question. Do you recollect Bethlehem Church?
Answer. No, sir.
Question. By looking at the map do you think you could recognize the point where you were?
Answer. I might.
Question. Look at the map before the court, if you please, and point out the place, if you can.
Answer. (After looking at the map.) I recollect that where our brigade lay the railroad was in view, and also the road we took next morning.
Question. According to the measurement upon the map, an inch to the mile, how far is that from Manassas Junction?
Answer. It is probably some two miles.
Question. When you say that the rebel battery was silenced, do you mean that it was incapacitated, or that it ceased firing, or was withdrawn?
Answer. I thought it was withdrawn.
Examination by the accused here closed.

Examination by the court:

Question. At what time on the 27th of August did your division arrive at Warrenton Junction, and how far had it marched that day?
Answer. I am under the impression that we arrived there about *noon;* the time of the day is not fixed distinctly on my mind. I do not recollect the camp beyond Warrenton, which we left; I might recall it by looking on the map. (Examining the map.) We marched from some point on this road (indicating on the map the road referred to) by Bealton, and then down the side of the track to Warrenton.
Question. Was your brigade the leading brigade?
Answer. I do not recollect whether it led that day or not.
The examination of this witness was here closed.

Brig. Gen. *Charles Griffin,* called on the trial for petitioner (G. C. M. Record, p. 162), after referring to General McDowell's arrival at Dawkins' Branch and going to the right, testified as follows:

I received an order almost directly after General McDowell had left to recall my pickets [Sixty-second Pennsylvania, which were deployed in front to the left and south of Thomas Nealon's], and orders to move my command *to the right.*

Now, from whom did that order come? It must have come from this petitioner in consequence of McDowell's verbal instructions and General Pope's orders. The petitioner says, nevertheless, that as he went back to where his troops were he saw the enemy gathering in such force in his front, that he had to send down the road towards Manassas Junction, to rear of his column, to direct King's division under Hatch to remain with him. General Griffin further said:

I attempted to go to the right and moved probably 600 yards, until, with the head of my column, I crossed a railroad said to run to Gainesville. Here we met with obstructions which we could not get through.
It was reported by somebody, I cannot say who, "You can't get through there." We then faced about and moved back to the hill where the battery I first referred to was stationed.
As we were getting to this hill the enemy's batteries opened upon us.

These batteries, the witness said in 1862 (G. C. M. Record, p. 162), opened on petitioner's head of column about one o'clock—the very time Brevet Major-General Sturgis fixes it (Board's Record, p. 711), but take notice that, up to that moment, *after* Griffin had been withdrawn, the petitioner did not believe the enemy were in force in his front, as is apparent from his conversation with Sturgis.

My brigade was then placed in position in rear and to the right of the batteries, and remained there during considerable artillery firing; I cannot say how long. * * *

Further, as to the enemy and large clouds of dust which he noticed from Thoroughfare Gap, witness said:

I have stated that the enemy seemed to be coming from Thoroughfare Gap. In fact, there is no doubt if that point was Thoroughfare Gap, that the enemy was coming through there *all day.*

Neither petitioner nor Longstreet have claimed *here* that. the latter had more than 25,000 men present at any time during the 29th of August, so that petitioner's statement on his trial that he believed Longstreet had a force present on the 29th of between 10,000 and 15,000 men was nearer the truth. (G. C. M. Rec., p. 266.)

On cross-examination as to the obstacles which made him retire when going to the right and the efforts he made to overcome them, Brigadier-General Griffin said:

I led off my column. We ran up into some little, thick pine bushes. We halted there. The next order I got was to move back again.
Some one reported that we could not get through. I made no reconnaissance whatever myself.

Further on he was questioned by the court as follows (G. C. M. Record, p. 169):

Question. You say that you had failed to get through to the right during the day of the 29th August. Will you state what efforts were made by you or by General Porter to get through on the right during the day?
Answer. *I merely obeyed orders. My position was at the head of my brigade. What efforts General Porter made I am not aware of.*

After this supporting of batteries, Brigadier-General Griffin evidently received orders from petitioner very similar to those received from petitioner by General Sturgis at 1 p. m. when those rebel guns opened, for he says (G. C. M. Record, p. 163): "We had started back towards Manassas Junction," when another order came from petitioner near sundown to attack, and General Griffin says he faced his command about immediately and started back.

He says, as to the point where this order came to hand (G. C. M. Record, p. 163):

We were probably *a mile and a half or two miles* from the position referred to in my previous testimony as occupied by this battery [Hazlitt's U. S. battery].

In his examination by the court he said (G. C. M. Rec., p. 168), as to this retreat by Morell's division: "I should think my brigade, as I have stated, moved a mile and a half or two miles—not far from a mile and a half."

This evidence of petitioner's witness was not apparently satisfactory, for it showed a good deal in the nature of a *retreat,* and certainly a falling back for a considerable distance.

Maj. *G. K. Warren,* Corps of Engineers, who was then colonel Fifth New York Volunteers, commanding a brigade under him, was called before *this* Board to prove that the falling back was not as great as Griffin had said, sixteen years ago, when his recollection was fresh.

This movement of Griffin appears to have been by Morell's order and about 5.30 p. m. Warren admits he himself fell back a hunderd yards or so (Board's Record, p. 19), but says there was no retreat.

In the 6 p. m. recently discovered dispatch of petitioner to General McDowell last before recited is this remark:

Failed in getting Morell over to you. After *wandering about* the woods for a time I withdrew him, and while doing so artillery opened on us.

Here, it will be perceived, petitioner has reported to McDowell that he had made some sort of effort to do what McDowell says he ordered

ordered him to do, viz, to put his forces in where they could be joined to the left of General Pope's army.

The petitioner would not have made such a report if McDowell *had ordered him to* REMAIN *where he was.*

Further, this report gives as excuses for not getting Morell over that the character of the woods through which he wandered prevented, and that even scouts could not get through, despite the fact that there was the straight and unobstructed Sudley Spring's road as well as the Five Forks road. From the evidence of Brigadier-General Griffin just above cited (and he was petitioner's witness on his trial,) it is plain that no part of the Fifth Corps "wandered about the woods" on that day.

The artillery opening is mentioned as merely a subsequent incident, and not as the controlling cause, as petitioner would have us believe, why he withdrew Morell.

Capt. *J. J. Coppinger*, Twenty-third United States Infantry, then captain Fourth Infantry, a government witness, testified as follows (Board's Record, p. 948):

Question. The next morning you marched for what place?
Answer. Manassas Junction.
Question. From there, what direction did you take?
Answer. Towards Gainesville.
Question. Do you recollect a place named Bethlehem Church?
Answer. I have an indistinct recollection of a small church on the left of the road.

Although that church was an indistinguishable mass of ruins according to the witness Leachman, nevertheless *all* the witnesses on that road seemed to know that there was a "church" there. All refer to it as Bethlehem Church, and recollect it, and speak of it in their evidence.

Question. You went out on that road; do you recall any incident connected with that march out on the road towards Gainesville?
Answer. Do you mean the passage of other troops?
Question. You went out on that road; when did you receive a command to halt?
Answer. When, I think, about two shots close to the edge of a wood—two shots, I think, were fired; just about that moment our command halted.
Question. From what direction?
Answer. Front and right.
Question. Then what did your regiment and brigade do?
Answer. Halted, *and were ordered to face about.*
Question. Then what?
Answer. We were marched to the rear in column of fours.
Question. To what point?
Answer. I cannot give you the point; but the next point I recollect is being on a side road which leads off towards the battle-field of Bull Run. Perhaps it would be better if I were to say that my memory of that battle-field—I was left on the field between the lines senseless, until the next day, and my memory of both those days is somewhat spasmodic. Some things I see as clearly as anybody I see in this room; and there are intervals of which I have a very poor recollection. Now, between the time of our being marched *here*, and our being halted, I don't recollect. (Witness indicates points on the map.)
Question. As to this point of fact—these shots being fired, and you countermarched to the rear—how soon after the shots were fired was the order for you to move to the rear?
Answer. I think almost immediately.

The Board will notice how this witness corroborates what was said by the petitioner to General Sturgis after those shots were fired, when Sturgis called his attention to the fact that there must be a gun up there; that he had just seen the glint of a gun, and the petitioner said he was mistaken (Board's Record, p. 711).

Question. Do you recall with any certainty how long or how far you marched to the rear?
Answer. We marched quite a distance to the rear, I think from one to two miles, if

not more; but I am almost certain that the command was, "Halt; about face," and within three minutes I think, and perhaps a shorter time, we were in motion to the rear.

Question. During that day did you move to the front again; if so, when?

Answer. We were moved on a cross-road, which led us the next day to the battle-field. (Witness indicates in the direction of the Sudley Springs road.)

Question. When did you say you made that move at the cross-road?

Answer. I cannot give the time.

Question. Some time that day?

Answer. In the afternoon.

Question. Did you encamp there, or did you go back again?

Answer. We passed the night there; stacked arms, and, I think, lay down by our arms.

Capt. *George M. Randall*, Twenty-third United States Infantry, a government witness (Board's Record, p. 725), testified as follows:

Direct examination:

Question. On the 29th of August, 1862, where were you, and what rank did you hold in the service?

Answer. Second lieutenant, Fourth Infantry, attached to Sykes' division.

Question. Where were you on that morning?

Answer. We were at Bristoe Station.

Question. Moved up from there to Manassas Junction?

Answer. Yes, sir; from Manassas Junction we took position on the Gainesville road beyond Bethlehem Church.

Question. When you were at Manassas Junction were there any indications of an action? If so, what were they?

Answer. Yes, I think so; I heard very distinctly heavy firing; as near as I can recollect, it was about half past nine or nine o'clock in the morning.

Question. How long did you continue to hear that?

Answer. I do not recollect; I heard artillery firing during the day several times, and I think along about three or quarter to four o'clock in the afternoon I heard it again; quite a brisk firing at that time.

Question. How far did you get upon the Manassas and Gainesville road?

Answer. I think we moved about three miles, probably four miles beyond the church.

Question. Did you go up to the front?

Answer. Very near it, sufficiently far that I could see the opening between our lines and where the rebels were supposed to be; at that time we were in a belt of timber; the head of the column, as near as I can recollect, halted at the edge of it.

Question. What indications were there of an enemy in front of you?

Answer. I heard several shots exchanged, and also some few shots from the skirmish line.

Question. Anything more?

Answer. That is all.

Question. Did you see any enemy?

Answer. I did not.

Question. What did your brigade then do?

Answer. I think some time in the afternoon we countermarched probably about two and a half miles, and then halted and bivouacked for the night.

Cross-examination by Mr. BULLITT:

Question. About what time did your company get up into the front?

Answer. I think about eleven o'clock.

Question. How near to the front were you?

Answer. I suppose we were three-quarters of a mile from the front; sufficiently near so that we could see the open space.

Question. You say three-quarters of a mile from the front; what do you call the front?

* * * * * * *

Question. Did you change your position that day at all to the right or left?

Answer. I think not. I think we moved to the rear.

Question. You have no recollection of being moved back into the woods?

Answer. I think we halted in the woods.

Question. The only move you made was to march back about two miles?

Answer. Yes; that is all I recollect.

Question. How far back in the woods were you?

* * * * * * *

Question. Will you mark the point to which you suppose you went back?

Answer. We went back about two and a half miles or two miles, but the exact point it is impossible for me to mark; we may have moved up *here* [in the woods] and taken a zigzag.

* * * * * * *

Question. Then you took your position in the woods, and then you subsequently countermarched toward Bethlehem Church. Now, I want to know whether you made any other movement after you had passed Bethlehem Church, and got up toward Dawkins' Branch, except first to march to the point where you first halted, then you got into the woods, and afterward countermarched about two miles back to Bethlehem Church; did you make any other movement during that day?

Answer. No, sir.

* * * * * * *

Question. Will you explain what you mean by countermarching in that particular instance?

Answer. We marched to the front, and then faced the column about and went to the rear.

Question. Did you countermarch by brigade?

Answer. By regiments and brigades, as near as I can recollect.

Question. By which, regiments or brigades?

Answer. By brigades, I think.

Question. You were in the leading brigade as you went forward?

Answer. I was in the leading brigade, Sykes' division.

Question. When you countermarched and marched to the rear, where were the other two brigades of the division?

Answer. I think they were going to the rear.

Question. You did not pass them?

Answer. No, sir; I think not.

Question. Did you march in the road, going back?

Answer. Yes, as near as I can recollect.

The late Bvt. Maj. Gen. Robert C. Buchanan, U. S. A., retired, called by petitioner before this Board (Board's Record, p. 215), testified as to the movements of the brigade he commanded in Brigadier-General Sykes' division, after they left Manassas Junction on the 29th, as follows:

Question. Which way did you move then?

Answer. We had been moving by the right flank; we then moved by the left flank; we moved down by the road which takes us near a church, which I have since heard called Bethlehem Church, in the direction of Gainesville.

Question. Where did you halt then?

Answer. Near that church and in advance of it.

This witness also recollected the church, despite the witness Leachman that it was wholly fallen.

Question. In what position were your troops then?

Answer. At that time directly on the road.

Question. How were you formed when you halted there?

Answer. We were formed in line of battle immediately after we halted.

Question. How long did you remain in that position?

Answer. I cannot tell you.

Question. During the balance of the day, I mean.

Answer. We did not leave that ground that day except under various instructions that we got to countermarch; from time to time we countermarched of course on the same ground.

Question. You did not leave that ground?

Answer. No; except towards night we changed our direction, I think on to a little road that led us off to the turnpike.

Question. Practically, you remained in that position during that day?

Answer. During that day.

Question. Do you recollect any stacking of arms?

Answer. Yes; they stacked arms from time to time.

Question. When you did that what position was your line in—still in line of battle?

Answer. Always; always ready.

Serg. *Solomon Thomas*, Eighteenth Massachusetts Volunteers, Martindale's brigade, Morell's division, a government witness (Board's Record, p. 840), testified as follows:

Question. Where were you on August 29, 1862?

Answer. With General Fitz-John Porter's corps, Eighteenth Massachusetts, Martindale's brigade, Morell's division.

Question. Do you recollect being at Manassas Junction on that day?
Answer. I do.
Question. Did you move off on the Gainesville road?
Answer. We moved up on the line of the railroad. We moved more in a direct line in front, though we were intending to move to the right.
Question. How far upon that road did your regiment go?
Answer. We went upon that road nearly to a small creek, or what had been originally a small creek; it was dry or nearly so at that time.
Question. What did you do there?
Answer. We then halted, and the Thirteenth New York, or a part of it which was thrown out as skirmishers—a battery was planted in our front a little to our right, in the fields, and as the skirmishers of the Thirteenth advanced we were deployed to the right, into the woods; our right rested in the woods. We halted and lay down. This was probably ten o'clock in the morning, I should say; might have been a little later.
Question. How long did you remain there?
Answer. We remained in that position—I should say it was half past four when we were called to attention and right-about face, and moved out from that position, left in front, upon the same road that we moved down on in the morning. I don't know the distance, but we had been marching some time.
Question. Back toward Manassas Junction?
Answer. Yes; toward Manassas Junction—when an officer came riding from the Manassas Junction way, having a dispatch, and rode up to General Porter and handed him the dispatch. Then we were commanded to halt; we did. General Porter dismounted and sat down by the side of the road and leaned his back against a tree—quite a large tree—and read the dispatch, and went up and remounted and called us to attention and right-about face. We marched back upon the same road we had come on, moving then right in front, until we came near the position of the road where we had moved into the woods on the right in the morning. We then moved out to the left, into an open field. The artillery was brought into the field and parked in our front. We were formed in line and were ordered to stack arms; we did so. Orders were received that there should be no fires made to make any coffee; that we were to remain perfectly quiet. The adjutant received orders that if there were any orders received during the night he should deliver those orders to the commander of each regiment in person, so there should be no loud words spoken; and we were to remain. Me and some of my comrades spread our blankets and were preparing to lie down for the night. As we sat down, before we got ready to lie down, we heard upon our right a shout which we knew was a charge—from the shout; then we heard musketry discharges.
Question. What did you understand at that time?
Answer. I felt at that time that we were expected to charge on the rear and flank in conjunction with what was going on in front.
Question. About what time in the day, in reference to sunset, was it that you were halted on your way back to Manassas Junction, and that an officer came up with a dispatch?
Answer. I should judge from the position of the sun it must have been somewhere from five to half past five o'clock.
Question. During the day did you hear any indications of a battle going on; if so, what were they and where were they?
Answer. Our immediate front we heard an occasional discharge of musketry, and, in fact, they were pieces of railroad iron fired from a rebel battery right over our right; and two pieces lodged in the rear of where I lay, probably forty feet in our rear. Some of the boys went and dug them up, and one of them was 18 inches in length, the other was about 15. We thought of bringing them home, but they were rather heavy, so we left them on the field. Then, while we were lying there, beside that we heard, upon our right, distant firing all day, but not continuous; there were intervals that we could hear artillery distinctly.

Capt. *A. M. Randol,* First United States Artillery, a witness for petitioner, testified (Board's Record, p. 93) that his battery moved back to within 150 yards of petitioner's headquarters for water, and arrived there at 4 p. m., and remained there. This was east of Bethlehem Church—a building which this witness recollects.

Lieut. *S. M. Weld,* formerly petitioner's aide-de-camp, said (Board's Record, p. 270) that General Sykes' division was moved back to near the junction of the Sudley Springs and Manassas and Gainesville road, some fifteen or twenty minutes' march from Morell, and that Warren intervened.

General Sykes' right was near petitioner's headquarters, and his left one-half mile back.

Bvt. Maj. Gen. Z. B. Tower, U. S. A., then of Ricketts' division, McDowell's corps, said (p. 446) that as his brigade moved up they met regulars on the Sudley Springs road about dusk; an hour after he left Manassas—probably two miles distant. They were on his right.

Thus we perceive that much of petitioner's corps was moved back considerable distances, and the regulars 2⅔ miles to the rear from Dawkins' Branch, and were in bivouac when King's division of McDowell's corps, under the supervision of McDowell himself, was having its gallant fight with Longstreet.

They were put out of sight and removed from a position of usefulness.

An examination of the dispatches sent that day by petitioner will lead to the conclusion that he did not intend to fight under General Pope if he could help it.

PETITIONER'S DISPATCHES.

Just before I began this argument the petitioner, through his counsel, undertook deliberately to explain some of his dispatches and his conduct to which those dispatches refer.

His first statement substantially was that Brig. Gen. Charles Griffin, who went with his brigade to the right, came back after Major-General McDowell left; and the fact that batteries opened just as he got back shows, as petitioner would have us believe, that he did see enemy's batteries as he was returning to his column from the last McDowell interview.

Griffin's evidence, however, does not confirm this (G. C. M. Record, p. 162). The latter remained over by the "little pine bushes" halted—making no effort to push ahead or find out if there was any serious obstacle in his way until ordered back by petitioner.

The pretense had been made of obeying McDowell's orders—it was enough for an excuse—and when petitioner's counsel deliberately states, for his client, that "petitioner had no knowledge of the woods towards Five Forks" he increases the measure of his responsibility for failure.

There is probably nothing which more conclusively shows his intention to do nothing that day than this absolutely utter indifference to these roads through Five Forks, by which he could have joined General Pope's left, had he been so disposed.

To say that Griffin was moved to the right because petitioner intended to *make an attack* shows—seeing it was begun immediately after McDowell's departure—that it was under his, McDowell's, orders to petitioner to put his forces in there where the dust was rising off to the north and west, back of Meadowville Lane.

The next explanation petitioner has ventured upon, with great deliberation in the argument of counsel who last preceded me, is that his dispatch No. 29 (Board's Record, p. XXVI), to McDowell expressing an intention to retreat, was written for the reason that Lieut. (now Maj.) S. N. Benjamin's battery, Second United States Artillery, ceased firing near Groveton about 1 p. m.; that then firing practically ceased and began near 3 p. m. near Sudley Church, from whence the petitioner concluded our forces were retiring, and that General Pope was therefore doing what he for his own purposes asserts General Pope contemplated, viz, " falling behind Bull Run."

Hence petitioner decided to withdraw.

I speak only from my notes of the learned counsel's closing remarks just before I began this argument, and would like to know if I interpret him correctly.

Mr. BULLITT. That is, that there was a lull in the firing of the artillery about that time; it may be a *little* later. Perhaps you do not exactly catch my meaning. My meaning was that the firing lulled. I do not mean to say that there may not have been shots.

The COUNSEL FOR THE GOVERNMENT. That is as I understand it, an occasional shot or so.

The limits of this argument will hardly permit *all* the irreconcilable statements of this petitioner to be followed and contrasted or commented upon.

As to this latest utterance, it is sufficient to say that it is not founded on Benjamin's evidence, for that officer distinctly says (Board's Record, p. 614) on cross-examination by petitioner's counsel, that he, Benjamin, took position at Groveton about 12½ p. m. and remained at that point *over three hours.*

When we look at the latter's direct examination we find what a stubborn and gallant fight he made from 1 p. m., against eighteen guns placed from 1,000 to about 1,500 yards from him.

These guns during that fight were added to by eight more, making in all twenty-six guns that Benjamin had to contend with.

Altogether, from 1 p. m. to at least 3½ p. m., there was an unusually *heavy* cannonading in progress right at Groveton itself, and thence northwesterly to the enemy's position—possibly heavier than at any other time during that battle.

The petitioner's excuse, therefore, is answered by Benjamin's evidence.

During all that long afternoon until the final general assault, there was heavy fighting on the whole of Jackson's line, as has been shown by citations in this argument.

The *third* statement in this latest utterance is, that petitioner's dispatch No. 28 (Board's Record, p. 423) to Morell, to push over and aid Sigel, was written *about* 3 p. m., and the movement over by way of retiring, but with direction to Morell to aid Sigel if he found he could do so.

The idea, says petitioner through his counsel, was that Morell should fall back to the northeast. In other words, the petitioner would have us believe that he undertook to carry out his expressed determination to withdraw to Manassas by sending Morrell's division in a *contrary direction.*

The correct explanation is naturally found in General McDowell's orders to petitioner before he left him.

In his reply to the Hon. Zachariah Chandler, in his defense before his court-martial, and in his opening statement here, has not this petitioner, as we have seen, insisted that the very ground over which he ordered Morell to go was broken country and impracticable?

If he could order his leading division, the one nearest his assumed powerful enemy, to march over that country by a flank movement at 3 p. m., it is plain there was nothing *then*, in his judgment, before him to prevent such a flank movement.

Nevertheless, when judicially asked why he did not do it under the joint order and McDowell's concurrent orders, he says there would have been "danger and disaster" in obeying, and that it would be a fatal military blunder.

However, if this petitioner believed at 3 p. m. that he could of his own volition order his leading division to push over and aid Sigel, what was there to prevent the rear division under Sykes being sent either by "Five Forks" or "Sudley Springs" road to our struggling troops, whom he admits in his dispatch he thought needed aid?

It was but a momentary order, the execution of which was never attempted, for it was followed by No. 33, from petitioner to Morell, to hold on to his present place, but it shows that he knew what was required of him and that it was not impracticable.

The petitioner says now, through his counsel, that the two dispatches he sent, addressed, one to General McDowell and the other to Generals McDowell and *King*, expressing an intention to retreat, are identical, and were sent by different messengers *before* Lieutenant Weld went with another message at 4 p. m. (G. C. M. Record, p. 129), to the effect that General Morell would now be strongly engaged; that there was a large force in front of him, &c.

Let me remark that this very message which Weld did take at 4 p. m. was one that would have had the effect to lead both General McDowell and General Pope to believe that the petitioner was making every effort to do his share in the operations that were then being conducted.

The assertion that the two dispatches, one to McDowell and the other to McDowell, and *King* were identical, or in other words contemporaneous, does not seem to be borne out by the facts.

Petitioner had located his own headquarters in the forks of the Sudley Springs and Manassas and Gainesville road. (Petitioner's Opening Statement, p. 40.)

The Sudley Springs road *was open all day* to our men, and wholly unobstructed to messengers and orderlies.

Possibly he sent the one to General McDowell before 4 p. m., because it is the dispatch which came into and has remained in General McDowell's possession.

The explanation of why General Pope did nothing, so far as the petitioner is concerned, with reference to that dispatch expressing an intention to retreat, was because Weld, the petitioner's aide-de-camp, came at 4, or between 4 and 5, to General Pope and said that they, viz, petitioner's forces, would be strongly engaged. This is merely a supposition. However, we find that at 4.30 General Pope ordered him to push into action at once.

Accepting for argument the petitioner's explanation, that he sent a dispatch to McDowell about 3 p. m., announcing his determination to retreat to Manassas, it seems plain that it was the following one, which General McDowell has produced before this Board, viz:

GENERAL McDOWELL: The firing on my right has so far retired that, as I cannot advance, and have failed to get over to you, except by the route taken by King, I shall withdraw to Manassas. If you have anything to communicate please do so. I have sent many messengers to you and Gen'l Sigel, and get nothing.

F. J. PORTER,
Maj. Gen'l.

An artillery duel is going on now—been skirmishing for a long time.

F. J. P.

If petitioner did not actually send this dispatch to McDowell until after he sent Lieutenant Weld to General Pope at 4 with word that petitioner "would now be strongly engaged" (the two messages being contradictory), he may have received General Pope's 4.30 order before writing to McDowell, and saying he should withdraw.

We have an excellent clew to the time at which the first note announceing an intention to withdraw was brought to General Pope's notice in Major-General Heintzelman's diary, in which he says:

> Forty-five minutes past five, General McDowell on the field at headquarters. Heavy firing on our center. Kearney reports he is driving the enemy back. *General Porter reports the enemy driving him back, and he is retiring on Manassas.*

Thus while the gallant Kearney was rolling Jackson up on the right of our line, petitioner, without either pushing in or moving up the Sudley road towards the Army, calmly declares what he proposes to do, although his loss by the artillery fire was the most insignificant.

Through Major-General Sigel's report of the 16th September, 1862, it appears he expected petitioner's corps to come in on his left (Board's Record, p. 505), and Heintzelman in his diary notes somewhere between 2 and 3 p. m., "We are hoping for McDowell and Porter." (Board's Record, p. 611.)

McDowell by the way had put King's division under Hatch in support of Reynolds until it was withdrawn and brought up near stone house by General Pope's own orders. (G. C. M. Record, pp. 94 and 221.)

The message at 4 p. m. by Lieut. S. M. Weld to Generals McDowell and Pope that Morell would be strongly engaged (G. C. M. Record, p. 129), was one calculated to allay suspicion and lead to the belief that petitioner had been trying to engage the enemy.

Instead of that the corps was put in concealment and no measures for *attack* projected until about 6 p. m., and then the only contemplated movement was by two regiments supported by two others. (P. XXXIII, Board's Record.)

Petitioner says that after Lieutenant Weld was sent at 4 p. m. this message was sent:

> Gen'l McDowell or *King:* I have been wandering over the woods and failed to get a communication to you. Tell how matters go with you. The enemy is in strong force in front of me, and I wish to know your designs for to-night. If left to me I shall have to retire for food and water, which I cannot get here. *How goes the battle?* It seems to go to our rear. The enemy are getting to our left.
> (Signed)   F. J. PORTER,
>   *M. G. Vols.*

The context shows it must have preceded the last-cited dispatch to McDowell announcing a determination to retreat to Manassas, and thus more widely separate the wings of the army.

The *second* dispatch of petitioner, declaring his determination to retreat, was as follows:

> [No. 36.]
>   *August 29th,* 1862.
>
> GENERALS McDOWELL *and King:* I found it impossible to communicate by crossing the woods to Groveton. The enemy are in strong force on this road, and as they appear to have driven our forces back, the firing of the enemy having advanced and ours retired, I have determined to withdraw to Manassas. I have attempted to communicate with McDowell and Sigel, but my messengers have run into the enemy. They have gathered artillery and cavalry and infantry, and the advancing masses of dust show the enemy coming in force. I am now going to the head of the column to see what is passing and how affairs are going. I will communicate with you. Had you not better send your train back?
>   F. J. PORTER,
>   *Major-General.*

It is the one which caused the amiable, kind-hearted President Lincoln, when he read it, to say the petitioner deserved death, because without a stroke even to help our Army which appeared to be retiring from the firing of an advancing enemy, he himself announced *his* determination to withdraw to Manassas, still further away from the direction the petitioner assumes the firing was taking.

On the trial in 1862, General Pope testified that he received this one *direct* from petitioner between 7 and 8 p. m. (p. 31, G. C. M. Record), and had retained it among his papers.

As his own and petitioner's headquarters were each at the unobstructed and open Sudley Springs road, and as petitioner knew where his headquarters were from his own aide, Weld, and Capt. Douglas Pope, he probably received it within half an hour after it was written—that being the time of travel between the two stations.

As to the *first* dispatch of petitioner to McDowell, expressing an intention to retreat, the latter has said before this Board that his *impression* is that he received it after the day was over (Board's Record, p. 809). This is at variance with Heintzelman's diary. General McDowell was at Pope's headquarters on the evening of the 29th, soon after the receipt by the latter *direct* from petitioner of the *second* dispatch (to McDowell *and King*) and was shown it by General Pope; hence his present impression. (G. C. M. Record, pp. 22 and 24.)

It is asserted by petitioner that the fact of the discovery by General McDowell among his papers of the dispatch dated 6 p. m. (next to be cited), in which petitioner reports he failed in getting Morell over to him, is conclusive proof that Major-General Pope's 4.30 order had not then come to petitioner's hand.

It must not, however, be forgotten that the 6 p. m. dispatch was *not* to General *Pope* but General *McDowell*.

It was a report under his previous instructions. It was not an explanation to General *Pope*, why he, petitioner, did not move into action at once. It gives the impression, however, that he is trying to do something.

He said: "I am trying to get a battery but have not succeeded as yet." If he meant a rebel battery, his preparations for assault were certainly not such as indicated any great force in his front. If he meant he was trying to get a Union battery, he had certainly six on duty with him.

If at six o'clock he was trying to take a rebel battery, why did he not make the effort four hours before. His efforts we know went no further than writing and sending an order.

According, therefore, to his own admission this petitioner permitted between three and five hours to elapse before he made report to General McDowell of what he had been doing.

Was it a report based on fact?

Is there any proof in this case that any part of his corps that day "wandered over the woods" in the vain effort to get through, or did petitioner do it himself?

The answer is, there is no such proof.

Another thing to be noticed is that the petitioner in some of these dispatches puts in the name of General *King*, although it is in evidence that early in the morning he, petitioner, was informed that General King had gone to Centreville sick, and that Hatch was in command of the division, and that he himself gave General Hatch orders that the division that was King's should follow him.

The following is the 6 p. m. dispatch which petitioner now says was a *duplicate* of the one reporting he had been wandering over the woods and wanting to know *how goes* the battle? This statement, from what has just been said, is apparently not borne out by the facts.

Gen'l McDowell: Failed in getting Morell over to you. After wandering about the woods for a time I withdrew him, and while doing so artillery opened on us. My scouts could not get through. Each one found the enemy between us, and I believe some have been captured. Infantry are also in front. I am trying to get a battery, but have not succeeded as yet. From the masses of dust on our left, and from reports of scouts, think the enemy are moving largely in that way. Please communicate the way this messenger came. *I have no cavalry or messengers now.* Please let me know your designs; whether you retire or not. I cannot get water and am out of provision. Have lost a few men from infantry firing.

F. J. PORTER,
Maj. Gen. Vols.

Aug. 29—6 p. m.

The inquiry again arises, is *this* report founded on fact? Did he make any efforts, sustained or vigorous, to get Morell over to the right, or did Morell wander about the woods for a time with his division?

The answer is, he did neither. His assumed difficulties in the way of sending messages is answered by noticing where his headquarters were—right at the open and direct Sudley road to Pope's headquarters, then at Buck Hill.

Notice, however, that even at this hour (6 p. m.) he reports the enemy *coming down on his front*, so that it is plain Longstreet could not have been there in full force deployed by 11 a. m.

Further, why did this petitioner leave this report until 6 p. m., when McDowell had ordered him to attack about noon?

If McDowell did not give him an order to attack when he was with him, which was not countermanded, and petitioner was no longer subject to those orders, why did he report he had attempted the very thing McDowell said he did order him to do?

But there is something more in this dispatch which requires comment.

Petitioner says in it, " I have no cavalry or messengers now."

Was this true? Let us look into it.

The following is the evidence of Bvt. Brig. Gen. Jno. P. Taylor, then captain commanding squadron First Pennsylvania Cavalry, and others of his squadron.

The Board will recollect that he testified to coming down from Gainesville that very morning when General Ricketts' division left it, coming down this very Manassas and Gainesville road that the petitioner was to go up on, down here to the Sudley Church road and to Manassas Junction, and there met the head of petitioner's column starting back under the orders that General Pope had given him. Now, at this point in his testimony, we have got Bvt. Brig. Gen. Taylor back with a squadron up to Dawkins' Branch, at head of petitioner's column. His evidence is as follows (Board's Record, p. 905):

Question. Where did you bring your squadron to a halt?
Answer. The day was warm; there were frequent halts made, I presume. I can scarcely say the distance that we marched; it was some miles when the command halted. There was an engagement going on a little diagonally to our front and right; that was some time in the after part of the day.

* * * * * * *

The WITNESS. We remained there until after night. The engagement continued on until after dark; there was heavy infantry firing and artillery. We were with the advance with Morell's division, and I remember distinctly after halting my squadron was formed in front of us, there being some skirmishers thrown out immediately in our front. The enemy turned and fired two pieces. One of the shots fell immediately in our front. We moved a little to the left, and my command remained there until the command moved in the night.

Question. Then you got to the point where General Porter's corps was halted on that day?
Answer. We were in the advance with Morell's division when it halted, but the point I cannot say. We did not reach Gainesville.

* * * * * * *

Question. What enemy, if any, did you see in your immediate front?

Answer. We could not tell what they were, but there was infantry heavily engaged at sundown. They were cheering and yelling, and there was musketry rising from the trees where the firing was.

Question. Was that in your front?

Answer. To the right of our front—diagonally across. It might have been a mile, or near two miles.

Question. From what time in the morning did you hear the sounds of battle?

Answer. We heard cannonading during the day, all day, and there had been some the day before.

* * * * * * *

Question. Did you know what your squadron was ordered to report to General Morell for?

Answer. The order was to report for orderly duty; that was the substance of the order.

Question. Were you behind any ridge or hill?

Answer. I don't recollect any hill right in front of us, and I recollect seeing an engagement in sight, and it seemed to be descending ground.

Question. What sort of an engagement did you see?

Answer. Infantry and artillery.

Question. How many infantry engaged?

Answer. I could not tell—the firing was in woods. We could see the smoke of the musketry rising above the trees, and could hear the cheering and yelling, as if a charge were being made.

Question. What time of day was that?

Answer. Near sundown; perhaps after sundown.

* * * * * * *

Question. What number of troops did you suppose to be engaged, from what you saw or heard—a large army, a division, a brigade, or a regiment?

Answer. There was a brigade at least engaged, and there may have been a division.

Question. Could you see the rebel troops?

Answer. After it began to get dusk we could see the flashes of their muskets.

Question. See the Federal troops?

Answer. No, sir; could see the smoke of the musketry and the flashes of the muskets.

Question. You laid in that field all that afternoon, did you?

Answer. During the time that we lay there I cannot say how long; we were there until dark.

Question. What did you do then?

Answer. Went back in the night.

Question. Where did you go then?

Answer. We moved back in the direction of Manassas with the same command, and on the next day, the 29th, I was under General Griffin's command, and at Centreville he ordered me to——

Question. On the next day, the 29th?

Answer. On the 30th. Went back during the night, and at some time on the 30th this command halted at or near Centreville. We were ordered to encamp and tie our horses in a clump of woods a little to the right of Centreville, in order that any orders that were given us they could send.

Question. What did you say in reference to a skirmish line that was being thrown out by General Porter—was there any on the 29th?

Answer. My impression is there was a skirmish line in front of us, and that is all that was in front of us. There were no Federal troops in front of us.

Question. Did your squadron go on skirmish duty?

Answer. No, sir; it did not.

* * * * * * *

Question. What was the number of the squadron you had with you?

Answer. I could not tell you the number; we might have had 50 men and may have had 75 men. Our number was originally about 90 men.

* * * * * * *

Question. I understand you to say that you laid idle, doing nothing, from the time you halted until you left there that night?

Answer. No, sir.

Question. Did not go upon skirmish duty?

Answer. No.

Question. Were not sent on any duty to carry dispatches?

Answer. I have no recollection of any.

Question. Or perform any duty at all that you can recollect?

Answer. No, sir. I got this information from a diary that I kept at the time.

15 G

Capt. *R. J. McNitt*, First Pennsylvania Cavalry (Board's Record, p. 913), testified as follows:

Question. Did you see any enemy that day?
Answer. No, sir; not, to the best of my knowledge. There were a couple of artillery shots fired when we were in that neighborhood. Towards evening on that day I saw smoke from infantry firing, and cheering of infantry apparently about sundown, along in the neighborhood of sundown.
Question. What direction was that from where you were?
Answer. That appeared to be a little to our right, I should think.
Question. Was there any action then going on between any of the troops of your corps that you were with there and the enemy?
Answer. Not as I recollect.
Question. Did you hear any other cannonading during the day? If so, where?
Answer. We heard some scattering cannonading through the day, but it appeared to be a good distance off, over towards the Warrenton pike.

* * * * * *

Question. Did you do anything up there?
Answer. Not very much.
Question. You have no recollection of having done anything?
Answer. Not a great deal. We remained there until we turned and came back again.
Question. Were you mounted or off your horses?
Answer. When we stopped, we generally got orders to dismount and rest our horses. If we did not stop for half an hour we dismounted.

William H. Ramsey, private Company B, First Pennsylvania Cavalry, testified as follows (Board's Record, p. 914):

Question. Do you know of any battle going on on that day? If so, where was it?
Answer. Yes; there was heavy infantry firing to our right and front towards the evening, and artillery firing during the day.
Question. Could you hear anything else which would indicate an action besides the musketry?
Answer. Yes; cheering; both rebel cheering and our cheering.
Question. Were your command used for anything on that day after you came to that halt? If so, what?
Answer. Not to my knowledge. There was not a man used, to my knowledge.

John Hoffman, private Company C, First Pennsylvania Cavalry, testified as follows (Board's Record, p. 915):

Question. Did you hear any firing that day?
Answer. Heard some firing on the right?
Question. What kind of firing?
Answer. Artillery and infantry.

William H. Bayard, private Company C, First Pennsylvania Cavalry, testified as follows (Board's Record, p. 916):

Question. While you were there at that point did you see any enemy in your front?
Answer. Well, no; I did not.
Question. Did you hear any firing?
Answer. There was some firing down to the front and the right.
Question. How far off?
Answer. I judge it was along a mile or a mile and a half; something like that.
Question. What was the firing, infantry or artillery?
Answer. Infantry and artillery both.

William Reddy, private Company C, First Pennsylvania Cavalry, testified as follows (Board's Record, p. 917):

Question. While you were at this place, where you were halted with this body of infantry, did you see any enemy in your front? If so, what was it?
Answer. Not in front exactly, but on our right in front.
Question. About how far away?
Answer. About a mile, or a mile and a half.
Question. Was there any firing on your front that day?
Answer. Not on our front, but there was to our right.
Question. What was that firing?
Answer. Artillery and infantry firing.

Question. Was there anything else by which you could tell that there was an action going on?
Answer. Not in particular, any more than the firing I heard off to the right.
Question. Did you see any artillery in your front that day?
Answer. I don't know whether there were two pieces or one, but anyway there were from two to four shots fired. I could not tell which.
Question. Where from?
Answer. From the enemy's side.

Cross-examination by Mr. BULLITT:

Question. Do you recollect what time that firing occurred—that infantry and artillery on your right?
Answer. Early in the afternoon; toward evening.

By the RECORDER:

Question. How long did you hear that artillery firing to your right?
Answer. All the time we were out there.

The evidence of Brevet Brigadier-General Taylor and men of his squadron would be sufficient as to whether there were any available cavalry there, but on the original trial Col. *E. G. Marshall*, Thirteenth New York Volunteers, a witness for petitioner, said: "Whilst my command was being got into line prior to my going on this duty, my brigade was behind some others. *General Porter had sent some dragoons* of another regiment to the front, and my brigade was waiting in the road to get into position" (G. C. M. Record, p. 191), and on General McDowell's court of inquiry petitioner himself swore he had on the road up to Dawkins' Branch a small cavalry escort (Board's Record, p. 1010).

The presence of this cavalry would, of course, contradict the assertion of petitioner in his report that he had none, and it became necessary, in view of the fact that he had borrowed orderlies from Colonel Schriver and General Pope, to show he had none.

Accordingly Maj. Gen. *G. W. Morell* was recalled as a witness by petitioner, but he did not recollect (Board's Record, p. 968).

Then Captain *Augustus P. Martin*, formerly petitioner's chief of artillery, was called, who "saw no cavalry except a few orderlies." (Board's Record, page 1127).

In the closing arguments here, petitioner, through his counsel, has ventured the explanation substantially that he did not know of this cavalry, and did not think they were there; but it must not be forgotten that the petitioner, moved up with Morell to Dawkins' Branch with the head of the column where the cavalry were, and himself ordered out skirmishers.

At or about 6.30 p. m., *half an hour* after he had reported to McDowell he had neither cavalry nor messengers, he sent a dispatch (No. 38) to Morell, in which he said, after ordering him to put his men in bivouac for the night, "*I wish you would send me a dozen men from that cavalry.*" (G. C. M. Record, p. 153.)

Lieut. *Stephen M. Weld*, then aide-de-camp to the petitioner, also testified on this subject as follows (Board's Record, p. 262):

*   *   *   *   *   *   *

General Porter sent out some cavalry skirmishers They were halted on the side of the hill facing west. The cavalry crossed the plain at the foot of this hill and went into the woods, not a great distance in, nearly as I can recollect: I saw them going in a little distance.

Thus it appears plain that the petitioner, in reporting he no had cavalry, in his knowledge reported that which had no foundation in fact.

Assuming for argument that he did not know he had a squadron of cavalry at his front, the statement itself shows how little he knew what was being done at the head of his column nearest the enemy.

The fact of the previous non-production by Major-General McDowell, until the request of this Board, of the three dispatches received from petitioner, has been made the subject of animadversion.

The acknowledgment of receipt on an envelope usually fixes time of receipt; but neither the government nor petitioner have been able to produce any such record in this present investigation, except in the solitary instance of Lieut. E. P. Brooks.

Petitioner's witness (Board's Record, p. 281), Major Ruggles, swears that at General Pope's headquarters it was customary to receipt dispatch on the envelope and return it by bearer, and yet petitioner has exhibited none such or proved contents of *alleged* missing reports of his.

Singularly enough, the petitioner has produced here eight or ten dispatches which he either did not have or did not recollect of on his trial or when he was a witness before General McDowell's court of inquiry. In fact, he did not then recollect even having given an order to Morell to "attack" with two regiments, supported by two others.

FORCES OF PETITIONER AND CO-OPERATING FORCES.

It may be desirable, right here, as showing some of the inconsistencies to which I have referred, to allude again incidentally to Piatt's brigade, which the petitioner, in his opening statement, declared was not with him.

Substantially we find, in looking at Assistant Adjutant-General Locke's evidence before this Board, aside from what General Sturgis and General Piatt have specifically testified to on the subject, that they were there; that he (Locke) saw them at the intersection of the Sudley and the Manassas and Gainesville roads marching to the rear.

Then Locke says that he was not aware that they had been "assigned to us" at that time; but, on page 454, he admits, on further examination, that they were "attached."

Griffin, in his evidence on the original record, also mentioned them being there; and we have seen introduced here by General Sturgis a dispatch that he received that very 29th of August from the petitioner, while there with him (Board's Record, p. 717), ordering him at daylight, August 30, to march off and follow the corps when they were ordered to join General Pope.

By reference to the maps it will be found that from Bristoe Station up to Gainesville there was a *direct* road. There was also another road up, via Milford, which ran into this Manassas and Gainesville road, and so on up to Gainesville, to the left of Thomas Nealon's.

The evidence of Capt. G. H. Dobson and of Prof. G. L. Andrews, of the United States Military Academy, is to the positive effect that Major-General Banks' corps were in Bristoe Station from the 28th up to and including the 29th and 30th, part of the 30th at least.

To contradict that has been brought here Brevet Major-General Gordon, of the United States Volunteers, to say that, instead of the corps being at Bristoe, they were a mile and a half farther away, toward Warrenton Junction.

By referring, however, to the record of stations of the corps during August in the official monthly report of Major-General Banks of the men he had and positions, dated August 31, 1862, now in this record, as an exhibit filed in the Adjutant-General's Office November 12, 1862, we find that the evidence of Professor Andrews (Board's Record, pp. 1095 and 1096) and of Captain Dobson is particularly confirmed by the statement that the several brigades and divisions of General Banks' corps were in Bristoe, having arrived there on the 28th.

Now, on the 27th, two days before the battle, as appears by one of the petitioner's own dispatches (No. 20, p. 90, petitioner's opening statement), he was ordered to hold himself in constant communication with General Banks; and that very morning, the 29th, General Sturgis had come from a position in the rear of General Banks up to and joining the petitioner at the front, reporting to him there near Dawkins' Branch.

It is also in evidence (of Brevet Major-General Gordon) that at Bristoe Station the cannonading and sounds of battle could be heard distinctly, and that they were anxious as to the result (Board's Record, p. 1214). These are confirmatory statements connected with the evidence of Captain Dobson himself. (Board Record's, p. 1134):

George H. Dobson, called by the Recorder, and examined in the city of New York on the 23d day of November, 1878—present, the Recorder, and Mr. Maltby, of counsel for the petitioner, and the petitioner—having been duly sworn, testified as follows:

Direct examination:

Question. Where do you reside?
Answer. Baltimore, Maryland.
Question. What is your occupation?
Answer. Lumber merchant.
Question. Were you in the military service of the United States in August, 1862; if so, in what capacity?
Answer. As captain of Company A, Third Regiment Maryland Volunteer Infantry, Col. David P. De Witt.
Question. With what rank did you leave the service?
Answer. I left the service as captain.
Question. Where were you on the morning of Friday, August 29, 1862?
Answer. At Bristoe Station, or in that vicinity.
Question. To what division, brigade, and corps did you belong?
Answer. Second Brigade, Prince; Second Division, Augur; Banks' corps. It was either Prince or Augur at the time you mention in command; one was captured and the other wounded.
Question. Do you know of any movements of your regiment, brigade, and division on that day; if so, what were they?
Answer. I believe on that day our regiment with some other troops, I don't know how many, were moved in the direction of Gainesville; it was given out that they were to go to Gainesville, as I understood.
Question. At the time?
Answer. Yes; I think it was given out that they were going to Gainesville.
Question. At what time did your regiment and those other troops leave Bristoe Station?
Answer. I could not say exactly. I could tell you what time they halted and about the distance they marched, so you could form some idea of the time. I believe they halted about half past three or four o'clock—between three and four o'clock—and the distance was about three or three and a half miles.
Question. In what direction?
Answer. Said to be in the direction of Gainesville. I was simply a line officer; I had no opportunity, as a general officer would have, of knowing those things.
Question. Of knowing what?
Answer. Of knowing where we were destined.
Question. What direction did you take on leaving Bristoe Station?
Answer. We took the direction of one of two roads that led from Bristoe Station towards the enemy's front; that is what we understood.
Question. Now as to the points of the compass, the road that you took?
Answer. I could not tell from my knowledge then.
Question. Northeast or southeast?
Answer. I could not tell from the direction of the compass at that time.
Question. At what time did you say you halted?
Answer. Between three and four o'clock.
Question. What then occurred, after halting, within your knowledge?
Answer. To me individually?

Question. Yes; state all.

Answer. A gentleman came and invited some of the officers of the regiment to take dinner with him in the neighborhood.

Question. Was that to the front or rear of the position in which you were halted?

Answer. A little to the front of us.

Question. Go on and state what you then did, and what sort of a place it was that you went to?

Answer. I was one of a number who accepted the invitation, and when I got to his house it was too late for dinner; he had had his dinner, but he gave me something to eat. I was then, to the best of my recollection, inside of our own lines; our pickets had been thrown out upon the road a piece. When I got through eating, our pickets were driven in towards our regiment, and I was inside the enemy's lines; they fired at me as I came out, three or four shots. I escaped and went back to the regiment.

Question. Then what was done?

Answer. I think we went back to Bristoe Station.

Question. About what time in the day was that?

Answer. I could not tell you exactly; it was late in the day, between four and five o'clock, when I went up there, I suppose.

Question. What description of force of the enemy was it that drove in our pickets?

Answer. I don't know; I suppose the cavalry videttes that were stationed on the road when we came out. We did not see our pickets driven in; the house sat back from the road some distance; simply cavalry videttes that had dismounted and tied their horses to the fence-posts.

Question. The enemy's cavalry?

Answer. Yes, sir.

Question. On which side of the road was this house as you went up?

Answer. On the right of the road as we went up, to the best of my memory.

Question. Did you see any artillery?

Answer. No, sir.

Question. Did you know, or were you informed at the time, of the purpose of this movement of these troops out in this direction?

Answer. No, sir; I had no means of knowing that, except from hearsay at that time. I do not recollect that I ever heard any object at all.

* * * * * * *

Question. As to the number of regiments, as near as you can recollect, how many regiments were there?

Answer. If I am not mistaken, there were the whole of our brigade of infantry and a Maryland battalion, the Purnell Legion.

* * * * * *

Question. How long had your brigade been in Bristoe at this time, the 29th of August?

Answer. I think they came there either on the night of the 27th, or early on the morning of the 28th; I have had the impression that it was the 27th; I am not positive.

Question. What was the strength of the corps on that day?

Answer. General Banks' army corps?

Question. Yes.

Answer. We roughly estimated it at 10,000 troops; that was the general idea that prevailed with us at that time.

* * * * * * *

Cross-examination by Mr. MALTBY:

Question. Who commanded your brigade on the 29th?

Answer. I think the colonel of the One hundred and eleventh Pennsylvania, Steinberner.

Question. Who commanded that division?

Answer. I think it was General Greene.

Question. What is his first name?

Answer. I don't know; he was commanding the brigade before General Augur got wounded.

Question. What regiments were in your brigade?

Answer. The One hundred and eleventh Pennsylvania, One hundred and second New York, one Ohio regiment, and our own, Third Maryland, and the Fourth and Sixth Maine Batteries.

Question. That all?

Answer. I think so.

Question. In which brigade were you?

Answer. Second.

* * * * * * *

Question. On the 29th, when you made this march, as you supposed, in the direction of Gainesville, how was your regiment occupied before you marched?

Answer. Simply at rest.

Question. What caused you to think that you moved in the direction of Gaines-ville? You say it was given out; who gave it out?

Answer. It was generally talked of in the mess that I messed with; that is the information that I got.

Question. You had no information from superior officers?

Answer. Yes; the mess that I messed with were all my superior officers.

Question. With whom did you mess?

Answer. Messed with the field and staff officers of the regiment; they were my superior officers at that time.

Question. Was your regiment the leading regiment?

Answer. I think it was the leading regiment on that occasion; we were known as the second regiment in the brigade; I think it was the leading regiment at that time.

Question. What causes the impression that the whole brigade was there with you at your advanced position that day, in the direction of Gainesville, as you understood it?

Answer. I only judged from the body of troops that were marched up; I do not say positively that the whole brigade was there.

Question. What causes the impression?

Answer. The cause of the impression was the large body of troops; it was quite an imposing string on the road—a couple of thousand men, perhaps.

The petitioner has sought to induce us to believe that Wilcox's division of Longstreet's special command was shoved down from the north of the Warrenton pike into the neighborhood and to the rear of D. R. Jones' division, because of some movements of the petitioner. But when we come to look at the record of what the petitioner did during the day, we find that he did not do anything, that he made no tentative movement of any description until six o'clock, when he gave an order which was not carried out.

Thus we are obliged to look to some other quarter for the explanation of Wilcox's division being shoved down there; and we find it in the movement of this brigade of observation of General Banks up in the direction of Gainesville.

This affords a slight indication as to the position I have taken here that General Lee during that day was merely occupying a *defensive* position, not with a view to assault in any sense whatever, because the position that General Banks held upon his right flank was one which, if he, Lee, had not held on to Gainesville and kept his forces where he could put them into position if necessary interposed between Gainesville and the direct road from Bristoe to Gainesville, and through Haymarket to Thoroughfare Gap, through which last point his, Lee's, re-enforcements were coming, he would have been in very much the position that Jackson would have been in had the previous orders of General Pope in every respect been complied with.

Therefore, I find the explanation of the movement of Wilcox's division down there to coincide with the movement of this brigade of observation up from Bristoe towards Gainesville to a point about half way between the two places.

Captain Dobson's evidence on the subject, putting this movement after three o'clock, coincides exactly with what is stated in the official report of Wilcox (of October 11, 1862, Board's Record, p. 530), that it was between four and five that he, Wilcox, was moved down there to be ready for any contingency, and what Wilcox has testified to before this Board. (Board's Record, p. 230.)

But if we assume what the petitioner would have us assume, that the fact of his (petitioner) lying along that Manassas and Gainesville road, stretched in column, all day, with a little skirmish line of one small regiment thrown out in the woods in front, was the reason why Wilcox came down to the point indicated, then we must apply the remarks of Charles Marshall, his own witness, to him (Board's Record, pp. 160, 161, 169, 170, and 171), that late in the day General Lee became perfectly satisfied that

218

there was no apprehension of an attack against his (Lee's) right; that he could spare him, and therefore moved back Wilcox to the north of the road to assist Hood, who was then about pushing into a severe action against McDowell's corps, because Hood required to be supported. Marshall himself also says that the occasion of Wilcox being sent south of the pike was the report of troops advancing from Bristoe, which threatened their right flank.

▸ After Wilcox returned to the north of the Warrenton Turnpike D. R. Jones, with his three brigades, was left alone to watch the national forces on their right, as "Kemper's troops were never anywhere except just to the south of the Warrenton pike on the right of Hood; they never were *anywhere* else." (Board's Record, p. 166.)

PETITIONER'S FORCES ON THE 29TH.

Much has been said by the petitioner with reference to the condition that he was left in when General McDowell took, at the suggestion of the petitioner, King's division from the rear, and carried it up to apply it intermediately; that he was thus in almost a defenseless position; that his troops were too few to do anything, although it appears that late in the day his own commanding officer on the skirmish line, Col. E. G. Marshall, did not think more than a brigade had got on his front. Nevertheless it has been stated here with great earnestness that he could not do anything, because he had no supporting forces; that the absence of King's division left him utterly helpless; that it would have been an unmilitary movement for him to push forward against what he now assumes to have been 25,000 of the enemy, instead of the 10,000 or 15,000 that he assumed on his original trial. But when we come to look at the official returns we find that his plea or pretense here that he had no sufficient support, or that his forces were not enough, must be taken *cum grano salis.*

Sturgis had come up to him, having passed Banks' corps that very morning, and the petitioner had been directed, two days before, by General Pope, as appears in evidence, to keep in constant communication with Banks.

In looking at the official return upon muster of Major-General Banks' corps for the 31st of August, he having remained quietly all of two days without being in action, we find that General Banks reported specifically for the 31st the entire number present for duty, commissioned and enlisted, with him, as 10,361 (see attached exhibit), which coincides very nearly with the rough estimate that Captain Dobson said that very morning of the 29th that the officers put upon the number of men that were there.

Even Professor Andrews, United States Military Academy, has made an estimate of, at least, 5,000 or 6,000 for duty present there at Bristoe under Banks. (Board's Record, p. 1095.)

Now, let us see what were the forces of the petitioner and the co-operating forces.

Here was Banks on his left at Bristoe; here was King's division moving up the "Sudley" road to go into position, and Ricketts' just behind—Ricketts' division having, according to the petitioner, 8,000 men, King's division having 7,000.

Next let us see what the petitioner had. His assistant adjutant-general, Locke, before this Board, admits (Board's Record, p. 454) that when the petitioner marched from Bristoe on the morning of the 29th the corps was "well in hand." The next day (30th August) they appeared to be well closed up; and that the corps lost between 2,500 and 3,000 men that day."

General Butterfield thinks (Board's Record, p. 463) that the two brigades of Morell's division under him lost over 2,000 men on the 30th. The other brigade had marched off to Centreville and did not get into action.

Sykes' return (*vide* exhibits) shows that his division of regulars on the 30th lost 917 men.

At Bristoe, at 9 a. m. on the 28th of August, the petitioner previously reported to Burnside that he had kept his command well up (No. 22, p. 91, petitioner's Opening Statement).

Therefore, such being the case, his command being well up on the 29th, and well in hand, having moved but slowly from Warrenton Junction up to Bristoe and thence to the point where we have him now (31st August), in order to ascertain what his actual strength was on the 29th, let us take his *official* report that he has himself put in (Board's Record, p. 457), the official return which he made of his forces at Centreville on the 31st August, 1862, and subtract therefrom the losses of the 30th.

The return that has been put in of Piatt's brigade showed that he had on the Manassas and Gainesville road with the petitioner 824 men for duty on the morning of the 29th.

On the 31st, according to the "official return" put in here by the petitioner, at Centreville, the total enlisted of Sykes' division present for duty was 3,601 and 322 officers. From this computation I exclude those who were sick, in arrest, or confinement; but of course I include those who were present on extra or daily duty, for those men were under arms and part of the actual force.

Of Morell's division there were officers for duty and on extra or daily duty 300, and of enlisted men present for duty, or on extra or daily duty, 5,959.

In that official return he puts as part of his force 19 batteries of artillery. He had actually with him six batteries of artillery, as appears by the evidence; whether he had all the other batteries available I do not know. But I take those six batteries and average them, 19 being the total number of batteries reported, and I find that it gives an average of 12 officers and 344 men.

I exclude in this calculation 592 officers and men present sick. Thus the petitioner had present at Centreville on the 31st of August, when muster came, according to his own report, a total of 11,362; that is, including Piatt's brigade.

Now, Locke says that the corps on the 30th lost between 2,500 and 3,000. Butterfield says his *own* loss in Morell's division was over 2,000, from the two brigades of the division under him, and he thinks those two brigades went into action with about 6,200 men.

Sykes reports 917 as the loss from his own division, whose numbers he roughly estimated on the trial in 1862 as 4,750 present on the 29th (G. C. M. Rec., p. 179.) Assuming a less loss than either Butterfield or Locke have done, viz, 2,164, the estimated number found in the *nominal* unsigned report of General Pope, adding this to the number actually present on the 31st of August at Centreville at muster, and we find that the petitioner had on the morning of the 29th at his service, exclusive of sick men or men in arrest and confinement, or any but those who were present under arms ready for duty, 13,526 men.

If I add to that the difference of losses between 2,164 in General Pope's nominal report, and 3,000 as stated by the petitioner's chief of staff, there will be added nearly 1,000 more men to the computation.

That this is not an unreasonable estimate, we find that ten days before, when his tri-monthly report was made by petitioner, Morell's division had present for duty 6,731, omitting those who were in arrest or confinement (*ride* exhibits), besides many absent.

Thus this petitioner, assuming as he did, in January, 1863, that Longstreet had between 10,000 and 15,000 men in front of him, nevertheless had enough men subject to his own orders to have made a movement that would have had every prospect of success.

And even if he had had less it would have been no excuse for not making a movement against the enemy that was near his front so as to prevent that enemy, if possible, from assisting the rest of their forces on another line of operations.*

If instead of taking petitioner's *official* returns offered by himself, we take the recollections of *his* own witnesses, we may form some idea as to the reliability of his "Opening Statement" (p. 5) that he had on the 29th of August, 1862, *less* than 9,000.

Brigadier-General Sykes, on the trial in 1862, testified that he had in his division of the Fifth Corps on the 29th, 4,750 present under arms, including three batteries of artillery. (G. C. M. Rec. p. 179.)

Brigadier-General Butterfield has said before this Board that when he went into action the next day in command of two brigades of Morrell's division, he had about 4,200 men. (Board's Record, p. 462.)

Griffin's brigade of Morrell's division, with Morrell himself, was then (the morning of the 30th) at Centreville. (G. C. M. Rec., p. 148.)

It had actually under arms 1,569, *possibly more*, but that is the number admitted by petitioner. (G. C. M. Rec., p. 241, and Board's Record, p. 452.)

Added to these the number Brigadier-General Piatt reported he himself had under petitioner on the 29th, viz, 824 (petitioner's exhibit, Board's Record, p. 1123), and we have a total of officers and men actually on duty under petitioner's *immediate* orders, under arms, on the 29th, of 11,343, as shown by his own witnesses.

Official returns.

1.—Piatt's brigade, viz (Board's Record, p. 1123): Present 824
2.—Petitioner's corps. (His monthly return 31st August, p. 457 Board's Record, excluding 591 present sick, *ride* Seventh Article of War.)

(1.) Sykes' division:
Officers for duty and present on extra or daily duty 157
Enlisted men present for duty..... 3,211
Enlisted men present on extra or daily duty 390

Total Sykes' division........................... 3,758

(2.) Morell's division:
Officers for duty and present on extra or daily duty 300
Enlisted men present for duty............ 5,345
Enlisted men present on extra or daily duty 614

Total Morell's division 6,259

Artillery:
Six batteries arranged on an average basis of 19 batteries reported in the corps.
Total officers 12
Total enlisted 344
356

11,197

Add killed and wounded on the 30th August, as per General Pope's nominal return 2,164

Total present for duty under petitioner 29th August 13,361

As Francis S. Earle, who was Morrell's assistant adjutant-general and petitioner's witness, says that Morrell told him, on the morning of the 29th, that he (Morrell) then had about 6,000 men under arms (Board's Record, p. 416), this would increase the number actually present beyond the above computation, and make it 11,574.

To these should be added the squadron of First Pennsylvania Cavalry, under Bvt. Brig. Gen. (then captain) John P. Taylor, between 50 and 75 strong (Board's Record, p. 909), and corps headquarters staff and mounted orderlies.

Again, all that day there were near to this petitioner, in proper position to have assisted him if necessary in a very short time, Banks' corps of over 10,000 men, and Ricketts' division of 8,000, exclusive of artillery.

STUART'S HILL.

In the closing argument of the petitioner something was said as to this commanding promontory called Stuart's or Monroe's Hill, which has so singularly been left out of this map, but which has played such a prominent part in this argument, and which it has been sought to show had but a slight elevation, some 10 or 15 feet, above the level of the country.

As contradictory of that we have the evidence of Bvt. Brig. Gen. E. D. Fowler, of the Fourteenth Brooklyn (Board's Record, p. 548), Capt. W. W. Blackford, Confederate engineers (Board's Record, p. 695), who speak of this commanding position; and of Jubal A. Early, of the Confederate service (Board's Record, p. 849), who said as follows, after preliminary remarks, that an hour or two after sunrise Jackson showed him a commanding ridge about a mile from the Warrenton pike, which we know as Stuart's or Monroe's Hill:

It was a commanding ridge and commanded a view of all the open country in front to the "Warrenton pike," and all of the fields to my left and General Jackson's right.

And Mr. Monroe, who lives there, says that from that point you can see Manassas and Centreville, Bull Run Mountains, and Thoroughfare and Hopeville Gaps. The witnesses last brought in here by the petitioner have shown that the ridges on each side of "Dawkins' Branch" near the railroad, and for several hundred yards from each side of the railroad, can be seen from Stuart's Hill; though that is a matter of which the Board—it being a question of topography—would take judicial cognizance by reference to anything that would give information upon the subject without necessarily having it in evidence, just as the Board would satisfy itself, if occasion required, as to the position of the sun or moon at a given time. It is to be regretted that the Board has not visited the country. I find, however, in my own notes, made on that hill last August from personal observation, the following remarks:

High commanding ridge; can see Carrico's, three-quarters mile; Centreville, Thoroughfare Gap, Gainesville, Warrenton pike one spot, Britts' under the hill, also Leachman's.

In the report of Col. E. M. Law (quoted by petitioner's counsel), of Hood's division Longstreet's command, he said (Board's Record, p. 536) his brigade moved forward, commanded by Generals Longstreet and Hood, until it reached a commanding position in front of the enemy, about three-quarters of a mile from the Dogan house. That report must be taken with considerable allowance, for, according to the officer who made the statement, it would have brought them down here in the valley at the foot of the natural glacis eastward, and directly under the guns of the Union force, which he says opened on them, and far within their range. That brigade could not have gone up on to "Stony Ridge," because Henry Kyd Douglas, adjutant-general of Jackson, according to his evidence, did not appear to know of Longstreet's arrival until *late* in the day. In the position counsel would place him, Major Douglas would at once have discovered the brigade. As it was north of the pike, it possibly attained the same ridge as Cooper's battery.

The next to be considered is the method of procedure of this petitioner.

METHOD OF PROCEDURE.

Next to be considered is the method of procedure of this petitioner, and in this connection it is to be noticed:

First. That he did not hesitate to avail himself of the libels of his former senior counsel against the court that tried him; against the witnesses who gave evidence against him; against the Judge-Advocate-General who reviewed his case, and indirectly against President Lincoln himself. (Board's Record, p. 994.)

Second. That he sought before this board to continue a cross-examination, voluntarily concluded by him sixteen years ago, of several who were witnesses before his court-martial, for the purpose of throwing doubt upon their statements on direct examination, when it was not possible that, after the lapse of such time, any witness could recall vividly all the circumstances then in his recollection upon which he based his statement of facts. (Board's Record, pp. 1108 and 1114.)

The history of jurisprudence will be searched in vain for such another like procedure.

Third. His conduct towards Major-Generals *McDowell* and *Pope*.

1. As to Major-General *McDowell.*

This officer's whole military career, during the eventful days of August, 1862, stands in striking contrast to the petitioner's.

He and Maj. Gen. N. P. Banks and Maj. Gen. J. C. Fremont had commanded independent corps—when Major-General Pope was called from the West—and the three corps were assembled and constituted the "Army of Virginia." All were seniors to General Pope, and McDowell was his senior both in the Regular Army and volunteers.

This, however, did not prevent him from *loyally* and earnestly, to the fullest extent, supporting General Pope in all his plans and movements, so far as he was made acquainted with and understood them. Indeed, the petitioner, throughout this case, has endeavored to make it apparent that General McDowell was an officer in whom the Commanding General, Pope put implicit confidence.

This admission, though made for *other* purposes, shows what a *loyal* and earnest man to do his duty—his whole duty to his country—McDowell was, for the times were critical, the capital was in danger; yet, although he must undoubtedly have had those feelings which any military man would have experienced at seeing his junior put over him (which a special law permitted), yet it did not influence either his official or personal action towards his commanding general, and no dispatch can be found from him criticising or reflecting on his commanding general.

Major-General Fremont asked to be relieved, and Major-General Sigel succeeded to the command of *his* corps.

Major-General Banks, who was by his date of commission next in command under General Pope, and General McDowell, continued in the sphere of duty their government put them in.

The methods, for example, by which it has been sought by petitioner to throw the responsibility of not fighting on this respected officer would be a fit subject of animadversion were it not that the petitioner's case shows too many unfounded statements and contradictions in his own behalf.

One little point has been dwelt upon by him, viz, that General Mc-Dowell would not admit that Longstreet's forces were those mentioned in General Buford's dispatch, which McDowell showed petitioner at Dawkins' Branch on the morning of the 29th, as the force coming in to Jackson's aid. He holds up McDowell's own previous orders of a day or two before, in which General McDowell referred to Longstreet as pushing for Thoroughfare Gap.

This is wholly collateral to petitioner's own conduct, but is part of a consistent plan of intentional misconstruction.

General McDowell has said that when his officers reported "Longstreet" was at a place, he himself assumed the fact and said "Longstreet"; when the report did not say Longstreet, but merely an "enemy," he did not say "Longstreet."

The fact that there were then no corps organizations in the Confederate army, and only divisional commands, the senior ranking officers having control of wings or detached portions, is sufficient answer to this.

However, the petitioner is concluded by his own evidence in the Mc-Dowell court of inquiry, in which the petitioner then showed that he himself *had no recollection of such conversation.* (Board's Record, pp. 1009–1013.)

General McDowell *did* show him General Buford's dispatch, and whether it was D. H. Hill, Hood, McLaws, Jones, Kemper, Longstreet, Anderson, or Lee, he gave him all the information he had as to an ENEMY.

In point of fact, it is now plain it was Lee himself who came forward with this fragment of his army.

2. The next collateral point which was presented was in order to show an assumed bias or prejudice of General McDowell against this petitioner, to whom the former had previously been so good a friend.

After the unfounded statements published by this petitioner had been distributed, the late Prof. Denis H. Mahan, United States Military Academy, appears to have written to General McDowell on the subject, suggesting the propriety of replying, and inclosing a copy of the publication.

Probably the most dignified way of doing this was the very mode adopted by General McDowell, who caused extracts to be taken from the reports of Stuart, Longstreet, and Jackson with reference to the battle of the 29th August, and published them without comment.

In looking at Longstreet's report we find he reports that at 4 p. m. the Union forces began to press forward against General Jackson, and that he sent forward some of his own command to attack.

The extract taken from Jackson's report of the battle, it is asserted, applies to the 30th; that it is so stated.

It narrates, however, that at 4 p. m. Longstreet undertook to do precisely what he said in his own report he did do.

It appears by Assistant Adjutant-General Henry Kyd Douglas' evidence (of Jackson's staff) that the report was written by Colonel Charles

James Faulkner, of Jackson's staff (Board's Record, p. 704), who was not present during the battles of the 29th and 30th, but made it up from eports subsequently received.

That which he ascribed to the 30th, and which General McDowell has sworn he thought belonged to the 29th, actually did have reference more to the first day's battle (the 29th) than the second, and was merely corroborative of Longstreet's and Stuart's reports, which preceded it in the little two-page pamphlet published by General McDowell at the request of his friend, the late distinguished Professor Mahan, and others, in answer to the petitioner's incorrect publications.

Longstreet's and Stuart's reports were sufficient to have been published without the corroborative extract from Jackson's, but as the petitioner has sought to turn attention from his own conduct on the 29th to General McDowell's *subsequent* acts, this explanation is due the latter.

It should be added that Jubal A. Early (Board's Record, p. 858) says that Faulkner, in writing it for Jackson, "confounded the facts in the report."

We know (Board's Record, p. 522) it was never filed by Jackson, but found among his papers.

However, when General McDowell ascertained that a claim was made that that report of Jackson applied to the 30th rather than to the 29th, it appears that he forwarded it to the Adjutant-General for the purpose of having the extracts which he had published compared with the official record as to whether those were extracts in relation to the operations of the 29th of August, as the heading to his little printed publication assumed they were.

The reply of the Adjutant-General was, as we have seen (Board's Record, p. 755), that it was "a true copy from the original report," and that there were but some slight verbal corrections to be made, taken from the rebel records.

Assuming the report has reference to the 30th, as stated, and which I have always contended and do believe applied to the 29th, nevertheless that which *does* apply to the 29th in the report is of the same state of facts, only in different language.

It is entirely collateral to this investigation, but the fact that such a thing has been brought in, as it were, incidentally, shows that the same line has been pursued consistently by the petitioner, from the time of the findings of the court-martial, of attack on all concerned.

Had he attacked on the 29th, as was *his* duty, probably these attacks would not have taken place.

PETITIONER'S CONDUCT TOWARDS GENERAL POPE.

3. The third is as to General Pope, who, it appears by the action of the 29th, was attacking, yet in the arguments of counsel we find a position ascribed to him very different from attack.

General Pope has furnished, I believe, all the information bearing on this case of petitioner within his power—his original dispatch-books, his letter-books have been put by him at the service of his counsel through myself as counsel for the government.

During the course of this investigation, one of petitioner's counsel stated that General Pope and General McDowell had been *"fully examined"* on the original trial. (Board's Record, p. 106.) In the course of the argument for the petitioner, at the close, it was stated that General Pope knew but little of the actual facts.

Such being the case, and he having been *very fully examined* and *cross-*

examined on the original trial, we can see the petitioner's method of procedure in asking this Board to bring General Pope here as a "government" witness, so that he may be asked merely his "opinions" (Board's Record, pp. 1016, 1018, 1020), and, after correspondence had been had with General Pope, *then* acknowledging that what they really wanted him for was to "cross-examine" him on his original evidence of 1862. (Board's Record, p. 1114.)

As to General Pope's desire to further this investigation, we find that as long ago as the 18th of April, 1874, he addressed a communication to the President, upon learning that the petitioner had made a new appeal, urging the very fullest examination by a properly constituted board.

The petitioner, however, has said that his (petitioner's) appeals were unheard or unheeded; that he from the time of his conviction had sought for "justice," the indirect assumption being that the court of nine general officers which convicted him could not give him justice.

But the President of the United States (Grant) who succeeded President Johnson, and who had two of these appeals before him, gave, it appears by his own letter in evidence here, the matter his personal attention, read the evidence, and came to the conclusion that the petitioner was not entitled to any rehearing.

This conclusion is found in President Grant's reply to General Pope of the 9th of May, 1874. (Board's Record, pp. 1176, 1177.)

If this petitioner had any sort of a case when all the witnesses were alive and everything was fresh in their minds during the lifetime of President Lincoln, and if President Lincoln himself was so ready to give the petitioner a new hearing as the latter would have us believe, why did he not put the matter before President *Lincoln?* However, the action of the only living ex-President shows that the petitioner's case received due and careful attention, that it was passed upon, and that the appeal was rejected.

General Pope's subsequent attitude towards this petitioner during this investigation has been shown in the voluntary transmission by him, for information or use of the latter's counsel, of all his original dispatch and letter books (Board's Record p. 1215), and by the following telegrams:

FORT LEAVENWORTH, KANS., *October* 21, 1878.

To Gen. J. M. SCHOFIELD,
West Point, N. Y.:

I have received your despatch of the seventeenth, in which you state that "in view of the fact that the counsel for the petitioner have stated that they believe that justice to their client requires your presence here, the Board requests that you appear as a witness before them at Governor's Island next Thursday, twenty-fourth inst." In reply I have to say that if the petitioner considers my presence as a witness necessary, he should apply to have me subpœnaed as a witness for him. Only as a witness for him or for the government can I be expected, with any semblance of legality, to appear as a witness in the case. To do so on a mere request of the Board would be to place myself in a position not only false, but in every respect extraordinary and unknown to the laws of or to the practice of the civil and military tribunals of the country.

While I stand ready to appear before your Board in any position known to law or practice, I cannot appear as a volunteer witness in the case on mere request, and without knowledge whether I am called for the government or the petitioner. As you state that I am requested to appear as a witness because of the statement or suggestion of the petitioner, it is to be inferred that I am called as a witness for him; but this fact is not definitely stated, nor does your telegram convey a subpœna, but only a request. To subpœna, regularly issued, to appear as a witness for either side, I will cheerfully and promptly respond. I am entirely willing to appear as a witness in the case, and desire simply to be placed in the same relation to the Board and the parties in controversy as that occupied by all the other witnesses.

JNO. POPE,
Brig. Genl., U. S. A.

FORT LEAVENWORTH, KANSAS, *October* 29, 1878.

To Major A. B. GARDNER,
Recorder and Counsel for Government, Governor's Island, New York:

I am informed by the Secretary of War, in telegram of this date, that the President declines to order me to appear or not to appear before your Board as witness, but leaves the matter to my discretion. In view of this fact and of the telegraphic instructions of the Secretary of War for the guidance of the Board, copy of which the Secretary has sent, I must adhere to the position taken in my telegram of 21st instant to General Schofield. Nevertheless, although the counsel for the government refuses to subpœna me as witness for the government, and the petitioner declines to subpœna me as a witness for him, and therefore I am subpœnaed by neither party, if the Board require any information in my power to give on any points brought out in this investigation, I will cheerfully give it either by sworn replies to written interrogatories, or, if the Board deem it necessary, by appearing in person before it for this purpose, on due notification to that effect.

JOHN POPE,
Brevet Major-General, U. S. A.

THE ASSAULT MADE UPON THE CHARACTER OF MR. BOWERS.

4. The petitioner's method of procedure is here well exemplified. The absence of any motive on Mr. Bowers' part should have protected him from the remarks in the closing argument of counsel, which, when published, as this Board has no judicial power, will be actionable.

Mr. Bowers said petitioner's headquarters, at the time, were in the earthworks at Centreville, which the latter's chief of staff corroborated. (Board's Record, p. 1043.) He said petitioner had a tent. In rebuttal some of the latter's witnesses said he had none—others a tent-fly. (Board's Record, pp. 1036, 1040.)

As Mr. Bowers is a lawyer of prominence and respectability in West Virginia, and only came here on the repeated summons of this Board, leaving, with Capt. R. McEldowney (another witness), professional engagements in the United States circuit court at Wheeling with inconvenience, he is entitled, in view of the cross-examination to which he was subjected, and the actionable language used towards him, to have this statement.

His evidence shows he never was a spy, never within the Confederate lines. He was in command of a detachment of scouts, in government service, under and with the military family of Brig. Gen. R. H. Milroy, United States Volunteers, until the latter was relieved from duty, when he again accepted a lieutenancy in the volunteers, until the close of the rebellion, and was then honorably discharged. (Board's Record, p. 953.)

PETITIONER'S CONDUCT ON THE 30TH.

As he was not convicted of anything he did on the 30th, while serving under the *immediate* observation of General Pope, and as the evidence offered by him on his trial in 1862, as to what he did on the 30th, was properly ruled out by the court after argument (G. C. M. Rec., pp. 118, 133, 252, and 280), I have, as I stated in my opening argument in rebuttal, refrained from going into that subject at all only from the belief that it was not germane to the case.

ANIMUS.

We now come to the consideration of the *animus* of the petitioner towards his commanding general.

In the opening statement of petitioner, all the dispatches which he cites up to the 26th August, 1862, show that he evidently considered

General Pope's army as yet a separate command, with which he was merely to co-operate.

Before the petitioner came under General Pope's immediate command he was under Maj. Gen. G. B. McClellan's.

On the 25th, when he began to get near that army, he began to be troubled with doubts, and in his dispatch to Maj. Gen. A. E. Burnside (marked No. 8) says, "*Does General McClellan approve?*"

And again on same day to General Burnside, who was his immediate commander, he asks (No 10), "Are my arrangements satisfactory?"

When, on the 26th, he found no forces of the enemy in front of him, below on the Rappahannock, but his own corps in close proximity to General Pope's, he wrote to the latter to know where his command would be most useful.

That night he received his first order from Major-General Pope. It was dated 7 p. m., signed by Major-General Pope, and requested the petitioner to "Please move forward" in a certain direction.

This at 11 p. m. petitioner acknowledged, and said his (Pope's) instructions would be obeyed as rapidly as possible; that his forces had been disposed of under instructions from the General-in-Chief. (Board's Record, p. 316.)

Possibly this reply had something to do with the query of General Pope to his chief of staff, Col. George D. Ruggles, whether petitioner would fail him. (Board's Record, p. 280.)

The petitioner asserts (on page 19) that he "had used extraordinary exertions to join General Pope," but this pretense of zeal fails in the light shed on this transaction by his own witness, General Burnside, when the latter swore on the trial (p. 185, G. C. M. Record) that the accused "used no energy or dispatch in joining the command of General Pope, and in his military movements in that direction, beyond those which his duty as an officer required him to use."

We now arrive at the point when he has received his first order from General Pope, and is told by the latter that he, Pope, "does not see how a general engagement can be postponed more than a day or two" (No. 16), and orders him to *hurry up* one of his divisions *as rapidly as possible,* and to put the other where he can "easily move to the front."

This is not what the petitioner apparently expected. He had no desire or intention to fight the new campaign under any but his old commander. He shows he is troubled at what he has already done, for he sends a dispatch to Major-General Burnside in which he says:

Have just received orders from General Pope. * * * I shall move up as ordered. * * * inform McClellan, that I may know I *am doing right.*

What had the commanding general of the Army of the Potomac to do with deciding this point if the accused was in General Pope's command?

On the other hand, if that commander's opinion was asked in order to ascertain whether he had been rightfully ordered by General Pope, how much could he have considered himself as a subordinate previously?

The truth of it is, the petitioner, as was testified to by General McClellan (on p. 197, G. C. M. Record), joined General Pope's command because he received orders *direct* from Major-General Halleck, General-in-Chief, so to do.

General McClellan further swore that "when the accused was making his efforts to leave the Peninsula, he did not know that he was to be placed under the immediate command of General Pope."

The petitioner admitted his hopes and wishes in his opening statement (p. 72) before this Board when he said he "thought that the main body of the Army of the Potomac was landing at Aquia Creek" [that is just where General Lee seems to have had an idea that the main body would land and get in his rear on the 29th] "and would join the Army of Virginia by the line of the Rappahannock; that the Army of the Potomac and the Army of Virginia, under their respective commanders, McClellan and Pope, would co-operate and be manœuvered by one head—General McClellan."

Said he: "I did not then know or suspect that it had been decided that General McClellan was to have nothing to do with the campaign."

In another place (p. 80) he said that before he left Harrison's Landing he was informed that General McClellan would command both armies.

It will be a subject to be considered in the light of other dispatches how far this petitioner permitted his wishes as to commanders to control his official conduct.

The next dispatch to be noticed is as follows:

No. 13.

WARRENTON, 27, p. m.

To General BURNSIDE:
*   *   *   *   *   *   *

Everything here is at sixes and sevens, and I find I am to take care of myself in every respect. *Our line of communication has taken care of itself, in compliance with orders.* The army has not three days' provisions. The enemy captured all Pope's and other clothing; and from McDowell the same, including liquors. No guard accompanying the trains, and small ones guard bridges. The wagons are rolling on, and I shall be here to-morrow. Good night!

F. J. PORTER,
Major-General.

This dispatch shows the feelings which the petitioner had towards the Army of Virginia, which already had been enduring fatigue and privations in the effort to protect the national capital.

The historian has yet to note the causes why General Pope's line of communications was interrupted at Manassas Junction and his supplies destroyed while he himself was holding an extended line of defense under superior orders.

Whether it was a corps or army commander who was responsible is foreign to this investigation.

However, this petitioner knew his special allusion, in the last-quoted dispatch, to General McDowell, was and *never* has been founded in fact.

That dispatch was followed by No. 20 (G. C. M. Record, p. 99):

[No. 20.]

(From Warrenton Junction, August 27, 1862—4 P. M.)

GENERAL BURNSIDE, *Falmouth, Virginia:*

I send you the last order from General Pope, which indicates the future as well as the present. Wagons are rolling along rapidly to the rear, as if a mighty power was propelling them. I see no cause of alarm, though this may cause it. McDowell is moving to Gainesville, where Sigel now is. The latter got to Buckland bridge in time to put out the fire and kick the enemy, who is pursuing his route unmolested to the Shenandoah or Loudoun County. The forces are Longstreet's, A. P. Hill's, Jackson's, Whiting's, Ewell's, and Anderson's (late Huger's) divisions.
*   *   *   *   *   *   *

Everything has moved up north. I found a vast difference between these troops and ours, but I suppose they were new, as to-day they burned their clothes, &c., when there was not the least cause. I hear that they are much demoralized, and needed some good troops to give them heart and, I think, head. We are working now to get behind Bull Run, and I presume will be there in a few days if strategy don't use us up. The strategy is magnificent and tactics in the inverse proportion. I would like some of my ambulances. I would like also to be ordered to return to Fredericksburg, to push towards Hanover, or, with a larger force, to push towards Orange Court-House. I wish Sumner was at Washington, and up near the Monocacy, with good batteries. I do not doubt the enemy have a large amount of supplies provided for them, and I believe they have a contempt for the Army of Virginia. *I wish myself away from it, with all our old Army of the Potomac, and so do our companions.* I was informed to-day by the best authority that, in opposition to General Pope's views, this army was pushed out to save the Army of the Potomac, an army that could take care of itself. Pope says he long since wanted to go behind the Occoquan.

* * * * * *

Most of this is private, but if you can get me away, please do so. Make what use of this you choose, so it does good.

Don't let the alarm here disturb you. If you had a good force you could go to Richmond. A force should at once be pushed on to Manassas to open the road. Our provisions are very short.

F. J. PORTER.

After telegraphing, this dispatch will be sent to General Burnside.

This was followed by another dispatch, viz:

BRISTOE, 9.30 a. m., *August 28*, 1862.

My command will soon be up, and will at once go into position. Hooker drove Ewell some three miles, and Pope says McDowell intercepted Longstreet, so that without a long detour he cannot join Ewell, Jackson, and A. P. Hill, who are, or supposed to be, at Manassas. Ewell's train, he says, took the road to Gainesville, where McDowell is coming from. We shall be to-day as follows: I on right of railroad; Heintzelman on left; then Reno, then McDowell. He hopes to get Ewell and push to Manassas to-day.

I hope all goes well near Washington; I think there need be no cause of fear for us. I feel as if on my own way now, and thus far have kept my command and trains well up. More supplies than I supposed on hand have been brought, but none to spare, and we must make connection soon. I hope for the best, and my lucky star is always up about my birthday, the 31st, *and I hope Mc's is up also.* You will hear of us soon by way of Alexandria.

Ever yours,

F. J. P.

General BURNSIDE, *Falmouth.*

On the very morning he received General Pope's order to move on Centreville (29th August), stating that it was very important that he should be there at an early hour in the morning, that a severe engagement was likely to take place and his presence necessary, he sat down half an hour later and sent this dispatch to General Burnside (p. 103, G. C. M. Record):

BRISTOE, 6 a. m., 29.

To General BURNSIDE:

I shall be off in half an hour. The messenger who brought this says the enemy had been at Centreville, and pickets were found there last night.

Sigel had severe fight last night; took many prisoners. Banks is at Warrenton Junction; McDowell near Gainesville; Heintzelman and Reno at Centreville, where they marched yesterday, and Pope went to Centreville *with the last two as a body-guard,* at the time not knowing where was the enemy, and where Sigel was fighting within 8 miles of him *and in sight.* Comment is unnecessary.

The enormous trains are still rolling on, many animals not having been watered for fifty hours; I shall be out of provisions to-morrow night; your train of forty wagons cannot be found.

I hope Mac's at work, and we shall soon get ordered out of this. It would seem from proper statements of the enemy that he was wandering around loose, but I expect they know what they are doing, which is more than any one here or anywhere knows.

* * * * * *

Comment on this almost seems needless, but it explains possibly why he did not give Pope a hearty support in that day's action.

He pretended to have no confidence in Pope; and in his appeal to the President of 10th October, 1867, p. 53, he went on to say that if his dispatches to Burnside—

Manifested confidence in General McClellan and a distrust of General Pope's ability to conduct the campaign (as claimed by the prosecution), they but expressed the opinion pervading our Eastern armies.

General Burnside, a witness for the accused, in his testimony (p. 181, G. C. M. Record), said he

Saw in Porter's telegrams exactly what he heard expressed by a large portion of the officers with whom he happened to be in communication at the time—a very great lack of confidence in the management of the campaign. It was not confined to General Porter.

The petitioner's late counsel, Reverdy Johnson, in the pamphlet to which I have referred, in undertaking to excuse or explain his, petitioner's, telegrams to General Burnside, said (p. 31):

Not only was the honor of the flag involved, but the very safety of the capital. *Porter saw that both were in danger by what he believed to be the incompetency of Pope.*

Here, I submit, is one of the reasons of the accused's fatal inaction on the 29th August, 1862.

He apparently does not appear to have received any replies to his dispatches here quoted to General Burnside or to others criticising the campaign.

The moment he found himself actually under Major-General Pope's orders and joined to duty with his army, and his late commander not at the front, he says:

I wish myself away from it, with all our old army of the Potomac, *and so do our companions.* * * * If you can get me away please do so.

If he really spoke in this dispatch for his general officers, some explanation might be found for the advice they gave on receipt of the 1 a. m. order, though, as has been shown, petitioner did not make known to them its urgency.

All the time he is looking for General McClellan and hopes his "lucky star is up."

Even when he gets an order, at 5.30 a. m. on the 29th August, to move forward at once, as a "severe engagement was likely to take place," he does not do so until 7 a. m., and, meanwhile, writes a long note to General Burnside, in which he says:

I hope Mac's at work, and we shall soon get ordered out of this.

All these expressions taken together afford in connection with his acts a clew to the motives of the petitioner. He was not satisfied with the commanding general that the government had placed over him. His service, therefore, was reluctant and of the most dilatory character. Either really or apparently he pretended to distrust his then commander and did trust another, whom he was hourly looking to see come forward, for he said that very morning he *hoped they would make connection soon* (G. C. M. Record, p. 119), and he did not propose to help Pope in any of his serious movements where he could possibly avoid it.

At any moment Sumner's or Franklin's corps might arrive, and with them the commanding general of the Army of the Potomac from Alexandria.

The countermarches and singular movements of petitioner in coming up to Warrenton Junction from the Rappahannock have not been specially inquired into, but apparently exhibit hesitation or delay. (Board's Record, pp. 842 and 948.)

The evidence of Asst. Surgeon Wm. L. Faxon, Eighteenth Massachusetts Volunteers, Morell's division, is noticeable.

Sykes' division, which first arrived on the 28th August from Warrenton Junction to Bristoe, was moved beyond it and put in position. Morell's division came up later in the day into Bristoe.

Dr. Faxon testified as follows:

By RECORDER:
Question. At what time did you arrive at Bristoe Station with your regiment?
Answer. I judge about the middle of the afternoon.

Question. During that time did you see General Porter?
Answer. I saw General Porter only as I crossed the run at Bristoe.
Question. Where was he at that time?
Answer. He was at a little house on the left hand of where I crossed; that is, on the side toward Washington. He and his staff were at a little house; I think it was a kind of peach orchard; I think most of them were sitting down.
Question. Describe what you saw and heard, so far as General Porter was concerned.
Answer. As I crossed the run I heard General Porter make this remark: "Go tell Morell to halt his division;" and he added, "I don't care a damn if we don't get there." I am very particular about those words, because I recollect them, and I have spoken of them.

* * * * * * *

By Mr. CHOATE:

Question. You put this and that together and thought it referred to getting to Bristoe didn't you?
Answer. No; I never have drawn any conclusion, except that the man had some motive in his mind, in view of the disaster that followed; because a general commanding a division if he had a motive of that kind should have kept it to himself.
Question. In view of what disaster that followed?
Answer. Second battle of Bull Run.

* * * * * *

Question. What other circumstances were there that impressed General Porter's remark upon you at the time it was made?
Answer. I said in view of the disaster that followed, our defeat at the battle of Bull Run, and the general talk thatevery body made about the displacement of McClellan and the appointment of Pope. That was a matter of common report in the Army as well as everywhere.

The next noticeable utterance of petitioner is at Dawkins' Branch, August 29, where, when petitioner of his own volition, after the fire of the few cavalry skirmishers of Stuart's, sent out Col. E. G. Marshall, he directed the latter *not to bring on a general engagement*. (Board's Record, p. 678.)

Then follows the remark of petitioner when General McDowell gave him his orders at the Manassas Gap Railroad, to put his troops in there, that he could not do so without getting into a fight. (G. C. M. Record, p. 85.)

After this comes petitioner's remark to General Sturgis, when the latter, after McDowell had gone and petitioner was back to his column, called his attention to the glint of a gun, showing a force, that he, petitioner, *thought he was mistaken*.

Then follows petitioner's orders to General Sturgis, after that section did open on him, for Piatt's brigade to march back to Manassas Junction and take up a *"defensive position."* (Board's Record, p. 712.)

Then comes his, petitioner's, orders to Morell to put back and conceal in the bushes all his division, after the feeble effort to move to the right. (No. 31, p. 95, petitioner's opening statement.)

Before and after this, we have the conduct of petitioner in putting his headquarters two and five-eighths miles to the rear of Dawkins' Branch, from between 12 and 1 p. m. up to night. (Petitioner's statement, p. 40.)

Next to be noticed is the conduct of petitioner in not making known to General Sykes, who was with him for hours, the fact of receipt of the 4.30 order to push into action at once. (G. C. M. Record, p. 178.)

Lastly, on that day we have this series of telegrams, in two of which the petitioner expressed a positive determination to withdraw to Manassas without having attacked, viz:

General McDOWELL: The firing on my right has so far retired that, as I cannot advance, and have failed to get over to you except by the route taken by King, *I shall withdraw to Manassas.* If you have anything to communicate please do so. I have sent many messengers to you and General Sigel and get nothing.
(Signed)   F. J. PORTER,
                                                    Major-General.

An artillery duel is going on now—been skirmishing for a long time.
                                                    F. J. P.

General McDOWELL or KING : I have been wandering over the woods and failed to get a communication to you. Tell how matters go with you. The enemy is in strong force in front of me, and I wish to know your designs for to-night. If left to me I shall have to retire for food and water, which I cannot get here. How goes the *battle?* It seems to go to our rear. The enemy are getting to our left.

(Signed) F. J. PORTER,
Major-General Volunteers.

General McDOWELL: Failed in getting Morell over to you. After wandering about the woods for a time I withdrew him, and while doing so artillery opened upon us. My scouts could not get through. Each one found the enemy between us, and I believe some have been captured. Infantry are also in front. I am trying to get a battery, but have not succeeded as yet. From the masses of dust on our left, and from reports of scouts, think the enemy are moving largely in that way. Please communicate the way this messenger came. I have no cavalry or messengers now. Please let me know your designs; whether you retire or not. I cannot get water and am out of provision. Have lost a few men from infantry firing.

F. J. PORTER,
Major-General Volunteers.

AUGUST 29—6 p. m.

AUGUST 29, 1862.

Generals McDOWELL and KING: I found it impossible to communicate by crossing the woods to Groveton. The enemy are in strong force on this road, and as they appear to have driven our forces back, the firing of the enemy having advanced and ours retired, *I have determined to withdraw to Manassas.* I have attempted to communicate with McDowell and Sigel, but my messengers have run into the enemy—

Although at this very time he was away back by the Sudley road, where he had a direct road perfectly open and unobstructed to General Pope's headquarters, or to any of those generals who were there—

They have gathered artillery and cavalry and infantry, and the advancing masses of dust show the enemy coming in force. I am now going to the head of the column to see what is passing and how affairs are going. Had you not better send your train back? I will communicate with you.

F. J. PORTER,
• *Major-General.*

These, by themselves, afford evidence which might be deemed conclusive that the petitioner was disloyal to his commanding general, Pope.

Of this, however, we are not left to conjecture, for during his trial, when the official reporter, Wm. Blair Lord, after the day's adjournment, called on him on business, accompanied by Mr. Waterman L. Ormsby, this petitioner, in a moment of unguarded impulse, declared he "was not loyal to Pope," but, as testified to by Mr. Ormsby, he "was loyal to McClellan." (Board's Record, pp. 651 and 968.)

These witnesses, the one for many years and now the official reporter of debates in the House of Representatives, and the other for fifteen years superintendent of transferring in the Continental Bank Note Company, indicate, additional to their characters and appearance, the amount of trust to be reposed in their accuracy.

Nothing which can be said in this argument as to this language can add to the force of that said by Mr. Lord in the private letter he wrote at the time to his wife on the subject, which is as follows (Board's Record, p. 980):

I have been a little bothered about General Fitz John Porter. I had to go to his room on Monday to get some papers that belonged to the court that he had had to copy. One of the reporters of the New York Times was along with me. While in the room, after some conversation, General Porter made the remark, "Well, I wasn't loyal to Pope; there is no denying that." Now, that is really the charge against him before the court-martial—that he did not do his duty as an officer before the enemy, and that he did not act rightly towards General Pope, his commanding officer. General Porter said what he did in the privacy of his own room; without thinking of the effect of his words. After thinking it over, I have concluded it better not to say anything about it now, though I would not promise as much for that newspaper correspondent.

Mr. Lord, from motives of delicacy, did not communicate information of this interview to the Judge-Advocate-General until the evidence in the trial in 1862 had been closed, consequently it was not used.

This petitioner, judging from his utterances and acts, on the 29th August, 1862, was apparently willing "to leave Pope to get out of the scrape," an alternative proposition which it appears from the record of this Board (p. 750) he was not the only general officer of the Army who was prepared to adopt.

The petitioner's remarks, as overheard by Mr. B. T. Bowers, then lieutenant First Ohio Battery, on the 31st August, that he did not wish any honors or courtesies shown to General Pope (Board's Record, p. 955) were not a necessary piece of evidence to show his *animus*.

The conduct of this petitioner in the eventful days of the August campaign of 1862 has now been reviewed.

He cannot say that he has not had the *utmost* latitude in the production of anything favorable to his many-sided case.

Punishment in the systems of laws prevailing in enlightened nations is not so much to visit condemnation on the individual as to deter others from committing the like offense.

Gladly would General Washington have pardoned Adjutant-General John André, of the British army, in October, 1780, but an example was necessary for the future safety of the state.

It must not be forgotten in the examination of the details of petitioner's case that the strength of the evidence against him lay much in the consideration that it presented a series of acts having throughout a character in common and bearing on their face a common motive; that they began upon his being placed under the command of a particular officer; that they continued so long as he remained under that officer; that they exhibited a half-compliance, non-compliance, or positive disobedience to both the letter and the spirit of successive orders received from that officer; and that his hostility to that officer was clearly proven, both in his dispatches and utterances.

Again, what may be called the method of his defection looked to a retirement of the army in which he found himself to a point in rear of the field of operations, where, by the fact of this retirement, and the assumed failure of the general under whom he was serving, he might come under another command; and his own private dispatches confirmed this aspect of the case, since they showed this to have been his ruling thought and desire.

It was, in short, the consistency of these acts with each other, their contrast with the previous conduct of the same officer, and the key to their purpose furnished by his own words, that trebly indicated his accountability, and bore the minds of the court to his conviction.

Of the less flagrant of these acts, perhaps of every one except his turning his back upon the field on the afternoon of the 29th and failure to push in, it may be said that this or that, had it stood alone, might, without knowledge of his *animus*, have been covered up or explained away so as to have left him the benefit of a doubt.

It was more difficult to do this with several taken together.

It was impossible to do it with all.

I have now concluded the duty put upon me, a duty among the most disagreeable in all my professional experience.

In performing it, I have felt that the honor of the service required every exertion on my part to ascertain the facts, so that the President, the historian, and the public might read this case and know it had been as fully investigated as possible, in the absence of any judicial or quasi-judicial power in the Board.

www.ingramcontent.com/pod-product-compliance
Lightning Source LLC
Chambersburg PA
CBHW020111030726
47498CB00006B/2049